BLADE OF FURY

Ranjith Radhakrishnan is a Bengaluru-based entrepreneur. This is his second novel.

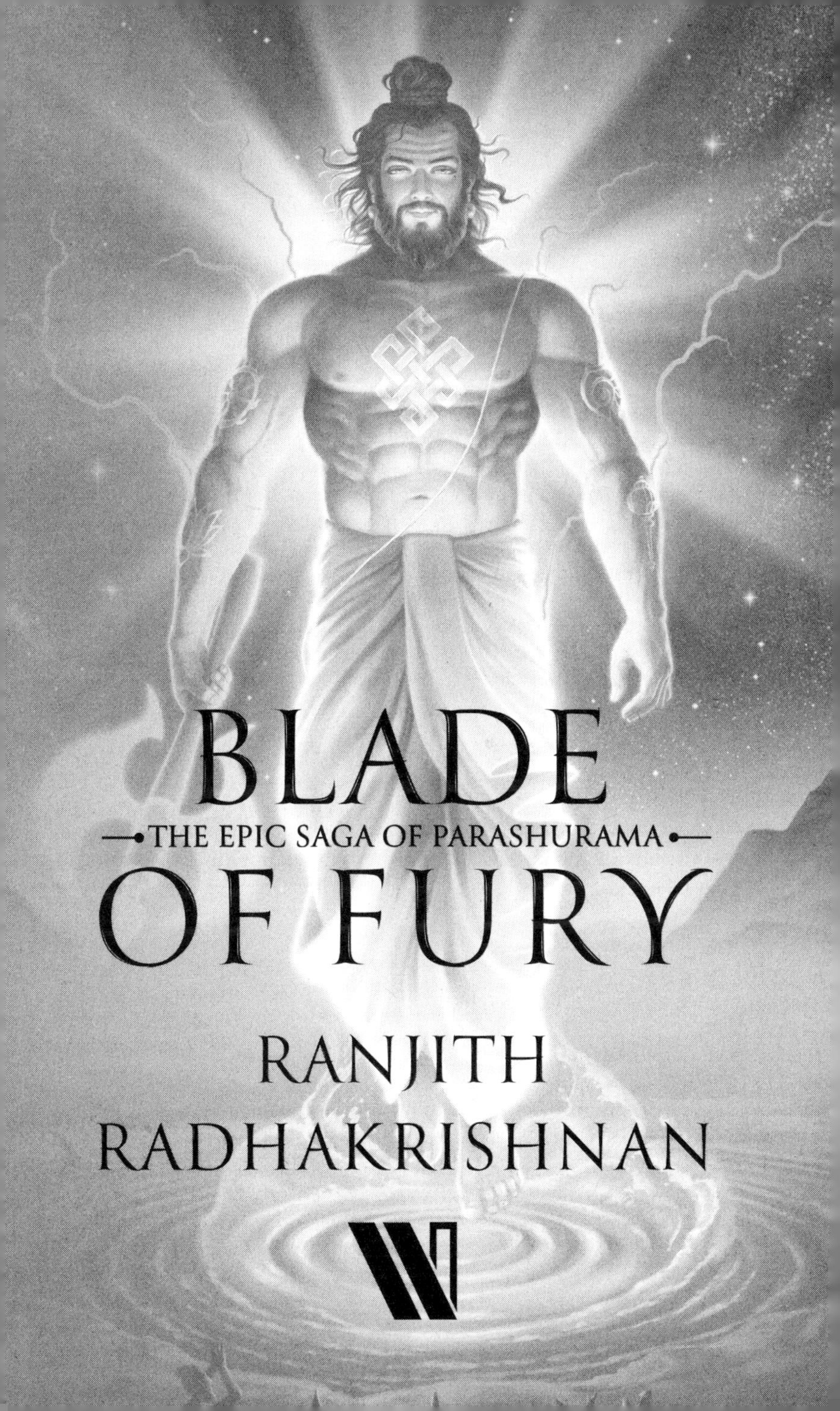

BLADE OF FURY

THE EPIC SAGA OF PARASHURAMA

RANJITH RADHAKRISHNAN

Published by Westland Books, a division of Nasadiya Technologies Private Limited, in 2025

No. 269/2B, First Floor, 'Irai Arul', Vimalraj Street, Nethaji Nagar, Alapakkam Main Road, Maduravoyal, Chennai 600095

Westland and the Westland logo are the trademarks of Nasadiya Technologies Private Limited, or its affiliates.

ISBN: 9789371977562

10 9 8 7 6 5 4 3 2 1

This is a work of fiction. Names, characters, organisations, places, events and incidents are either products of the author's imagination or used fictitiously.

Typeset by R. Ajith Kumar, Delhi

Printed at Manipal Technologies Limited, Manipal

Samarpitam idam grantham
Tava paadaambuje sadaa |
Mahadevi mahavidye
Jnanadeepa prachodite ||
Tvat-kripa bhaasate lokaan
Sanatani paraatpare |
Maatrurupe maheshaani namaami
Parameshvarim ||

For

Priya and Sudeep,

May the beloved auspicious light

shine undimmed.

Contents

I

Three Loops and a Half

The chariot sped through the forest and the night, whisper smooth and arrow straight. The ruin that was Mahishmati and the bloody carnage of twenty-one Akshauhinis lay far behind. The shattered legacy of a samrat who had it all—strength, valour, majesty, divine blessings and utter dominion over Prithvi—but had squandered it at the altar of ego. A few muhurtas ago, righteous wrath had scythed his pride down, his armies and his many-splendoured capital ruthlessly cut and burned like weeds, and his strength and life ground in the mill of karma and tossed aside like chaff.

The rise and fall of Chakravarti Samrat Karthavirya Arjuna will be remembered and spoken about until the end of this Manvantara. Perhaps even beyond. Legends and fables would bloom, their fragrance strong and heady, but petals prickly. Bards would sing of how the earth sighed in relief and spun lighter on her axis as she turned her perpetual homage around the sun. In their ballads would be a name that would gather awe in the listeners' imagination and spark primal fear in the oldest part of their lizard brains. Their breath would turn cold at the mention of the dread weapon, and they would huddle closer together when they would hear of his indomitable fury. The weapon had found its match and master, and would forever prefix his name ... Parashurama.

Mahodhara held the reins lightly, letting the horses determine their course and pace. Akrita was curled up on the floor of the chariot, deep in slumber. Rama rested against the ratha's centre pole, brow lined with beads of sweat even in the cool of the night. His eyes were closed, but the pupils moved behind the shut eyelids, his mind lost in rambling thought and untethered from reality. The inferno of rage that fuelled the annihilation of Arjuna and his vassals had simmered down. Somewhere in the night, that sense of absolute clarity Rama had achieved after embracing mrithyu had escaped, from him, without him being aware. The brilliant stillness inside him had turned into a stormy disquiet. Rama didn't understand it, and this added to his unease. He had dozed off in the ratha and the pounding in his head had begun.

Rama was caught between worlds. He sat still as a statue, but felt disconnected from his body, as if he were outside of it, floating in the air beside the chariot, moving with it, and gazing down at himself. Inchoate worry gnawed at him. His mind raced from the thrill of victory and despair at Arjuna's death in one moment, to disgust at the triumph and glee at his end the next. He tried to remember the vision of the Supreme Goddess and came up short. His brain thumped inside his skull like a hundred hammers were pulverising it. He couldn't form the agnikund in his mind or focus on the banalinga or kalasha. The fury of the Parashu seemed far away ... buried deep underground. Nightmare visions danced before his mind's eye.

He saw himself walk upon the dead and dying, their flesh

squelching beneath his feet. The dim world was littered with bodies as far as the eye could see. The dying cried to him for help as their open, gruesome wounds spouted blood. They begged for a quick death to end their agony. He laughed at them, mocking their pleas. Hands grasped at his legs in supplications of mercy, and he kicked them away. Vultures perched on his shoulders; armies of wolves followed in his wake. The pisachas and vetalas came to him, salivating rivers of ichor, offering bitten-off flesh as homage. This was the eclipse world of death and fear and torture. And he was the god of it. He roared his supremacy. With the thunder of his roar, his body grew in strength and size. It grew humongous, reaching for the dim stars. And then ... he sprouted a thousand arms.

NO! Rama's mind screamed.

No, neti, neti ... he kept repeating as if that one word would somehow rescue him.

He found himself back in the chariot, and another vision bloomed: Arjuna lay curled beside him, smiling up at him. The chariot was huge; he seemed high up in the air. He looked over the front rim of the ratha. It was yoked to Sahasrabahu. The ratha careened over his father's ashram, trampling hut and human ...

No ...

The vision disappeared, and Rama gazed down at Akrita as he slept; his slender neck was white against the dull golden floor of the ratha. Rama felt an irresistible urge to cut that neck. Cut it, just like he had cut his mother's, but a clean slice this time. Blood would leak and the floor of the ratha would be a glorious red. Rama's hands reached for the Parashu ...

No ...

He was immortal. He would see yugas come and go. Arjuna was merely long-lived. He would live forever. He had beaten Arjuna here, too. The samrat was no match for him. He was superhuman. He would conquer the earth; all crowns would rest at his feet. He would stride across the world like a colossus, rule till the end of time and collect tribute ...

No! Rama's mind screamed. *I'm human.*

Guru! The Guru would have answers. He could save him. Something was terribly wrong with him, and the Guru would know how to correct it. Relief coursed through Rama, lifting his spirits and giving him hope.

He couldn't remember the Guru's name. He remembered nothing about him. Rama wept with grief.

A sound vibrated within him. Two separate syllables repeating themselves. Rama couldn't hear it clearly. He concentrated as hard as he could and then gave up in defeat. It was either too loud or inaudible; he didn't know which. He cupped his ears in mind-numbing pain and in his imagination, blood coursed out of them, between his tight fingers and down his arms.

He tried again to form the agnikund, to imagine the banalinga and kalasha. He failed again. His mind throbbed and pounded as he cast about frantically for an answer.

Rama teetered on the edge of insanity.

'Acharya!'

The word seared through him, loud and sharp. Rama startled awake, struggling to focus his eyes on Akrita kneeling before him.

'What happened?' Rama stuttered.

Akrita looked closely at Rama before answering. 'We've been trying to wake you for a while now. You were lost in some dreamworld, it seems, or maybe it's just battle fatigue.'

Rama didn't answer. He looked around slowly to get his bearings. It was shadowy and still all around.

'The ratha has stopped,' he blurted aloud. He shook his head and blinked rapidly to clear his mind. There seemed to be an ocean of water sloshing around in his head and shaking it made his vision and mind pitch and yaw like a ship on stormy waters.

'The horses refuse to move,' said Mahodhara. 'They cannot actually. There is a barrier a few feet ahead. An invisible barrier. I went and checked it. Neither I nor the horses can pass through it. And I see only black up ahead. It's somehow blacker than the night. From the barrier, there is no trail and no jungle ahead. Everything is there to the sides. We've been trying to wake you since.'

'I don't see black. I only see a fork in the road,' said Akrita. 'I see it from here by the light of the stars. But the horses refuse to move.'

Rama was confused. He struggled to his feet, clutching at the centre pole to steady himself. The world swayed this way and that. Rama fought the urge to retch and waited for his vision to settle.

Finally, he said, 'I see a fork in the road.'

Mahodhara checked for himself. 'I still see nothing,' he said. He turned to face Rama and Akrita. 'Which way is ours?'

'We are very close to the ashram. That way home,' said Akrita, pointing right.

'That way,' said Rama, pointing left.

The three of them stared at each other in confusion.

They walked to where Mahodhara said the barrier was. He pressed his hands against something invisible, indicating its presence. Rama put his hand out and felt nothing. He took a couple of steps forward and a tingling sensation, almost a shiver, ran down his body. Akrita too stepped forward after him.

'Did you feel anything?' Rama asked. Akrita shook his head.

They watched Mahodhara as he came closer and up against the barrier, his right foot still lifted mid-stride.

'I can't come forward,' Madodhara said. Rama moved towards him and held his hand out. 'Hold my hand and move forward.'

Mahodhara clasped his hand and tried to move. Rama felt him strain and tried to pull him through but to no avail. Mahodhara let go of his hand and threw himself at the barrier. He bounced off. There wasn't the least bit of give in the barrier nor a whisper of sound as Mahodhara tried again. Rama put his hands out, upturned, feeling for its contours. He paused when he felt that tingle again and ran his palms up, down and sideways. He moved to the side of the trail, keeping his hands tingling. It was there too, and it wasn't hard to guess that it stretched away into the forest. An invisible barrier, perpendicular to the ground, straight up and down as far as he could reach.

Rama kept his hand on the barrier. 'Press your hand against mine,' he told Mahodhara. He did as Rama asked, and his eyes widened in surprise.

'I can't feel your hand,' he said.

There was nothing between the two hands pressed together, yet they didn't feel the touch of skin on skin. All Rama felt was the tingle. Akrita was touching the air with his palms. 'I don't feel anything,' he said in confusion. Rama groaned inwardly. What in the name of Mahadeva was this?

He didn't think too much about it; he didn't understand what was happening and the more he thought, the more the hammering in his head increased. Rama cradled his forehead in his palms and whispered, 'We'll walk from here. The ashram is close.'

'Are you alright, Acharya?' Akrita asked. Rama didn't reply. 'Why is this happening? What is this barrier?' he continued.

'We'll just take that road home and figure it out,' said Rama.

'This road, Acharya, not that one,' said Akrita.

'I know the woods better than anyone else. That way is home,' said Rama, an edge creeping into his voice.

'Acharya, I know that, but this is the way. I don't know how I know it, but I know it for sure.'

Rama grit his teeth in irritation. His right fist clenched as if tightening itself around the handle of the Parashu, and he realised he'd left it in the chariot. *Lucky for them,* he thought to himself. Rama willed himself not to move, afraid that if he did, he would assault Akrita or Mahodhara. The pounding in his head increased and his vision turned watery. He realised he was holding his breath. He exhaled slowly, trying to ease his annoyance. Akrita and Mahodhara glanced at each other, concern writ large in their eyes. This was not the Rama who had taken on the world's mightiest monarch and his army single-handedly.

'Mahodhara, you go home ... wherever that is. I'll summon you when I need you,' said Rama. He held up his palm before Mahodhara could reply. He looked at Akrita.

Akrita knew what was coming. 'No,' he said resolutely.

'Yes,' said Rama, 'You take the trail's right fork. I'll take the left. Let's get our things.' Rama walked back to the ratha to fetch his weapon. Akrita controlled his urge to object. An inner sense warned him that Rama would brook no demur. He silently complied.

Rama paused a few steps into the left fork. He saw Akrita walk reluctantly on the right trail and disappear behind the thick foliage separating the two paths. He glanced back. Mahodhara and the ratha were gone.

He looked around carefully to find his bearings. His eyes struggled to see through the inky murk of the forest at night. The moon hid behind clouds, and the stars had disappeared. *How can I even see this much?* Something unnatural was afoot. He controlled his breath to calm his nerves and get a feel of his surroundings ... to become one with the jungle. Rama strove in vain. He felt completely disembodied and disinterested as if this was happening to someone else, someone he didn't care for. He was a mere spectator. A profound sense of loneliness washed over him, dampening his spirits, sapping his energy and causing his shoulders to slump. Rama stood still for a long while and slowly inched forward.

A hazy silhouette of a thicket of banana trees stood to the left of the trail. He walked past it, searching for natural signposts along this path. He soon fell into his easy, long stride and a while later, a sudden odour flooded his nostrils, his brain even. There was no mistaking it. Pungent and musky, half alluring and half unpleasant. The air was heavy with the scent of gandhapushpas. His head reeled with the all-pervading smell, but he couldn't spot a shrub or flower. The forest was dead silent. No rustle of leaves, no scurrying of small foragers, no crickets, no cicadas, not even a whisper of wind. As he trudged on, a realisation dawned on Rama: this wasn't how he remembered the trail. This was a trail like none other. It was completely flat; there was no unevenness to it. No ridges and hollows on the surface, no roots protruding from the earth, no rocks, no pebbles or gravel. No rise and fall of the path, and the path was dead straight as far as he could see, no twists or turns. Even the undergrowth stopped exactly where the path started, framing it in two parallel straight lines.

Rama trudged on in the eerie stillness. He didn't know how long he walked; he'd lost all sense of time. He put one foot in front of the other and moved along until he came to a second cluster of banana trees to his left. The trees seemed taller than the ones he'd seen before. An alarm went off in some deep corner of his mind, but the relentless pounding distracted him from pursuing it. The two-syllable sound was louder and clearer now, but he still couldn't make out what it was. Sometime later, the heavy odour of gandhapushpas hit him again. He plodded on.

He came to the third stand of banana trees. These were even higher. Rama paused to study them and then, realisation hit him like a shock wave. It was the same set of trees; he was sure.

He was going around in a circle.

Rama stood stunned, his aching mind racing to find answers. The invisible barrier was definitely for him, no doubt about that now. He hadn't seen Akrita ever since they took the diverging paths, but he doubted Akrita was having the same experience. The barrier was to stop Mahodhara, and the fork in the trail was designed to lead Akrita away. Clever to split them like this. Who was doing this?

Puzzled, his mind screaming, Rama stared at the trees. He'd seen them at the very start of the road and then twice again. That made two complete circles. The longer he stared, the more an inexplicable feeling took root within him—the trees weren't taller, but he was sinking lower, as though being buried deeper into the earth. He looked at the ground, but it was level. It hadn't dipped. A nimisha later, he saw his body wasn't casting a shadow on the trail. He checked around him. No shadow at all. He looked down at himself. The darkness had seeped into his body. Like it was a shadow itself. Mystified by his surroundings, Rama walked on cautiously. A little later, that unmistakable odour again. Halfway along the arc of the circle. He continued and returned to the banana trees once more. Three loops now.

What was the meaning of this? What purpose? Rama had no answers.

He broke into a run, frantic yet unheeding. What if he was caught in this loop forever? He had so unwittingly stepped into the trap.

He stopped, gasping with effort, expecting the odour of gandhapushpas to hit him. It didn't. Rama's vision was swimming. This was the spot. He was sure. He'd been this way thrice now. Rama whirled back the way he came, Parashu uplifted and ready, worry wracking his brain. Nothing.

He turned around and froze. Something was right there, straight ahead of him. Something big. And red.

2

Red Tusker

It stood immobile before him. A mammoth tusker, three times larger than any he had seen. *Three and a half times,* his mind told him. It glowed a brilliant red in the night, looming sky-high, dwarfing Rama with its sheer size. Rama's grip on the Parashu tightened. Its call to him, its urge to fury, was distant, almost undetectable like it had been buried yojanas deep somewhere. *In the ground.* The tusker simply stared at him, absolutely, unnaturally still.

'Mahadeva!' Rama whispered. The banalinga wouldn't materialise in his mind. Neither the kalasha.

Perhaps he should back away. He took a soft step back and felt the invisible barrier press against his back. There was no path behind him. He didn't have to look, he simply knew it. He considered getting off the trail and plunging into the darkness. Some deep instinct warned him against it. There was no way but forward.

Rama glanced sideways and the pounding in his head resumed with renewed ferocity, nearly throwing him off balance. He looked at the tusker and the agonising throb stopped immediately. This was no ordinary phenomenon.

Something greater was at play, his mind whispered. But the whisper was lost in a sudden splash of clarity. The presence of the Parashu stormed into him, and his rage ignited. The Parashu responded instantaneously. Rama roared and charged with an upraised Parashu to scare the tusker.

The elephant's trunk shot towards him, improbably fast and long. It twisted sinuously around Rama's torso, and as Rama flung the Parashu, the tusker flung him upwards.

The earth fell away, and so did the atmosphere. Rama drifted into space ... the sun, the planets all so far away from him. *This cannot be happening*. A brief flash illuminated the void, and the emptiness of space was suddenly alive with surging waves of energy rushing past him. The waves battered him as they swept by. Then, something rushed towards him and halted abruptly. It formed into a translucent, human-like shape, studied him with an intense gaze, and then faded into nothingness. *This was another dimension of existence*. The swells of energy congregated around ... the tusker. It was here. Rama glanced at his outstretched arm. The Parashu was still where it was a nimisha ago. He summoned it with his mind. It was sucked into this dimension ... and remained suspended halfway between him and the tusker.

In a blink, Rama was transported to Indra's court, the tusker looming magnificently behind the grand throne. Rama and his Parashu's appearance surprised Indra. He sensed the tusker behind him and turned ... Rama was whisked away.

He saw rishis and renunciates gather around the tusker and engage in rigourous tapasya. The world disappeared in a flash.

Rama was travelling at an incredible speed, but he felt no momentum. His body seemed frozen while the world around him swirled and transformed into newer versions of itself.

A different world, different rishis. Rama was in awe of their joy and resplendence. They bowed to the tusker.

Another world. Beings of light stood watching silently, the tusker among them. The Parashu still floating halfway between Rama and the tusker. 'Immortal like us,' a being whispered, 'ignorant yet. So much to learn.'

Rama was thrown into emptiness. *This is like the emptiness in the banalinga*, his mind said. Four faces, incredibly huge, appeared in the emptiness. Rama revolved around them. Deep wisdom and compassion shimmered across the four faces, each crowned with millions of stars and framed by white beards that seemed woven from the finest silk. The tusker perched atop the heads, dwarfed by their size. The eyes on the faces opened and Rama gasped, a thrill of bliss coursing through him. Brahma! Rama pressed his palms together to worship, but he plunged downwards ...

He found himself standing on a surface of varied colours. White, black, purple, gold and yellow. Nagas teemed all around him. Brilliant gems studded their long sinuous bodies, glowing as they snaked past him. Millions of them slithered by him towards a point ahead of him. A great naga stood alone on a rise before him. *The one around Mahadeva's neck when he wrought the Parashu. Where was the tusker now?* Rama spotted it. The Nagas wound around each other, weaving and intersecting till their slithering bodies formed the tusker, as if in homage. The rubies on their bodies shone with the same red glow. His Parashu was here too, hanging midway between them.

The world of Nagas disappeared and Rama found himself before hordes of danavas, daityas and asuras. The tusker stood nonchalantly amidst the hordes. They saw the Parashu, they looked keenly at Rama. A nimisha later, they roared and charged at him. He was whisked away again.

Different world, different nagas. Many-hooded, they all hissed at him. In the distance, Rama saw many lower their hoods as they bowed to the tusker.

Another world. A world of illusion. He was in a city, magnificent in scale and beauty. Spires reached for the sky, wide roads lined with gold, regal palaces as far as the eye could see. The city tilted upside down and righted itself sideways. Rama's mind lurched. He moved forward a step and found himself ten paces to the right. Mountains moved of their own accord. Rivers flowed and disappeared underground in a blink. Trees grew wings and took flight. Rama found himself hanging from a precipice. The next moment, he was falling upwards. Everything moved and twisted and turned and morphed. Only the tusker stayed immobile.

Rama was in another world, in a magnificent royal court. An asura sat majestically on a throne. Incredible power radiated from him, his effulgence like Indra's. A dwarf Brahmin stood beside him, smiling at the tusker. 'Sixth avatara,' said the Brahmin, 'Parashurama!' The asura bowed, his palms together, whispering, 'Mahabali salutes you, Parashurama.'

Blink. Rama was in a mine this time. Goblins scurried around, picking nuggets of gold, prospecting for veins of the metal. They looked him up and down and, finding nothing that glittered, dismissed him from their consideration. This world, too, vanished.

Rama found himself in a richly decorated boudoir surrounded by beautiful women. Many were scantily clad; others were in a state of complete undress. They caressed him, nibbled at his ears and pressed their soft bodies against him, whispering descriptions of outrageous carnal acts they were eager to perform for him. Goblets of wine were held to his lips, urging him to sip, with promises of indefatigable stamina. Lust gleamed in their eyes, their smiles were laced with flirtation. The tusker watched. Rama shut his eyes.

For a nimisha, he was back on the forest trail, watching the Parashu speed towards the tusker. Then, he was propelled sideways this time into another world ... worlds ... just like his own. He was there in all of them, different Ramas performing different things in each. Rama watched each version of himself closely ...

In one world, he was seated on the earth, drawing a special geometric rune on the surface before him.

In another world, he was chanting prayers to Mahadeva and Ma Gauri.

Then, he was seated in padmasana, his divine bow beside him. A being of light blazed before him. He caught snatches of the words he was chanting ...

... *Vedaahametam Purusham*

Mahantamadityavarnam Tamasah Parastat ...[1]

Rama's lips moved of their own accord as he heard himself intone. He knew this. It was the Purusha Sukta.

I know this Great Purusha who shines like the sun beyond darkness ...

Another version of him appeared. He was in an ashram writing on a brown palm leaf ... Again, a new world ... The energy of the Sudarshan chakra whirled around him as he chanted, sitting cross-legged with his pupils turned

[1] *Rig Veda*, tenth Mandala

up and only the whites of his eyes showing. A being of light, different from the first yet curiously the same, stood resplendent before him.

Sahasra Sirsham Devam Visvaksham Visva Sambhuvam[2]

Rama knew this too. The Narayana Sukta.

The thousand-headed and thousand-eyed ... Imperishable ... All-surpassing ...

The beam of light burst forth from the forehead of the Rama that chanted. It merged with the light of the being that stood before him. The Sudarshan chakra whirled as it grew smaller and moved in the light from Rama's forehead to the being. The being turned to the Rama that watched and spoke in a voice ever so gentle, 'You've returned what belongs to me. We will meet in another yuga, if you know what to do now.'

Rama stood frozen, uncomprehending. And then, the realisation flashed in his mind. And these weren't different worlds, these were different points in time in his future life! He held the power of the divine chakra, the power he had extracted from Arjuna. This was the being he had to hand it over to. Who was he? Before Rama could ask, the vision disappeared.

Another vision and he was chanting something again. A single word, a single syllable. Rama listened carefully.

The vision remained the same this time, but now he was chanting another syllable. And Rama knew then what it was all about. These were the two syllables he had heard unclearly in his head.

[2] *Taittiriya Aranyaka*, tenth chapter

He came crashing back into the world where he stood on the path before the tusker. The Parashu sped towards the tusker as it withdrew its trunk. It waited for it, accepting its strike and its power.

The Parashu cut off the elephant's left tusk. The tusk disappeared. The Parashu hung in mid-air; it didn't return to Rama. The tusk appeared again and vanished once more.

And Rama knew what he had to do ...

He sat on the trail of three and a half loops and eased himself into padmasana. He didn't call forth the fury of the Parashu, form the agnikund in his mind or focus on the banalinga or kalasha. Rama closed his eyes, controlled his breath and emptied his mind.

His self-realisation had been won on the battlefield. The Supreme Goddess had, in her infinite grace, bestowed upon him a glimpse, a blessing and power to accomplish a specific purpose. To kill Arjuna and rid the world of his blight. The extraordinary power had restored him to life, but now, he had to find himself again. His self had floated away like an untethered kite, buffeted by the winds of emotion and thought. The disembodiment had set his mind racing, and he had fallen prey to negative emotions and fantastical delusions of the mind. He had to secure himself to *his ownself*. He had to ground himself in this world. Rama had to find his foundation, and to do that, he had to go back to the start.

The tusker had taken him through the fourteen worlds to show Rama what an infinitesimal part of creation he was. To rid him of his deranged delusions of grandeur. It showed him the things he still had to achieve. What they were, he had no idea. That, too, he must realise by himself. It had shown him what to do and waited for Rama to understand.

The red tusker was Mahadeva's son, the lord of beginnings and remover of obstacles. Ganapathi.

'Vinayaka, mighty leader!

'Gananatha, chief of the Ganas!

'Lambodara, O big-bellied one!'

Rama pressed his palms together as he prayed and bowed to the deity. And Ganapathi spoke in his mind.

'The three and a half loops are the coil of the kundalini serpent that lies at the base of the spine. It is the Muladhara, the first chakra of awakening. That is where you have to start, Rama. You had to attach yourself to it. Your journey to awaken the great Ahi inside you starts here. And it was a lesson that had to be taught through action because your mind was too high in the clouds to understand oral teachings. The Parashu and your prowess made you a danger to everybody around you. The syllable is the key.'

As with all good gurus, Ganapathi had shown him the door and waited for him to open it.

He surrendered his five organs of perception. Gyanendriyas.

He surrendered his five organs of action. Karmendriyas.

He surrendered his five functions of life force. Panchaprana.

He surrendered his five subtle elements. Panchatanmatra.

As twenty-first, Rama submitted his self to Ganapathi, the Lord of the Akasha tattva, the aspect of reality which encompassed the four tattvas of Agni, Vayu, Apas and Prithvi within itself.

He prayed to Ganapathi to bless him with Avakasha, the possibility to ground himself.

Rama gave himself over to instinct.

He traced a circle on the ground. The symbol of Akasha. He drew a square inside it, the symbol of the earth. He uttered the first syllable. *Lam.*

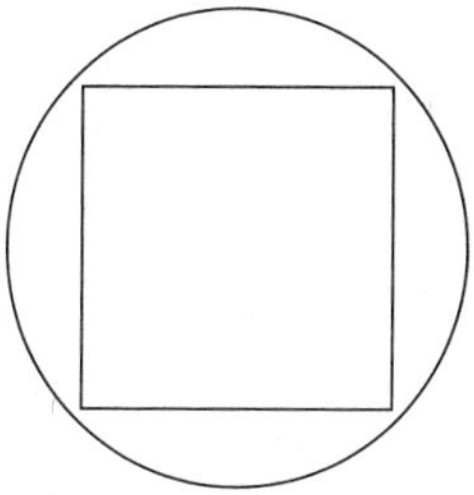

He elongated the ending of the syllable as he intoned with his exhalation and let its vibration run through his body. He focused his attention on the base of his spine and an ineffable sense of settling into himself came over him. Of being whole. Of being Rama again.

'The syllable, the beeja-akshara, of the first of seven chakras in your subtle body, Rama.'

The agnikund, banalinga and kalasha finally flashed in his mind. Rama expressed his gratitude to Ganapathi. He opened his eyes. The tusker and Parashu were gone. Rama was not done yet.

He drew vertical and horizontal lines inside the square to divide it into nine equal squares. He inscribed a number in each like he had seen himself draw in one of the dimensions.

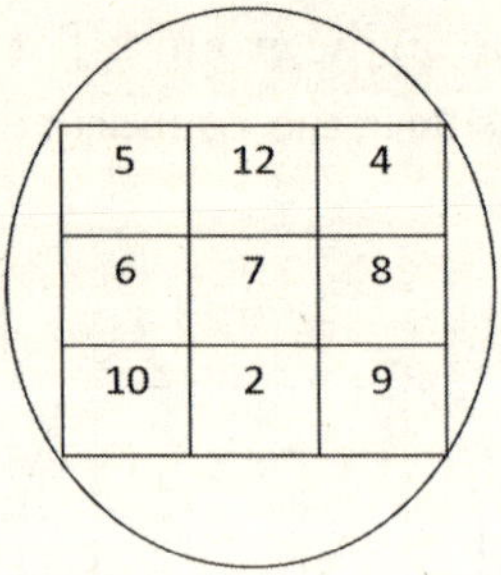

A Sarvatobhadra square. Each column, row and both diagonals added up to twenty-one. He closed his eyes and chanted the second syllable, elongating it again.

Gam.

A resplendent form took shape, its colour the red of the rising sun. An intense feeling of well-being flooded Rama.

'Devam Balaganadhipam,' Rama uttered as he worshipped an infant Ganapathi.

Rama's pupils rolled up and the whites of his eyes stared at the deva. He formed the agnikund in his mind again.

Gam. He repeated the monosyllabic mantra four times and with each intonation, he drew the Sanskrit letter on the ground to form the auspicious symbol. A swastika.

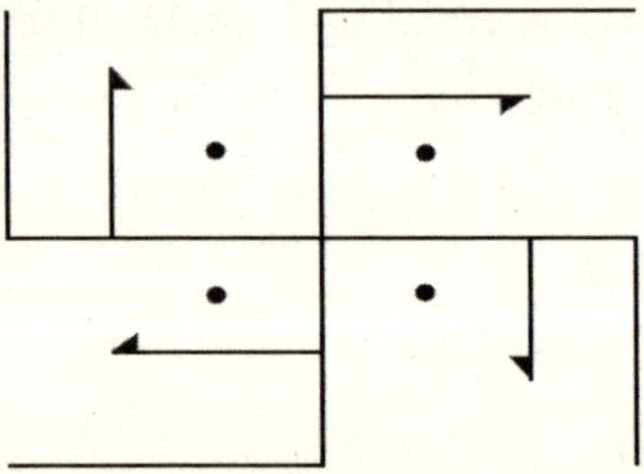

He prayed to Ganapathi and beseeched his aid. He summoned the power of the Parashu and submitted it to Ganapathi as homage, as atonement for the strike that broke the tusk. The red form rippled and transformed. Five elephant heads appeared on a gigantic golden human body. A magnificent lion supported the seated form on its back. Ten arms held a variety of objects, the significance of each being of great import. Six arms held the noose, rosary, mallet, garland, fruit and sweet. It was the remaining four arms that filled Rama with delight. One was in Abhayamudra, gesturing his protection. Another in Varadamudra, symbolising his blessing. One held his broken tusk and the last the Parashu.

The lion roared, and Rama shuddered with joy.

'The syllable is my beeja-akshara, Rama. Learn it!'

'*Om Gam Ganapathaye Namaha*!' Rama intoned in gratitude.

'Perhaps you will be worthy of the seven.'

Ganapathi disappeared in a brilliant flash. Rama emerged from his trance, wondering what the Ganapathi meant about the seven. The seven chakras? He had no inkling. The Parashu sat in his lap. He grasped it and touched the head of the axe to his forehead. The pounding was gone. So too were the anxiety, despair and anger. His mind was clear as sunshine.

Rama closed his eyes, and he was back with Mahodhara and Akrita. He didn't let the surprise or bemusement show on his face. Ganapati had made him run in circles, whirled him across dimensions, shown him what he must do in the future, blessed him with knowledge, and returned him back in time to just before they parted ways with Mahodhara.

'We are very close to the ashram. That way home,' said Akrita, pointing right.

'That way,' agreed Rama and pointed to the right.

'Go home, Mahodhara. There's nothing to worry about. I'll summon you when I need you.'

'I'll get our belongings,' said Akrita.

'Yes,' said Rama as he held Mahodhara close and bid farewell.

Guru and shishya made their way home in the darkness.

3

Brothers Five

Rama and Akrita walked into the ashram a little after dawn had broken. The hubbub around the ashram was muted, with the disciples going about their duties and chores with a palpable wariness, like a hungry herd of deer in verdant grassland. They had to fend for themselves but knew that predators lurked. Rama couldn't blame them. The quiet ashram had seen a tumult of activity, both human and divine. The inmates gave Rama a wide berth, not pausing to greet him or Akrita, with whom most of the younger ones were friends.

Rama hastened to his father's hut and found his brothers seated together on the stoop. They almost jumped off their perch when they saw him walking towards them. Their eyes roved over his body in horror. *The dried blood and dust and turmeric*, Rama realised. He hadn't thought of washing it off. They flinched when they saw the Parashu, as if seeing it for the first time. *They wouldn't have noticed it in their grief last time around.*

'Rama ...' Vasu's voice was strangled with worry and fear.

'I'm alright. It's not my blood,' said Rama, and instantly regretted it as his brothers' faces blanched.

'How is father? Has he recovered fully?' Rama asked.

Brutwakanva stared blankly for a moment and nodded, his mouth forming words that had no sound. He gulped and stammered, 'I believe he is alright.'

Rama moved to go into the hut.

'He isn't here,' said Brihudyanu.

Rama whirled, 'Why? What happened?'

'That's what we want to know. That's why we waited here for you,' said Vishwa.

'What? How would I ...?' Rama paused. 'Father told you to wait for me here?' he asked, baffled.

'He asked us to tell you to wait till he returns,' said Vishwa.

'Wait here? But I'm not going anywhere,' said Rama. He put the Parashu down on the stoop, and the four brothers hastily moved away. Kanva nervously plucked at his janeu. 'Tell me what happened after I left.'

'Father recovered completely. He woke up a day after you left. But ...' said Vishwa.

'He didn't say a word. He drank a pitcher of water and sat silently. Ma assured us he was alright and asked us to stay silent. They lit a lamp here, right where he was lying, and both went into dhyana. They didn't speak or eat a morsel of food,' said Brihudyanu.

'We didn't know what was happening; so, we just waited beside them. And suddenly Ma's body turned red again,' said Kanva.

Rama gasped. 'When? When did it turn red?'

'Yesterday ... Close to dusk,' said Vasu. 'Why?'

Rama looked at his brothers for a long time. 'That was the time I died,' he whispered. His brothers looked at each other, struggling to understand what had transpired. 'But I came alive again.'

'You died and came alive!' Brihudyanu said in a hushed voice.

'And I killed Arjuna.'

His brothers froze. Brihudyanu's jaw slackened.

'And slaughtered twenty-one Akshauhinis of Arjuna's army. And laid waste to Mahishmati,' added Akrita.

Brihudyanu swooned. He went stiff-legged and toppled backwards. But Rama caught him before he hit the ground. His brothers were still staring at the spot where he had been just a nimisha ago. Slowly, they turned to face him. 'How ...' Vasu trailed off. Rama carried his brother to the stoop and gently laid him on his back. His brothers turned to Akrita.

'Acharya can move incredibly fast now, among other things,' he explained.

'What happened then?' Rama asked.

'Ma's body returned to normal, and they came out of dhyana a short while later. They were beaming with joy,' said Kanva.

So they knew. But how? And what else did they know? Rama wondered.

'Father gathered all the darbha grass he could find and walked away into the night. He instructed us to wait for you at the ashram. That was the only thing he said.'

'And what did Ma say when he left?' Rama questioned.

'She said pay my respects to the seven, and may Mahadeva answer your prayers.'

'Darbha ... Seven ... That means ...' Rama turned to Vasu in surprise.

'I think so too,' said Vasu. 'Vishwayonika!'

There was silence among the brothers, and Akrita looked at each of them. 'What is this Vishwayonika?' he asked nervously.

'The Saptarishis worship Mahadeva in a special form. A linga of darbha. Why they do it and how is known only to them. The ritual is secret, and the lore about the linga is known only to the Seven. Nobody has seen this linga or knows why the Saptarishis use it, only that they use it sparingly. Even Ma doesn't know anything. That linga is called Vishwayonika,' said Vasu.

'Father has used the Vishwayonika only once before. To learn the secrets of Dhanurveda and divyastras. He learnt the mantras from Mahadeva but never used them,' said Vishwa.

'He did in a way,' said Rama. 'Father taught me the mantras. I could master the divyastras so quickly because of his teaching. Otherwise, it would have taken me years to learn even one of them. It has helped me truly understand a weapon. I mastered the Parashu because I understood it well enough to unlock its mysteries and reveal its potential and power.'

'You learnt the divyastras! It seems you should be telling us what's happening. There is so much we don't know!' said Kanva.

Rama paused, unsure how much to divulge. 'Akrita will tell you all he knows later.'

'But Acharya, I don't know everything. You didn't tell me about the barrier.'

Rama sighed. 'The barrier was a lesson for me, as well as a blessing. It came from Sri Ganapathi.'

Akrita looked at him in confusion.

'There is no end to surprises from you, is there?' asked Vasu.

'Akrita will tell you whatever he knows,' Rama repeated. 'But where is Ma?' he asked.

Vasu wrung his hands in despair. 'Ma's gone to the settlements. There's been an outbreak of Masurika.'

Rama gasped. *The red plague!* The pox was highly contagious but extremely rare.

'I hope the patient has been isolated,' he said.

'Not one,' Vasu wailed. 'Dozens of them, across settlements. Completely healthy people developed red spots all over their bodies within a matter of nimishas.'

Vasu squatted down and hit his forehead. 'Dakini was weeping when she came for Ma. Ma left immediately, asking all of us to stay within the ashram. It's not natural, Rama, this outbreak. It is demon's work.'

Rama stood stunned.

Rama floated on the languid waters of the Narmada. It felt so good to be clean, to soak in the cool waters, disconnected from the world and its worries and its lures. Akrita had finished his wash and prayers and returned to the ashram. No doubt, Rama's brothers would hound him for answers. It was wonderful to be alone in the forest, to move with the river's gentle current, watch the morning mist lift off the surface of the water, breathe in the air with a thousand scents, see the distant hills emerge in the sunlight and hear the awakening of life all around. He swam lazily to the opposite bank of the river and back. His muscles stretched, delighting in the gentle effort. He swam back and forth a dozen times before he emerged from the river and dried himself off, squeezing the last droplets of water from his beard and tying his hair in a knot on the top of his head. He ached to tarry, to drink in the sights of the beautiful vista and roam his beloved woodland, but he had to return to the ashram and decide whether to wait or go in search of his parents. He wrapped a clean dhoti around his waist, finishing by scooping one end up between his legs and tucking it tight against the small of his back. He picked up the clothes he had washed and made his way back with a sigh.

He was almost at the ashram when Akrita came running up. He grabbed the clothes from Rama and said, 'A visitor for you. The man didn't mention his name.'

'He asked for me?' asked Rama with some surprise.

'He asked for Parashurama,' said Akrita.

The man sat on the stoop of Jamadagni's hut in sukhasana. Long, lustrous black hair framed his face. His thick beard extended to the middle of his chest, and he wore a pale yellow dhoti and angavastra over a hard, fleshy body. A neat circle of sandalwood paste and vermilion had been drawn in the centre of his forehead. There was an aura of authority and erudition about the man. Black, intelligent eyes watched Rama carefully. His brothers had welcomed him, and the now revived Brihudyanu placed a small clay tumbler of water beside the man. Rama noticed his feet. The man hadn't washed them with the water from the jug kept at the entrance for just this purpose, yet there wasn't any dust on them at all. Well-tooled leather sandals stood neatly at the entrance.

Rama pressed his palms together. 'Pranaam.'

The man gestured for Rama to sit as if the ashram was his and Rama was the guest. A melange of floral scents, subtle but decidedly feminine, rushed into Rama's nostrils as he sat before the man. Rama wondered at the incongruity between form and fragrance. The man made no move to identify himself, and Rama wondered if it would be rude to ask immediately. He glanced at his brothers and Akrita. They were as puzzled as he was.

'My father, Saptarishi Jamadagni, and my mother, Renuka, aren't here now. What can their sons do for you?' said Rama.

'Renuka Chinnamasta,' said the man in a powerful voice that seemed to emanate from deep within. His enunciation was smooth and there was an odd lilt to his speech, but it was one that was used to unquestioning obedience. 'And it is me who can help you. Help the man that killed Sahasrabahu.'

Rama stared at him warily.

'Who would you be, mahodaya?' asked Vasu. The man laughed mockingly, a challenge dancing in his eyes.

He wants me to deduce it. Perhaps he was being mischievous, or this was some test. Rama felt a mild irritation. He was in no mood to play games with a stranger. Rama nodded, accepting the unspoken task. He rose and entered the hut. He came back with the Parashu. The man's eyes locked onto it. He tried hard not to flinch, but Rama noticed the slight quiver that ran through him. Rama sat and held the Parashu at eye level between the two of them.

'I slew Arjuna with this. I hacked his thousand arms and beheaded him.'

The man's right eyelid flickered. The left eye stared at the axe, mesmerised by its presence. He tried to pry his eyes off the axe, and the right eyelid flickered furiously. It was beyond his control. Rama moved the weapon to his right. The man's right eyeball tracked it, the left one stayed still. Rama studied the man's left eye as he moved his axe slowly. It needed close scrutiny to know, but the left eyeball was certainly artificial. The man was blind in his left eye. Suspicion grew in Rama, but he couldn't be certain yet. Was it mere coincidence that he'd seen Vamana and Mahabali earlier? He laid the axe down and spoke softly, 'Long ago, a man tried to stop the flow of water from the spout of a kamandalu. To prevent Mahabali from making a pledge to Vamana. He lost an eye in the process.'

The man tore his eyes off the Parashu as chagrin flashed upon his face, and Rama knew who he was.

'Welcome, fellow Bhargava, in the name of our clan father, Brighu.' Rama put the Parashu down. 'Welcome to our ashram, Daityaguru.' Rama introduced the visitor to his brothers. 'He is the son of Brighu and Kavyamata. Shukracharya.'

His brothers prostrated themselves at the feet of their forefather. Rama stayed put, watching as they paid their respects to the man known the world over as the guru to the asuras.

'You look as young as us,' Vishwa said in awe.

Shukracharya chuckled. 'One who can manifest beauty, see and enjoy it in all things, never grows old. It is one of the secrets of the Mrita-Sanjeevani,' he said half-jokingly. He winked at Akrita. 'Do you see beauty, young man? In the smile of a lovely girl, perhaps?'

Akrita blushed.

'Well done!' said Shukracharya to Rama.

Rama's reply had no amusement in it. 'You didn't come to meet the man who killed Arjuna. You came to meet the man who annihilated your horde of asuras.'

'I'll say it right, Rama,' said Shukracharya. 'I came to meet the man who slew the Asuras and the avatara who slew Arjuna.'

'Avatara!' Vasu gasped. 'Rama, what is he talking about?'

'They don't know?' Shukracharya asked slyly.

Rama bit his tongue. So, Akrita hadn't told them yet.

'Your brother has sparked the amsha of a deity in himself. He has become an avatara. I'm curious how he managed to do something like that,' said Shukracharya. Rama kept quiet. There was something in Shukracharya's voice when he delivered his final words—a subtle shift in intonation. Rama couldn't quite place it, but it felt different. 'I've come to help you rule, Rama.'

'Rule?' Rama blurted. *Yes! Be the samrat!* said a voice in his head. It was the voice of yearning and power and not the one he was used to hearing. A voice that was from him, yet somehow other.

'Killing Arjuna isn't the end. It is *an* end. And a beginning.'

'I've destroyed the balance of power,' Rama countered Shukracharya. 'Arjuna's dominion is over. The kingdoms he subjugated will win their freedom. There is no one now who matches Arjuna's prowess.'

'True! But there is one greater. You! You are the fulcrum of power. Your next move decides the fate of the world.'

'That is a fantastic exaggeration, Daityaguru,' said Rama. *Not really*, said that power-hungry voice again.

'An avatara of a deity appears on earth. He wields a weapon so formidable that no one knows the true extent of its power. A weapon given to him by Mahadeva himself. When has some such happened before, Rama? I'm afraid I don't exaggerate enough!'

There it was again. An almost imperceptible strain in Shukracharya's voice.

Shukracharya leaned forward. His eyes had a hard glint

in them, and his voice had dropped. 'What did you do with Arjuna's power? What was the secret?'

Rama stared back. 'Mahadeva, you said, and ... "deity". But you didn't mention the name of the deity whose avatara I am—Mahavishnu. You can't bring yourself to speak his name. So, is that what this visit is about? Your desire to thwart the Protector?'

Rama waited for a retort. There was none.

'You raised two mighty samrats, Hiranyakashipu and Mahabali, in your relentless quest to overthrow Indra. You failed both times after initial success. Two avataras of Mahavishnu put paid to your plans. One tore Hiranyakashipu apart, another put Mahabali in Sutala. He is to be the next Indra in the coming Manavantara, but he no longer abides by your advice. He worships Mahavishnu.'

'You seek to influence who you think is the next avatara. To bring him over to your side. Your idea of crafty vengeance. I'm right, am I not?'

Shukracharya watched Rama with a wry smile.

'How are you so sure I'm an avatara, Daityaguru?'

Shukracharya's smile broadened. 'I wouldn't be Daityaguru if I didn't know this much. You hold Arjuna's power, do you not? You didn't destroy it, you extracted it, if I deduce right. Answer, Rama.'

Rama didn't reply.

'I'm right, then,' Shukracharya asserted. 'Avatara. Parashu. Sahasrabahu's secret power.' He shook his head in wonder. 'There is no being as powerful as you in the three lokas except for the gods themselves.'

Rama laughed. Ganapathi had shown him the fourteen lokas and how Rama was just a speck in it. The Daityaguru's knowledge did have its shortcomings. Once again, he was grateful for Ganapathi's guidance. He had grounded Rama in more ways than one.

Shukracharya laughed, genial and self-effacing, as if embarrassed that Rama had to listen to ramblings that didn't make sense to himself even.

'I'm just a mortal,' Rama probed. 'A mortal's lifespan is but a fraction of a nimisha in the grand scheme of things.'

Shukracharya's eyes twinkled. 'There are ways to overcome that. I can help with that too. Anyway, many mortals have lived long past their lifespans by the strength of their tapasya or by the blessings of the Devatas. Didn't Arjuna rule for thousands of years?'

Rama smiled. The man had no idea of his blessing.

'Speak your mind, Daityaguru.'

'Choose your options, Rama. Rule on earth as the Chakravarti Samrat. I'll make the Asuras swear their allegiance to you. A blood oath, if you wish. Use them and win over Devaloka if that is what you desire. Rule the three worlds of asuras, mortals and devas. Establish dharma and peace, and flourish. Nobody can help you better than me. Not even Brihaspati.'

True, said that eager voice in Rama's head. *My ambition must match the power I now wield. Daityaguru will be a great ally. Samrat of three lokas! I will rule*. Rama shook his head to quiet the voice. Shukracharya watched him closely as Rama mulled it over. The first option was a credible proposition. But would the asuras accept his overlordship? He didn't think so. Maybe they would pretend to do so, and Shukracharya had some covert means to nullify a blood oath. Option two was a lie. Option three was the true intent—an appeal to dharma, leveraging Rama's good intentions and sense of justice to cloak it, making the plan seem altruistic and palatable. Shukracharya wished to use him as a tool for his purposes. A powerful instrument that can be controlled by him, all the while seeking the means of making it redundant once the goal is won. He probed some more.

'You deem me worthy of this pursuit?'

'You are a Bhargava in the truest sense of the word! The progress of humanity owes everything to the Brighus. Bhargavas brought agni to humankind, taught men about the gods, worship and yagna, and revealed the intricacies of the soul and science. The Bhargavas enhance life in this sacred land in a hundred ways and form the bridge between man and divinity. And now a Bhargava is an avatara! The story of civilisation is the history of Brighu and his children. Brighu, Chyavana, me. Our clan produces superlative men. Jamadagni is one of the Seven Seers. Renuka carries an aspect of a Mahavidya. You spoke of mortality, Rama. A Bhargava defeated death and became a chiranjeevi. Markandeya.'

Shukracharya came closer to Rama, his index finger jabbing the air. 'You, my child, can be the greatest in Brighu's clan. I will guide your path. I will teach you to rule!'

Rama glanced at his brothers. They were listening in rapt attention, mesmerised by Shukracharya's speech. Only Akrita watched with doubt in his eyes.

Shukracharya resumed, his demeanour changing to that of a guru instructing an ignorant shishya. 'Arjuna ruled with an iron fist, true. But his genius was the implementation of a simple plan. He let the defeated kings continue as titular heads of their respective kingdoms. He let them live in their palaces, nay, confined them there, as a symbol of their helplessness.

Every key position of power in each kingdom was entrusted to his people.

'The high priest in each kingdom is his man, and so is the senapati. The soldiers are all Haihayas, from the five clans that make the horde. Soldiers of the defeated kingdoms are either dead or have switched loyalties to save their families from enslavement or slaughter. Arjuna's vrajapati oversees the pastures and farming. His jivagribhas police the cities. His govinkartanas control the forests and produce thereof. All disputes are settled by madhyamasis trained and dispatched from Mahishmati. And do I need to mention it? Revenue is collected by his bhagadugha, accounted by his akshavapa and held by his sangrihitri. Every suta and messenger is his. Thousands of spies report to Jayadhwaja, his son and spymaster. He established absolute dominance through a network of those who owed clan allegiance or fealty to him. It is an iron frame that he has put in place. So, even if Arjuna is dead, the iron frame endures.'

Shukracharya paused, studying Rama to see if he understood the weight of his words.

'Arjuna's iron frame stretches across the seven dweepas, from the east where the Chinas dwell to the land of the fair-skinned barbarians far west of the Sindhu. It reaches from the frost-covered northern regions, through the desert-dwelling lizard-eaters to the southwest of Gandhara, and down to the mighty dark-skinned tribes further south. It spans the ocean to the west of the white skins, extending to the two dweepas populated by numerous tribes who learnt civilisation from the seafarers and voyagers of this sacred land. How long before the iron frame snaps a trap for you?'

'I will do as I've done before,' Rama replied. '*Paritranaya Sadhunaam Vinashaya cha Dushkritaam.*'

Shukracharya nodded. 'You need no help with the destruction of evil, but you will need me to protect the good. You need a guide to navigate the quicksand of politics. Rise to the call, Rama. Serve dharma.'

'Arjuna followed dharma, too. He was lauded as the best among men. Yet, the corruption of power grew in him like a bonfire in a dry-wood forest. It consumed him,' said Rama.

'Bah! For all his power and supremacy, Arjuna remained a half-barbarian all his life. A thousand lifetimes wouldn't help him rise to the mettle of a Bhargava,' Shukracharya spat.

'Did you make the same offer to him, then?'

Shukracharya didn't answer.

'You didn't. And I know why. You disdain mortals and their fleeting lives. You don't think them worthy of your attention, let alone your guidance. Why then do you come to me? The answer is evident. You can't find an asura willing to challenge the devas, or perhaps there is one, and he disdains you. Am I right, Daityaguru?

'Or is it worse? The devas, I hear, have the secret of the Mrita-Sanjeevani. Your advantage stands nullified. Do they all disdain you now?'

Shukracharya remained quiet.

Rama pitched his voice low, 'I am right. You are left with no recourse but to approach mortals to fulfil your quest for revenge upon the devas. It is not me who needs you. It is you who needs me.'

Shukracharya's eyes were cold and wary. 'Be that as it may, it seems we have a venture well-found.'

Rama pondered his response for a long time. His brothers grew fidgety, while Shukracharya sat still.

'There are many things you are unaware of. A couple that bears telling, so listen carefully. There is a second Bhargava who has gained immortality. You speak to him now,' Rama finally said.

Shukracharya and Rama's brothers gasped in surprise. A couple of nimishas later, he crowed with delight, 'Chiranjeevi! Suits our plans wonderfully.'

'There is more. Arjuna and I have something in common. A guru. The divine Avadhuta. Guru Dattatreya.'

Shukracharya was shell-shocked at the revelation.

'I tread the path he lights. All I've achieved, nay, been granted, is the result of Saptarishi Jamadagni, Ma Renuka and Guru Avadhuta's guidance. What need do I have of yours?'

Anger flashed across Shukracharya's face. 'Make your decision now, Rama. The Avadhuta is of no use in worldly matters. He couldn't stop Arjuna from turning to adharma. You could do better by seeing the value of my advice.'

An alarm went off in Rama's mind.

'I will think it over for a while,' he replied carefully.

Shukracharya rose to his feet and alighted from the stoop. He wore his sandals. 'Strike when the iron is hot, they say. Some men wait for the iron to grow hot, and there are men like you who strike the iron so hard and so much that it turns hot, and then strike it again. You've heated the iron, Rama. Strike!'

Rama stayed silent, and Shukracharya walked away from the hut. 'Time doesn't stand still. Neither for Brahma nor for a chiranjeevi. My offer leaves with me.'

Time is of the essence, Rama told himself. *But why? Why did he come now, at this moment?*

Perhaps Shukracharya knew Jamadagni was away. He knew Jamadagni would dismiss his offer, so he sought to turn

Rama's mind in his absence. But that left Ma. She was as sharp as a tack and would pierce right through the fluff to the nub of the matter. The answer flashed like lightning in Rama's mind.

'Daityaguru! The Masurika! Is that your doing? You sparked the outbreak to draw Ma away?'

Swirls of black smoke spiralled around Shukracharya. He turned in the midst of it.

'Your answer, Rama?'

The Parashu flew to Rama's hand. The smoke enveloped Shukracharya. In a blink, smoke and man disappeared without a trace.

Jayadhwaja stood on the balcony and stared at Naraka unfolding before him. A circle of fire, smoke, destruction and death lay around the imperial palace in Mahishmati. The palace had been untouched by the destruction but was denuded of its pride and infallibility. It stood as a symbol of defeat. The capital of the world was reduced to rubble, and the palace stood mute, an impotent spectator. Twenty-one Akshauhinis of the famed, all-conquering Haihaya army lay dead around the fort and in the streets. Fires had broken out inside the city as the terrified populace fled the looters and arsonists who had a free run of the city. The royal guard dared not venture out of the palace grounds, and the elders, women and children of the royal family huddled together in the humongous hall where Arjuna had once held court. Jayadhwaja's world was aflame and his inheritance reduced to ashes. He turned away from the sight.

The palace was built to a gargantuan scale, an edifice

worthy of Sahasrabahu. Normal humans felt puny in it, and Jayadhwaja even more so. He was short, hardly five and a half feet tall, and swarthy. He rubbed his bloodshot eyes and scratched at the sparse stubble that timidly grew in dirty patches on his cheeks. His inability to sport a moustache worthy of a Kshatriya gnawed at him. His brothers were all taller and displayed majestic facial hair, but it didn't matter. He was the eldest and heir to the throne, and that was all that counted. That, and revenge. Jayadhwaja ground his teeth in anger as his stocky legs walked the dimly lit corridor that snaked around and above him.

His four surviving brothers—Shura, Vrishasya, Vrisha and Shurasoma—stood silent. Their wounds were dressed in strips of blood-stained cloth, their armour battered and rent, their shoulders slumped in defeat.

'Is any general, any officer of the army alive?' enquired Jayadhwaja.

It was Shura who answered. 'Only Mahaveera survived.'

'Chandragupta? Raikava?'

Shura shook his head. 'Don't know if they are dead or alive.'

'Other ministers then?'

'A few junior staff hid themselves or were lucky. The rest were dragged out of their mansions and lynched, along with their families and servants. By our troops when Para ...' Shura's voice petered off. '... when under the influence of the Twastrastra.'

'Say the name,' said Jayadhwaja.

Shura stayed quiet.

'Say it!' Jayadhwaja hollered, his words echoing off the walls.

'Parashurama,' Shura mumbled. Jayadhwaja looked at his brothers' faces. After a moment's pause, each of them whispered the name.

'How will you find the courage to fight him if you cannot even say his name?' Jayadhwaja demanded.

'But how can we fight him? He killed the most powerful man on earth,' Vrisha blurted.

Jayadhwaja stared daggers at him. He drew close to his brothers. 'Are we warriors or eunuchs?'

Silence reverberated through the walls.

'Come!' said Jayadhwaja, walking into their parents' private courtroom.

'See well, brothers. Brand what your eyes see into your memory,' he said, pointing at the two dead bodies laid out together on a wide table. 'Samragni and samrat of the world, our parents. Do not dare take your eyes off them.'

Jayadhwaja's eyes roved over his mother's face and Arjuna's decapitated head. The dead bodies lay without the pomp and circumstance befitting the monarch of the world and his queen. No flowers, no flourish of fanfare, no attendants. The five sons stood wordlessly.

'Does vengeance not make your blood boil? Do your hearts not hammer away in your chest with uncontrollable rage? Has grief numbed your valour, or is it fear in disguise?'

The brothers stood mum.

'Answer me!' Jayadhwaja shouted. The lone lamp at the feet of the dead bodies flickered.

'Forget the throne and kingdom, but remember them. This is personal. We owe it to them.'

'Yes, Jyeshta. You are the eldest and heir. We will follow your lead. But the man ... Parashurama is extremely powerful, and he has that axe. And divyastras. We need a plan,' said Shurasoma.

'The situation is dire. The Haihayas' legacy is at stake. It all began thousands of years ago from here, Mahishmati. From here, we will make our power felt. But there are challenges, and sacrifices must be made,' said Jayadhwaja.

'I'm recalling most of our troops from the foreign outposts. The fastest ships need to carry this message from all ports east, west and south. Some commanders may not respond. They will wait to see how the wind of fortune blows. A few may rebel once the news reaches them. We will deal with them later. Some territories furthest from us, in the dweepas across the oceans, are lost for good, I'm afraid.

'It is a small price to pay for keeping it all together here. There is hardly anything you can call civilisation in those parts. But the centre must hold or all is lost.

'This is our motherland. From Sindhu to Kailasa, from the Brahmaputra to the Mahasamudra and the shores east of it—this is the zenith of human progress, the one land that must be preserved. We cannot lose this sacred land to rebellion. I will gladly sacrifice anything outside our motherland to maintain our sway here. Do you agree?'

His brothers nodded.

'There are no ministers, no advisers, no one to read the stars. We only have us. Speak up if you disagree. I would rather change plans than fail,' said Jayadhwaja.

'Some of our own may rebel,' said Vrisha.

'The Kshatriya code of honour still holds sway. Many are kin and tied to us through marriage. Still, nothing tempts more than a whiff of opportunity, and nothing kills the spark of ambition better than a show of indomitable force.

Time is of utmost importance. We must move fast,' declared Shura.

'We have no inkling of Parashurama's plans. So, let's assume the worst. We cannot allow him the opportunity to unite the old kingdoms against us. He destroyed twenty-one Akshauhinis single-handedly. He can build an empire with a handful of troops. We cannot allow it,' said Vrishasya.

'Indomitable force, yes,' said Jayadhwaja. 'Many will sense opportunity and their ambition will drive them to grasp it. Kill them, wipe out their families, their bloodline, their loyalists and servants. Raze their mansions to the ground. Be ruthless; use assassins if needed. We cannot appear weak.'

'Time,' Jayadhwaja continued. 'There is one advantage we have. It will take time for the news of this devastation to reach the ears of our generals, vassals and rivals. No messenger dove could've left the city with all the vultures and hawks feasting on the dead. We must consolidate ourselves before the news spreads.'

'Vrisha, you head to Avanti. It now houses our largest treasury, since the one here was burned. It also has four Akshauhinis garrisoned there. General Chandraketu is my son-in-law and loyal to me. Divide the troops into four units. Keep a quarter and send the rest to Shura, Vrishasya and Shurasoma. I will hand you written orders for the same.

'Shura, the kingdoms of Kambhoja, Gandhara, Kuru and Panchala should be brought under your control. Vrisha, you are in charge of Avanti, Matsya, Shurasena and Chedi. Shurasoma, to you I assign Kosala, Vatsa, Malla and Kashi. Magadha, Vrijji and Anga to you, Vrishasya. I will deal with Dakshinavarta. I will make the Andhras, Pandyas and the other clans of the south bow to me. But first I must bring control and order to Mahishmati. I think the royal guard will suffice.

'Leave your families here. Take your guards and attendants. Release your messenger doves only when well away from the city. Coordinate with Vrisha where your respective armies will meet you.

'Are we together, brothers?' asked Jayadhwaja. The four of them nodded in assent.

'There is one simple message that you must send. Chakravarti Samrat Karthavirya Arjuna is dead. Yuvaraj Jayadhwaja is samrat now. Obey and show fealty.'

Shura moved to the small table beside the dead bodies. He picked up Arjuna's gold and diamond embedded crown with reverence. He gently placed it on Jayadhwaja's head with Vrisha's help. The four brothers hailed the new samrat.

'*Veera Bhogya Vasundhara*! Victory to Samrat Jayadhwaja!'

The samrat lifted the crown off his head and returned it to Shura. 'Place it beside the throne. I'll wear it again only after that wretch is killed.'

Jayadhwaja walked to the dead bodies of his parents. He bowed to them, tears running down his face. He pulled a dagger from his waistband and cut his right palm, allowing the blood to pool. The new samrat grasped Arjuna's feet with it.

'I swear a blood oath of vengeance! Death to Parashurama! Death to the Brighus!'

His brothers followed his lead. Each swore the same blood oath. They embraced each other and walked away to prepare for Arjuna's and Manorama's final rites. The blood dripped from Arjuna's feet.

4

Blood Flowers

Rama sat against the wall of Jamadagni's hut. He carefully replayed the conversation with Shukracharya in his mind. He needed not to miss anything of importance. His brothers and Akrita broke into excited chatter, exploring theories and possibilities. All of what the Daityaguru said was true in a sense, but his truth was riven with ambition and self-interest. He had used all the tricks he could think of, even dangling clan loyalty and dharma as baits to ignite the ambition he had hoped was inside Rama.

But he was right. The job was only half done. Arjuna's 'iron frame' sees benefits and self-sustenance in maintaining the status quo. He had merely cut the tree. He must burn the deep roots to finish the task. The first thing would be to appoint a successor, a new samrat. Rama wondered who that might be. *A son of Arjuna, surely.* There was one at the temple in Mahishmati. Yuvaraj Jayadhwaja. Did he or any of Arjuna's children survive the battle? Rama had lost count of the number he'd slaughtered.

Twenty-one Akshauhinis, his mind reminded him in that old, familiar voice. Rama shut his eyes and the enormity of the killing crashed into him. Millions of lives met their death at the tips of his arrows, the edge of his blade and the extraordinary power of his divyastras. Visions of corpses, battered bodies and pools of blood filled his mind. A city sacked by its citizens. Embers of fury ignited in his mind; he quickly suppressed them. It wasn't the soldiers he thought about; it was their dharma to fight, and they too had dealt with death elsewhere. It was their families who would bear the brunt of the irreparable loss. So many families would have lost loved ones. Ageing parents would have lost their source of comfort and support; wives, the love and security of their husbands. Some, nay many, families, their sole breadwinner. The light of carefree laughter would have died in the eyes of countless children. Their grief, their desolation, shattered hopes and inevitable curses settled like battle smog in his mind. Rama shut his eyes tighter and grit his teeth in pain.

His mind, screaming in agony, was torn in different directions. *The greater good. You've destroyed the fount of misery.* The innocent eyes of a child waiting for her father formed in his mind. *Greater good for her?* Suddenly, thousands of children were before him, staring mutely, their eyes bottomless pits of despair, of irreplaceable loss.

The eyes accused him. Rama's breath caught at the sheer malevolence on the faces of the children. Their image burned into his mind. There was no shield against it, no divyastra to counter this.

Make the world better for them. You have to. You owe it to them. How?

The visions disappeared. One word flashed like lightning across his mind. The other voice. Loud and clear.

Rule!

Rama's eyes flew open. Was this Shukracharya's doing? Did he play tricks with his mind or merely till its soil so a deep, sullen desire already present in him could sprout? Indeed, it was curious that he wanted to speak to Rama alone as if he was sure Rama's parents would disapprove.

Rama pushed himself off the wall, aware that his brothers and Akrita were watching him.

'I'll see if I can trace father's trail and find him, and then I'll go see Ma,' he said into the silence.

'No, Rama,' said Vasu. 'Their orders were explicit. Father wanted to be left alone and Ma wanted everyone in the ashram to stay within its confines. Respect their wishes.'

Rama sighed.

'They can handle themselves, Acharya. Surely you don't think otherwise. Amba wouldn't want her son to survive a battle and then succumb to the disease. Staying home is the best way to stop the spread,' said Akrita.

'But this is Daityaguru's doing,' Rama argued.

'Maybe. Maybe he wants you to presume so. But Ma has the power of a Mahavidya to call upon. You should take care of yourself first. Eat and rest. Battles within one's soul can be harder than battles with weapons,' said Vishwa.

'I'll get you some food,' said Akrita, walking away to the hut which housed the ashram's kitchen.

'We'll see to the lessons. It's late already,' said Kanva.

'They'll be back soon,' Brihudyanu joined in. 'Everything else can wait.'

They dispersed. Akrita returned with an ewer of water and laid out rice pancakes, curry and fruit on a banana leaf. Rama ate and then drifted off to sleep.

It was the pungent, acrid odour that woke Rama from his fitful sleep. It was nearing dusk. He'd slept the daylight hours away! Dakini was leading a handful of men into the ashram, each holding clay pots of varying sizes and shoulder bags bursting with herbs. One of them was toting an enormous bunch of neem leaves. Dakini's face was marked by anxiety; tension stiffened the shoulders of the men. Rama rushed to her, eager for news of his mother.

'Ma?' Rama asked as soon as he reached her. Dakini gestured for the others to carry on, passing on her herbs and pots to the men as they walked by her.

'She's at her wit's end. The disease rages,' Dakini replied.

Rama was taken aback. 'If Ma cannot help, then …?'

'She says it's an unnatural outbreak. Masurika has no cure, but we isolate the person and help relieve their pain to some extent. It started with two people. They were perfectly healthy, but were infected with the disease in an instant, as they stood. We isolated them quickly and Amba started to treat them when a score more broke out with red spots before our very eyes. Dark magic. That's what Amba says it is. And then later in the morning …'

'This morning? About a couple of muhurtas past dawn?' Rama interrupted.

'About then. Why? How did you know?'

Rama didn't answer. That was the time Shukracharya had left the ashram.

'What happened then?' he asked.

'The disease turned virulent … like it had taken a life of its own; like it was hunting down people.' Dakini was almost in tears.

'How many infected now?'

'More than a thousand, Rama. It appears on people in an instant and then it manifests full-blown. They collapse where they stand,' Dakini wailed.

'A thousand!' Rama exclaimed.

'A dozen settlements upstream are affected. Even the forest nomads have come pleading for help. It is vile, malignant magic.'

Upstream. Rama looked at the tops of the trees, watching them sway in the breeze.

'We are downwind from the settlements. If this is airborne, then the ashram is right in its path,' Rama gasped. 'What did you bring?'

'Neem leaves to smoke; it will help purify the air. Nagadaman leaves and bark for fever. Mandukparni for sedation. Tincture of manjishta, neem and tulsi, medicated ghee, and an ointment of chitraka, dalchini and meethavish.

'All this would help if it was a natural outbreak,' said Rama. 'How does Ma plan to counter the dark magic?'

'I don't know what she's doing. She said something about there being no other way. She's assembled all her patients in the forest clearing, the big one near the sal trees. The volunteers who helped move them are also down with the disease. I was preparing the medicines with Varnini so I haven't got it, by the grace of Mahadeva. They all hang onto life by a thread. Amba weeps in despair.'

Rama's blood turned cold. 'Come,' he said as he hurried away, the Parashu flying into his hand.

They ran past Rama's hut. The banalinga was still there beneath the tree. Rama had hoped his father would be here, but there was no sign, no intangible sense of a presence, human or animal, around. They ran to the first settlement,

Rama maintaining a pace that Dakini could match. The main square and the roads were all deserted, and the small mud and stone dwellings stood in melancholy, as if crouching in the earth. Dusk was turning into night, yet the lamps were unlit. Even the small lamps on the doorsteps and at the foot of the tulsi plants were without light. Fear and gloom hung over the settlement; Rama could almost smell its stinky, sweaty odour, like the fear that erupted when a man-eater made a kill. Except, there was no defence against this assassin. It was going to be a fearful night, and ominous days lay in wait if a cure or counter wasn't found. They sped on without a pause. The same bleak atmosphere had ravaged all the settlements they passed, till at last, Rama and Dakini plunged into the thick forest that skirted the clearing.

They had walked a dozen steps when Rama stopped all of a sudden, tense and vigilant, sensing movement ahead. His eyes scanned the forest, watching patterns of light and shadow in the bright moonlight, alert for the slightest change. Dakini crouched behind him. Rama listened to the sounds of the underbrush, searching for a telltale sound.

There, ahead of them, something was in the bushes, something that kept close to the ground. Rama wasn't sure what it was. The leaves of the gokshura plant rustled. Rama almost let the Parashu fly when an arm emerged. It was slim and dark ebony, with a clump of festering pustules on the forearm. It clawed into the dirt and soil of the forest floor and pulled itself forward. Thick black hair and a head emerged from the foliage. The hand moved forward again, groping for purchase. Fingers wrapped around a small protruding rock and with a painful heave, half of a woman's torso came into their view. Her swollen face, tattoos grotesquely misshapen, turned towards Rama and Dakini. She tried to stretch her hand towards them. The hand fell, and the body sagged into the ground. A pustule bloomed on her cheek.

'Matangi!' Dakini whispered in shock. 'The tribal chieftain's wife.'

The woman desperately heaved herself forward one last time, and her distended belly emerged from the undergrowth.

'Devi Ma! She's with child!' Dakini sobbed.

Rama pointed to her other hand. It was clasped around a small ankle. She was dragging another child. He rushed forward.

'Rama! No!' Dakini screamed. 'She's already got the disease!'

Rama gently pried the foot out of Matangi's hand and reached into the undergrowth. He almost dropped the child in disgust. He laid it on the ground, turned away, dropped to his knees and vomited. Behind him, Dakini did the same. The child was more of a big abscess than a human being. About four years old, its whole body was covered with pustules, swollen and distorted. A round red spot grew on its ankle. It blistered rapidly and filled with an opaque fluid. The blister burst, and putrid pus oozed out. The child lay completely still.

'Mahadeva!' Rama muttered as tears streamed down his cheeks.

'Is the child dead?' Dakini's voice trembled.

The child's arm shot up suddenly, and its fingers grasped Rama's throat with surprising strength. It opened its mouth, and Rama retched at the rotten stink that emanated from it. The mouth was filled with sores.

'My offer still stands. Agree, and all this will go away,' the mouth said. 'Rule, Rama!'

Fury exploded in Rama. 'NO!' he screamed. *Listen to him*, the other voice in his head screamed.

'Not even to save this life?' the mouth laughed. 'The air hunts your people, Rama.' The arm dropped, and the jungle went quiet as a grave.

Matangi's breath rasped as she tried to say something. Big red spots spurted across her body. Rama didn't think twice. He slid his arm underneath her shoulders and heaved her upright easily. He put his axe arm behind her knees and lifted her in his arms.

'Bring the child,' he whispered to Dakini as he walked forward. Matangi snuggled into his chest. Her blisters broke, and the pus smeared Rama's chest and arms.

'Thayee ... Amma ...' Matangi croaked. He knew she was calling for Renuka. The reek from her mouth was nauseating. Rama hurried as carefully as he could, biting down on his lip in anger and disgust. His skin crawled as the pus spread over it. He was thankful for the moonlight illuminating his path, praying that he could get them to Renuka on time and that Ma could do something about it.

The terrain dipped gradually, and the odour of smoked neem leaves, wood fire and herbal preparations hit him. The smoke hung still and heavy. Ma had chosen the clearing well. The space was in the lee of the wind and away from the settlements. Rama hurried past the last shrubs and into the smoke. He could barely make out the moon in the sky and the bright twinkle some distance from it. The planet Shukra, Rama noted with chagrin, named in honour of the Daityaguru. He inched forward, eyes adjusting fast to the smoke and dark. He stopped short at the horror before him.

Bodies lay all across the clearing, some completely still,

some thrashing wildly, limbs jerking like marionettes, screaming as waves of pain wracked them. Each of them was covered with red spots or blisters oozing pus. Many were slathered with turmeric and some ointment, but the spots and blisters had pushed past them, taking on ghastly hues. They moaned and cried in anguish, tears and pus flowed from their eyes. They had voided themselves, the urine and excrement mixing with blood and the discharge from the sores. The stench was everywhere. Rama couldn't even smell the neem smoke now.

Alone, in the centre of the clearing, Renuka sat in padmasana with her eyes closed. All around, her small band of helpers had collapsed because of the disease.

'Rama,' Dakini gasped. She fell to her knees as Rama turned, and then collapsed to her side, still clutching the child. It rolled out of her grasp as she arched the small of her back upward with a mind-numbing scream and started to thrash about. Red spots broke out all over her. Blisters appeared in a blink, filled with the whitish purulence. She gasped for air, her eyes begging Rama for help before they closed as her entire body swelled. She went still.

Rama laid Matangi on the ground as his mind raced for an answer. He knew enough about medicines, but that wouldn't help against this magic. He felt helpless. No, he felt worse. He felt useless. He stared at the Parashu. Rage pounded through him, but what was the use of that? It was a weapon. It could cut, it couldn't heal. He turned towards Renuka. She was still in dhyana.

What is she doing? Rama's mind screamed. He looked down at his body. No red spots anywhere. Was he immune to this? Or, was Shukracharya sparing him deliberately so he could witness the suffering of others and finally come pleading for his help? Rama dismissed the thoughts. He shut it all out, concentrating on his breath, controlling it. In a moment, he was in dhyana. He formed the image of the clearing in his mind and gazed at Renuka with his mind's eye.

She was untouched by the dark magic. Was the Daityaguru savouring her failure or keeping her as the last gambit for Rama to surrender to his offer? Rama could see the force of tapasya emanate from her. She was emitting prodigious amounts of it, giving it all she had. It came off her in waves of golden whorls. Rama traced the whorls. They were fighting, desperately seeking to contain the spirals of red that sought to escape their clasp. The red spirals were the magic of the disease. Renuka was straining with the effort. This was all her. Where was the Mahavidya?

The red spirals glowed, growing darker, denser and stronger as Renuka tried to nullify them, suck their power away and contain their impact to the clearing. She was preventing it from breaking free, and it was taking all the strength she had. Rama probed, seeking the extent to which Renuka had spread her power. It was a gigantic circle, all the way from the settlement nearest to the ashram, across the river, deep into the forest and further upriver to encompass a dozen more settlements. A great, wide golden circle striving to keep the red within itself.

Mahadeva! How long had she been at it? How long more could she hold on? Panic coursed through Rama. Give up, accept the offer and spare the people the pain. Surrender now to win another day. *Eliminate the magic of the disease and deal with Shukracharya another day*, his mind suggested. No, who knows what other tricks he had waiting to force Rama to do his bidding? Fight now, defeat him, and then punish him. Rama decided not to back down. He had to help Ma, but what could he do?

The dome!

The dome the asuras had formed over Indrapuri was Shukracharya's magic. It had sucked away the power of the devas and rained decay on them. Could Rama form it and use it for his purpose?

He envisaged the agnikund in his mind and channelled the power of the Parashu into it. The outer circle of the rune on the Parashu glowed. Rama felt power surge through him. Incredible, glorious power. This wasn't the kundalini shakti, this was all him. The power of an avatara.

He formed the transparent dome in his mind, encompassing both golden whorls and red spirals. Not a solid dome, a fluid one. Not hard, but incredibly soft and flexible. A dome made of millions of watery, gossamer-fine spider webs. Tough enough to contain the two forces, soft enough to mould itself around the red spirals if they tried to force their way through, and flexible enough to snap back into place once the force dissipated.

The red spirals attacked immediately, seeking to puncture the dome. They hammered into it, and thousands of red cobwebs erupted on the inner surface, the force of the assault scattering and dying out across the soft interior. The battering was ferocious and unrelenting. Even then, the dome held!

The golden whorls withdrew into Renuka. A sigh of relief escaped her, and the tension in her body lessened. Rama didn't know what else he could do. He hoped Ma did.

A dead calm spread through the dome. The force field shifted suddenly around Renuka. She started to suck the red towards her, to draw the magic of the disease to her. The spirals pounded frantically against the dome. The dome held.

Rama felt a gasp of air near his left ear. He cleaved his mind and turned the whites of his eyes towards Dakini. She floated stiffly in mid-air, right beside him. Her pus-filled eyes stared at Rama. He knew what was coming.

'Desist, Rama,' said Shukracharya through Dakini's mouth.

Rama's voice was icy and menacing. 'Stop this now, or you make an enemy of me.'

'I desire no enmity with you, Rama. I was wrong about doing this. But I cannot stop it now. Renuka has taken control, and I cannot withdraw it. Remove the dome and I will annul the magic. Only I can do it, she cannot. I never thought she would suck the magic into her. It will kill her. I do not want that sin on my head. Trust me, I give you my word.'

Rama didn't trust him. 'Begone!' he said through clenched teeth.

Dakini collapsed to the ground. Shukracharya's voice was gone.

The red spirals swirled around Renuka, fighting to flee from her. *What is Ma doing?* Rama panicked.

Renuka opened her mouth. Rama gasped, almost falling out of his dhyana. She was taking the disease into herself. *No! No!* His mind wailed. *There must be another way.*

Suddenly, Chinnamasta was there. An ear-splitting, keening laughter rang around the clearing, shaking the ground. Renuka's tongue lolled improbably long. The red spirals turned into liquid fire. Chinnamasta drank it all. The spots, blisters and scabs, the pus, the stench, the blood and excrement—they sloughed off the bodies lying in the enclosure as the victims all writhed. She drew it all to her and opened her mouth wide. Rama's vision was filled with Chinnamasta's mouth and tongue. That was all that could be seen. The brilliant red of the tongue and the utter blackness inside the mouth. His hair stood on end. It all disappeared into the black.

Renuka's body turned blood red. As the gaping mouth devoured the disease, the pupils of her eyes shone like iridescent rubies, and thousands of flowers bloomed on the surface of her red skin. Flowers big and small—champa, gandhapusha and kaner, hemapushpa, chitrapushpi and navamallika, palasha and suvanchala. The stench evaporated, and a sweet, joyous fragrance filled the air.

Rama saw Dakini breathe in great lungfuls of air, her skin becoming whole and clear again. Men, women and children revived as the magic left them, restoring their health. Relief and disbelief played on their faces as they examined each other. Slowly, they turned to Renuka Chinnamasta and stared wonder-struck, rapture dancing in their eyes. Matangi lay still on the ground.

Mahadeva! Was it too late for her? Was her unborn child dead? Rama prayed it wasn't so. He beseeched Chinnamasta to help her, to do something. The Mahavidya laughed, gentle and soothing. In a blink, she was inside Matangi's body. Rama and the others stared in amazement. Renuka's face was on Matangi's body, and Matangi's face was on Renuka. A warm crimson glow covered Matangi's body as Renuka rubbed her palms in circles across her belly. The glimmer poured into her mouth and spread across her body. In a nimisha, it dispersed out of her nostrils and faded away. The disease melted away from Matangi. The swelling disappeared. Matangi's body was restored, without blemish, and she revived. Renuka's face was on her own body again.

The tribes-people rushed to Matangi as she held her child to her and wept. She pushed herself to her knees and looked at Renuka with adoration.

'Amma,' she whispered. Her hand caressed her belly. 'Yellara-amma! Mother of us all!' Her people took up the chant and soon everyone joined in, all on their knees, gazing at Renuka's red, fragrant body.

'Yellara-amma! Yellara-amma!'

The red disappeared from Renuka's body. Rama no longer sensed Chinnamasta's presence. He let the dome fade away. He emerged from dhyana and walked towards Renuka. The blistering heat wave drove everyone away from her and closer to the periphery. Renuka's skin bubbled from within as she threw her head up to the skies and screamed. Rama didn't know if it was the sound of rapture or agony.

A cool mist gathered, encircling just Renuka and trapping the heat around her. Thunder boomed in the skies and lightning streaked all around. An enormous downpour descended on her like a waterfall from the sky, pummelling her skin, and soaking into her. Vapour radiated from Renuka, billowing into the clearing. A shock wave ran through the place with a dull thud. The heat, mist, rain and vapour disappeared in a blink.

Renuka sat calmly in dhyana. Indra stood before her, muttering an incantation under his breath.

'Incredible things happen around you, Rama,' he said, approaching him. 'I don't know how she did it, but Renuka has digested the evil magic. It gave off the enormous heat. She would have cooled down on her own, but it would have taken her a couple of days more and would have been excruciating. I thought it would be fitting to spare her that, given what she's been through.'

A coolness now emanated from Renuka, along with the fragrance. It brought a benign calm to the tense crowd, slowing their rapid breathing and soothing their nerves.

'She has rescued you from the fire of your pyres,' Indra said to the crowd. 'She's breathed the cool air of life back into your lives.'

They listened quietly and bent to touch their foreheads to the ground before Renuka.

'Shitala Devi!' said someone.

They chanted again, 'Shitala Devi! Renuka Yellara-amma! Shitala Devi!'

'Thank you,' said Rama.

Indra smiled and answered the question at the back of Rama's mind, 'I was informed that the Daityaguru was in your father's ashram. I also know he is a Bhargava. Whatever else he came for, you should understand he has only one burning ambition. To unseat me from my throne. He will go to any lengths for that.' Indra paused a nimisha. 'Wonder what he's cooking up now?'

Rama understood. 'He wanted me to join forces with him. Many arguments, inducements and big words were used to convince me. Without a doubt, Devaloka and your throne were discussed. He wanted me to rule. This terrible magic was to pressure me into agreeing to his offer. I said no, but ... I'm not sure. I have to think it through. But I will not align with the Daityaguru. Neither do I have my eyes on your throne.'

Indra stared at Rama for a long time and then glanced at the Parashu.

'You have my word,' said Rama. Instinctively, he formed the agnikund in his mind. He held his palm out, and agni bloomed between his fingers. 'I give you a fire oath,' he said. 'Agni Sakshi.'

Indra nodded, and they embraced each other. 'There is something you can help me with,' said Rama and whispered something in Indra's ears.

Indra put his thumb on Rama's forehead and whispered an incantation.

'It is done,' said Indra. He opened a portal and stepped through. The portal blinked out.

Rama turned to the crowd. Everyone was seated before Renuka, waiting for her to emerge from dhyana. They were still chanting her name. Dakini and the other helpers were examining each of them, giving them something to drink from a clay cauldron.

Rama sat down to wait for Renuka to wake.

5

Throne

A muhurta later, Renuka opened her eyes. Gasps and awe-filled murmurs ran through the crowd. They chanted loudly and repeatedly, but no one moved towards her. Renuka scanned the crowd, found Dakini and beckoned her. She spoke to Dakini, who ran out of the clearing to do her bidding. Rama didn't think it right to listen in. Renuka closed her eyes.

A short while later, Dakini rushed towards Renuka, carrying two jute bags, one of which was filled with strips of cotton. She placed the bags at Renuka's feet. The sky darkened around Renuka. An inky blue-black sheath of air gathered around her. Streaks of lightning emanated from her body, traipsing through the dark air. Dakini staggered back with a strangled cry. Renuka opened her mouth, and a swarm of brown motes rushed out of her mouth and into the bags Dakini held open before her. The crowd gasped. Rama rushed, unsure what this new phenomenon was. He stopped at the edge of the semi-circle formed by the crowd when he realised the motes were dried pustules of the disease. His hair stood on end, and he froze at the sight and the immense power radiating from his mother's mouth.

The outpour stopped, and the air and lightning faded away. Renuka opened her eyes. She saw Rama, but her gaze shifted until she found Dakini. She whispered instructions again. Dakini and a couple of other helpers carefully took the bags away. Without another word, Renuka rose and walked past Rama and into the crowd. The crowd parted to let her through, and she walked right to the middle. They withdrew a few steps as she walked, filled with awe and fear. The chanting had stopped and a heavy silence permeated the clearing. Wide, unblinking eyes were fixed on her. A baby wailed in the crowd and was urgently shushed. Renuka smiled, the same innocent smile that belied her age and her power, and in a nimisha, the crowd surged to her. They touched her and whispered her name, beseeched her blessings and gushed with gratitude. She had a few soothing words for all of them as they broke down around her. Her loving hand caressed the children. The wondrous fragrance wafted in the air as she moved amidst the press of people.

It was a long while before they took their leave, Renuka instructing her helpers to light torches and escort the tribes to their settlements. She assured Matangi of the safety of her unborn child and told her what to do in her native tongue. Dakini handed Matangi a small clay pot of medicated ghee. At last, Renuka decided it was time to return to the ashram with Rama and Dakini.

'Preserve the dried pustules carefully,' Renuka told Dakini, 'We will use them to prevent another outbreak. They will help the people fight the disease and kill it naturally, without getting infected.'

She continued with her instructions as they walked in single file, with Rama leading the way. She made no mention of him, nor did she ask him anything. Rama wondered why, a trifle irritated.

'A small piercing should be made on the left forearm for men and the dried pustule placed in it. Wrap it with the cotton strips. For women, the piercing should be on the upper arm, between elbow and shoulder,' Renuka was saying when Rama stopped and turned to face her.

'Ma,' he said.

Renuka paused. A slow smile played on her face as she touched Rama's cheek, her eyes expertly noticing and analysing the cuts and bruises on his arms and torso.

'Rama. What news do you bring?'

Rama was flabbergasted. He opened and closed his mouth a couple of times before he blurted, 'Arjuna's dead.' He heard a sharp intake of breath from Dakini.

Renuka's smile broadened as she replied, 'You wouldn't be here otherwise.'

Rama was tongue-tied.

'But ... But ... So many incredible things have happened ...' he sputtered.

Renuka held a finger to his lips. 'Yes. But have you understood it all? We must hear it all, but there will be another time for it. Not here, not now. And certainly not when hunger eats me. I haven't been this hungry since I was a child. Go on, lead the way to the ashram.'

Rama walked on in confusion.

'Thank you for the dome,' said Renuka. Rama kept mum.

'What dome?' questioned Dakini from behind Renuka.

Nobody replied. They walked in silence in the moonlit forest. Back at the ashram, Renuka slept as soon as she'd eaten.

Rama woke early, finished his morning rituals and waited for Renuka to return from the riverside with her pot. She came empty-handed. She caught Rama staring at her empty hands but didn't acknowledge it. Instead, she said, 'Your story can wait till your father is back, Rama. And leave him be. He'll be back when it is time.'

'When?' Rama asked.

Renuka shrugged and walked away to guide the shishyas in the day's lessons.

Rama sat on the stoop. Everyone had something to do. Even Akrita had disappeared, busy with his lessons and happy in the company of his friends. Rama wondered what story he'd tell them all. He conjured ideas and plans in his mind, turning things over endlessly in frustration.

'So many things to be discussed. Where is father?' he muttered to himself.

Rama resumed his practice and drills, burning the new moves he had learnt into muscle memory and making mental notes about the flow and pace of the movements. He analysed the weapons he had made his own and the ones he'd seen being used, how they'd been deployed, their uses and disadvantages in different situations. He thought of going to his ashram and sitting in dhyana before the banalinga, but the turmoil inside him needed physical expression. Finally, he decided to cut wood, throwing himself into hard labour and submitting these complicated thoughts to the monotonous thwack of the axe hitting wood. No, the Parashu wouldn't do. It was a weapon, not a tool. He borrowed the biggest woodcutter's axe from the store and whetted the blade. He lost himself in the task till the blade gleamed like new. Rama set out into the jungle in the afternoon heat. Some firewood, perhaps, or maybe a new beam for the pathashala. One of them had a crack in it.

He meandered through the woodland, selecting and dismissing trees and branches. He twirled his axe as he walked, constantly shifting it between his hands as he let his thoughts stray as they pleased. Rama noticed the spoors of various animals through sheer force of habit but veered off from their trails. He wanted to be alone. Even the company of these creatures wasn't welcome to him now.

Dusk turned to night, and he roamed, dimly aware of resting animals and the creatures of the night prowling or foraging in the dark. He walked through a pride of lions, hardly taking note of them, and they quietly let him pass, watching him all the while.

Deep into the night, Rama stopped to rest against a dead sal tree. He looked up at the stars and the moon to judge the time. It was only a couple of muhurtas before the break of dawn. He made himself as comfortable as he could at the foot of the sal and dropped into a quick nap. His last thoughts were about Guru Dattatreya. Why hadn't the Guru reached out to him?

He woke with the first light of dawn. Immediately, his warring thoughts were back. But they seemed to have organised themselves into the semblance of an order. The thought that occupied his mind most prominently was the Parashu. He'd picked the biggest and heaviest axe in the ashram and twirled it like a toy with very little weight. He had either grown stronger, or the Parashu was so heavy that this axe felt much lighter in comparison. Perhaps both. He'd never thought of the Parashu as heavy. It was weighed just right for him. Rama realised he hadn't seen another mortal wield the battle axe. Surely Arjuna would have tried ... and succeeded. The Parashu was hovering a hair's breadth above his forehead when he'd come back from that other world ... or was it another dimension?

Only Mahadeva and Nandin have held his weapon, and they weren't mortals. Moreover, Arjuna was the embodiment of the Sudarshana chakra. Nandin's hands had a visible tremor when he held the Parashu. Was it fright, weight or both? Rama made a mental note of this.

Sudarshana chakra ... Muladhara chakra ... Sahasrara ... thousand petals ... thousand prongs ... His mind went off on a tangent and his musings were replaced by another thought.

The scrolls and manuscripts in father's hut. He'd read precious little about the kundalini shakti, but he couldn't shake the feeling that he *knew* more. He'd just have to put all the pieces together. There may be some mention in his father's library. He hoped that there were no riddles or prophecies.

The third thought jolted him upright. There was one story Jamadagni hadn't told him, and he'd never thought of asking. He was absolutely convinced the story was of vital importance. He berated himself for not thinking of it earlier. Father was away, but Ma would know the story. She knew about the Guru.

Rama scrambled to his feet and rushed home.

Rama caught Renuka as she was leaving the hut.

'I have to talk to you,' he said.

She held up her hand to remonstrate, but Rama was insistent, 'It is about Guru Dattatreya. I want to know the story of his birth.'

Renuka was mystified. 'Why is that so important now?'

'I don't know, Ma. But I want to hear it. I have to hear it.'

Renuka sat on the stoop and Rama sat opposite her. He was getting impatient.

'Dattatreya's parents are Atri and Anasuya. A saptarishi and a mahasati, no less. The spiritual power they have earned is beyond measure, so it isn't a wonder that Dattatreya was born to such a couple. He was a blessing bestowed on Anasuya.'

'A blessing?' Rama interrupted. 'Who blessed her?'

'The divine Trimurthi—Brahma, Vishnu and Mahadeva together. A blessing to mark Anasuya's success at a test devised by them.'

'A test here too?' Rama said.

'Yes. A test of her chastity, her penance, adherence to dharma and her presence of mind. They came to her hermitage when Atri was rapt in tapasya. They demanded to be fed by her but imposed one condition. She had to offer them food while naked.'

'What? Why would they impose such a humiliating condition?' Rama exclaimed.

'That was the test. Tell me, what does Anasuya do now? Deny the Trimurthi and anger them? Or accept the condition and bare her beauty against her wishes before men other than her husband?'

Images from the past flooded Rama's mind. The test by fire invoked, Ma Chinnamasta, the naked couple writhing below her. He pushed them away and focused on searching for an answer.

He thought aloud, 'The soul is eternal, the body just a garb the atma wears in this life. It changes garb across deaths and rebirths. It doesn't really matter in the cosmic sense. Yet, in a particular life, the atma is tied to a body. Dharma and chastity demand that it be shared only with one's beloved, to uphold the sanctity of love and matrimony. She could've done as she pleased if she was unwed.

'On the other hand, the Trimurthi know all there is to know. Nothing is hidden from them. To see a naked mortal is nothing to them. So, why ask this?

Renuka smiled and kept quiet, letting Rama work it out.

'She could agree. It is the Trimurthi, after all. What is there to hide from them? There should be no false modesty before them. Atri would understand, wouldn't he?

Renuka didn't answer.

'She could disagree. Even the Trimurthi cannot demand this. Denying them would uphold dharma, even if it angered the gods. And Atri ... surely he would empathise with her predicament?'

Renuka didn't answer.

Rama was silent for a long while. He threw up his hands in defeat. 'I don't know the answer. What did she do?'

Renuka laughed, 'Anasuya agreed. But she was clever and outwitted them. So tremendous was her power of tapasya that she turned all three into babies, and suckled them at her breast.'

Rama stared wide-eyed. The answer had thrown him deep into contemplation. Renuka watched closely, wondering what thread of thought Rama was teasing out.

'Mahadeva!' Rama whispered. 'I've been blind to the truth. And it has been right in front of me all this time.'

'What truth, Rama?'

'*Remember the beginning.* The guru told me this, and so

did Nandin. I thought they only meant the beginning of all that happened here. Then it took on other meanings, other beginnings. And then the very beginning of it all. You told me the beginning of the guru's story, and I just realised something.'

'What is it, Rama?'

'Let me think it through. Let the thought settle and sprout and then go beyond the mind. I will have answers for you soon.'

Renuka nodded and rose. Rama rose along with her and moved into the hut.

'There are some things I need to find and read.'

'Good that you haven't forgotten the Brahmin part of Brahmakshatriya,' said Renuka as she walked away.

Rama looked at the texts lined on the shelves. There were forty or fifty of them, big and small. He didn't know where to start, so he chose at random and scanned through them. Some were in verse; others were commentaries. This wouldn't do, he needed to do more than read; he needed to study and understand. Rama moved to stack aside the texts he'd already studied as a shishya and the scrolls on Dhanurvedaand Ayurveda. He had committed most to memory. That came easily to him. He paused. What if these known words had another shade of meaning, a subtle layer of nuance that he'd missed earlier and could understand better now? Rama sighed. He had to temper his impatience and pore over them all. For that, he needed Vishwa's help. There was no one better than him in understanding the grammar of the texts and the scores of meanings that could be gleaned from words and phrases. He picked one, sat cross-legged on the stoop and touched the bunch of palm leaves to his forehead, seeking the permission and blessings of his gurus and pitrus and conveying his gratitude to the learned men and women who had written this knowledge down. Finally, he began.

For nine days, Rama continued to read, putting the texts aside only for his ablutions, sandhyavandana, a little food brought by Akrita when he was hungry and snatches of sleep when it overcame him. At first, he took the scrolls and leaf bundles to Vishwa, interrupting his teaching sessions. Soon, Rama compelled Vishwa to forsake everything else and sit by him, asking and arguing, poring over minutiae, till he was satisfied. Nobody disturbed them. Renuka passed silently by, as did his brothers. Akrita came only to leave food and take away empty utensils.

'Acharya is on the hunt again,' Akrita whispered to Renuka as they stood watching Rama from the pathashala on the ninth day. He was staring into the distance, lost in thought.

'And he won't rest until he finds his answers,' said Renuka. 'He explores something new, some new path. My instincts tell me so.'

'He knows your magic, Maathey. I missed telling you this earlier. He knows to make pots from river sand just like you do and to extract water from stone.'

Renuka beamed with both wonder and pride. A couple of nimishas later, she looked deep into Akrita's eyes and asked, 'Do you sleep well, Akrita? You saw a war like none other. The blood and gore. The scale of destruction. I hear the stories that the newcomers in the settlements whisper. Arjuna, his army and his city, all smashed. Seeing all this can make one lose his mind. The trauma would be deep and powerful. Yet I see no such signs in you.'

'I was there, and I saw it all, yet I seem to remember it second-hand,' Akrita searched for the right words. 'I see it in my mind as a series of paintings. It removes any fear or pain or trauma when I recall the war. A voice repeats in my head, calming me. The voice says only one word, over and over again. Swasti-astu. It protects me.'

'The voice of the woods. The Avadhuta's voice,' said Renuka.

'No, Maathey. I don't hear that voice anymore. This voice that protects me belongs to acharya.'

Surprise flashed in Renuka's eyes.

'I remember acharya's every action during the war. All that I've seen is etched in my brain. The incredible power, the glory of it.' Akrita went quiet and seemed lost in thought. Renuka slipped away.

A muhurta later, Rama rose, walked to the store and picked the smallest axe he could find. He strode out of the ashram and into the jungle. Akrita trailed in his wake. After a while, Rama beckoned him.

'How goes your study of the Vedas, Akrita? I haven't had time to teach you much, but father and Ma would've instructed you.'

'They both did, even your brothers. It is a blessing. To learn so much, to be taught by the Bhargavas.'

'I am on a different quest now. I will need your support.'

Akrita beamed. 'Forever and always, acharya. Mahadeva bless me that I'm always by your side.'

A twinge of sadness played across Rama's mind. Akrita was mortal. He would shed this body when his time came. So would his brothers and his parents. So much death would be witnessed by one fated to be chiranjeevi. All his loved ones would pass away, leaving only memories. Despair clutched at Rama's heart, and he fought it desperately. He turned to Akrita and placed his hand on his slim shoulder. Rama looked straight into Akrita's eyes. Innocent, expectant, filled with absolute belief in his guru.

'I will do all I can to help you progress spiritually, Akrita. To evolve into a self-realised soul. To give you true happiness.' Rama paused a nimisha. 'All that I've undergone, all that I've done, teaches me something. Something important. I've studied about it. I've thought a great deal about it. It has permeated my subconscious mind. I need to meditate on it now. That is the only way to realise whatever it is that is just beyond the grasp of my mind.'

Akrita nodded.

'I'll ask questions of you about what you've learnt. Answer as best you can. Ask me questions if need be.'

Guru and shishya walked and talked. Rama made for the dead, burnt-out Sal tree. They reached as dusk was falling. Rama set to work, using the small axe to hack and hew at the dead wood. He lost himself in the work, not caring about the passage of time, giving over to instinct and letting his mind work out the answers as his body laboured. An impulse that told him that there was some shape in the tree that needed to be revealed. He continued long into the night, working with the light of the stars, his body sweating even in the cool, damp night air.

He finally dropped the axe and sat on the seat he had fashioned for himself. Rama sat in siddhasana, slowed down and controlled his breath, and went into dhyana. Akrita silently watched.

Jayadhwaja stared at the crown placed on the throne. He'd sworn he wouldn't wear it till he'd had his revenge. The crown would remain where it was until he had crushed that wretch and beheaded him. Parashurama, the killer of his father and guru. Slayer of the man he'd idolised and yearned to become. He didn't have a thousand arms like Arjuna, but he'd win it all back with just two. And that would make his exploits and glory all the greater. He would carve his name into itihasa, a son who outdid his superhuman father. Jayadhwaja slipped out of the tunnel that led from one of the secret underground chambers of the palace to the garden, a yojana from the cremation grounds. Arjuna had a network of tunnels built ages ago. The entire extent of it was known only to the deceased samrat, Jayadhwaja and a few trusted spies.

The spy ahead of him, a distant relative, carried a torch that shone bleakly in the eerie, dense darkness of Mahishmati. More than a week of heaping corpses together and burning them, and yet thousands upon thousands remained, strewn like malignant sores of some rabid disease. A disease, that's what Parashurama was, Jayadhwaja thought, and he would find a cure to rid this world of him.

The survivors had fled the city, and those that had escaped capture by the royal guard. The rest were forced into cleaning the city and burning the corpses. His brothers would send more men. To rebuild, to recoup. And then ... Vengeance. Jayadhwaja balled his fists in anger and quickened his step.

He was used to the stench now, and the scavengers and rodents and vultures. But what brought his blood to boil were the flies. The capital of the world was reduced to a city of flies. Millions of them had invaded the city, and their incessant buzzing set his teeth on edge. And along with them came their predators. Birds, beetles and mites swarmed. A small voice in his head mocked him, *The samrat of flies, that's what you are.*

'Has he come alone, Tarakaksha?' he asked aloud to dispel his thoughts.

'Yes, samrat. Maybe ... No,' said the spy. 'I see one man, but I feel surrounded in his presence. As if a thousand eyes were on me. Like unseen things are waiting to pounce. He makes my skin crawl, samrat. That man terrifies me. Is it wise to meet him alone, without protection?'

Jayadhwaja didn't reply. They hastened on, hearts of anger and terror pacing towards the cremation grounds.

'Who is he?' Tarakaksha asked after a while. Jayadhwaja kept silent, his mind recollecting the military campaign from years ago.

Mayong. A place steeped in mystery and lore. Entire tribes devoted to expending supernatural powers to gain supremacy and wealth, to wreak havoc against each other. They boasted about their ability to harness these powers, claimed it ran in their blood, that they learnt in their mothers' wombs. They gloried in their prowess till the powers turned upon them, and took their price. Cruel, gruesome deaths, and souls cast into oblivion. But utilising these powers was a heady and addictive practice, and the tribes were willing to pay the price. Nobody learnt to control the energies they invoked, and they failed to expand their domain. Mayong was feared, and nobody ventured there. Of course, nothing worked against Arjuna. He just pummelled them into submission.

Until one family learnt. The powers didn't bite back. They grew in eminence and might. They declared themselves as rulers, and in an act of breathtaking ambition, turned their powers against Arjuna. Arjuna dismissed the threat with arrogant disdain. Manorama did not. She waged war, her troops aided by an army of Vedic rishis and priests. White magic against the black. And he, Jayadhwaja, eager to prove his mettle to his all-powerful father, had been in the van of the battle.

It had been a long, terrifying campaign, but he had prevailed. He had wiped off the entire royal family. All except one, the prince. A mere child of eight years surrounded by the corpses of his family, he mewled and begged for mercy, his eyes riveted on Jayadhwaja's bloody sword. He'd ordered the child to rise and meet his fate. The child obeyed. And then Jayadhwaja had noticed the child's eyes. The pupils were mere pinpricks, and they oscillated even as they stared back. The child had pulled Jayadhwaja's sword to his chest and pushed his heart against the razor tip. He'd jerked the tip out with a groan, collected his heart blood and sworn a blood oath of fealty and service to Jayadhwaja.

Jayadhwaja had seen the raw power the tribes of Mayong could harness. They had contempt for the rules of the Vedic priests and had outmatched them more often than not. It was their feeble army that was the chink in their armour. He'd decided to let the child live, though he wasn't sure he'd survive the self-inflicted wound. He ordered the child to learn his craft, build his strength and come to him to render his service.

The child had come back now, three decades later.

Jayadhwaja and the spy wound their way through the smouldering pyres; the heat dispelling the cold of the night and the flies and slathering their bodies and clothes with sweat. They came upon him at last, seated cross-legged and alone on the bare earth, behind a small burning pit.

The man was resplendent, matted hair and beard framing his shining face. His body was covered with prodigious hair, and buffalo hide was wrapped around his waist. Amulets covered his arms, ankles and neck. Every finger had a ring. The pinprick pupils danced in the whites of his eyes, and a small smile played on the twin daggers of his lips. There wasn't a drop of sweat on his body.

He remained seated, pressed his palms together and extended his arms towards Jayadhwaja. He bent his head.

'Swagatam, samrat. The life you had once spared is at your service.'

'So, you're back now ...' Jayadhwaja started.

'Not that name, samrat. I beseech you not to call me that. That is an old, discarded name. A name for a different person. This is a new me before you.'

Jayadhwaja said nothing. He simply waited and watched.

'I offer my powers to you. I offer my aid in your endeavours.'

'Powers, you say? Abhichara? Your black sorcery. It was of no use against my father,' Jayadhwaja taunted.

'Too little power, too much ambition, then. My forefathers failed. But I've built on what they knew. I understand more, hence I am more powerful. Arjuna is dead. Brought down and slain despite his enormous authority and power. Are you stronger than him? And mightier than Parashurama?'

'So, you know that name?' said Jayadhwaja.

'Your soldiers can't forget it. I'm sure even these flies know it by now.'

'Why should I trust you?'

'I swore an oath with my heart's blood. That oath cannot be broken. Heart blood is bound with the powers I channel. I'm a warlock. Break the oath, and I lose everything. And I don't intend for that to happen.'

'How did you survive that wound?'

'There are ways. I knew enough even then.'

'Why do I need your help?'

'I know you have divyastras. Too few and not as powerful as Arjuna's or Parashurama's. Will they stop the Parashu? I can sense and evaluate the power within you, samrat. Not enough. You fight a Brahmakshatriya. An avatara!'

Jayadhwaja startled. Tarakaksha drew a sharp breath.

'I know all this, samrat. He is an avatara of Mahavishnu. Word will spread; the world will know soon.'

Jayadhwaja's mind reeled. Vengeance suddenly seemed a fool's dream.

'How do you know all this?' he stammered.

'There are ways.'

Jayadhwaja contemplated for a while, staring into the burning embers in the pit.

'What is in it for you?' he asked.

'A challenge and a curiosity. The man kills his mother, she comes back to life. With some powers too, it seems. The man dies on the battlefield, yet he comes back and thrives. Man dies, avatara comes. It is a curiosity. The scale of killing and destruction is unparalleled. Like Rudra himself did all this. Ah, the power to do all this. To get that is a challenge. You can rule the world, samrat. I don't care about it. Now, if I can bind Parashurama's power ...'

'Why weren't you here for the war?'

'It happened so quickly. I left from the far shores of the Brahmaputra as soon as I knew what was happening. The most powerful man in the world, he who cannot be killed. Twenty-one Akshauhinis. All dead in three days. Three days! And he did it single-handedly! Incredible!'

Both of them stared into the ablaze pit.

'Avatara!' Jayadhwaja whispered in awe.

'Not born that way. No. He grew up mortal like all of us. And then became one. Wonder how?' The warlock stared away into the night. 'A twist in the play of dharma.'

'You perform Abhichara, and speak of dharma?' Jayadhwaja was surprised.

The warlock laughed. 'Dharma, adharma. Divine, mortal. Man, woman. Day, night. Good, bad. The universe is a play of dualities. Many, many dualities. Two sides, two halves, two opposites, sometimes more. But never less than two. Those Vedic fools lie.'

'Where two opposites meet, divine and mortal, Parashurama stands. Between dharma and adharma, stand I. I use both for my purposes and don't care for either.'

The warlock's voice grew louder. 'I play with energies. I bend them to my will. Use them to impose my writ. Use my powers, samrat. Kill your enemy. Rule the world.'

'I already do,' said Jayadhwaja.

'No, samrat. You merely sit on the throne. Parashurama rules. If you know what I mean.'

Jayadhwaja glared at his visitor.

'Forgive my insolence. But what if Parashurama attacks now? Will you survive?'

Jayadhwaja had no answer. At least none that he wanted to say aloud.

'Avatara or not, I will avenge my parents. The Haihaya flag will fly proud again.' After a nimisha, he continued, 'I wish I knew what he's planning.'

'I can help with that,' the warlock replied.

Jayadhwaja looked into his eyes. The pupils vacillated at a dizzying speed.

'There are ways. But first, we must secure the throne, the loyalty of the kshatriyas.'

He drew an urn from behind him.

'An oil infused with spells. It has many ingredients, but what is most important to you is that it contains a drop of blood of each kshatriya clan in Bharatvarsha. I will bind their fealty to you. Dawn approaches, samrat. After your ablutions and prayers, anoint yourself with this oil from the top of your head to the soles of your feet. Circle your throne, counter clockwise, twenty-one times. Then sit on your throne. Naked.'

Jayadhwaja's expression was a mixture of disbelief and bemusement.

'Now we need to prepare for a ritual to see what Parashurama is planning. I need to collect a few things from these grounds. Your man can help.'

Jayadhwaja nodded.

The warlock and spy walked away. Jayadhwaja sat alone, absorbed in his thoughts. Slowly, he grew aware of an inexplicable feeling of menace all around him. As if he was surrounded and watched. As if a horde of obscene, craven eyes and slavering maws lingered around the fire pit. He caught movement out of the corner of his eye, a grotesque shadow slithering towards him. He turned. There was nothing there. He shivered slightly and stared into the fire.

They returned with the first feeble light of dawn, bearing broken skulls, bones, teeth, skin, tufts of hair and ash from the pyres. Tarakaksha looked like he was ready to retch.

'Rich pickings, easy pickings,' said the warlock. 'Just in time. Dawn breaks. The time of sandhya, of dark and dawn both. Powerful time.'

He arranged the collected items beside him as he sat before the fire. He retrieved a small pouch from his waistband. It was full of a fine powder and the warlock sprinkled a fistful of it into the fire. The flames soared.

'One last requirement. A living body. A life to be taken. It is necessary.'

Tarakaksha was confused for a nimisha. Then realisation hit him. He turned to Jayadhwaja. The samrat stared back without expression. Tarakaksha turned to flee and froze mid-stride as the warlock's spell caught him.

The warlock whispered his chant as he drew a small golden knife from his waistband. He walked around Tarakaksha, carefully inserted the knife into the left side of the spy's body and cut across the width of the stomach. Tarakaksha grimaced in agony, but his screams died within him. No sound escaped his lips. The warlock tapped him on his forehead and he fell backwards, flat on the ground. Blood oozed from the cut. The warlock wiped his blade clean with his fingers, raised his fingertips to his mouth and tasted the blood.

'Oh! He belongs to the Talajhanga clan. I can tell by the taste. Good, good,' he whispered.

He went down on his knees, tucking the knife away. Jayadhwaja sensed the sudden excitement in the air around him. As if those invisible maws wanted a taste, too. The warlock used his hands to widen the mouth of the cut, chanting something indecipherable. He pulled Tarakaksha's intestines out.

'You can't die, not yet. I need you conscious,' the warlock smiled at Tarakaksha.

He examined the intestines with great care as Jayadhwaja stared at the scene, horror-stricken.

'Parashurama is in the forest, some distance away from his ashram. He's alive, unhurt. Alone, except for one other. Perhaps a helper. He meditates. He seeks something.' The warlock was quiet for a couple of nimishas. 'He seeks some kind of ... Power!' he exclaimed. He turned to Jayadhwaja. 'Don't believe me yet? You shall see for yourself.'

He chanted mantras Jayadhwaja had never heard before.

'Come, Howler,
Come, Mouth of Flames,
Come, Body of Thorns,
Come, Tusk-fanged,
Come, thou of a thousand cloven hooves.
Take this living corpse,
Give me sight here of that I seek afar.'

The chant seemed to be repeated by a thousand invisible mouths around them, snarling, croaking, hissing, spitting. The warlock placed his pickings into a broken skull. He held it in the fire and sprinkled more powder into it. In a nimisha, everything inside the skull liquefied into a thick, greasy brown sludge. His hand, holding the skull to the fire, remained unhurt. The sludge bubbled with the heat. He came to Tarakaksha and eased his mouth open.

'A few nimishas more, my friend, then, peace of oblivion,' he whispered, wiping the sweat from Tarakaksha's forehead. Tarakaksha's eyes begged him to stop the torture, to end it all. The warlock poured the molten sludge into the open mouth. Jayadhwaja tore his eyes away.

It wormed its way down the throat. The warlock snapped his fingers, and the flames in the fire pit curved upwards, rushing into the mouth, down the torso and out of the wound. It formed an arc from Tarakaksha's body to the fire pit. The warlock threw some pyre ash at the flaming arc, and suddenly, they were staring at a forest vista.

Jayadhwaja and the warlock stared with unblinking eyes. The saffron dawn sun rose behind Parashurama. He sat in dhyana with his helper beside him. Parashurama sat on an old, dead tree trunk. It had been cut and fashioned to look like a throne. There could be no doubt about it.

'So, that's him, the avatara. A rishi who sits on a forest throne. He fancies himself king,' the warlock whispered.

Anger erupted inside Jayadhwaja. Filthy abuse poured from his lips. The warlock examined the vista. The image faded away.

'That's all we can see now,' said the warlock. He caressed Tarakaksha's forehead again. 'It's over, it's over. Sleep, my friend, sleep the long sleep. Let the pain go.'

Tarakaksha's stiff body relaxed. A spasm of relief played across his face.

'Die.' The warlock snapped his fingers. Tarakaksha's body crumpled into skin and bone. The flesh inside had vanished.

The light in his pained eyes died away.

'Go now, samrat. You have the loyalty of the Kshatriya clans and a powerful ally at your command. We will bring this avatara to heel together.'

Jayadhwaja rose. 'You have my gratitude. More than you can fathom.'

'I can fathom,' said the warlock. 'There are ways.'

Jayadhwaja walked away and turned. 'You didn't tell me your name.'

The warlock plucked Tarakaksha's eyes from their sockets and smiled.

'Dantakrura.'

6

Trikona Prashna

Rama eased out of his dhyana. He remained seated and kept his eyes closed. Much insight and the faint stirrings of a plan had sprung in his consciousness. He let it play in his mind now, evolving and growing wings. He was half sure of what he needed to do, and he was eager for any new understanding that could help him find the way forward.

A faint sound tickled his ears, one incongruous with the melody of the forest at dawn. His instincts had immediately noticed and paid attention. A habit baked into him by a lifetime spent in the woodland. He strained to hear more, unwilling to open his eyes yet. Slowly, the sound became clearer.

Not hoof, not paw, not slither, not claw. No, it was something softly slapping against the earth, and at a distance directly ahead of him. Not rock, not metal, yet something solid. *Wood!* Rama was mystified. He opened his eyes as soon as the answer came to mind.

Padukas! The simple wooden footwear worn by sages and renunciants. And something more, another sound. Of wood striking the earth. He broke his meditative asana and stood up, letting blood course down his legs. He listened to the off-beat rhythm drawing closer. Six padukas, so three individuals. And three other pieces of wood. *Sticks*, he deduced. Or perhaps long staffs, if they were rishis coming this way. Akrita approached and stood beside him.

'Three people approach,' said Rama.

'Where, Acharya? I can't see anyone.'

'They are in that thicket, across this clearing. They are too far to see. We should see them in about a fifth of a muhurta.'

Three men emerged from the thicket, just as Rama had predicted.

'They look like rishis or sadhus,' said Akrita.

All three were dressed in white dhotis, with angavastras thrown over their shoulders. They carried long staffs in their right hands, grey hair tied into a topknot on their heads and flowing salt-and-pepper beards. There was no ornamentation on their bodies except for their janeus. They approached at a rapid pace.

'They look so much like Saptarishi Jamadagni,' said Akrita. Rama saw that and sensed more. The three men had enormous spiritual power. In his mind's eye, their tejas, the brilliance of their power, outshone the dawn sun.

'They are not ordinary individuals,' said Rama.

The three men had their eyes fixed on Rama. They stopped six strides away from the duo, standing three abreast.

'He's made a throne for himself,' said the one on the left, glancing at the tree.

Rama looked around in surprise. He stared at his handiwork. He had done it by instinct, in the dark of night, but there was no mistaking it. It was a rough-hewn throne. He'd scooped out the wide base of the trunk and evened it out for a seat and two rough armrests. But it was the backrest that froze him cold. It was an upward triangle, and stretching from the seat to its apex, at its centre was the outline of the staff of the Parashu. The arching blades flared above the triangle, and he knew if he sat on it, the bindu on the axe cheek would be level with his Agya chakra. For the briefest of moments, he saw himself, shadow-like, sitting on the throne. *Samrat Parashurama!* that other voice proclaimed. *Bow your head, pay homage, beg favour.*

'He fancies himself a samrat,' said the man in the middle.

Rama whirled back to them. 'What? NO!' he exclaimed.

'We shall see,' said the man on the right.

They struck their long staffs into the earth together. The thump shook Rama and Akrita.

'Ramabhadra!' said the man on the left as he moved away further forward towards the left. 'I hear of your prowess and exploits. I come to take the measure of you.' He stopped and turned towards Rama.

'I am Vishwamitra.'

Rama's jaw dropped in amazement.

His grand-uncle! The Kshatriya who'd become a Saptarishi. The Seer of the Holy Gayatri. The man born of the other portion of blessing wrought by Rama's grandfather, Richika. He'd waited so long to meet this great sage, and here he was.

Before Rama could prostrate himself and pay his respects, the man on the right moved.

'Jamadagneya! Son of Jamadagni. I hear of your tapasya and divine boons. I too come to take measure. I am Gautama.'

Rama was utterly stunned, and he could sense the same in Akrita. Thoughts exploded in his head. Another Saptarishi.

Something serious was afoot. He turned to the man in the middle before he could speak. The man stood immobile, and his face gave nothing away.

'Bhargava Rama! Rama of the Brighus. I hear of the Mahavidya, the Parashu and the death of Karthavirya Arjuna. I come to take measure. I am Kashyapa.'

Rama heard Akrita exclaim in surprise and prostrate himself to each in turn, but his mind worked furiously. A third Saptarishi! And his father had disappeared into this forest to perform some secret, sacred ritual. Had he stumbled into a meeting of all seven? Was he in violation of a rule? He was sure he wasn't. What measure were they here to take?

Rama looked at each. They gazed at him expressionless. In a flash, Rama saw that he stood in the centre of a triangle formed by the three Saptarishis. *You are the bindu!* His mind screamed.

'Gather your wits,' said Vishwamitra.

'Harness your thoughts,' said Gautama.

'Answer our questions,' said Kashyapa.

Rama froze. Something of enormous importance was at stake here, but he just couldn't figure out what. They were here to test him. *Test your wisdom, test your understanding*, his mind whispered. *Your presence of mind. Like Anasuya. Trimurthi then, three Saptarishis now.*

He controlled his breath and focused his attention. He closed his eyes, bowed his head and pressed his hands together.

'I pay my respects to all three of you. I submit myself to your demand.' He dropped his hands, opened his eyes, and waited. 'I will answer if I know.'

'What is desired by all men but comes not when demanded?' asked Vishwamitra.

Odd question to start, Rama thought, but he would answer as best he could.

'Good sleep. The most generous of thieves. It takes away your thoughts and leaves dreams,' said Rama.

'Who is the most impatient guest?' asked Gautama.

'Hunger.'

'Who is true renunciant?' asked Kashyapa.

'One who is connected to all, but attached to none.'

'Who is the best witness?' asked Gautama.

'An honest man.'

'Who is the best witness against an honest man?' asked Gautama again.

'The man himself.'

'Where do hope and desperation reside at the same time?' asked Kashyapa.

'In an empty purse.'

'What, when broken, leaves a scar in the mind?' asked Gautama.

'A broken heart.'

'What is life?' asked Kashyapa.

'Breath is life. Breath is not one's creation. One is breath's creation.'

'What is breath, then?' Kashyapa again.

'Prana is breath. Breath is the physical aspect of this non-physical shakti.'

'What is prana?' asked Gautama.

'It is the sankalpa, the intention of the Divine. San is to become one with, and kalpa, time.'

'What is the sankalpa?' asked Vishwamitra.

'Inexhaustible compassion. It is the unmanifest divine, manifested.'

'Then what is god?' asked Kashyapa.

'Prana-shakti is a part of Parashakti. If I take a drop of water from a river, I can talk about it and its qualities. But when I put it back, you can't tell where the river stops and the drop begins. The drop, the river, everything is Parashakti. Parashakti is god, is the ultimate reality.'

'Drop in the river, you say. What is stronger, fire or water?' Vishwamitra asked.

'The child of both. Fire father, water mother. From the fire of the sun, and the water of the ocean comes salt. Be salt.'

'Which is more powerful, love or hate?' asked Gautama.

'Neither. Awareness is more powerful. Awareness makes your love stronger or shows it to be passing fancy. Awareness shows if your hate is justified and if it should cause righteous anger. Or, if it is just a result of misunderstanding, or worse, petty jealousy.'

'What is intelligence, and what foolishness?' asked Kashyapa.

'To turn even poison into medicine is intelligence. Intelligence learns what should be added to the poison, and what subtracted. When to partake, and how much and who and why. To turn even medicine into poison is foolishness. The deliberate misuse of intelligence is malice. To turn poison into medicine to earn and hoard coins is greed. To boast of it is pride. For fame is vanity. To resent another's intelligence is jealousy. To steal the fruit of another's intelligence is avarice. To not use intelligence to discover more uses of the poison is sloth.'

'All this greed, malice, vanity and the rest are ultimately

foolishness. So, context, in the light of available knowledge, decides what is intelligence, and what foolishness.'

'Who are a man's best friends?' asked Vishwamitra.

'Imagination, a sense of humour, wisdom and discipline. To aspire to who one can be. To tolerate who one is now. To know the path forward. To have the resolve to walk it.'

'What is friendship between men?' asked Vishwamitra again.

'To understand. To be understood. To inspire each other to walk in dharma. It is millet and mountain air. Both mundane and pure. It is common, everyday trust and support when you attempt to scale heights.'

'What is harder than a diamond?'

'Truth is harder than diamond. Abide in it, and it becomes a warm blanket when cold lies abound.'

'What is virtue, and what is vice?'

'They are sometimes opposite; sometimes tied at the hip. Context and dharma decide between the two. If the sun was modest, it wouldn't be the sun. It takes pride in its brilliance, and justly so. If the moon was constant, it wouldn't wane. In its fickleness lies the tides of the sea. If a mountain was self-effacing, it wouldn't rise. Its flamboyance gives us rain.'

'What is humility, then?'

'Humility is a man honestly judging if his efforts were correct and enough. It is the willingness to do more if required. It is the true friend to one's aspirations. And aspirations must always be proud and noble.'

'What is wisdom?' asked Gautama.

'An intelligent question is half wisdom. The correct answer gives it fullness.'

'When does knowledge expand into wisdom?'

'When knowledge knows its limits. When one decides what one doesn't want to know, else it becomes knowledge for its own sake.'

'Which text is the repository of wisdom?'

'No one text. Wisdom is found in man, nature and god. All can perceive to a lesser and greater extent. But be warned, a god that writes one text and claims complete wisdom is a false god.'

'What is the essence of the Shrutis, the Vedas?' asked Kashyapa.

'The cognition and the relation between jeeva, jagat and Brahman. Atma, creation and Paramatma.'

'What, then, is the greatest teaching of the Vedas?'

'That the self is the saviour of the self. Know oneself and know the Supreme Truth.'

'What is the mind?' asked Vishwamitra.

'It is manas, ahamkara, buddhi, chitta and atma. Manas is the collector of sensory input. Ahamkara turns these inputs into a personal experience. Buddhi makes evaluations and judgements. Chitta is the memory of all one's experiences, to which one keeps adding. The witness to all this is the atma.'

'What is the body?' asked Gautama.

'For the ignorant, it is flesh and bone. For you, it is a temple of one column, nine doors and five divinities. The spine, the nine bodily orifices and the five elements, the pancha mahabhoota. You aim to make a tenth hole in the top of your skull and gain liberation.' Rama paused, wondering if he must proceed. He thought differently and was unsure how his thoughts would be received. But what better men to present before?

He continued, 'I know it as a garden of lotuses. The seven

most important lotuses are aligned on the same column, the spine. The column has three channels, Nadis. Ida, Pingala and at the centre, Sushumna. It is in the sukshma sharira. The subtle, not the gross body. Open the seventh lotus, the topmost, the lotus of a thousand petals, and gain liberation.'

'What is the Sushumna nadi?'

'It is the janeu of the enlightened.'

The three Saptarishis paused. A long nimisha later, Vishwamitra resumed the questions.

'You spoke of awareness, of righteous anger, Ramabhadra. What is righteous war?'

'It is righteous to wage war against the ignorance of mind, the malady of body and the impulses of your samskaras and vasanas. Your karmic impressions and desires. Win, and you have the empire of the soul.'

'Yet you waged war against Arjuna. Why?' asked Kashyapa.

'Arjuna embodied the arrogance of the mind. He was a malady to the body we all live on, the earth. His desires wrecked civilisation, and his power impressed many ignorant men to follow in his wake. My righteous wrath destroyed them all. I rendered justice. Three days of justice are worth a lifetime of prayer. My war was a dharmayuddha.'

'What empire did you win?' asked Gautama.

Rama was suddenly aware of the throne behind him. 'No earthly empire. I relieved people, this civilisation, of its misery. But I gained a treasure worth more than an empire. I gained understanding.'

'What is the armour of a warrior?' asked Kashyapa.

'Courage.'

'What is the armour of a sanyasi?'

'Patience.'

'What is civilisation? What does it require?'

'It is cooperation amongst men and women based on dharma. Its requirements are four. Teacher, trader, king and storyteller. For knowledge, treasury, power and art.'

'Storyteller?' Kashyapa asked again.

'A civilisation is remembered and remembers through its bards, poets and storytellers. To forget your stories, to not tell them, to ignore them, to not understand them, to mock them, is to slide into decay and decadence. It is to turn from a pride of lions into a flock of sheep. It is a slow death. Worse, it is a cheap death. A storyteller is no less important than the other three. He is the only one who has the gift to animate space and enliven time.'

'What is poison for the four varnas? What should they most beware of?' asked Vishwamitra.

'Dogma is poison for a Brahmin. To use prejudice to arrive at conclusions. To know the rule but not the context. Lust for power is the poison for Kshatriyas. To think might is the only right leads to Matsya Nyana, predation not protection of the weak. But to be powerless is also a sly venom. A Kshatriya must wield power. To love coin more than value is the poison of a Vaisya. It will lead to greed, earning without rendering correct value. To believe one is the lowest and least of the four varnas is the poison of a Shudra. It ferments victimhood and resentment for others, and will grow mediocrity in art, craft and produce.'

'What is the antidote?'

'Dharma is the antidote.'

'Which four men are the four ashramas? What are their shadows?'

Rama stared at Kashyapa in confusion. His mind scrambled

for answers and found nothing. How could he not know? He silently scolded himself. *So embarrassing*, said the other voice. He composed himself and focused on the questions; they had to be understood correctly. He knew the four ashramas, but four men? Four kinds of personalities, perhaps. And shadows? Light falls on an object, and its shadow is formed. The shadow was of the thing, but not the thing itself. A shadow was dark. Dark ... where the light doesn't fall. The light of what? Knowledge or awareness or consciousness, maybe. So, something unknown or disregarded or unconscious. Rama thought hard. The Saptarishis waited.

'The four men are the warrior, the king, the magician and the lover. Their shadows are the imbalance in them, through lack of awareness or viveka,' said Rama finally. The Saptarishis observed him with quiet interest. It was obvious they wanted him to continue. 'The first ashrama is brahmacharya. The brahmachari is the warrior whose armour is self-discipline and self-growth. His weapon is learning. The shadow is when the weapon is used to bully or when the discipline is excessive. Then, his armour becomes restrictive and stunts self-growth. The first is cruelty to others, and the second to oneself. The grihasta is the king, one who takes responsibility and wields authority in family and society. His shadow is the abuse of power, to be a tyrant. Or the inability to wield power, to be a weakling. In vanaprastha, a man is the magician. A wise old man with understanding and wisdom to guide others and transform lives. His shadow is to use his wisdom to manipulate others, or to be innocent of any understanding and to feign wisdom he doesn't possess. A sanyasi is the lover. He sheds possessions but is full of love for the world. A love that is in service to the divine and all existence. His shadow is to force his love on others like an addict. Or, to be impotent, to just live up to expectations but not love truly. Unwholesomeness defines their shadows.'

'What is degeneracy, and what is wholesomeness?'

'An interest in and the pursuit of the profane is degeneracy. Defeatism, profanity and the path of least moral resistance is degeneracy. A yearning for beauty, innocence and purity is wholesomeness. There is nothing profound about the profane. Wholesomeness gives birth to hope.'

'What is yoga?' asked Gautama.

'Yoga is abstinence from unwholesomeness, observance of auspiciousness, control of breath, withdrawal from distraction and bending the body to straighten the mind. Such a mind can concentrate on the divine, meditate upon it and attain absorption in it. Yoga is a collaboration with divine grace. It is to make the seven lotuses bloom. It is to raise kundalini.'

The Saptarishis exchanged glances.

'What is enlightenment?' asked Vishwamitra.

'Expansion of awareness is enlightenment.'

'What is sadhana?'

'Generosity of attention to a point of focus is sadhana.'

'What is devotion?' Kashyapa asked.

'Love for the divine and its veneration is devotion. It should be of the heart, not of the tongue. The devotion of the tongue is akin to an egg broken from the outside; life ends, and no grace will be won. Devotion of the heart is an egg broken from the inside. Life begins, and divine grace is won.'

'What is dhyana?'

'Dhyana is the fasting of the mind. It is the Rajamarga, the royal highway to knowing the divine. It winds through the carnival of distractions, the mansions of ambition and attainment, the gardens of love and attachment and the tunnels of boredom. In the end, the light of realisation awaits.'

'Then, what is moksha?'

'Moving from life to death is mere existence. Moving from death to eternal life is moksha.'

'What is auspiciousness?' asked Gautama.

'Self-purification is auspiciousness.'

'What is dharma?'

'That which is true to Ṛta and Satya. Dharma is the anvil of the world. What is forged in it sustains and nourishes. What breaks on it never would sustain and nourish.'

'If dharma is the anvil, what is the hammer?'

'Karma is the hammer. If correct, the result will be upheld; if not, it will collapse. Mind the correctness of karma, not the result. That will take care of itself.'

'What is Sanatana dharma?' asked Kashyapa.

'It is a path to create warriors of truth. It is the path and light of the Vedas, the road to immortality. It is older than the sun, yet as new as sunrise. We live in this world of death, mrithyuloka. Sanatana dharma is the Maha Mrityunjaya mantra of this world.'

'Yet, you stray from the path, don't you?' said Vishwamitra.

Was it a question or a taunt? Rama was unsure.

'I do not. I never will,' he answered firmly, indignation evident in his answer.

He turned to Vishwamitra. 'Gayatri is considered Vedamatha. Mother of Veda. The base of all mantras is the Pranava. Om. Only a fool can deny it. The path I walk is already glimpsed in the Vedas. I seek to add to that knowledge. I speak from the truth of my self-realisation. The experience that defeated death, and made me an avatara and chiranjeevi.'

'And what is this knowledge?' Kashyapa asked.

'Sri Vidya. Sri is auspiciousness. Sri is Shakti and Shiva. Vidya is knowledge and the means to obtain it.'

'Proclaim your path then,' Kashyapa ordered.

When I meditated on Mahadeva I saw a bright, endless pillar of light. This light is the Supreme Consciousness, the ultimate source of everything. Imagine it like a vast ocean of light, and each of us is a tiny drop in that ocean. Every drop—every soul—contains a spark of that divine knowledge. This Supreme Consciousness is all that exists, and it's called Parashakti, or Lalitha Tripurasundari. She is the beautiful one beyond our normal states of being awake, asleep or dreaming. She is everything!

From her, the gods Brahma, Vishnu and Shiva get their roles: Brahma creates the world, Vishnu keeps it going, and Shiva brings things to an end. She's like the mother of all existence—past, present and future. Everything is her energy, and she's playing a grand game, called her lila.

She also shows us a way to connect with her through another part of her game. This is like a conversation between her two sides: the masculine, Shiva, and the feminine, Shakti. Shiva represents stillness, while Shakti represents movement and change. Some people think these two are separate, but they're actually one—Parashakti is the unity behind them. She is both beyond the world and within it. When people don't see this unity, they're caught in maya, which is like an illusion that hides the truth. Her energy creates this illusion, but we can use that same energy to wake up and realise the divine knowledge in every soul.

In short, everything is part of the divine mother's energy,

and by understanding her, we can find the truth within ourselves. I honour her as the divine mother!

'To understand moksha, understand maya. The path to moksha lies in maya itself. That is the beauty of her lila.'

Rama paused, searching for a reaction from the Saptarishis.

'Explain your path more,' said Vishwamitra.

'Not many can truly worship the abstract and the formless. That's why we have the material, with form and attributes, to worship. Yet, jagat mithya, Brahman satya—the world is unreal, only Brahman is real—cannot be comprehended by ordinary mortals. To them this maya, this jagat, and everything in it is real. Not unreal, not mithya.

'I proclaim, Yes! It is real. Because this maya is Shakti too. It is real to the five senses and the mind. They need a path that gives material and spiritual progress.

'*Bhogam cha moksham cha karastha ev.*'

Rama stopped suddenly. It seemed like he was preaching to the Saptarishis, individuals who had mastered the knowledge of the Supreme Truth. Did they think him a fool? Did they mistake his conviction for arrogance?

'Go on,' said Gautama gently.

Rama sighed in relief. They wanted to hear him out. Moreover, putting words to his thoughts helped him to untangle his mind and clarify things. Was this the purpose of their visit?

He continued, 'The mind is a creation of nama-rupas, names and figures. It is a vector of the past, not of the present. It has one weakness. It cannot observe and think at the same time. I will teach how to use observation to stimulate awareness, not the thought process. The kundalini must not rise to the mind. That way lies ruin.'

'Why mustn't the power of the Ahi rise to the mind?'

'The mind is a time-travelling fool. The past is memory; we make a spectacle of it. We exaggerate the present as if it will stretch forever. We make a tragedy or comedy of it. Of the future, we care too much or too little, a farce it is. To raise such extraordinary power to the mind is to flirt with insanity. Kundalini belongs not to time but to the eternal, the soul. This I will teach.'

'Teach?' said Kashyapa. 'Who then is a guru?'

'If a mortal is akin to a clay lamp, the light of the wick is the atma. For most, it shines dim. In a guru, it blazes. A guru shows the path by his light. A guru is a margadarshak.'

'What is diksha?'

'It is a consecration. The prana pratishta of knowledge in a disciple.'

'What is guru dakshina?'

'It is a solemn oath, a yagna to sustain and grow the light the guru has given you.'

'Who is a yogi?'

'A yogi is a cremation pyre on two legs. The wood is vidya, the fire his sadhana and he burns his untrue self.'

'Who is a true guru and who is false?'

'One who shows the way and walks it himself is a true guru. One who merely preaches is false. A true guru is rain; a false one is thunder. It is rain that grows life, not thunder.'

'What is obedience to a guru?'

'Shastanga pranama to a guru is obedience; licking his padukas is not. Both the guru that demands the licking and the shishya who does it are knaves.'

'Are you the guide then of this path?' asked Gautama.

'Guide and pathfinder both, by the grace of my pitrus,

Mahadeva and Guru Dattatreya. One of many, I'm sure. Each mortal has the essence of a guru inside him or her, a guru tattva. I, the outer guru, will teach to awaken the inner guru. This I will perform in cooperation with the shakti in maya. I will stimulate the guru tattva through the senses, not the mind.'

'Who are the pitrus?'

'They are the day before yesterday and the day after tomorrow. Yesterday is memory, and tomorrow is hope, but the pitrus are greater than both. They are tradition, culture, learning and progress of civilisation. They are observance of tradition, refinement of culture and the urge to better ourselves. To honour the pitrus today is to respect yesterday and to receive blessings for tomorrow.'

'How will you stimulate the guru tattva?' Vishwamitra asked.

'Five stimulants for five senses. Bells for the ears, mantra for the tongue, fragrance for the nose, paste for the skin and vigraha for the eyes.'

'Vigraha? A murthi?'

'*Visheshana grahyate iti vigraha*. That form, vigraha, that helps to observe, not think.' A vigraha is an instrument that helps devotees feel the divine in a personal, visible way. It's not just a statue but a sacred focal point that supports worship, devotion and spiritual growth, guiding the devotee towards a deeper connection with the divine.

The Saptarishis glanced again at each other.

'This is new,' said Gautama.

'Beg pardon. It is as old as the Vedas. *Om Namah Shivaya* is the mantra. The yantra is the Shiva linga. Many have unknowingly walked the path already. Do you doubt it now?'

'The Panchakshari and the Gayatri are your mantras?' asked Vishwamitra.

'I revere them. The Panchakshari and the Navakshari have given me enormous blessings. I will continue to revere and chant them.'

'That is not the implication of my question.'

Rama thought for a nimisha. 'I understand, O Great Rishi! Thoughts need language, and language needs meaning. Meanings would engage the mind.'

Vishwamitra smiled.

'Normally, when we think, we use words, and words have meanings. Those meanings keep our mind busy. But music is special—it can touch our mind without needing words. There is a kind of "music" called Beeja-akshara, or seed sounds. These are simple syllable sounds that don't have a meaning you think about. Instead, they connect directly to a specific energy, a part of the divine power called Shakti. These sounds engage your heart and soul without making your mind analyse.

'The path of the lotuses is paved with seed sounds that make the lotuses bloom. Two have been revealed to me. Beeja-akshara of Ganapathi is Gam. That of the lowest chakra, the first lotus, called Muladhara, is Lam.'

'If Om is the sound of creation, what is the sound of maya?' Gautama asked.

Clever question, but Rama was prepared for it.

'O Great Saptarishi, since it is the sound of Maya, and Maya engages the mind, the sound must have a meaning. The sound of Maya is Tathasthu.'

'What then is the yantra of your path?' asked Kashyapa.

Rama stood befuddled, and a while passed. The Saptarishis

truly knew how to take measure. He searched for an answer, and then it hit him. It was obvious; it was BRILLIANT! Mahadeva had shown it to him. The shakti he held in his hands. How deeply the gods teach! He knelt to trace the yantra on the ground and answered with exhilaration.

'The yantra is the bindu.'

The Saptarishis looked at the yantra. It was the rune on the Parashu. A bindu and a circle.

'Parashakti is the bindu. She is all points of the circle and all points in between. The path starts here and ends here. It begins now, here, as you are. The bindu is the path.

'My path is death. The path of true death, and the doorway to eternal life. So, my first command of this path is "Die, yogi, die". Die and awake to life.'

'Who is an avatara and what is an avatara's purpose?' asked Vishwamitra.

'A descent of the divine into a mortal form is an avatara. Its purpose is to help man ascend to his true moral height. An avatara is morality that has found a blade.'

'Who are the Saptarishis?'

'All true rishis are the eyes, ears and lips of Parashakti. The seven Saptarishis are foremost among them. Rishis are also poets, and Saptarishis are greater poets. It is not because of the quality of their verse, but how they have composed their lives. Their life is the poem.'

The Saptarishis fell silent.

'Well answered,' said Kashyapa.

They glanced at each other, and a message danced across their eyes.

'I propose,' said Vishwamitra.

'I second,' Gautama nodded.

'I concur,' agreed Kashyapa.

Vishwamitra and Gautama walked to where Kashyapa stood. They faced Rama.

'We have taken measure, and you have measured true. Blessings upon you! May you walk forever in the light!'

Rama prostrated himself before the three. Akrita followed his lead. They rose and waited to do whatever the Saptarishis wanted next.

'We take your leave,' said Kashyapa, and turned away.

Rama was taken aback. What was the meaning of all this? Why had they come? He needed an explanation.

'Wait!' he called out.

They turned in unison as if expecting his call.

'One question. That is all we will allow,' said Gautama.

Rama struggled to conceal his consternation. The Saptarishis remained inscrutable. One question! Rama racked his brain for the right one, picking and discarding the options his mind threw up in a frenzy. It had to be something only the Saptarishis would know. He made his selection.

'The Shiva linga of the Saptarishis. Why is the linga called Vishwayonika?'

The faces of the rishis displayed surprise.

'One question and he picks the one we cannot answer,' said Vishwamitra.

'From our judgement, we should have expected no less,' said Gautama.

'Only a Saptarishi can know that, Rama,' said Kashyapa. 'Walk your path, and realise the answer.'

They turned away.

'Wait!' Rama called again, 'I have a request.'

They turned to face him.

'If you think me worthy, would you participate in and conduct a yagna for me?'

'Certainly,' Kashyapa agreed instantly.

'I have a boon from Indra. It enables me to speak to the person I intend by utilising the powers of my mind. When the time comes, allow me to call you.'

The Saptarishis knew what to do. They each placed their thumbs on his forehead.

'Tathasthu!' said Vishwamitra with a smile.

Rama watched their retreating backs until they crossed the clearing and disappeared into the thicket. He turned and gazed at his throne. He had created this through instinct alone, and he learnt to trust it a long time ago. An idea had flashed in his mind when Gautama had asked him about what empire he had won. He had glanced at the throne and the idea had come to him.

'So be it,' said Rama to himself. 'If I must be samrat, I will.'

7

Dikṣha

Rama stared into the distance, lost in thought.

'Gurudeva,' Akrita interrupted. 'If you deem me worthy, I ask you to initiate me into your path.'

Rama didn't have to think at all. 'It will be a privilege to have you as my first initiate, Akrita. I am truly blessed.'

They performed their sandhyavandana, and a short while later, Rama sat again on his throne in siddhasana.

'Sit close,' he told Akrita.

Akrita sat in padmasana to Rama's right at the base of the tree and closed his eyes.

'How many sit before me?' Rama asked. Akrita bit down on his lips before he blurted out the obvious answer.

'I don't know, Gurudeva.'

'Three sit before me, Akrita: who you were, who you are and who you want to be.'

'I was a leper, I am a shishya and want to be a rishi.' Rama waited. Akrita thought harder, and then he had it. 'My past lives, my present life and my future ones.'

Rama nodded. 'What connects them?'

'Karma. Prarabhda karma, the portion of past actions of past lives, is responsible for this life. My actions now determine the future.'

'Which are the three attributes you need?'

'Icchashakti, to start this journey with will and confidence. Jnanashakti, the wisdom to navigate it. Kriyashakti, to sustain it with disciplined action.'

Rama nodded. 'In my dhyana, I saw a mirror. Guru Dattatreya planted a dream in my mind. I could taste colours, see melodies and hear shapes. I realised later that both the mirror and the dream were lessons. Let's use them. Close your eyes, Akrita.'

Rama spoke softly now. 'Imagine a full-length mirror in your mind's eye. See yourself in it. It doesn't matter if you can't remember every small detail of your body, what matters is the emotions the image brings up. Pay attention to them. Feed the emotions into the image in the mirror. Let the image remain constant or change at will. Now, wipe that image away, and resolve that you are also wiping those emotions away.' Akrita's right hand moved as if removing something in the air in front of him.

'Now imagine who you want to be. Perhaps a guru or a rishi. Feel the emotion of it. See it, hear it ... use all your five senses. Imagine it in the finest detail, and savour it.' A beautiful smile suffused Akrita's face. After a while, Rama asked Akrita to open his eyes.

'Later I will teach you how to awaken the Ahi in you. So do what I've just taught you after every sandhyavandana. May you attain what you want to be!' He gently placed his right palm on Akrita's head. Rama's pupils rolled up and the whites of his eyes stared at Akrita.

'*Athatho Deeksham Vyakhyasyamah*,' Rama intoned, 'Hence, we unfold initiation.'

Jayadhwaja sat before Dantakrura on the cremation grounds. It was past midnight, and he'd come alone this time.

'I've done as you instructed,' said Jayadhwaja.

'And how do you feel?' asked Dantakrura.

'Stronger, more confident.' He paused. 'More virile.'

Dantakrura laughed. Jayadhwaja looked around, feeling the invisible eyes on him again.

'Who or what is watching us?' he asked.

Dantakrura raised an eyebrow. 'How many people sit here?'

'Two.' said Jayadhwaja.

'Six.' said Dantakrura. Jayadhwaja looked around. There was no one.

'When two people meet, six people are present. Each man as he sees himself, each man as he sees the other and each as he really is. Two pairs of eyes, six visions,' Dantakrura explained.

'What does that have to do with what I feel?'

'Why, nothing at all.' Dantakrura chortled.

'Do your pupils ever stop moving?'

'I see well enough. Better and more than others.' Dantakrura was abrupt.

Jayadhwaja didn't bother to hide his concern with the situation. 'How do we deal with Parashurama?'

Dantakrura took a brief pause before he answered. 'I've gathered information about him from your surviving soldiers. Let us discuss what we know. Avatara. Spiritual powers.

Parashu and divyastras. I deduce he is extraordinarily strong physically. Some of your soldiers described his bow.

'Ah! You forgot that. The Parashu took away all your attention. That bow is divine. It takes enormous strength to draw a war bow. An ordinary mortal cannot do it. Parashurama's bow was twice the size of a war bow. Hence, he is immensely strong physically. You agree?'

Jayadhwaja nodded.

'If he can slaughter twenty-one Akshauhinis, assassins would be of no use, I think. Unless … it is a special kind of assassin.'

Dantakrura was quiet for a long while. 'I only have second-hand information about him. I must take measure of the man.'

'Just kill him and be done with,' Jayadhwaja insisted.

'And if the attempt to kill fails? He thinks it's all over. He already sits on a throne. We fail to kill him, and he becomes aware that he still has enemies. Where will you hide from death if an avatara decides to kill you?'

'When news reaches him that I'm samrat, he will think of me as the enemy.'

'The city was his to destroy. And Arjuna's throne and empire. He could've killed you. Yet, he just walked away. Why would he bother about you? But … but … now, he sits on a throne. A puzzle. A duality …' Dantakrura went quiet again.

'Special assassin, you were saying,' said Jayadhwaja when the silence had stretched on and on.

'Yes.' Dantakrura came out of his reverie, 'One that has brought the greatest of men crashing down from lofty perches. The urge that overcame the great Vishwamitra even. A woman.'

'You mean to invoke an apsara?'

'Why should I? I will pick a suitable mortal woman, and imbue her with a fascination, an allure, an attraction, a charm that will put an apsara to shame. Yes, he will submit to her, through her to us. Then, his life is yours, his power, is mine.'

'Whom will you send?'

'I will find one near his ashram. I cannot read minds like your father, but I can see through the eyes of small animals. Animals that are quiet and commonplace, and hence, go unnoticed.'

Dantakrura looked off into the darkness as if gazing back at all the invisible eyes there. 'I will need all my powers,' he murmured.

'What if ...?' Jayadhwaja didn't complete.

'... it fails?' asked Dantakrura. 'Listen to this, samrat. Once, during my travels, I chanced upon a devotee singing praises to his devi. He sang beautifully, but I remember only one line from his song. *Bhogam cha moksham cha karastha ev.* I was struck by the wisdom of it.

'Where do pleasure and moksha lie, samrat? In the loins of a woman! The few nimishas of oblivion, the split-second moksha that men chase so hard, they find it there. But the devotee didn't know that, he was blind to reality. He thought it was bhakti and philosophy.

'Bah! Vedic fools! They walk the forest and see no trees.

'I suspect Parashurama is a brahmachari. Untouched by a woman. When the heat of a woman's loins calls him, he will come running. When the yoni beckons, all men are pashu.

'And if it fails, I will have taken measure. Go now, samrat. Enjoy your virility. I must prepare for the first skirmish with our enemy.'

Jayadhwaja walked out of the cremation grounds and towards the tunnels hidden behind the rocks and vines in the garden. He stumbled into someone in the dark, and his hand reached for the dagger in his waistband.

'Jyeshta,' said Shurasoma. Alarm turned into irritation as Jayadhwaja snapped back, 'What are you doing here?'

'Watching ... Abhichara, jyeshta? This is wrong.'

Jayadhwaja jerked the dagger out. 'I'll do whatever it takes to kill that rotten knave.'

Shurasoma stepped back. 'But jyeshta, Abhichara can recoil against the doer. Haven't our acharyas and priests taught us?'

'And where are these worthies now? Dead. Or absconding. So easy to preach when all is easy, to signal virtue and morals when all is well. That man is the only one who has come to our aid, and he's sworn a blood oath. Need I remind you? So have you.'

'Yes. And I'll stand by you, jyeshta. No matter what comes my way, even if it's death.'

'Don't die now, Shurasoma. Go!'

Shurasoma stared and stuttered. He turned and disappeared behind the vines. Jayadhwaja waited till he was sure his brother had gone. He felt his annoyance melt away, and the feeling of strength and virility return. As if he were years younger, and there was fresh blood and vigour in his body. No, he wouldn't go to his queen's boudoir now. Charu no longer held his fancy. He needed someone fresh. A new queen, once this was all over. Many new queens. But he desired a woman now. There would be whores around, Jayadhwaja thought as walked into the city, and desperate women. There always were at times like this. He found one soon enough. He threw a small purse at her, and her eyes gleamed as she caught it. She pulled him into the darkness of the alley.

8

Visitors

Rama and Akrita trudged home, hungry and happy. Soon, dusk would fall. They would make it in time for the evening prayers and then eat something.

They came upon the first settlement on the way home. A host of familiar faces greeted him, and the sprinkling of unfamiliar ones was easy to identify. They saw him, heard his name called or whispered, and fright flashed across their faces. They stood bewildered when the old settlers approached him with easy respect. There was no pomp and show, and no one stood on ceremony. Some youngsters came to touch his feet. Rama was immensely popular amongst them, and the newcomers immediately rushed to do the same, as though seeking permission to stay.

Akrita tried to dissuade them, and Rama tried hard to smile and look as non-threatening as he could. None of them would meet his eyes, and they rushed away from him as soon as they could. They'd all be from Mahishmati or small settlements around the city. He was Sahasrabahu's slayer. They were expecting him to be a monster, or at least have no love lost for Arjuna's former citizens. They didn't know him, didn't know what he stood for or intended to do.

More women than men, Rama noted. The couples were all middle-aged or old. Most would have lost someone in the war. They carried hate for him in their hearts even if they were careful to hide it from their faces. But the eyes of some men glittered with a strange light, and Rama understood. Men who were formerly of some means and position, now snatched out of the ease of the city and thrown into the rough living of the forest. They who had power and pelf and had lost it in the carnage wrought by him. Men who probably still owed allegiance to Arjuna. Men who may seek vengeance. Rama carefully observed the new arrivals as they tried to touch his feet or bid namaste from afar.

Rama and Akrita came to the second settlement, the one just before the ashram, munching on jamuns given to them by a passing band of forest tribes. They'd gushed their gratitude to Renuka and told him Matangi and her unborn child were hale and hearty. They tried to give him everything they'd collected from the forest: herbs, honey, roots and hides. Rama had gently turned them down, and finally accepted the jamuns. He'd taken his leave quickly when the old matriarch talked of his marriage and how she had a few suitable candidates for him to consider. The girls eyed Rama openly, appraising him. Taking measure, he thought wryly. The matriarch held forth on the importance of child-bearing hips and strong thighs, and how there was a season when even men and women should rut. Akrita won a heroic battle not to chortle with amusement.

They walked through the second settlement as fast as they could, Rama spotting the unfamiliar faces and guessing at their pasts. That one there was an old army man, no anger in his eyes, just stoic acceptance. Not cavalry. He wasn't bow-legged, probably a mace wielder or broadsword man, judging by his shoulders. That handsome couple definitely came from a rich, comfortable life. Their bodies looked well cared for and unused to toil. Probably stopping here with a group and seeking the fastest way out to a city somewhere east. That group were workers of some sort, that a gaggle of housewives and their children, that man with the sword was Anantha, and that ... wait!

A smile bloomed on Anantha's face as Rama's eyes rushed back to him.

'Pranaam, Swami. Greetings to the Uddhatr!'

'Anantha!' Rama was happy to see him.

'Only you?' asked Akrita.

'Only me. The rest follow slowly, all of them.'

'Come, we'll talk as we walk,' said Rama.

They were at a distance from the settlement when Anantha resumed.

'You left without telling anyone,' he said.

'I am sorry about that, Anantha,' Rama apologised.

'I found your trail out of the grove easily enough, but by then, Bhargavi was all aflutter. The Nagamandala had changed, and she didn't know how that happened. Do you?'

'Not really.'

'Bhargavi thought it best to leave you alone, though I wanted to follow with a few men. There must be a reason you left without a word, she said, but after a few days, the wait and lack of news made us weary. Bhargavi performed her rituals, consulted her stars and proclaimed that we must all move and come to you. I started with a squad that very day and reached here a day ago. I learnt your ashram was close, but that you weren't there. You'd gone into the jungle and probably would return this way. I sent the squad back with the news and waited.'

'Where are the rest of the Malaya Kshatriyas now?'

'The last I heard, they were south of the Vindhyas. There, they met another branch of Malaya kshatriyas, our brothers and sisters, who'd gone to Bhrigukachcha, the land of your ancestor's ashram at one time. A rishi and patni are with them now, it seems, and they are all eager to meet the Uddhatr.'

'What is news here, Swami? What have you been up to?'

'Samrat Arjuna is dead. Gurudeva here slaughtered him,' Akrita reported, his expression deadpan. Anantha gasped.

'He also slew twenty-one Akshauhinis.' Anantha's jaw dropped.

'All by himself.' Akrita was enjoying himself. Anantha walked silently, reeling under the shock of the information.

'He laid waste to Mahishmati.' Anantha stared at Akrita in a daze.

'Oh! Gurudeva also died and came back to life.' Anantha stopped moving.

'Enough, Akrita,' said Rama, as he moved on.

Akrita waited till he thought Rama was out of earshot and whispered, 'Just like me.'

He caught Anantha by his forearm and pulled him along. 'There's more, but I'll tell you later. Seems nobody from this ashram dies. They go and come back.'

They entered the ashram and one of the young shishyas ran towards Rama. 'Pranaam, acharya. Visitors from Mahishmati are here to see you. They are with Amba.'

Rama hastened past the huts of the senior sanyasis. Anantha froze mid-stride.

'Yes, that too. Come along,' said Akrita.

Two men sat on the stoop with Renuka. Rama recognised Raikava, the priest he'd seen at the temple in Mahishmati. He'd never seen the other man before. They rose in unison, faces pale as if they'd seen an apparition. A nimisha ago, Rama wasn't standing there, and now he just was.

'Raikava, high priest of Arjuna,' said Rama. He looked at the other man. The man gulped and tried to form words. No sound came from his mouth. He tried several times, desperation showing on his face as he failed each attempt. He gave up in frustration and threw himself at Rama's feet.

'Chandragupta. The chief minister of Samrat Ar ...' Raikava's voice faded away as anger flashed in Rama's eyes.

'Why is he at my feet?' Raikava quailed as Rama's raptor gaze pierced through him. The menace in his voice was unmistakable. Chandragupta clutched Rama's feet, babbling something Rama didn't understand.

'He was with Arjuna when Arjuna came here. He's the one who discovered Surabhi,' said Renuka. 'Let it be,' she continued before Rama could react. 'He's already got his punishment. He's lost everything he had. Family, status and wealth. So has the priest. They escaped the carnage by the skin of their teeth and come here for forgiveness.'

Rama sighed deeply. 'Get up,' he said.

Chandragupta rose and stood immobile, not even dusting the dirt off his clothes and face. Rama motioned them to sit and introduced Anantha to Renuka.

'Speak,' he said to Raikava.

'Surrender. Forgiveness. Refuge. Please find it in your heart to render these to us,' Raikava spoke low. Rama studied them. Both were dirty, weary and didn't look like they'd eaten a decent meal in days.

'Surrender, I accept. Forgiveness, I give,' Rama replied. 'Wash. Eat. Rest. I'll decide anything else later.'

Rama asked Akrita to make arrangements for them and Anantha. Akrita led them away, while Rama held Anantha back.

'Watch them,' Rama said. Anantha nodded and followed the trio.

Rama sat and told Renuka about the Saptarishis. She thought awhile and said, 'I can't figure out why they came, or what this taking measure means. Perhaps they have a task for you. They readily agreed to help, didn't they?'

'Have all seven of them gathered in the forest? Atri, Bharadwaja and Vasishtha, too?'

Renuka shrugged. There was nothing more to be said. Rama washed, performed his sandhya, ate and fell into a deep, dreamless sleep.

Jayadhwaja sat before Dantakrura, the fire pit between them.

'I'm at a loss, samrat. I cannot find an answer. It is a curiosity.'

'You can't find a suitable woman. How can that be?' said Jayadhwaja.

Dantakrura brushed his question away. 'No. Not that. Where are the souls, samrat?'

'Souls?'

'I use souls to scry and better understand Parashurama. So much killing in Mahishmati, so many souls awaiting deliverance, so many I can use. And I have utilised them to delve into their memories and final moments. Some, of course, have been taken by Vetalas and Pisachas. The others I study were killed by Parashurama's arrows, by his divyastras and by the weapons of their fellow soldiers when they turned on each other.

'But I cannot find a single soul killed by the Parashu. Why?'

Jayadhwaja shook his head, mystified himself. 'Why is it important?'

'What happened to them? What has Parashurama done? I've never come across such before. Does he have the ability to obliterate souls, or has he trapped them? That takes incalculable power.'

'Are you backing out?' Jayadhwaja demanded.

'Never have I had such a challenge. No, samrat, I do not step back.'

'So, what do we do next?'

'We prepare for the ritual. I have several requirements and some particular items. The texts caution against the lack of these.'

'What texts, Dantakrura?'

'Ah! It is an irony,' Dantakrura crowed. 'Saptarishi Jamadagni was the High Adept of the Atharva hymns. Hymns, *seen* by Atharvan, one of the names of the clan father Brighu. There is another seer who has hymns in the Atharva. Angirasa. The true father of Abhichara, though he wouldn't want to be called that.

'Only fifteen hymns of Angirasa are counted amongst the Shrutis. The rest were deemed forbidden magic. Improper. Fools! Those hymns are known to me and my ilk, and we have built on their knowledge. That disrespect, that omission from their prim and prudish collection, has come back to bite the scion of Brighu.'

'You mean to cast a spell on Parashurama?'

'No. As the son of the High Adept of Atharva, Parashurama also knows the chants and spells. Perhaps he already has protection, or he may know instantly when a spell is cast on him. Why show our hand so soon? I have found a woman for my spell.'

'What do you need, warlock?'

'Twelve sers of rice, forty-eight more of beaten rice. Ninety-six sers of gud, twelve of ghee, forty-eight of sarshapa tailam, three of navaneeta. Twelve bundles of tambula of twenty-four each ...' Dantakrura rattled off a long list.

'You'll have them.'

'I'm not finished. Slough of jalasarpa, the abdomen of varaha, ligaments of markata, the bile of gau, hair of shalyaka, the tail of uluka, the dung of jatuka, blood of grudrah, milk of mahishi, the marrow of riksha, eyes of kak and gorochana of aja.'

Jayadhwaja blanched.

'Duality, samrat. Clean, unclean. Customary, strange,' Dantakrura laughed.

'Is that all?'

'Most important. The skeleton of a whore.'

'By when do you need these?'

'Don't fret, samrat. Without haste, but without waste, you'll collect them all. We perform the ritual on Kali Chaturdashi, the fourteenth night of the waning moon.'

'But that's tomorrow,' said Jayadhwaja.

'Better set men to the task immediately then,' said Dantakrura.

Rama reached his ashram after his morning rituals. For a muhurta, he set about cleaning the two cottages and the space between them. He approached the banalinga and kalasha and stopped. He had set them down to face east. The kalasha was now facing north. Had he inadvertently turned it when he had prayed to the Devi when battling Mahadeva? No, he hadn't. He wondered if he should turn it back east again. Puzzled, he mused it over for a while and decided to let things be.

Rama cleaned the banalinga and kalasha, filled the kalasha with water and worshipped the Lord and His Consort. He focused his attention on the centre of the three eyes on the banalinga and slipped into dhyana. There was no mirror this time, no unending space and deep silence. Instead, he was in the mountaintop temple of Indrapuri. The temple was completely different. The twin banalinga was still there, but there was another sanctum a few steps from him. Rama walked to it. He turned to face a murthi of Bhadrakali. He closed his eyes and bowed to it, straightened himself and looked at the first sanctum. The banalinga faced east, and the Devi, north. Just like in his ashram.

Mystified, he looked around. There was another sanctum and two alcoves carved into the wall surrounding the temple. He took his bearings again. The third sanctum was in the north-eastern corner. A murthi of Ganapathi. He bowed and moved on. The first alcove had a murthi too. It took him a few seconds to recognise the deity. Veerabhadra, guardian of

Mahadeva temples. He paid his respects. The second alcove had a rectangular slab. The carvings were indistinct as if the images were caught under the surface of the black stone, straining against it, waiting to come forth. Seven carvings on the slab. He thought long and hard, but couldn't figure them out.

The mountain and temple blinked out, and he was before the mirror. His whole body gleamed in the reflection. Seven points of light shone along his spine. The seven chakras, the seven lotuses, and he knew their names. He'd gleaned that much from stray lines in all those texts he'd pored over. Others had only glimpsed what he was now witnessing in its entirety.

The bottom point was brighter than the rest. Yes, he knew the beeja-akshara to that one, the Muladhara chakra. He thanked Ganapathi again. What about the light on his forehead? He called it forth, the amsha of Mahavishnu. It glowed, furious as ever. He extinguished it. The sixth point of light between his eyebrows stayed dim, unlike the Muladhara. It would light up, it would bloom when he found its mantra. He would find the mantra for each. What was given as a blessing of Parashakti would be earned by him this time around.

Numerous fine, golden channels of energy ran through his body, emanating from his spine. This was his subtle energy body. Not the gross physical one. Yet, each affected the other. Seventy-two thousand channels. The three primary ones ran up his spine. Ida, Pingala and Sushumna. This too he'd read in the texts. He was seeing it in his dhyana now.

Ida and Pingala ran on either side of the Sushumna, and all three went up the spine. Ida and Pingala criss-crossed at the chakras, while Sushumna ran straight through. Rama stared at the image for a long while and eased out of dhyana.

He walked back to Jamadagni's ashram. He didn't know what the temple was supposed to show him, but he had surely understood the significance of the reflection. He had to discover the mantras of each chakra. And if the first discovery was anything to go by, he would have to perform some action, here on prithvi, to uncover them. He was a Brahmakshatriya. It would take realisation and action to reveal them all. It wouldn't be so for ordinary mortals. They would have the beeja-aksharas if he succeeded in this endeavour.

'So be it,' he thought to himself and grinned. 'Tathasthu.'

A bunch of people had crowded around Renuka's hut: his brothers, Akrita, Raikava, Chandragupta, Anantha, Dakini and Varnini. All were awaiting Renuka's return from one of her forays into the forest to collect her herbs. An idea flashed in his mind, and he rushed into the hut, brought out the Parashu and laid it flat on the floor. He asked Akrita to pick it up. Akrita looked from him to the Parashu and back, reluctant to touch it.

'Go on. It will not harm you. Just pick it up,' said Rama.

Akrita gave it all he had, but the axe didn't budge an inch. Anantha tried next, and then Anantha and Akrita together. They failed to move it. Rama's brothers pitched in. Shoulders and arms, back and legs, muscle and sinew straining, the six of them lifted the Parashu a couple of inches off the floor. A nimisha later, it crashed back, bruising their fingers. They grinned sheepishly and launched into theories and possibilities.

Renuka returned, handing the herbs to the girls and listening to the excited babble. She reached for the Parashu.

The image of Chinnamasta in that otherworldly realm flashed in Rama's mind. Renuka couldn't budge the Parashu. Rama picked it up with one hand, and the group fell silent. Rama was turning it all over in his mind when a familiar sound tickled his ears.

Padukas! No doubt about it. The sound came from the edge of the ashram, coming the same way he'd come. No long staff. And a second sound, something soft treading the earth, following the padukas. Two people, one behind the other, and the second person wore footwear of hemp or leather.

'Two people come,' said Rama. They waited for them to appear. A few nimishas later, the first person rounded the corner of the hut. Jamadagni had come home at last.

He wore the same white dhoti and angavastra as the three Saptarishis Rama had encountered in the forest. Padukas adorned his feet, his right hand grasping a bundle of palm leaves and a tangle of darbha grass, while his left hand carried an umbrella made from dried, woven coconut leaves. Rama had never seen that umbrella before. Despite its simplicity, it looked ceremonial, like it was marking an occasion formally. Rama dropped the Parashu. Jamadagni's eyes found Renuka and the light of some unspoken message played in them. Rama sensed the absolute stillness in Renuka.

Rama moved towards Jamadagni when the second man emerged round the corner. Disbelief and anger exploded in him, stopping him cold. The second man was Shukracharya.

Jamadagni held up his right hand before Rama could react, gesturing for Rama to hold his peace. He removed the padukas as Rama's brothers rushed to wash his feet, take his umbrella and angavastra and bring him water. Jamadagni handed the palm leaves and darbha to Renuka.

'It is time,' he whispered to Renuka. The words were meant for Renuka's ears only, but Rama heard them loud and clear. Something changed in Renuka. Her eyes took on the timeless gaze he'd seen in Chinnamasta's eyes. Her eyes wandered for a nimisha. She looked at her husband with a strange smile in her eyes and on her lips and embraced him.

'Time it is, then,' she said with her lips beside his ears. No one else heard, except Rama. He wondered what it meant.

They held each other, wrapped in a cocoon of their own world.

'The Daityaguru comes to apologise,' said Jamadagni as they eased apart. 'I met him on the way back here. He tried apologising to me. I told him I'm not the one who should forgive.'

The man pressed his palms together and bowed to Renuka. 'I regret my actions. Please accept my apologies.'

Renuka nodded her acceptance absent-mindedly. *Did she even hear him?* Rama wondered.

'My apologies to you, Rama. Neither motive nor approach was correct. I shouldn't have tried to compel you.'

He said it unabashedly and plainly, without artifice. Rama stared back without a word or gesture. His evident resentment lay thick on all of them, hushing everyone.

'Parashu of Mahadeva,' said Jamadagni, breaking the awkward silence. He picked it up with ease and touched the cheek of the blade to his forehead. A collective gasp rippled through the crowd. 'No. Parashurama's Parashu,' he said half to himself. He looked it over, taking in the arc of the twin blades, the rune and the menace of it. He stared at it for a long while.

'Much heavier than it appears,' Jamadagni mused. He put it down and turned to the group. 'Is there no work for all of you today? And who are these three men?'

Rama's brothers and the girls left, whispering amongst themselves. Rama introduced Anantha, Raikava and Chandragupta to Jamadagni. The trio prostrated themselves before the Saptarishi and then the Daityaguru.

'Aren't you going to resolve this?' Jamadagni asked Rama as he looked at Shukracharya. Rama sighed, picked up the pot left by his brothers and gestured to Shukracharya. The Daityaguru removed his shoes, let Rama pour water over his feet and stepped onto the stoop.

'There's much to talk about,' said Jamadagni as he sat. Renuka and Shukracharya sat with him. Rama followed to complete the circle. The trio gathered closer.

Jamadagni intoned in a soft voice,

'*Om sahana vavatu ...*' He waited till everyone repeated and continued as all joined in.

'*Saha nau bhunaktu,*
Saha viiryam karavavahai,
Tejasvi navaditamastu,
Maa vidvissaavahai,
Om shanti, shanti, shanti.'

May the divine guard teacher and student,
May it nourish us,
May we cooperate with energy,
May our study enlighten us,
May there be no divide or hate,
May there be peace.

Rama thought for a nimisha. There was a shade of

formality to their conversation. Things were going to be asked, and things were going to be explained. He pressed his palms together and chanted,

'*Om purnamadah purnamidam,*
Purnat purnamudachyate,
Purnasya purnamadaya purnamevavashiisyate,
Om shanti, shanti, shanti.'[3]
Full is the outer, full also the inner,
From fullness comes fullness,
Taking fullness from fullness, even so fullness remains,
May there be peace.

Jamadagni smiled approvingly and gestured to Shukracharya to speak.

'Arjuna's eldest, Jayadhwaja, is now the samrat. His brothers travel far and wide, invoking clan and familial loyalty and the strength of arms to secure his position. His prodigious armies outside Bharatvarsha have been called back. The Kshatriyas consolidate. The order of things serves them well, and they will find sense in continuing it. Rama cut off the source of misery in this world, but the iron frame, Arjuna's system of administration, continues to thrive after his death,' said Shukracharya.

'Itihasa will proclaim Parashurama a great warrior. One who vanquished the undefeatable and slew the un-killable. It is a great accomplishment. The question remains—is that all he will be?'

All heads turned towards Rama. He wondered for a nimisha if he should talk openly before Shukracharya and understood that Jamadagni had already thought of it. He had bound this meeting with the sacred chant. Honour and

[3] *Ishavasya Upanishad*

self-respect would prevent Shukracharya from presenting a false front. Rama told them of the three Saptarishis and how they had 'taken measure' of him, watching his father all the while for any hint of what it was all about.

'So, you carved a throne by instinct. Will you be samrat?' Shukracharya asked. Rama didn't reply.

'Permit me to speak,' said Raikava.

Jamadagni nodded.

'As Arjuna's high priest, I put his blinkers on my eyes and obeyed every word. I performed his rituals and convinced myself that it was dharma. Deep down, I knew it wasn't. Many like me thought so, in secret. But we allowed fear into our hearts and the comfort and ease of the order of things to dull our souls. Brahmins like me have sinned. We require purification. We are ready to walk the path of dharma under Parashurama's protection.'

He turned to Rama. 'Punish our weakness, but allow us to make amends. Break the iron frame. Vidya is for everyone. Free it from the clutches of the elite.'

Chandragupta spoke as soon as Raikava finished, 'I was Arjuna's prime minister. I know the men and women in positions of power across Bharatvarsha. I know some spies. I know the traders who resent the back-breaking taxes but have only confided their displeasure to me in secret. I know the iron frame. I've been inside it for two decades. Allow me to help you break it.'

'Two allies, with knowledge and of importance. But one man cannot do it. You need an army, Rama,' said Shukracharya.

'He has one. The Malaya Kshatriyas. His people. Women and men willing to lay down their lives for the Uddhatr,' said Anantha.

'Uddhatr?'

'The man who will raise the land and settle us down. Parashurama is Uddhatr.'

'Raise the land?'

Anantha shrugged and looked at Rama. Raikava and Chandragupta exchanged glances. But Shukracharya caught it and asked them to speak up. Raikava told them of Arjuna's ill-fated temple and how Apava thwarted Arjuna.

'Do you remember the prophecy?' Renuka asked.

'Every word. It was why Queen Manorama insisted on the ritual that would tie her life to Arjuna's and in turn, protect him.'

'The yagna in the temple in Mahishmati—it was the first time I saw Arjuna,' said Rama. Raikava nodded.

'This is what Apava said:

A prophecy of fire and water.

Of fire that is the womb of water, and water that is the heart of fire.

When Mahakaal's dread weapon,
Descends to earth from heaven,
Its master, he will break the world,
Thirsty for blood will be the axe once hurled.
Lakes of warrior blood five,
The price, arrogance and folly contrive,
The fork in the path of dharma,
Lies solely in the samrat's karma.
To renounce, to reform, this choice he has,
To turn from the dark of tamas,
To flow with peace, like water,
And stop perchance, the slaughter.
Else, if he walks the path of fire,

To pander untrammelled desire,
Beware the golden horn,
For that day, vengeance is born.
If he swears a battle oath,
Lives forfeit would both.
For Sahasrabahu,
And master of Parashu,
This fate to escape from,
Is to unbecome, to die, to become.'

A moment of quiet settled over everyone.

'Arjuna chose the path of fire,' said Raikava.

'Surabhi was the golden horn,' added Chandragupta in a small voice.

'You died and then came alive?' Shukracharya asked Rama.

'To unbecome, die, become,' said Renuka.

'Fire and water,' said Jamadagni.

'Five lakes of blood?' said Rama.

'Yet nothing about raising the land,' said Anantha.

Only Akrita was quiet, deep in thought.

Chandragupta continued. 'Arjuna flew into a rage and became Sahasrabahu the moment Apava cursed him. He leapt at the Rishi, but Apava disappeared into thin air. Frustrated, Arjuna bounded away towards the Sindhu sagar, the western ocean. Jayadhwaja, Brihadbala, Suchandra and I followed. Before we found him, we saw devastation mounted on an unimaginable scale. Yojanas of the coast plunged into the ocean. Twenty-one yojanas' width of land submerged in one day. Massive waves brought unprecedented destruction upon prithvi.'

'Perhaps that is the land you must raise,' said Raikava to Rama, who said nothing.

'Your turn, Rama. Tell us about the Parashu, the war with the asuras and your journey till this moment. Akrita has told us what he knows. We wish to hear from you now,' said Jamadagni. Everyone leaned in expectantly, and Rama narrated his story.

It all began with his dhyana of the banalinga, the kalasha and the battle with Mahadeva. Akrita filled in with what he saw. Gasps and exclamations punctuated the narration. A hushed atmosphere of awe surrounded the group when Rama paused after the meeting with the Guru and the Nagas.

'Arjuna was the embodiment of the Sudarshana chakra. That is why I didn't see the chakra when I examined the light of the amsha in your forehead,' Jamadagni mused.

'And you extracted that power! Mahadeva! Truly, there is no being as powerful as you in the three worlds,' a stunned Shukracharya spoke.

Yes! That other voice in Rama's mind exulted.

'That power isn't mine to use. I used it just after I took it from Arjuna. A full Akshauhini of soldiers died in a nimisha. I will not use it again,' said Rama.

'Then you will have to find a way to return it to the source, the great Mahavishnu himself,' said Jamadagni.

'But why is it still with me, father? Why didn't it go to Mahavishnu as soon as I extracted it?'

'Perhaps there's something you need to accomplish, some purpose to this. I cannot explain it. Now continue with your story.'

Rama told them of his return to the ashram, Jamadagni's death and the vengeance he wreaked. He told them of that other-worldly realm and what happened there. He concluded with the incident on the way back to the ashram.

'How did you know I'll understand?' Rama asked Jamadagni.

'I didn't know. I hoped you would. The guru who taught you Dhanurveda, dying without a fight—I thought that ought to pique your curiosity. And that had to come from you alone. I cannot teach it to you,' said Jamadagni.

'But how did you know this was the way?' asked Rama.

'Ever since Ma Chinnamasta manifested in Renuka, and the amsha sparked in you to kill Arjuna, I've been thinking it over. All this cannot be mere coincidences. And remember the prophecy, too. What was said for Renuka was impacting you too. To unbecome, to die, to become. It gave us a Mahavidya. Why couldn't it help us defeat Arjuna? I found no answer until Arjuna came here and demanded Surabhi. Then it all came together. I took the chance. I hoped my son who beheaded his mother would see I too had swung on instinct and possibility.

'And it wasn't my time to go. A Saptarishi knows when the time comes. Renuka would figure out how to manifest Chinnamasta, or perhaps the Daityaguru would've come by with his Mrita-Sanjeevani to aid a fellow Bhargava.'

Rama nodded. The Saptarishis seemed to know a lot more than they let on.

'How were you able to lift the Parashu?' Renuka asked Jamadagni.

'It's because of my tapasya and knowledge of Dhanurveda. But I cannot use it or make it my own.'

'What have you deduced about the axe?' he turned to Rama.

'It is not just a weapon. It takes enormous spiritual power and wisdom to know its secrets. Perhaps only Mahadeva knows it all, but it would take a Brahmakshatriya to wield it as the Parashu. Else, it is just an axe with a blade that cuts anything,' Rama replied.

'Parashu? You call it an axe?' Jamadagni asked.

Rama shrugged.

'Has it grown heavier, Rama?'

'I'm not sure, but I think so,' said Rama.

'The verse about the Parashu. Tell me the fourth line, Rama.'

'Devourer of Soul.'

'That is why it grows heavier. All the men and asuras you killed, all have their souls trapped in the Parashu.'

Everyone gasped.

'Another responsibility. You have to find a way to give them deliverance. I don't know anything about this too.'

Jamadagni wasn't done yet. 'Invoke the bow, Rama.'

Rama stood, moved away from the stoop and invoked the bow. In a nimisha, his fingers curled around it.

'The bow of Vishnu! Twin of the bow of Shiva!' Shukracharya cried loudly. 'Will the wonders never cease with this boy?'

Jamadagni peered at the bow and smiled, 'Yes, it is Vishnu's bow. I've wielded it too. A long time ago.'

Rama let the bow disappear and sat down again.

'You wield Sharanga, twin of the Pinaka. Do you know how heavy the bow is? It is impossible to lift without great physical strength and immense merit of tapasya.'

Rama stared in surprise. It hadn't felt heavy at all.

'Have you come to a decision? About the way forward?' asked Jamadagni.

Rama sighed. Another taking of measure by another

Saptarishi, his father no less. Jamadagni seemed to read his mind. He smiled with a joyful, child-like twinkle in his eyes.

'The three Saptarishis who questioned you proposed something, and all seven agreed,' he said.

Then Rama's guess was right; all seven had gathered. Something important was agreed upon, and he had to know.

'What was agreed upon?'

'There are seven rishis for each Manavantara. They are responsible for upholding, propagating, protecting and teaching dharma. That's how we received the name Saptarishi. And we must pass on our position to the next seven, for the next Manavantara. Three of us took measure and found the first of the next seven. You.'

Rama gaped, stammered, swallowed and shut his mouth, oblivious to the excited babble around him. Words failed him. He threw himself at his parents' feet and stayed that way for a long while.

He sat back finally. 'I will destroy the iron frame,' his resolute voice cut through the chatter. It silenced everyone. 'Are there any more responsibilities?' Rama wouldn't keep the edge off his voice.

Renuka smiled. 'Who or what is an avatara?' she asked him.

'The one with all the responsibilities,' he answered flippantly.

Renuka laughed, 'I understand, Rama. You want to be left alone. But you've come so far of your own choosing and on the strength of your deeds. It's just that the story didn't end where you expected it to.'

'The dharma of ordinary people makes the world go round. The dharma of an avatara makes it go forward. You are a citizen of two worlds—a world within and a world without. Everyone is, to a lesser or greater extent, but an avatara is necessarily so. You are the bridge between the inner and outer worlds of others, simply by your strength in both worlds.

'You could argue that every rishi is so, even the Saptarishis. True, but not to the extent of an avatara. You teach dharma for the time, place and context in which humanity finds itself. So the descendants can learn from what their ancestors did. An avatara comes in dire circumstances and serves as a point of focus. A bindu, if you will. To attract all the strikes upon himself or herself. Because an avatara can, whether he or she knows it. To know it, to accept it, is part of the journey.

'Many people teach dharma and abide by it. An avatara embodies it. You are the embodiment of dharma. Only one such could have defeated the embodiment of the Sudarshana chakra.

'So, it follows that an avatara must absorb enormous pressure, face one trial after another, surmount Himalayan challenges, even cutting criticism and public outrage. An avatara is a living murthi of dharma, faith, justice and hope.

'I do not doubt in my mind, my son, that you are just that.'

When Renuka stopped speaking, murmurs of approval wove about the group and died away. Anantha spoke next.

'My question is this. A man so powerful, an avatara—he can do it all himself. What need does he have of us?'

'Sitting and praying for an avatara, waiting for him or her to solve all your problems, will not work. That is just stupid fatalism,' said Shukracharya. 'An avatara comes because ordinary people have adhered to dharma despite the odds; they haven't strayed from dharma regardless of the order of things. It doesn't need many, a few will do. But the few will be intractable in their defiance of adharma. When things go out of their capacity, the avatara arrives. To give succour, to take pressure.

'Even an avatara needs help. He can do it all himself, but will the lesson be learnt? For the first time, a mortal has sparked an amsha in himself. This avatara doesn't come, fulfil the purpose and leave. He stays and becomes chiranjeevi. People must gather to his flag. Otherwise, there is the danger that people may consider him just another tyrant imposing his will and doing what he thinks is right.'

'The Kshatriyas must know that all three varnas stand against them, and dharma-abiding Kshatriyas too, if you can find them. Parashurama is your figurehead, the glue that will hold you together. Already the world talks of him in awe, and in that most hard-won of things, respect.'

Raikava, Chandragupta and Anantha conferred amongst themselves.

'Has the Avadhuta spoken to you?' Jamadagni asked.

'No.'

'Why Rama? He came to you. You've done as he wanted. He didn't respond to Arjuna's call, and now he goes silent.'

'He came to me. I think he wants to see if I can figure out how to go to him,' said Rama.

'What learning did you take away from his story?' asked Renuka.

'That it was all about the mothers. And the *All-Mother.* Anasuya, Padmini and you, as mortal mothers. And Parashakti, the mother of all. It was the power, the shakti, in them and you, that set the trajectory for their children.'

'The fathers' love, the gods' blessings and the mothers' powerful tapasya. What put it all together with love and compassion, to bring forth Guru Dattatreya, Arjuna and me? The shakti that pervades all. That *is* all. Parashakti. It was her behind the scenes. It was all her play, her lila.'

Rama pointed to the rune on the Parashu. 'She is the bindu, she is the circle.'

'Circle? Shunya?' Shukracharya queried.

'Not shunya. *Poorna*. Not emptiness. Fullness. She is all there is. It is her path I tread. The hidden power she revealed to me, the kundalini, is what I must rediscover here. This is my greatest responsibility.'

'Did you know of this?' Rama asked Jamadagni.

'I expected your self-realisation to have something to do with the Mahavidya. But this I did not expect,' Jamadagni replied.

'She is Sri Vidya. The auspicious knowledge.' Rama pressed his palms together and bowed. 'Sri Maathrey Namaha!' he intoned. The others repeated after him.

'You have a second mother now, Rama. Devi herself. You are the twice-born, born twice. Truly, destiny rides your shoulders, and new paths open with the swing of the Parashu,' said Renuka.

'Ramabhadra,' Shukracharya mused, 'Rama-bha-dra. Dra means great, maha. Bha, meaning maya. And Rama rejoicing. Ramabhadra, the one rejoicing in mahamaya! An apt name for her devotee.'

Rama smiled and bowed to the Daityaguru.

'Make your plans, then. I will watch with interest.' He turned to Jamadagni and Renuka. 'Thank you for your hospitality and understanding. I take your leave.'

He descended the stoop, slipped his feet into his shoes and vanished with a final pranaam.

It was Akrita who broke the silence. 'High Priest, was Rishi Apava's prophecy for both Gurudeva and Arjuna?'

'Yes,' Raikava replied.

'To unbecome, die, become. We know what Gurudeva became. Arjuna died. What did he become?'

Nobody had an answer.

They began at dusk, sitting on opposite sides of the fire pit. The flames in the fire pit grew as the sun plunged below the horizon and night embraced Mahishmati and the funeral grounds.

'It is a complex spell I weave, samrat. The one in whom I must seed the allure and the one who must get attracted—neither is before us here. I must imbue the spell in the woman I've chosen and have her approach Parashurama. I need you to follow and submit to the seven laws. First, fix your purpose to seed this spell. Second, focus on the ritual. Third, be steady in demeanour; there must be no hurry, fear or excitement. Fourth, pour your soul into the ritual and purpose. Fifth, put all your intensity into the syllable I give you. Sixth, remember the duality, male and female, the man who will lust, and the woman who will generate the lust. And last, desire the completion and success of this ritual with all your heart.'

Jayadhwaja nodded his resolve. Dantakrura whispered his chants and spells as he cast his oblations into the fire. The skeleton of the whore lay before Dantakrura, and he touched every offering to various parts of the skeleton before consigning it to the flames. Sweat slathered Jayadhwaja's body as the fire grew. Dantakrura chanted long into the night.

The warlock stopped suddenly, breathed deep, raised his open right palm into the sky and ululated. Two sounds emerged from him, one from his throat, and one from his stomach. They formed an eerie melody, killing all other sounds, even the crackling of the burning wood. Dantakrura ululated again, long and strong, the pitch alternating between high to low. Jayadhwaja's hair stood on end.

'Come!' Dantakrura roared, 'Sambara, Nikumbha, Naraka, Tantukachcha.

'Come! Armalava, Pramila, Mandoluka, Ghatodbala.'

His voice dropped low as if whispering in a lover's ears,

'O Aliti and Paliti, approach. O Amile, Kimile, Vayujare, Prayoge, heed my call. Phake, Kavayushve, Vihale, Dantakatake, come. Come, Bhandirapaka. Come, chant with me.'

Jayadhwaja's body turned cold. The invisible eyes and the shadows seemed to have increased a hundred-fold. The air around the fire pit pummelled him, his ears throbbing like war drums were being beaten inside them. Something brushed against his back, as soft as a whisper, and his skin crawled and shrank from it. All around him was slobber, slither, hiss and gnash. Foetid breath hit him out of thin air. Jayadhwaja fought the urge to retch, to keep his terror from showing. He fought the urge to glance, to turn, to rise and run. He fought to remain sane.

'Our visitors have come, samrat! Close your eyes and chant the syllable. Once on inhalation, once when you exhale. Keep your awareness on the syllable. Many crore times must we chant this together.'

Jayadhwaja closed his eyes and chanted the syllable Dantakrura had given him. He chanted as if his life depended on it, jerking his attention away from the unworldly sounds around him.

Much, much later, he heard Dantakrura call out to him, 'Open your eyes, samrat.'

Jayadhwaja did so. The fire burned black, its flames leaping for the sky. Black, sooty and bubbling smoke from it flowed down, carpeting the earth. He couldn't see himself below the waist.

'Come, Chandali,' Dantakrura whispered. 'Come, Kumbhi, Tumba and Katuka. Lend me your aid.'

Dantakrura held his arms out to the side. His hands grasped invisible fingers, while the inaudible chanting continued. Suddenly, Dantakrura broke into song,

'Dusk and dawn,
Fire and ice,
Wind and ether,
Heart's blood and loin's sap,
Come, Bhutaketu,
This soul be mine till bone turns to ash.
Earth and sky,
Roots and leaves,
Serpent and eagle,
Heart's blood and loin's sap,
Come, Shraga,
This soul be mine till bone turns to ash.
Infinite night, infinite light,
Midnight sun and midday moon,
Honey and effluvium,
Heart's blood and loin's sap,
Come, Bandhamohini,
This soul be mine till bone turns to ash.'

'Come! I invoke thee! I bind you to my will! I order you to do my bidding!'

The frothing smoke left of Dantakrura parted with a thump to reveal the skeleton. Jayadhwaja had no inkling how it got there. The air was heady with a teasing, flowery fragrance. His heart pounded with a strange longing, and his loins stirred and roused. The skeleton glowed silver.

'She's come!' said Dantakrura in a delirium of ecstasy. 'Bandhamohini is here.'

He rose and went to the skeleton, scooping it in his arms and embracing it like a lover. He whispered something to the side of the skull, where the ears would've been. The warlock kissed the broken, yellow teeth. Something of great power roared away from the skeleton and into the night. Dantakrura laid the skeleton down with care. He whispered again and clapped his hands thrice. The black flame, the thick smoke and the unseen chanters all vanished in a blink. Jayadhwaja breathed long in relief.

He looked in the fire pit. No trace of the oblations in or around it. The fire burned low and the pre-dawn cold smothered the heat of the ritual. The skeleton lay still, not silver but dirty yellow, inside a circle of red ash. Inside the skeleton was a small heart. A small, red beating heart.

9

Circle of Allure

The warlock laughed quietly, supremely satisfied at the powerful magic he'd woven. He opened his pouch and brought out Tarakaksha's eyeballs.

'I can see. Both of us can hear each person talk.'

He muttered mantras under his breath, closed his eyes and placed the two eyeballs on his shut eyelids. The eyeballs adhered to his eyelids as he took his hands away. He turned to Jayadhwaja, and the samrat blanched, turning away to stare at the skeleton and heart in the circle of red ash.

'There are ways,' Dantakrura laughed. 'Let us wait for the lila of lust to play out.'

Rama walked away from the pathashala. Jamadagni was holding forth on the meanings of a sutra, and Akrita was running an errand for him. He reached his parents' hut and called out to his mother. No reply. He sensed someone coming round the corner of the hut and turned. It was a woman. He'd seen her before. Yes, it was that couple he'd seen in the second settlement, soft-bodied and quite evidently accustomed to a life of ease. She approached alone. And Rama couldn't take his eyes off her.

She came closer, stopping at an arm's length from him. She smiled nervously, and Rama's mind reeled. She was so utterly beautiful, why hadn't he noticed before?

'Amba?' she asked.

Her voice danced in Rama's ears. His vision was besotted by the curve of her lips, the fullness of them, the way they touched and parted as she spoke. She waited for a reply, and Rama couldn't get his words out. He was breathing heavily, unable to break his stare. Alarms went off in his mind, somewhere in some far corner. He didn't understand why.

'Wait,' he croaked. 'She'll come by soon.'

The skeleton suddenly spoke, its jaws jerking awkwardly. Jayadhwaja almost jumped out of his skin.

'Amba,' said the skeleton.

'Bait,' said Dantakrura.

Move! Something inside him screamed, but his feet refused to budge. He *had* to get away even though he wanted to stay. Stay, and let his eyes rove across her face, look deep into her light brown eyes. To comb his hands through that thick black mane, knotted loosely and framing her exquisite, radiant face. To trace that thin gold necklace down her neck and deep between ...

No, no. Rama willed his eyes to look away from her, only for them to return a nimisha later. She smiled a little wider, and Rama yearned to tell her a trifling to make her laugh, to cup her chin, to draw her close ...

She stared openly at him, a thrill running through her. She didn't know if it was because of her audacity or the attraction of his form. The sheer vitality and strength he radiated. And his eyes. Pupils of honey, alight with tapas. He stood so still, like a hymn to solitude, a quiet storm of calm.

Say something, that other voice in Rama's mind pleaded.

'That man ...' he fumbled. He paused, and the words came in a rush, 'That man I saw you with. Your husband?'

'Yes,' she replied.

Rama's heart plunged in despair. Anger and jealousy bloomed. That man didn't deserve her.

'He isn't here now,' she said.

His heart soared. The anger disappeared, but jealousy stayed.

Get away! Get away! his mind shrieked, sharp as a hawk's cry. *Go closer*, the other voice pleaded. Rama willed himself to turn away from her, sweat breaking through the skin of his brow and his palms. He walked away, not daring to cast a parting glance. His step quickened as he turned the corner of the hut, gasping in relief. Anantha rose from the foot of a tree to come to him. Rama furiously gestured to him to stay as he walked. His throat was parched. He needed water. There was someone ahead; he would ask her. Rama reached abreast the woman, turned and froze. It was *her*. Joy coursed through him. She looked at him with surprise, and Rama ached to hear her sweet, sweet voice again.

'What's your name?' he gasped.

'Bhumi,' she replied.

Rama rolled the sound of her name in his mind, savouring it.

'Bhumi,' he whispered.

The whisper seared through Bhumi's ears. Her name was on his lips, a voice like honey over steel, and she didn't know if it sounded like a prayer or a curse.

Fool! his mind rebuked him. Rama glanced around in embarrassment to see if anyone was a witness. He saw the stoop of his parents' hut. He'd gone around in a circle.

Bhumi giggled. His eyes snapped back to her, and he almost danced in the exhilaration of the sound. The sound of silver coins on stone. She bit her lower lip and it reddened—a pomegranate's promise. *How did you get back here?* a small voice inside him asked.

It took an enormous effort for Rama to drag his feet forward. He forced himself to go back the way he'd come, blindly stumbling forward. Again, relief coursed through him as he distanced himself from Bhumi. And then, he found himself before her again.

Bhumi's eyebrows rose in surprise.

'Are you Parashurama?' she asked softly, though she already knew.

Rama nodded desperately.

'The mightiest warrior on earth,' she said in awe.

Rama blushed. He felt his ears turn red. His heart thumped so hard he thought it would break his chest. The alarm rang insistently in his mind, but that was a mere drop compared to the torrent of heady, warm, arousing sensations that were drowning him.

Bhumi noticed the effect of her words. A surge of power coursed through her as if she had a secret weapon and he had no counter to it. 'Strong muscles you have,' she whispered. 'Unlike my husband. He's just a soft, flaccid lump. I like my men ... hard.'

Rama gulped, his head spinning with the dizzying visions her words were conjuring in his mind. *Take her in your arms*, the other voice begged.

Bhumi almost clapped her hand to her mouth, aghast at what she'd just said. Visibly embarrassed, she half turned to flee. Somehow, she found herself facing him instead.

'You don't love him?' he asked.

Rama's voice was hoarse, and his gaze pierced through her. It robbed her of words, of breath even. He had a predator's eyes. Wild and primal. A man-beast, her imagination blazed. A danger to anything in the jungle, one who scorned the warmth and safety of a campfire at night; the heat of his caged ferocity was enough.

Bhumi shook her head slightly and found her voice at last. 'Not all married women are wives.' Coyness overcame her and she dropped her gaze. Remember your vows, she told herself, a moment of sanity. Her fingers tried to grasp at her necklace, her mangalsutra, for support.

A thin strand of luscious black hair came loose. Rama yearned to tuck it behind her ear, into the raven tresses dense as a monsoon torrent. He breathed deeply and her scents swarmed into his lungs. She smelled of jasmine and the earth, and neem. Her hair smelled faintly of tailam. Bhringraj, hibiscus, brahmi ... Rama tried to list the ingredients to distract himself. Yet, his mind rebelled.

She wore no earrings, but her ears were pierced. The nudity of her ears was voluptuous, stoking burning lust. Rama's eyes roved. Except for the necklace, she wore no jewellery. Her dress, a length of pale green cotton, was wrapped twice around her waist, across and up her torso to her left shoulder, down the back and tucked in. The wrap stopped just above her knees, and she was barefooted. He felt miserable that she had no footwear to protect her delicate feet. Rama tore his eyes off her legs, and they settled on her right arm. He could see a faint tan line on her tawny skin, high up on the arm. She used to wear a blouse. He checked her right shoulder. There, where the shoulder met her neck, another tan line. The telltale sign of the cut of the blouse. He wondered how low on her bosom the cut went ...

No, no. He stopped that train of thought. *She was better off without a blouse ...* Stop!

A brief gust of wind flapped at the wrap across her upper body. For the briefest of seconds, Rama caught a glimpse of the soft bulge beneath, smooth as sandal paste. His mind, his body, his very breath was fire. She smoothed the stretch of cloth and folded her arms across. Her bosom strained against the cloth. *Mahadeva!* he almost called out. He brushed his palm down from his brow to shut his eyelids, guilt a whip across his mind. *Look! Look!* the other voice screamed.

'I've to go to the goshala,' he said through clenched teeth.

He dragged himself away and turned around the corner. Anantha stood mute as he watched Rama. Rama tore past huts and reached the goshala in a blink. He breathed lungfuls of air and sat down. He wasn't going anywhere. After a while, he controlled his breath and calmed himself down. Something was wrong, very wrong. He was lusting for a woman he'd just met. A married woman at that, and he didn't understand why.

Bhumi breathed deep, hoping for the tide of emotions in her to subside, wondering why she was so overcome by the sight of this man. The answer sprung in her mind immediately. Because you desire him, and you haven't felt this way in a long, long time. And Bhumi remembered the last time. In the court of Samrat Arjuna, when he had glanced at her in the visitors' gallery. The tug she had felt inside her then was the same as now, but somehow a thousand-fold stronger.

Rama rose, resolving to get away from the ashram. He raced towards the jungle. And halted in a blink. Before Bhumi. He'd gone around in a circle again.

She laughed, and it was the sound of merriment and abandon. It tinkled through his ears, to his heart, and down to his loins. She moved to the stoop and sat, crossing her legs. The wrap rose high on her thighs like a village gossip threatening to reveal secrets. She tossed her head back, and the slack tie of her mane came loose. Rama drank in the vision of her like a drunkard forsaking his abstinence.

Bhumi stared at Rama standing before her again, and her heart thrummed a drumbeat of forbidden want. There was no reasoning with it. The tug was desperate and insistent, threatening to shatter her modesty.

Get away! his mind cried, and he tried, struggling with all he had. *Go to her!* the other voice pleaded. He lowered his eyes with a soft moan, looking at the ground, and walked backwards. One step, two. It was so hard to move away. Three steps, four. A little easier now. *Why?* his mind screamed. Rama egged himself on.

'Rama,' Dakini called. 'You can't keep away, is it?'

He whirled towards her. How long had she been here? Had she seen it all? He'd not noticed her at all. He froze in embarrassment. Dakini came to him and held his arm, eyes dancing with mischief, and a knowing smile on her lips. He gasped with relief. He put his arm around her shoulders and held on for dear life. She led him forward to the stoop.

'Amba is with the forest tribes. She'll be here in the

afternoon,' Varnini said to Bhumi as she walked towards them.

Bhumi nodded, rose and walked away with an awkward smile. Rama hastily looked away from the sway of her hips and the tightness of the wrap around her behind. He exhaled when she disappeared around the corner.

Bhumi turned the corner and fled, half relieved that Dakini had come and half furious at herself. She tried to forget all that had happened but could only think of Parashurama's hands and how it would feel if they touched her.

'When did you come?' Rama asked as he sat on the stoop.

'Before you. Looking for a wife, are we? That one is married.' Dakini couldn't help giggling.

'Or do you have something else in mind?'

'Hush that loose talk,' Varnini scolded. 'Rama will marry a princess, just like his father. And where were you all morning? I searched all over.'

'Watching interesting sights,' Dakini said with a wink at Rama. The two women sat a few steps from Rama, chatting without pause.

Anantha walked towards the women, observing Rama with curious eyes. But he was soon drawn into an animated conversation with them. Rama quietly let the insanity inside him die down. He breathed easier, biding his time. Varnini, ever the busybody, walked away to the store. Dakini and Anantha put their heads together, talking softly. Probably talking about him, Rama thought. He didn't want to hear what they said. He was embarrassed still and absolutely at a loss about what had happened. Perhaps it was some sort of reaction to all that fighting and blood and killing. Or some kind of winner's fallacy, assuming that the world and its women were willing to throw themselves at his feet. But why this woman? Why was he so fascinated with her? He remembered the words of an old drunken rake in one of the settlements: women waited at the end of the race to offer themselves to the winner. They wanted the strongest, richest, most influential. It was just their natural selection. Men hunted beauty, but women hunted success. That there were predators on both sides, wolves amongst men, and sharks amongst women. Was she one of those? She was certainly appreciative of him and had a provocative way of expressing it.

She was undoubtedly from Mahishmati. Perhaps she was appreciating him for avenging some injustice meted to her by Arjuna. *Stupid, stupid* ... his mind chided, and he agreed. He was getting nowhere thinking like this. Going around in circles, his mind told him.

Rama rose only when he thought that the woman ... *Bhumi* ... had had enough time to return to the settlement. He needed to get out of the ashram to clear his head. Anantha insisted on joining him and he let him, glad for the company. He hoped she wasn't somewhere in the ashram. He desperately wished she was ... to look at her again, to run his eyes over ... *Stop.*

Rama kept his eyes lowered and set a fast pace, avoiding the settlements. His breathing eased when they entered the dense woodlands. Rama kept up the pace until he heard Anantha panting heavily. He paused to let him catch his breath and walked on, his walk as furious as ever. Sometimes, Anantha had to run to catch up, and he paused more often as Anantha grew tired. No matter how much he walked and thought, he could decipher neither head nor tail of the matter.

He knew Anantha was watching him keenly, but he didn't know how to explain things to him. He didn't even want to look at Anantha.

Rama suddenly figured where out he was headed. His throne. He came upon it soon enough and stood gazing at it. Rama saw himself sitting on it ... with Bhumi in his lap, caressing him, grinding against him, shrugging her wrap off her shoulder ... *STOP!*

He calmed himself down, sat on his throne in padmasana and tried to go into dhyana. Rama tried to ease into it, and then he tried to force it. He tried for a long time. It was impossible. His mind was filled with Bhumi's form, her smile, her lips, the sway in her gait, her touch. No, he hadn't touched her yet. He longed for it, to run all the way to the settlement for it.

He opened his eyes. Anantha had been watching him keenly. Rama was surprised to see the time of the day; it was past afternoon. He walked again, to get away from the throne, his pace slower but thoughts racing.

The sun was dipping towards the horizon when Anantha stopped him and insisted they go home.

'We're walking around in circles, Swami. We've passed this spot a dozen times now.'

Rama stopped like he'd hit a wall. He was no closer to an answer. Perhaps someone in the ashram could help. One of his brothers. Yes, that was best, he'd talk to Vishwa.

'Let's go home. You lead the way,' said Rama. By now, Bhumi would've come to the ashram, met Ma and gone. It was safe to return. He didn't trust himself to walk straight home, and Anantha could find the way with little difficulty.

'We are close, Swami. I know this part of the jungle.'

Rama nodded absently and walked in silence behind him, grappling with the shock of being unable to go into dhyana.

They came upon the settlement. The settlement in which *she* stayed. Both worry and desire bloomed in Rama. He should've told Anantha not to come this way. He was glad he hadn't told him. She was close, so close. He wondered which hut she stayed in. Anantha exchanged pleasantries with the people he knew, some of them newcomers. Rama turned in place, looking for Bhumi. Perhaps he should ask someone. He bit his tongue to stop himself. He wondered what she was doing now. Preparing for her sandhyavandana, no doubt. Bathing to cleanse herself. He physically shook his head to push away the images his mind had conjured of her bathing.

Anantha was speaking to one of the boys on the street when Rama willed himself to say, 'Let's go. Now.'

They reached the ashram at dusk. He thanked Anantha and walked ahead towards the pathashala. Anantha shrugged and slipped away. He didn't find anyone at the pathashala. Time for the evening rituals, he realised. Rama sat, waiting.

—

No one came to the pathashala. Rama rose and walked to his parents' hut. The door was open, the glow of a lamp spilt onto the entrance. He entered and found Renuka bent over a few small clay pots, checking them, covering their mouths with lids or leaves.

'Rama,' she said over her shoulder, 'Good you've come. Take these down to the storeroom and ...'

'Amba,' came a soft call from the stoop.

Rama whirled. He knew that voice. It was her, standing

before the hut, glowing in the light of Dakini's and Anantha's blazing torches. His breath caught. He couldn't take his eyes off her. He saw the slight dampness in her hair. She had bathed. Another swarm of images overpowered his thoughts.

'You're back. The medicine is ready. Your husband will sleep like a log, don't fret,' said Renuka. She handed a clay pot to Rama. 'Give this to her.'

Rama grabbed at the pot and moved forward soundlessly, eyes fixed on her.

'Both of them were coming here, and she asked for you ...' Anantha's voice petered out when he saw Rama wasn't paying attention.

Rama slowly descended the stoop, eyes gliding over her lips, her neck, to the softness of her palms held open to take the pot. She stepped forward, less than an arm's length away. He looked into her eyes. They were lined with anjana. A teasing invitation danced in them.

Bhumi's eyes flirted with his. She'd come as quickly as she could when she'd heard he was back in the ashram. He was magnificent to look at in the shadow of dusk and the light of the clay lamps. The ferality in him was breathtaking. She held the pot and stepped closer.

'Parashurama,' she whispered, 'I know what you want. I want it too. Do you not feel this urge beyond all reason?'

Bhumi's hands inched forward on the pot. Her fingers touched his hands. Rama felt a jolt of sheer excitement run through him. *Move away*! his mind wailed, on and on. Something clattered inside the hut. He didn't pay attention. Desire burned inside him. To clasp her, taste those lips and crush her soft body against his hardened muscles. *Do it now. Take her now!* the other voice was ferocious.

Sweat broke on his brow as he resisted his urges. He held still, waiting for the tidal waves of lust to subside, hoping to hold on to his sanity, his morals and his self-respect. The veins in his neck and forehead throbbed with the effort. He grit his teeth and clenched his fists, his nails digging into his palms.

Bhumi knew he resisted, she could see it in his face, and it stoked her desire even more. He was vulnerable, but only to her. He wanted her, and so desperately wanted to hide the want from her. A strange pride bloomed in her heart.

She handed the pot to Dakini and took another from her. She opened the leaf lid and held the pot up near his chin. 'Something I made. Sweet pudding. For you,' she whispered. Rama teetered on the edge. She dipped two fingers into the pot and held them to his lips.

'Lick my fingers,' her voice was honey. His jaws ached from the labour it took to hold them shut.

'What do you want?' he croaked. His voice was rough but hungry. He loathed it and craved it.

'The same that you want. Or will you lie to me?'

'This is madness,' he stuttered.

'It is the truth,' she replied.

'It is a trap,' he spoke at last.

'The prey seeks the trap,' she said.

Rama had no answer, and she smiled triumphantly.

'Come to me tonight. Find my hut. Stop resisting this. The night is kinder to surrender.' Her voice dropped lower, almost inaudible, but Rama heard her loud and clear. 'My husband will sleep like a log. I will wait for you. Bring your weapon. Not the axe, your spear.'

Rama had been transformed into a beast clawing at its cage. He licked her fingers and lost himself in the ecstasy of taste and wild imagination.

The clatter was tremendous this time, jolting Rama and everyone else. It gave him a nimisha of sanity. Renuka came to the doorway as Rama stepped back. He was sweating all over now. He swayed as he tried to move further back. Dakini held his forearm, concern writ large on her face.

'Are you alright?' she whispered. He put his arms around her, gulping down air, staring into the ground.

'We must go. My husband awaits,' said Bhumi. She bowed to Renuka, turned and walked away, accompanied by Anantha and Dakini, who repeatedly glanced at Rama with worry.

It was some time before Rama regained control of himself. He raised his head and looked at Renuka. She had a half-smile playing on her face.

'You mean to take a wife?' she asked.

'What? No ...' he stammered.

'Well, enough women are interested now. Several girls from the tribal clans are eager to make you theirs. A mighty yoddha as a husband would do them proud, they say. In fact, they are agreeable for you to choose more than one woman if you so please.' Renuka couldn't hide the mirth in her voice.

Many wives, many more concubines, the other voice laughed.

'But if you choose her,' Renuka gestured to where the three were standing nimishas ago, 'then that is good too. After all, she knows you well.'

Rama stared at Renuka in disbelief.

'Your Parashu keeps clattering,' she said, walking back into the hut.

The Parashu! Somewhere deep inside him, he knew it was the Parashu that made that sound, but his mad fascination had muted even that. Rama walked into the hut, gathered his Parashu and walked out. He called forth the power of it, and fury ignited in him. He let it course through him, revelling in the clear purity of rage. Rama twirled it around, practising a few drills in the small open space before the hut. He felt wonderful. He purposely thought of Bhumi and desire erupted in him, stopping him mid-stride. Rama stood still with the Parashu held out in front of him, a creature of rage and lust, vacillating between the two, helpless as the two potent emotions flooded and crashed inside him. In this tumult, silent as a serpent slithering towards its prey, was a small third emotion. *Shame.* Shame that he was so utterly fascinated, said the familiar voice in his mind. Shame that he didn't act to get what he so obviously wanted, said the other voice. A long while later, he laid the Parashu on the stoop and sat cross-legged before it, his mind utterly at sea. This wasn't a battle for the Parashu, it couldn't help him in this. It had recognised the danger his mind was warning him about, and responded, urging him to beware, to fight. This was a battle he had to win without it. Something deep inside told him that he battled death, and that some trap had been sprung. And he had no idea what it was, or how to escape it.

Dantakrura watched with the eyes he used to see through, camouflaged in the dark.

'The avatara realises his Parashu can't help. He sits bewildered, his mind addled with lust,' he told Jayadhwaja. I've chosen the woman well. She subconsciously craves him, desires him. My spell has brought her hidden feelings bubbling to the surface.'

Dantakrura grinned with satisfaction. It was a complex spell he'd woven. So many strands to the weave. Strands of allurement, compulsion, observation and trust. And he had put incredible power into it. This was an avatara, after all. A spell of this much power would've driven an ordinary man insane, a nimisha before his heart burst inside his ribcage. He was proud of the cunning in the spell, the twist other warlocks wouldn't have thought of. The allurement that Parashurama felt rebounded on the woman, overcoming her feminine reluctance to make the first move, to stoke her baser instincts, to turn her from a housewife to a seductress. It removed any suspicion from Parashurama's mind that her desire was a sham. It was a genuine and deep-rooted craving that she exhibited, and that had a power of its own.

The compulsion was linked to the man's nature. A man like this would resist, no doubt. But he would also go after answers. It was his basic instinct. Else he wouldn't have achieved so much. He would have the single-mindedness and the daring to pursue answers. Pursue he would, and be constantly puzzled. The spell was so complex, and nobody would even guess how he had used observation and trust. All this, woven into a single spell. A spell that was a thing of beauty. Imagination was truly the greatest ally of Abhichara. In shadows, imagination thrived, and he, Dantakrura, was king of the shadows.

'Bandhamohini has them both, samrat,' he said aloud. 'When they make love, when their bodies writhe together, she will drain his power. He will lose so much more than his seed. He will bawl like a child who has lost his favourite toy. You will have his head at your feet.'

Rama sat on the stoop, not daring to step away. The stoop was his refuge. It gave him a sense of security. A vain feeling. She could come here any time she wished, but it gave him solace, and he held on to it. Akrita sat with him for a while, silent, somehow guessing Rama's reluctance to talk. He retired for the night, leaving food for Rama. Jamadagni stopped beside Rama, noticing his silence and the untouched food. He sat opposite Rama and quietly watched.

'Examine what you know. Find the answer. Interesting ... wonder who did this?' said Jamadagni. He rose, walked into the hut, and shut the door. Rama sat in the darkness. He couldn't shake the feeling he was being watched, but dismissed it. He didn't want more to worry about. He ate but couldn't sleep. He burned with the desire to go to the settlement, to find her hut, to see those lips again ...

Rama tossed and turned on the cold, hard floor of the stoop. He wasn't going to find answers this way. Perhaps he should go to the settlement, get to the nub of the matter. Maybe he would find answers there. No, you just want to see the woman, to slake your lust, his mind chided. *To claim my conquest*, the other voice said.

He decided to walk. He considered taking the Parashu but immediately decided against it. A cool drizzle fell on him, calming his mind only for a nimisha. He imagined her body, wet in the rain, her dress plastered to her curves. He stood still, letting the drizzle drench him, waiting for the strong pang of lust to subside. It didn't, and he sensed himself walk. He walked past his ashram and paused. The banalinga and kalasha were here. He could sit before them and go into dhyana. What if he failed? The first fine strand of fear wormed its way into him. He didn't want to risk that.

The relentless urge to go to her tugged at him. He moved jerkily, not wanting to go, and wanting to run to her at the same time. Something tugged at his mind, urging him to pay attention, but he couldn't get a grip on it. He moved forward. That sense of being watched returned. He turned around in a circle but saw no one.

Rama walked into the settlement. Every instinct screamed at him to step away and return, an incessant chorus at the back of his mind. Every inch of his body thirsted for her. The drizzle stopped, and the heat in his body rose. He stood like a statue, confused, maddened and at war with himself. He lost count of how long he stood there.

Rama inched his feet sideways, fighting the urge, wanting to turn back. He inched his feet back, succumbing to the urge. In desperation, he intoned the syllable he'd heard during his encounter with Ganapathi ... Lam.

He stepped aside again, and the motion helped him move. It returned his addicted mind to where he was now. He continued chanting as he turned and walked, slowly and with great effort in each step. One step after the other, then one more, and again. He kept his eyes on the ground before him, following his own tracks home. A long while later, he slumped on the stoop of his parents' hut, breathing heavily from the exertion of every movement.

Rama chanted the syllable as he stretched out on the stoop. The mental relief was enormous. The thought that had caught in the back of his mind resurfaced. He let it be. He would sleep over it and see what the dawn brought. Rama slept like a log, dreaming of Renuka in the doorway, of drizzles and wet earth, and Old Shiva chanting *mara mara mara* ...

He woke a little before dawn, and could hear Renuka

and Jamadagni stir inside. He now had the answer. Rama wandered around the hut, eyes searching the ground. He saw the telltale signs. He was sure now. Rama waited. Anantha came, stifling yawns and asking if he wanted to go to the riverside. Rama nodded, and Anantha set off to get his things. A while later he arrived panting, and the two set off, with Anantha leading the way.

Dawn broke, the sun a semi-circular orange orb framed by the mountains and swaddled in mist. Anantha shivered. 'Cold today.'

'It rained last night. The chill will pass soon,' Rama replied.

Anantha led him to a grassy, secluded slope that tapered into the river. Rama waded in ankle-deep and scooped water to wash his face. He heard murmurs behind him and turned. She had come.

His breath caught at the sight of her as she walked past Anantha, with Dakini beside her. She was in the same garment, her hair was loose and that alluring smile played on her lips. She tied her hair up in a knot as she stood at the edge of the water. Her brows knit as she frowned at Rama. His heart plunged at her displeasure.

'I waited, you didn't come,' she complained. 'Are you playing hard to get? Or do you need encouragement?'

'I don't understand,' Rama managed to say.

She smiled and Rama's heart rattled against his ribs. 'I do. Poor Parashurama, a hero to everyone but himself.'

She tugged at the end of the wrap tucked behind her, and let it fall off her shoulder. Rama's eyes involuntarily wandered down from her lips to her bare breasts. Her nipples were hard in the morning chill. Dakini giggled as she took hold of the cloth and unwound it from around the waist. Bhumi wore nothing underneath, the soft triangle of hair dark against the fleshiness of her thighs. She stepped into the water, gasping at its coldness. Rama couldn't take his eyes off her nudity, her voluptuousness. *Don't even blink*, said the other voice.

'Beautiful, isn't she?' Dakini asked.

'Yes,' Rama croaked. He began to chant the syllable. It gave him a sliver of sanity.

Bhumi drew close to him, her hands reaching for his chest. His body burned with desire for her, urging him to submit, to worship her nakedness. It was all he could do to remain still.

'Aren't you ...?' she whispered in his ear as she tugged at the knot in his dhoti.

'Kiss me first,' he replied.

She turned her face up, offering her half-open lips. Her body was crushed against his. The calm grew in Rama as he mentally chanted. He cleaved his mind and went into dhyana.

Rama partitioned the mirror in his dhyana. One mirror showed him his golden body with the chakras and nadis. The Svadhisthana, the second chakra from the bottom, pulsed frenetically. The second mirror showed him the riverside vista. He brought forth the light on his forehead and shone it upon the second mirror.

At the riverside, Rama's pupils rolled up. The whites of his eyes stared at Bhumi. Bhumi, Dakini and Anantha gasped in shock.

Rama saw the magic wrapped around the three of them in the mirror. Thick, oily, black ropes of magic. The ropes covered all of Bhumi's body, but were different for the other two. They were thickest around Dakini's heart and Anantha's eyes.

A spell! A forbidden, complex spell, intricately woven,

made of distinct elements, fascination and compulsion amongst them.

'Clever,' said Rama at the riverside.

'Clever,' repeated the skeleton in the circle.

Rama studied Anantha in the mirror. He saw the eyes behind Anantha's eyes—a dead pair using spells to watch Rama right now.

'You watch me,' said Rama as he pushed Bhumi away. Rama pushed Bhumi away again as she reached to clasp him. 'Wait,' he ordered.

Turning to Anantha, he said, 'Blink if you can hear me.' Anantha's eyes stared for a long nimisha and finally blinked.

'You cast a spell on this man to observe me. He was the one who saw where I was and brought the woman to me. Then he waited and watched—so you could see me. He insisted on accompanying me to the forest to observe what I did. You made him return from the forest through the settlement, so you used compulsion on him, too. He told the boy on the street to inform this poor woman that I was back in the ashram, to come there herself. He watched me through the night, not sleeping a wink. But he made a mistake. No, you made a mistake. It rained last night. All the tracks were washed away, except mine going to the settlement. And his, following me. I can recognise his footprint anywhere. This morning, I saw faint footprints around the hut. His again.'

'Rama, she's waiting,' said Dakini coyly.

'You used my trust in this girl. She came to me, touched me and I felt relief. I held her close for reassurance, and it seemed to me that she approved of what Bhumi wanted. But that was not the spell. The cunning was that she touched me whenever I stepped backwards. I know Atharvan spells and the way to overcome their bondage is to find the specific invocation and chant it backwards. You didn't want my mind to make the connection when I moved back. Very clever, but I caught on when I realised my mother thought it was Dakini I had an interest in, not Bhumi. I have always seen her as my sister, and my mother's statement made me remember everything she did yesterday. Then, I knew.'

Rama invoked Agni into his mouth in the second mirror. He poured his power into the Agni and blew it at Dakini. The magic around her caught fire and burned away. Rama continued burning it till not a speck was left.

Dakini blinked and saw Bhumi behind Rama. Naked and waiting. She turned to Rama. 'Why is she here? Why is she naked? This woman is married, Rama.'

'Why are her clothes in your hand?' Rama asked softly. Dakini stood dumb.

He burned the magic around Bhumi. She broke out in a sweat at the riverside, beads escaping from every pore on her skin. She stood still as a statue, eyes unseeing and suddenly gasped. She stared at Rama with surprise, and down at herself. Bhumi wailed with shock and shame, using her hands to cover her nude form. She saw her clothes in Dakini's hands, and outrage overcame the shock. She snatched the wrap from Dakini and turned away, dressing hurriedly. Then she scampered away.

Rama gazed into Anantha's eyes.

'They are free, and you don't know how. I didn't need to know your chant or recite it backwards. A spell against an Atharvan. Ambitious of you. But the ambition was foolish.'

Rama invoked the power of the Parashu in his dhyana. He let it loose as he charred the coils of dark sorcery wrapped around Anantha. He sent it racing into Anantha's eyes in the mirror. Through and beyond, tracing the magic's path from Anantha to the warlock, consuming it in a fiery rush as it went.

Dantakrura snatched the eyeballs off his eyelids in the nick of time. The eyeballs exploded in his hands. An alarmed Jayadhwaja fell backwards. A few nimishas later, they gathered their wits, and looked at the ground before them. The skeleton and heart had turned into ash. There was no trace of the circle.

Rama dismissed the second mirror. He concentrated on the Svadhisthana and waited. In the deep silence, it came to him—the sound that wasn't a sound, the sound that he could see.

'Vam,' he intoned.

The feverish pulsing of the chakra in the mirror stopped and steadied into a constant, bright glow. The three channels lit up from the first to the second chakra. The second lotus had bloomed. He had controlled his lust despite being subject to fascination and compulsion, and being the target of a powerful spell. He had won over the most basic, basest instinct in a mortal.

Rama eased out of dhyana. Two confused faces turned and stared at him.

'Go to the ashram. Ma will need you soon,' he told Dakini.

She wanted to ask her questions but didn't. She nodded and walked away.

'Come, Anantha. Time for our sandhya,' said Rama.

Anantha nodded, bewildered.

10

Five Symbols

The samrat and the warlock sat in silence for a long while, both staring at the ash. A timid wind wound around them, lifting the fine ash into the air.

'We failed,' said Jayadhwaja.

'We learnt a valuable lesson,' said Dantakrura. 'And a startling fact. Knowledge and curiosity. No! Not a mere curiosity. A wonder.'

'What wonder?'

'You said Arjuna had killed Jamadagni. That he trampled the Saptarishi to death.'

Jayadhwaja nodded.

'Jamadagni lives, samrat. I saw him with those eyes.'

'Impossible!' Jayadhwaja screamed. 'Your witchcraft has turned on you. Or Parashurama destroyed your magic and put a spell on you instead. Your mind is deluded.'

'No, samrat. Parashurama destroyed my magic. How? I concede I do not know, but he hasn't cast a spell on me.'

'How would you know that?'

'I would know. Every warlock knows how to defend himself.'

'You don't know how he wrecked your magic. How would you know if he had cast a spell?'

'There are ways,' said Dantakrura, touching various amulets on his body. 'A spell is a spell, black or white. I will know. And so will he, if we try again.'

'I swear, samrat. Jamadagni lives and breathes. Send your spies to the ashram. Take my life if what I say is untrue.'

Jayadhwaja rose and kicked at the ash, screaming obscenities. 'My father died. Twenty-one Akshauhinis died. And his father lives. What justice is that? They've lost nothing except for that stupid cow.'

He whirled to Dantakrura, 'Can you get me that cow?'

The warlock shook his head. Jayadhwaja roared and kicked a pebble towards the fire pit. Dantakrura flicked his fingers, and the pebble changed trajectory mid-flight and flew away from them.

'I will have my vengeance,' Jayadhwaja stared daggers at Dantakrura. 'His father's head severed from his neck. I will do to his as was done to mine.'

'And don't forget the throne, samrat. Muster your strength, gather your armies. That man, Anantha, through whose eyes I watched everything unfold? He is a swordsman, not a sanyasi. He is a warrior. Perhaps Parashurama has an army we don't know about. I have learnt my lesson. Parashurama's power is incredible. I will have to find a way to nullify his power and counter his Parashu.'

'You lied,' said Jayadhwaja. The warlock stared at him in surprise.

'You said you could see only through the eyes of small animals. But you looked through this Anantha's eyes. You lied!'

'I needed the eyes of your spy and elaborate spells and rituals to see through that man's eyes. Now, I cannot. But I can see through the eyes of small animals and birds anytime I wish.'

Jayadhwaja paced silently. He turned to Dantakrura at long last. 'Find a way to kill him, or nullify his power. War comes, and I will wash the Brighus away in blood.'

'But first,' said Jayadhwaja as he walked away, 'vengeance.'

He walked the dimly lit streets of Mahishmati. Sentries were few and good citizens knew not to venture out after sunset. It hadn't been this way before. Mahishmati's streets had stayed brightly lit through the night, and the citizenry had revelled long into the night. That monster who called himself an avatara had shattered that safety. But there were men who liked the dark. And women. He wanted a different one today. The previous one had lost her charm the moment he was done with her. Just hearing what was happening to that wretched avatara had stoked his lust. Had the warlock cast a spell on him, too? He didn't think so. No, he didn't care if Dantakrura had. He wanted release from his intense anger at their failure.

Jayadhwaja waited and watched if his brother was spying on him again. He wandered the streets, doubling back the way he'd come, hiding in dark alleyways to confirm he wasn't being watched. Convinced that he wasn't, he searched for what he desperately needed. He found what he was looking for, in one of the gardens. She sat on a bench semi-circled by shrubs and trees. He walked to her.

'Good night for some fun,' she said.

'A lot of fun,' said Jayadhwaja.

He saw her eyes run over him, quickly appraising his worth, like a buyer at a cattle fair.

'Fun always has a price,' she said.

'The reward should be worth the price,' he replied.

'Darling, this will be the best night of your life.'

The woman bounced off the bench, and her hands were all over him, traipsing down his torso. She found his purse and crowed in delight. She groped lower. 'My, my,' she whispered, her voice now husky. He heard a noise in the shrubs, and his eyes turned towards it.

'Eyes on the fun,' she laughed, clasping his face in her hands and turning it towards her.

Jayadhwaja kneed her in the stomach and whipped his dagger out of the waistband around the small of his back just as two men crashed out of the shrubs. He ducked under the punch of the first man and kicked the second. He spun around as the woman, now fallen to her knees, lashed a torrent of vulgar abuse at him. The first man came at him again, the stench of sweat and cheap alcohol coming along with him. Jayadhwaja stopped his strike with his left hand and plunged the dagger into the man's stomach. The man grunted and clutched his midriff as blood spurted from the wound. He crashed to the ground. Jayadhwaja leapt away as the second man swiped at him, something glinting in his right hand. A knife, but Jayadhwaja knew by the swipe that he didn't know how to use it well. He'd relied on surprise and greater numbers.

He saw the woman stagger to her feet. Jayadhwaja slapped her hard. She fell back on the grass between him and the bench. She scrambled her way to it. The second man attacked again and Jayadhwaja slipped past him and behind, kicking him in the groin. The man screamed and fell. Jayadhwaja reached down and slit his throat.

He turned to the woman. She glanced back and saw the two dead bodies. Fright flashed in her eyes.

'Look at me,' said Jayadhwaja. 'Eyes on the fun.'

He retrieved the knife from the dead man's hand.

'I'm sorry, I'm sorry,' she wailed. Her shivering hands held the purse out to him.

'Shh! Quiet now! I paid the price. I want my reward.'

She kicked out at him from where she lay on the ground. He stabbed her foot. The woman shrieked. She looked around wildly for help. He sat on her, straddling her flailing arms between her body and his legs. He raised his dagger and plunged it towards her but stopped before it could scratch her skin.

'No, no, no. That would be too quick,' he whispered huskily. The woman mewled and begged.

'Do you know who I am?' he asked. She shook her head. 'No?' he screamed.

He stabbed her with both blades, a stab punctuating each word as he launched into his singsong soliloquy, 'I am the samrat of you and your dead friends and this city and this world and I will kill that avatara ... are you having fun ... I am ... and then I will rule ... so much blood ... it is glorious ... can you hear me? ... say you love me, and there will be none as powerful as me ... isn't the night so cold but your blood is so warm ...'

A long while later, Jayadhwaja rose and slipped away into the darkness as if nothing had happened.

Anantha apologised every couple of steps as they walked back to the ashram. Rama assured him it wasn't his fault, but Anantha wouldn't let it go. Rama explained again and asked him to reflect instead of apologise. That kept him quiet for a while.

'I don't know what to think, Swami,' he said finally.

'Whoever this mantravadin is, he had to choose you, Dakini and Bhumi. That means he's been watching me before deciding on the three of you. It also means he started his scrutiny only a day ago. Otherwise, he would have gone for Akrita, who's almost always by my side.'

'You are right, Swami. I didn't think of that.'

'So, how did he do it?'

Anantha thought hard as they walked into the ashram. 'I don't know.'

'Neither do I,' said Rama. 'Keep your guard up. We must find out.'

Rama sent him to find Akrita and inform him and walked to his parents' hut. Jamadagni stepped out as Rama approached. He peered at Rama.

'You found the answer,' he said without surprise.

'Yes, but I nearly fell into the trap. Did you know it was Abhichara?'

'Interesting! I had my suspicions, but I didn't look for a spell. When one has been an Atharvan for so many centuries, one gets to sense things. Every soul in its present body has its own distinctive rhythm. No matter what emotion takes hold of the person, that rhythm can be identified. But when the rhythm changes, becomes frantic or slow, then there is something unnatural making it do so. Your rhythm was frantic.'

'A new enemy for you, Rama. A mantravadin. I don't know of any who practises Abhichara. But I've heard of a land far to the northeast. Mayong. They seem to have made it their sva-dharma.'

'What spell was it?' asked Renuka as she came out.

'A web of different spells cunningly woven together. Compulsion and fascination, mostly.'

'Mohana, vashikarana,' said Renuka. 'Lust. I read it all wrong.'

'It wasn't on Dakini. It was on the other woman,' Rama paused awkwardly, '... I don't see Dakini that way either ... you know ... as a wife or anything ... like that.'

Renuka laughed. 'Fine. I'll spare you the blushes. The oldest trick in the world. The nemesis of so many rishis. So fascinated by the soul, they forget their souls also have bodies, and the bodies must be satisfied too.'

She lowered her voice, 'I think the desires of these rishis were so frustrated, they did the Abhichara on the rishis themselves.'

'You are embarrassing him,' said Jamadagni. Renuka took one look at Rama's red face and chortled with laughter.

'Well, we didn't make five sons by sitting in tapasya, did we?' she asked her husband. Jamadagni went still as a statue. Renuka didn't stop. She was enjoying this.

'Parashakti didn't give women beautiful breasts and rounded bottoms just on a whim, did she? There is a purpose, a pleasurable one. Some rishis get their minds addled by it.'

She turned to Rama. 'Maybe you should find a willing woman and embarrass the life out of each other. Like the tribals say, there is a time to rut.'

'Ma ...' Rama flustered.

Renuka giggled some more, and in a blink, her demeanour changed.

'You think you are ready ... But when the time comes ...' her voice trailed off.

Rama stared, puzzled. That timeless look was back in her eyes. She cupped Rama's face in her hands. 'Good, you didn't lose your morals,' she whispered and walked away. Rama turned to his father. Jamadagni's eyes followed Renuka until she was out of sight.

'What does she mean? What is she readying for?' Rama asked.

'Never mind,' said Jamadagni. 'I was thinking about the Parashu, and the souls within them. It is Mahadeva's axe, so I'm certain he can tell you how to release those souls. Those temples you see in your dhyana? Maybe it is a sign.'

'A hint to what I should do?'

Jamadagni nodded. 'The oldest temple in the world is in the oldest city in the world. Kashi. Mahadeva's own city, and your mother's birthplace. Perhaps your answers wait for you at Mahadeva's temple. And what better place to liberate souls than Kashi? Perhaps, start at Prayag and go to Kashi.'

Rama thought it over and nodded. 'A pilgrimage then, to Kashi. I also want to meet the Malaya Kshatriyas to put my plan into action. They are south of the Vindhyas now, east of here. I'll meet them, tell them what to do and then find my way to Prayag.'

Dusk deepened into night. Jamadagni, Renuka and Rama sat before the Saptarishi's hut, talking about the pilgrimage and Kashi, when Akrita burst upon them.

'Gurudeva ... Anantha ...' he blurted and stopped.

Before he could catch his breath and continue, Anantha had appeared before them. Rama looked at him and knew something was amiss in the way Anantha carried himself, the look in his eyes, the scabbard that wasn't strapped to his waist but clutched tightly in his left hand. He rose as Anantha stopped just out of arm's reach. Rama noticed the blood-red tilaka on his forehead and remembered the ritual at the sacred grove when he had first met the Malaya Kshatriyas.

'You are going to war?' he asked.

'I'm going to kill,' Anantha replied.

'Who?' Rama asked in puzzlement.

'Myself.'

'What?' Rama blurted.

'I let you down, Swami. I placed you in danger.'

'There was nothing you could do, Anantha. You can't blame yourself. Nobody thought of a threat like this, or that Abhichara would be used.'

'But he chose me for his spell. I cannot be close to you. I can endanger you again.'

'Anantha, listen to me. We know of the threat now. I burned down the spells. I can do it again. Anyway, I don't think that mantravadin is foolish enough to try this again. He's a clever fellow.'

'Yes, Swami. Very clever. Maybe we won't know of his next spell until it's too late.'

Rama bit his lip, cursing himself mentally for saying what he did.

'Anantha, you did no wrong. There is no need to punish yourself, forget taking your own life,' said Jamadagni.

'I betrayed the Uddhatr. We are his people, and it is my deep dishonour that I, this wretch before you, betrayed him.'

Rama threw up his hands and groaned in frustration at Anantha's stubborn insistence. The man was set on killing himself. 'A Saptarishi says you are innocent, yet you insist on this stupidity.'

'My conscience holds me guilty,' said Anantha.

'Your manasakshi? It is only a sakshi, a witness. How did your conscience become supreme judge, Anantha?' Renuka asked. 'The Vedas are the supreme judge. Then comes the teachings and actions of great saints and rishis of the past. Third, the actions and teachings of great men and women living now. Last is manasakshi, because one never knows what ideas have formed it. Jamadagni and your Uddhatr say you are innocent. Listen to them.'

Tears rimmed Anantha's eyes as he clasped his hands together with the sheathed sword between them. 'I cannot argue with all of you, and I cannot forgive myself, Amba. I come only for permission.'

'What permission?' Rama asked, anger showing in his voice.

'To die by my own blade,' said Anantha, holding out his sword. 'If I have served you well in the past, let me die by your hand.'

'Permission denied,' said Rama. A forlorn look came into Anantha's eyes.

'True judgement. I am not worthy of an honourable death. I will cut my throat myself.'

Rama groaned in anger and stepped forward to hold Anantha by his shoulders and shake some sense into him. Anantha shrank back.

'Your Uddhatr denies your betrayal. Denies permission, Anantha. Obey!'

'You are merciful, Swami. But I cannot live with this dishonour. What has to be done has to be done.' Anantha turned away.

'Wait!' Rama's voice was harsh. Anantha turned and looked into the unflinching stare whose intensity bore into him. He saw the rage dancing in Rama's eyes. He froze.

'I will be judge and executioner,' said Rama. Anantha offered his sword again.

'I have no use for that. I have a blade of my own,' Rama refused. 'You shall die by the Parashu.'

Anantha's eyes widened. He said nothing.

'Do you submit to death by the Parashu? Is that honour enough?' Rama's voice was cold as death. Anantha nodded.

'On your knees!' Rama roared.

Anantha dropped to his knees, his sword fell to the ground. Rama held out his right hand, and the Parashu hurtled out of the hut.

Rama brought forth the fury of the Parashu and it stormed through him, adding to the anger he was already feeling. The night went still, and the sounds of the forest and the ashram hushed abruptly. The air lay heavy upon them all. Anantha shut his eyes. Rama let the terrifying rage course through him, feeling the power imbued in blood and sinew, bone and muscle.

'Dharma will be judge and executioner.' Rama's wrath had coarsened his words. 'Look at me!'

Anantha's eyes stayed shut.

'Look at me when I kill you!' Rama screamed.

Anantha opened his eyes. Rama's pupils rolled up. Anantha's jaw dropped in fright as he saw the implacable wrath of an avatara before him.

'Blade, be true,' Rama whispered, committing himself to the killing. The Parashu turned golden.

Then, he screamed, the fierce voice rolling over the ashram like a thunderclap. 'Death comes calling. Yama awaits!'

Slobber ran down Anantha's open mouth. Akrita staggered back, Renuka clutched her hands to her chest and Jamadagni stared frozen where he sat. Nobody could tear their eyes away.

Rama shrieked his rage to the skies, raised the Parashu and swung down. And the world seemed to slow down. He could see the blade slice through the air, see where it would hit Anantha's head, how it would split him open in two halves, the blood and brain splattering in an explosion. He could see the glow of the lamp at the stoop, and the glimmer of the moon on the blades as it arced downward. It seemed so long to him, but it would be a fraction of a nimisha to Anantha and the others watching.

The Parashu thudded to a stop, at a finger's breadth from Anantha's head. Rama's hands shook as he pushed the Parashu to finish the swing. It didn't budge. He let go. The Parashu hung in mid-air for a nimisha and dropped to the ground. Anantha stared at the blade, almost cross-eyed. He shook like a leaf in the wind, mewls of terror and gasps of relief gushing out of his agape mouth. He laughed and cried as his hands wandered about his head and face, dishevelling his hair and scratching his skin, unable to believe he was alive.

'Judgement proclaimed,' said Rama quietly.

The Parashu flew back to him, as Anantha collapsed. They seated Anantha on the stoop and dribbled a little water down his throat, and let him be until he gathered his wits. Nobody spoke for a while, each allowing the tension to defuse. The sounds of the night slowly resumed, albeit a mite nervously.

'The rage of a Brahmakshatriya and avatara. Truly breathtaking! I will never forget the sight of it,' said Renuka. 'Did you know the Parashu would stop?'

Rama shook his head. 'He was innocent in my eyes, and I think the Parashu recognised that. I suspected it would. But I committed to killing him. I don't want him to think I was acting a charade. He can't doubt my judgement now.'

'Anantha was right about the spells, Rama. The mantravadin could target Akrita next,' said Jamadagni. Rama nodded.

'Saptarishi, I don't think he could if he tried,' said Akrita. 'I explained to Amba earlier how I'm not traumatised by the slaughter at Mahishmati because Gurudeva protects me.'

'I do?' Rama asked, puzzled.

'Your image, your murthi in my mind protects me. Your voice in my head protects me ...'

There was more, but Akrita was somehow embarrassed to continue.

'Tell us,' said Jamadagni gently.

'I composed a hymn, a stotra,' said Akrita. 'I don't know how I did it, and I didn't do it all at once. The lines always came to me after dhyana, when I recite my gratitude to Gurudeva.' Akrita's voice died down to a whisper. 'I believe it will protect those who love Gurudeva. The mantravadin will not gain access to our minds.'

Jamadagni's pupils turned up. 'Recite it, Akrita,' he said. Akrita gulped, composed himself and obeyed.

'Shankara priyam,
Mangala pradham,
Kshatriyaanthakam, Vikramaamsajam,
Parashudharinaam, Suraganaarchitaam,
Brighukulodhwaham, Bhavayaamyaham!'[4]

Beloved of Shankara,
Bestower of auspiciousness,
Destroyer of Kings,
Incarnation of valour,
The one whose weapon is the Parashu,
The one praised by the Devas,
The one born in the clan of Brighu,
Him, I cherish!

'Excellent!' exclaimed Jamadagni. 'It will indeed protect. Teach everyone this.'

Akrita beamed like the full moon.

'Name it, Akrita. That honour is yours.'

Akrita looked at the dumbfounded Rama. 'I've already thought of a name. Veera Rama Stotra.'

Anantha was at Rama's feet, begging forgiveness, before he could react to Akrita's hymn. Rama raised him and embraced him. 'Don't let your honour be so brittle. And don't assume responsibility for what you haven't done,' Rama whispered in his ear. He turned to Akrita.

Akrita pressed his palms together and intoned, '*Mathru devo bhava, pitru devo bhava, acharya devo bhava*. For me, all three, mother, father and acharya, are you, Gurudeva.'

---

[4] Dasavathara Stotram, translated by K. Padmanabha Warrier.

Rama embraced his student before Akrita could fall at his feet. He held Akrita tight, eyes moist and tongue-tied at the utter devotion his shishya had for him.

Rama wanted Raikava, Chandragupta and Akrita to accompany Anantha and him. He reined in his impatience as they waited for Anantha's squad to get back. Four days later, at dawn, it wasn't a squad, but two men who came. One was a young, lean, hard man Rama remembered seeing at the grove. He introduced himself as Ekavira. The second was a man about fifty years of age, stolid and short. Scraggy strands of hair passed for a beard and moustache, and he carried himself stiffly. Unlike Anantha and Ekavira, he didn't have a sword and had a soft belly and big eyes that wouldn't look anywhere other than at Rama. He carried a satchel of their supplies.

'Uddhatr,' he whispered repeatedly, as if speaking more loudly would offend Rama in some way.

'Who are you?' Rama asked.

'Bhamaha,' he replied as he made to fall at Rama's feet.

'No need for that. Rest today. We'll leave tomorrow at first light.'

At at the crack of dawn, Rama bid his goodbyes to his brothers, Dakini and Varnini, at his parents' hut. Jamadagni and Renuka walked on either side of him, insisting on coming along to the edge of the ashram. Akrita, Anantha and the rest followed in their wake. He bent to touch his parents' feet when they passed out of the ashram. Jamadagni and Renuka kept their palms on his head for a long while, whispering blessings and prayers. They hugged him close when he rose, and inexplicably, Rama didn't want to go.

He wanted to lead them back to their hut and then go out to the forest for his chores. He wanted to hear the mantras being taught and repeated. To watch the games the youngsters played in the evening. To chat with his brothers at the kitchen stoop, to tease Dakini and listen to Varnini's chiding. So little time he'd spent with them since that fateful day of the beheading. His heart turned away from adventure and affairs of the world and longed for the routine of ashram life. He looked at the ashram as he held his parents tight, and it seemed the ashram was holding him, embracing him with memory and comfort, love and sacredness, and pleading silently with him not to go.

A rush of sentiment filled his heart, a mix of cherishing and melancholy. A strangeness of bereavement when he was right there holding them. Of wanting to be a child again, to insist on sleeping in his mother's lap and climbing onto his father's shoulders. Of eating jamuns all day to his heart's content, and playing with his brothers. To hear Veera, no Nandin, shout instructions to him as he learnt the forms of weapons drill. To watch all this play out in his presence as a grown man. Of roaming the forest, lazing in the Narmada. Of wanting the sun to brown his skin and rain to wet his hair. Of wanting to never leave home. Home, where Ma made pots of river sand and squeezed the water out of rock, father sat in tapasya and taught the hymns, where wildflowers danced to the music of the wind, where trees brushed the sky, and the earth cocooned him in a verdant embrace.

Rama stood still, unable to say goodbye, savouring the touch of his parents' hands on the skin of his back—Jamadagni's coarse beard on his left shoulder and Renuka's forehead on his right. His world was complete. Arjuna was dead, and he didn't care a whit about the iron frame and the new samrat.

'Go,' said Jamadagni at last, easing away from him.

Rama nodded, unable to speak, unwilling to look them in the eye. Renuka's fingers brushed his cheek as he turned away. He heard the others bid their goodbyes and hurry to him. He glanced behind as he walked. The rishi and his patni stood still, their hands around each other. They were watching. Not smiling, not crying. He walked some more to the bend in the path and looked again. There was nobody there.

The group walked in silence, Ekavira scouting ahead and Anantha bringing up the rear. They followed the course of the Narmada eastwards, leaving the settlements behind, taking the trails through the woodland teeming with life and colour, tweets, whistles, snorts and buzzing. They walked without rest as the sun rose, reached his zenith in the sky and fell. Rama wanted to put as much distance between him and the ashram as possible, as if the ashram would pull him back in if he didn't.

They stopped four muhurtas after dusk, on a gently sloping bank of the Narmada. Anantha, Akrita and Ekavira set about building the campfire, collecting and stitching palasha leaves for plates and cooking the gruel. They sat around the fire, scooping the gruel off their plates with fingers, talking amongst themselves in a low voice in deference to Rama's silence.

Rama sighed as they sat around the fire after the meal was done, wanting to break the pensive mood he was in. A heavy heart could make even a short journey hard and long, and they still had a long way to go. He caught Bhamaha fearfully glance at the Parashu beside him and thought he'd make some conversation.

'Why don't you carry a sword, Bhamaha?' he asked.

Bhamaha's eye lit up. 'I knew you would ask me that,' he crowed. 'The virtue of our path attracts all, even the Uddhatr.'

Rama paused. It was a casual question, asked to start a fireside conversation, but it evidently meant a lot to Bhamaha. He caught Anantha and Ekavira glance at each other. They seemed to want to be far away from here. Bhamaha needed no prompting. '*Ahimsa paramo dharma*. Even the Uddhatr accepts.'

'I don't understand,' said Rama.

'You have come to give us freedom and give us our land back. That is your purpose, your responsibility and your duty to us.'

'Us?'

'The Ahimsamargis. The Children of the Earth. The enlightened ones. The ones you are beholden to.'

'Beholden?' Rama glanced around. Anantha and Ekavira refused to meet his eyes.

'We abhor violence, carry no weapons and eat no meat. We harm no one. We are pure. Live and let live, we say. An eye for an eye makes the world blind, we teach. Violence is for crude, base men. Men who are more animal than human, more pashu than manushya. We are above all that. We are true Sanatanis. Ahimsamargis teach everyone the true way. We accept all and convert them from pashu to manushya. You are beholden to men like us.' Bhamaha spoke like he was teaching a lesson. A lesson that only he fully understood, but was now constrained to teach others.

'I killed Arjuna and his army,' said Rama. He couldn't keep the edge out of his voice.

'Yes, yes. Anantha told me. Savage ... so much killing ... beastly.' Sadness filled his eyes as he looked off into the distance. 'I don't blame you. You don't know better. You are not as evolved a soul as us.'

Rama frowned. Incredulity flashed across the faces of Akrita, Raikava and Chandragupta.

'Gurudeva received darshan of Mahadeva, was blessed by him,' said Akrita.

'Yes, yes. Shiva gave him the Parashu. He recognised the Uddhatr's base nature and rewarded him accordingly.'

'What?' Rama blurted in amazement.

'You could have asked Shiva to make Arjuna non-violent. Then everything would've been fine. That's what I'd have done. And then Arjuna would've disbanded his armies. Peace would've reigned. World peace and love everywhere. Universal love. *Vasudeiva kutumbakam.*' Bhamaha's eyes turned glassy in ecstasy. 'But, no! You asked for a weapon to kill. So foul, so ignorant. But I don't think Shiva could've given anything better.'

Akrita gasped. Bhamaha wore his disappointment on his face. He held up his index finger to make his point. 'Meditate and manifest what you want. Sit calm and everything will be fine. Surrender to Mahavishnu. He will take care of it all. The universe will conspire to give you what you want.'

Rama was at a loss for words at the utter conviction this man had in all this stupidity.

'Then meditate and manifest your freedom,' said Raikava.

'I did meditate. We all did. Perhaps there was some lack in it. If it was perfect, the Almighty would've snapped his fingers and set everything right. Alas, we failed somehow. That's why the Uddhatr is here.'

'But he is violent,' said Chandragupta.

'Unfortunately, men like him must exist, so we are free to evolve even further. Arjuna visited misery upon us. Only another barbarian could protect us from him. A thorn to remove another. We will not commit himsa. He must. Half the job is done. Now he must come to our land, drive away the Haihaya army and give us our freedom and land.'

'I'm a barbarian?' Rama asked in a low voice.

'All savages like you are. Brutal, un-evolved beings, yet to bring the love of the Almighty into their hearts and minds,' said Bhamaha, like a saint explaining scripture.

'Suppose I give you your land, then what happens?' asked Rama.

'It's obvious, isn't it? Your job is done. You must kill yourself. We can't have another tyrant.'

Rama fought hard to keep his anger from rising. 'You want me to commit suicide, commit a mahapaapa?'

'Himsa itself is a mahapaapa. If you live by the sword, you die by it.'

'Utter drivel! Are you this foolish?' Rama roared as he rose to his feet.

Bhamaha cowered in fear, trembling like a leaf. He threw himself at Rama's feet. 'Please forgive me. We do not do violence even with words. We hurt no one, not even a fly,' he wailed. His hands shook as he clasped Rama's feet. 'I'm sorry to have hurt your feelings.'

'My feelings!' Rama couldn't believe his ears. 'How can you believe such nonsense?'

Bhamaha gulped, searching for words. He sat back with

his palms pressed together. 'I don't expect you to understand. After all, you are un-evol ...' He stopped short when he saw Rama's face. A nimisha later, his face lit up.

'Ahimsamargis will honour your sacrifice. We will cherish your memory. We will name our children after you,' he whispered fervently. 'I offer my life, if that will convince you to give us our freedom and land.'

Rama snarled in exasperation, turned and walked away.

Dantakrura listened with interest. He'd watched them make their way from the ashram, set up their camp for the night and searched for eyes and ears closer to the ground. He'd finally settled on the wild boar, imposed his will and magic and crept through the underbrush, till he was an arm's length away from the group. They were unaware of him, and he could see and hear all that transpired. He waited for the conversation to resume.

Rama stared into the night for a long while. He chided himself for having lost his temper with Bhamaha. People held absurd views, especially when it came to politics and religion, and they were welcome to it. Life didn't suffer fools gladly, and such people would have a rude awakening eventually. But he hadn't come across something so simplistically stupid and fatalistic. He still couldn't believe a grown man could believe in such an infantile philosophy. Rama sighed, he didn't want Bhamaha to feel isolated in the group, but he couldn't indulge his whimsy either. He walked back to the group and sat down. He could sense the irritation of the group towards Bhamaha.

'All is maya, all is maya,' Bhamaha chanted softly with his eyes closed, swaying back and forth as if some invisible hands were rocking him to sleep. Rama waited as he chanted on and on, like the words were a spell of protection. Rama cleared his throat, and Bhamaha stopped instantly, opening his eyes.

'All is maya,' Bhamaha started a nimisha later before anyone could speak. 'It means all this is not real. It is just an illusion. A rope in the dark appears as a snake. Reality is unknowable. Accept your fate and strive for nothing. Accept all. This is the essence of Sanatana Dharma. I'm a true Sanatani. The rest of you are not. Chant Mahavishnu's name and let go. Realise the truth.' Bhamaha went quiet as if all this was self-evident, and none could argue against it. Rama regretted clearing his throat.

'Gurudeva is an avatara of Mahavishnu,' said Akrita.

'No, no. He is a false avatara. Anantha told me all the stories yesterday. That's what they are. Stories. He lies and misleads you. Never mind an avatara, even a true bhakta of Mahavishnu wouldn't bring Shiva's name to his lips.'

Akrita huffed. Anger flared in the group, heat blooming in every person's eyes and faces. Bhamaha stared at them as if he expected no better from such 'un-evolved' souls. Rama raised his palm before anyone could speak, bidding them to keep silent.

Bhamaha spoke into the silence. 'And now he worships Devi.' He spat out the last word. 'These are all profane gods. Only Mahavishnu is to be worshipped. None else. The Devi temples have animal sacrifice. Meat as naivedya! As sacred offering! Sacrilege!'

He shook his head in disgust. 'Savages! Heretics! Is this the way to worship? Eaters of meat. Fallen people. All evolved souls are vegetarian.'

'I'm vegetarian, so is Gurudeva,' Akrita retorted.

'That's because you are Brahmins. But what's the use? You worship lesser gods.'

'I thought true Sanatanis accept all,' said Raikava.

'We accept purity. All this is impure.'

'You need the violence of the impure to safeguard your purity?' asked Raikava.

'Yes, yes. That is how they repent for their mistakes.' Bhamaha smiled.

'Karthavirya Arjuna didn't eat meat,' said Chandragupta. 'Usually, he had no problem if others did, but meat couldn't be cooked in the imperial palace. Once, a visiting dignitary unknowingly asked for meat during a royal dinner. Arjuna flew into a rage. Nobody knows why; one could never guess how Arjuna would react to situations. He skinned the dignitary alive. Ordered a cauldron be brought in, and cooked him in the heated oil.'

Bhamaha gasped.

'Arjuna ordered the body cut up and fed to the dignitary's aides and diplomats.'

Bhamaha scrambled to his feet, ran to the bushes and vomited. The group stayed quiet until he returned.

'A vegetarian brought untold misery to the whole world.'

Bhamaha had nothing to say.

'Let's leave the gods alone for the moment. What do you mean, reality is unknowable?' Rama asked.

'Our senses are inadequate. They give us an illusion of certainty. It is night now. It is dark all round us except here, near our fire. I'm sure there are animals around us, though my senses tell me nothing.'

'There is a small animal, a boar I think, right there,' said Rama, pointing to where it lurked. It grunted in surprise and fled, the underbrush shaking in the wake of its mad rush.

'Nevertheless,' said Bhamaha once he'd gotten over his surprise. 'It proves how lacking our senses are. They make a rope in the dark appear a snake. It is a lie. Reality is unknowable. This is what Sanatana Dharma says. This is what our learned intellectuals tell us.'

'That is not what Sanatana Dharma says. And your intellectuals have stuffed their heads with more than their intelligence can handle. A rope in the dark *appears* a snake, but is not so. The very statement says so. It urges you not to jump to conclusions and examine keenly what you see. To throw light on it. To realise reality. It asks you to use viveka, discernment. Use it to apply something very important. Context,' Rama replied.

'We don't see the stars when the sun shines. It doesn't mean they don't exist. When night falls, we see galaxies of them. The rope exists. So does the snake. Don't be fooled to think one is the other. Mistaking a snake for a rope can be fatal. You can die. You cannot say the snake is an illusion and hope to be magically cured. You must take an antidote. Listen well, Bhamaha. There is no enlightenment for deniers of reality.

'Further context is for spiritual seekers. To see beyond reality, to seek who or what made this reality, who or what exists in every anu, every atom of reality. To seek Brahman. It doesn't mean that all this is unreal in a physical sense. It means seek where it comes from.'

'Your senses are better than mine,' said Bhamaha. 'You knew there was an animal there. I did not. What is real is different for you and me. My reality differs from yours.'

'No. What is, is. You mentioned the possibility of there

being animals, remember? I confirmed it. You applied context. You are in a forest at night. The forest teems with a variety of animals, some that are nocturnal. It stands to reason one of them considered us prey or was curious because we are in its territory. You used your discernment. Viveka.

'Nobody is born equal. Two sons of the same man aren't equal, even if they are twins. A man is not equal to himself on some days. Some men have more abilities than others, some learn or acquire them. My senses are sharper. I used viveka, context and feedback from my senses, to tell you the truth.

'Reality exists independent of us. It doesn't disappear if you deny it.'

'But you had a personal insight. Your senses told you, mine did not. How can I believe without a personal experience?'

'Reality will tell you. You heard the animal run away.' Bhamaha searched for the right words.

'Was there anything illogical in what I said?' asked Rama.

'No.'

'Your conclusions are all wrong but somehow, magically, *un-really*, your twisted theory is right?'

'But ... But ...' Bhamaha didn't know how to counter.

'We are all men here, right?' asked Rama.

'Yes, yes. So what?'

'None of us can get pregnant. We never will have personal experience of it. So, are you saying women don't exist? Or that they are unreal, an illusion?'

Bhamaha went red with embarrassment.

'Do you see how ridiculous your idea of reality is?'

'An idea so stupid, only enlightened intellectuals will believe it,' said Akrita. The group chuckled.

Rama continued, 'Ahimsa is virtuous. One must avoid

himsa as much as we can. In thought, word and deed. But, listen carefully, a world without himsa doesn't exist. A tiger killing a deer is himsa, a deer tearing off grass to eat is himsa. The grass-depleting minerals of the earth to grow is himsa.'

'But that is all natural,' said Bhamaha.

'Exactly. Violence is also natural. Brahma cannot create without violence, however subtle it may be. Mahavishnu cannot sustain without it, nor can Mahadeva destroy. Srishti, stithi and samhara needs himsa and ahimsa. You think violence only destroys, it is impure and low. Violence is undesirable and uncomfortable, so you run from it. Hence, you think Mahadeva is lesser than Mahavishnu. Ahimsa also destroys.'

'What?' Bhamaha exclaimed.

'It destroyed you,' said Rama quietly. 'Let me guess. Arjuna's men did as they pleased, abused their power in your land, didn't they?'

Bhamaha gaped at the darkness, grief and despair etched on his face. 'Yes. There is a garrison of his army in our land. They are brutal. They run their swords through anyone who protests their misdeeds, trample the peaceful protestors beneath their war horses. Those men raped our women,' Bhamaha wailed. 'They made us their slaves.'

He wiped his tears and continued, 'When the Malaya Kshatriyas came to our land, wandering in their search for you, they fought Arjuna's army. They freed us. They protected us till their oracle said it was time to move on, that the Uddhaṭr was coming soon. We were at the mercy of the army again. Some of us left our homes and joined the Malaya Kshatriyas to see who this Uddhatr was. And bring him to our home to save us.'

'No, Bhamaha. You left because you were scared. You need the courage of another to live in your own land. Your ahimsa destroyed you; it destroyed your Kshatra, your warrior spirit. The army violated your women, and you did nothing. If you had hit back against the army when they started their atrocities, you'd have drawn a line. The army would've known that to cross the line was to invite trouble, to cause loss of their life and limb. It would have been a deterrent. A little himsa would've spared you so much misery.'

'But how could we know if we would succeed? What if the army hit back?' Bhamaha wailed.

'Of course the army would. You hit back harder. Escalate the cost of such misdeeds. Remember, it is your land. They are the conquerors. Life has no guarantees. All the more reason you should see reality for what it is. You cannot argue philosophy with an unsheathed sword. You should have fought. The Malaya Kshatriyas did. By sticking to ahimsa when himsa was needed, you have committed adharma.

'If you act like prey, the predators will come calling. It is a rule of nature, and a rule of power. To be peaceful is very different from being harmless. Everyone wants an Uddhatr or an avatara to come save them. An avatara is beholden to no one. His or her duty is to dharma alone. An avatara will bring justice to people who follow dharma, and smite down followers of adharma. Even if they call themselves enlightened, evolved or true devotees.

'An avatara isn't a mercenary who will kill anyone you point a finger at. He will judge, he will execute. Will you dare submit yourself to the judgement of an avatara? Will you suffer his wrath? What is wrought by men must be unwrought also by them. The divinities aid dharma, and when it is in peril, an avatara comes.

'Your ideas are not Sanatana Dharma. They are the very opposite of it. You say, accept all, an eye for an eye turns the world blind. World peace. Universal love. All will be fine. Attract what you wish. Where is viveka in these statements? Where is the context? I don't know who your guru is; who taught you all this. I don't wish to know. Beware of gurus who spout such nonsense, statements that are good to hear but are vague in meaning. The words can mean anything or nothing at all. They are like opium. They drive viveka away and urge you to escape from reality. Such teachings put an adult mind into a cradle of infantile fantasy.

'Nothing is won by heeding this nonsense, either materially or spiritually. It will only give you spiritual madhumeha, the diabetes of the soul. A soft, sweet collection of vapid ideas. Nothing hard to bite or chew on. Nothing hard to digest. There is no contemplation for the mind, no impetus for the soul, no stiffness to the spine. These ideas are like spiritual pudding for weak teeth, slack jaws and feeble minds. It destroys your spirit and makes your soul shrink. A true Sanatani resists, always upholding dharma. He stands tall and proud.

'You wouldn't put spoilt food in your stomach, yet you want a society, a civilisation, a culture, a way of life, a spiritual philosophy, to accept your rancid ideas.'

'Do I make sense?' Rama asked.

Bhamaha stayed quiet, staring at the campfire.

'Where is this guru of yours now?'

Bhamaha pressed his palms together. 'He's a paragon of virtue. He is Vishwaguru! His birth is divine, one who just cannot have been born to a mortal mother. So great was his love that he ordered us to work for the Haihaya army, feed them, clean their camp and give them most of our produce. All this shows them how evolved we are, how open our hearts are, how great our beliefs are. If only he were here. He'd have held the avatara by hand and led him home. Home to ahimsa. And you would have been grateful! Vishwaguru is the true samrat of this world, monarch of the empire of love. Hriday Samrat!'

'Answer my question, Bhamaha.'

'I think the army murdered him,' Ekavira said. Rama waited, not taking his eyes off Bhamaha.

'He left our land,' Bhamaha said in a small voice.

Rama sighed. 'A guru who forsakes his people.'

'No! He will come back! To end all our troubles ...' Bhamaha's voice stayed small.

'True ahimsa, perhaps. He ran from the fight,' Akrita laughed. 'And cuckolded an entire community before he went.'

'Your idea of ahimsa is incomplete,' said Rama. 'No harm to others is only the half of it. Also important is that others don't harm you. And sometimes that can be ensured only by himsa or the threat of it. These foolish beliefs have ensured you live life with palms pressed together in supplication. The hand never swings to land a hard slap, or makes a fist to punch away a dishonour.'

Rama paused momentarily and went on. 'Meditation will not solve everything. I'd like to see you meditate beside a hungry wolf or in a nest of vipers, and say all will be well. You couldn't meditate in a swarm of mosquitoes, even. All will not be well. Instead, all will be supremely unwell, Bhamaha.

'You are not the creator of this universe for it to do as you please. You will be rewarded and punished as per your karma, and you will not get more or less than you deserve. Even Mahavishnu's mercy must be deserved. So you must act, do your karma.

'*Kritasya karma, phalam anivaryam.* You can decide your karma and how you want to do it. But you have no choice but to get its phala, its fruit. Karma once done, phala, good or bad, will ensue.

'The karmas of your past lives decide the varna of your birth. Your gunas, qualities and the character you develop through your free will. Your purushartha decides what you do in this life. And what you will become in the next. Your fate, prarabhda, is free will you have exercised in the past. Why boast about it or feel sad? Why swagger if you are a Brahmin, and why despair if you are Shudra? What you do now is important. A Brahmin isn't enlightened and high, or a Shudra ignorant and low. To believe that is aviveka. There are evil Brahmins and noble Shudras. Same with vegetarians.'

'So you will eat meat?' Bhamaha quickly asked.

'The varna to which I belong because of my karma prohibits it. My gunas dislike it. So I don't. But if I went to a Devi temple, and the prasada given to me is meat, I will eat it.'

'You approve of animal sacrifice?' Bhamaha was finding his voice again.

'Parashakti manifests as gentle Saraswati, and as the fierce and terrible Bhadrakali. Different energies from the same source. Certain rituals and pujaviddhanas, ceremonial rites, need these sacrifices. You are free not to follow if it's not to your liking. There is no compulsion.

'Know this, "*Yo Vishnuh sah Shivo jneyo, yah Shivo Vishureva sah*". Vishnu is Shiva, and Shiva is Vishnu. Only fools see the difference. The source is the same. Parashakti. When you say "All is Maya", you take Bhagawati's name. Ma means moksha, and ya means giver. What is really said is "All is Bhagawati".'

Rama stopped talking. He knew what was coming. He knew what would be asked. Rama could almost see the thoughts form in Bhamaha's mind. He couldn't come so far and falter at the last step. Rama thought furiously about how he would go about doing it.

'How do you know it is Parashakti?' asked Bhamaha.

'Self-realisation. What I experienced is what I must show the world and help others experience. I must make this path so others can follow. Some have glimpsed before me, I see clearly. I must bring this vision to others.'

Bhamaha's eyes shone. The fallacy of his beliefs had been shown up. Here was his chance to get one back. Rama waited for him to ask.

'So, all this was a personal experience? No one else saw, felt or experienced anything. I agree with all you've said, but how do I know this is real? My senses don't say so. Nobody else's senses say so either. So, what is reality in this context?'

'I was there when Gurudeva came back from the dead. I saw him defeat and kill Arjuna.' Akrita was outraged.

'Saptarishi Jamadagni agrees, and so does Shukracharya.' said Raikava.

'If you say so. But both of them are Bhargavas. And Akrita is his shishya. How would I, a common man, know?'

'Isn't their word good enough? Isn't all that he's done proof enough?' asked Chandragupta.

Bhamaha stared at Rama. Chandragupta shook his head in resignation.

'Speak your mind,' said Rama to Bhamaha.

'Show me you are Mahavishnu's avatara.' Bhamaha folded his hands across his chest, unafraid now, sensing some sort of victory.

Rama's pupils rose, and the whites of his eyes stared at Bhamaha whose face went ashen. The growing suspicion that he had probably taunted an immensely powerful man sent a shiver down his spine. He suddenly wasn't so sure of himself.

Rama stood and moved to the edge of the water. He saw himself in the mirror in his dhyana. The light on his forehead blazed. He remembered the yantra that had descended on him in Ma Chinnamasta's eclipse world to celebrate his victory in her test. He called it forth in the mirror in his dhyana.

A square with four nested sides formed in the mirror, half on land, half in water. Six concentric circles of red lotus petals settled around him inside the square. He was the focal point, the bindu. He let the light on his forehead spread down his body, into the earth, water and the yantra. It flashed golden. The six circles rose, spacing themselves from Rama's feet to his head.

All of them watched, unsure of what was happening. The campfire erupted, climbing higher than the treetops, its orange-red flames dancing and whirling, amazing the group and pushing them back. The river morphed into sinuous coils of swirling water, weaving in and out like a million serpents. The fire rushed down on Rama, descending on the top of his head and splattering like water. The water spiralled up his legs, prancing like flames.

The fire and water met, thudding into each other and twirling around Rama, hiding him from the group. A keening cry arose as they twirled faster and even faster. The fire and water mixed, lacing into each other. A sudden deep hush descended, and the water and fire dropped, smashing into the ground and vanishing without a trace.

The campfire shrunk back to how it was before, but the flames didn't dance. They were frozen, stone solid. The water stood dead still in the river, as if it were a river no more, but a vast expanse of silver mercury, reflective as a mirror.

Rama loomed. He stood before them at his normal height, and yet he was as high as the mountains. Fire and water glowed and swayed on five spots on Rama's body. They traced distinct patterns onto his skin. Two spots on each forearm, two on his upper arms, just below the shoulders, and one on his chest. The patterns blazed, flowing like liquid, orange lava and solidified, holding the motif.

The five patterns were the five symbols of Mahavishnu—the lotus on the right forearm and the mace on the left. The chakra was on the upper right arm, and the conch was on the left. The srivatsa blazed at the centre of the chest.

The group watched, frozen in astonishment, faces upturned to the looming apparition, mouths agape, eyes unblinking, hair standing on end.

'The water,' Akrita cried suddenly. 'Look at the river.'

They scrambled to the river's edge. Mahavishnu's cosmic form stretched across the water. A calm, gentle, meditative face of extraordinary beauty and effulgence, framed by millions of faces on either side. Innumerable arms framed the glowing blue torso. Entire solar systems, galaxies and universes disappeared into him and emerged out of him. Thousands of deities, sages, birds, beasts, yakshas and nagas and uragas, gandharvas and apsaras and unknown, unimaginable beings emerged from his half-open mouth and vanished in it. A serpent of countless hoods stood above his head. A tune of indescribable joy erupted in their ears. A melody of sacred chants and blooming flowers, of lullabies and love songs, of silence and mountain mists. Of limitless grace and enduring love, of dancing damsels and cheerful chuckles, of moonlit nights and lovers' embraces. Every atom in their bodies sang in harmony, one with sheer rapture. All the world, all of existence was the sight and the sound.

An eagle of tremendous girth rose out of the shimmering still water. A bird of water and fire. It shrieked its triumph to the world as it swooped around Rama's looming figure and plunged headlong into the ground at his feet. A gigantic bull of water emerged. Snorting fire, it careened around him and leapt into the water. The water didn't ripple or spout; it stayed still as ever. The incredible spectacle remained unchanged, except for the central figure of Mahavishnu. In his place stood Mahadeva, the same gentle smile adorning his handsome face. The serpent wound around his torso like a kaleidoscopic yagnopaveeta, as universes crashed and erupted from him. The sliver of moon in his hair shone like a sickle of brilliant diamonds. Ganga, caught in the knot of his hair, leapt gleefully to meet her sister Narmada. The music of sheer joy played on.

The beat of the damaru echoed through the melody of chanting, increasing its tempo. The melody raced, like a war cry in battle, like the dundhubis of the devas beating as one. Like a traveller's first sight of home, like the crimson rising sun, like a cloudburst on parched land, like the thrum of the heart after first love's kiss. The bodies of the men shivered in the throes of exquisite ecstasy.

The melody rose to its divine crescendo and went dead

silent. A silence that held all of everything there was, is and will be. That held the essence of all sound. A quiet nimisha before the burst of creation and a nimisha after all was dissolved. The scintillating spectacle disappeared from the river. The silver of the river turned red. The group stared, transfixed, unsure if they were breathing, if their hearts still beat, unsure if they were dead or alive, if they were body or soul.

An inverted red triangle formed on the river. A red so deep, it addled the mind to look at it. A ferocious, majestic roar of a rampant lion tore through the utter silence. As one, the group turned to Rama.

The Parashu flew to his right hand. His body turned red like a rudrapushpa. His eyes and the Parashu blazed incandescent white, the symbols brilliant saffron. The looming body of Rama reached for the skies. The world turned crimson. The men cried in agony and ecstasy. In a blink, all was gone. Rama stood before them again, his honey-coloured pupils watching them prostrate themselves to him.

II

The Dance of Mohini

They set out with the first light of dawn after a sparse meal. Rama noticed the telltale fatigue and red eyes and guessed the group hadn't slept, probably discussing what they'd seen. The group treated Rama with a deference that soon became irksome. Everyone was reluctant to approach him. They hung on to every word he said as if he were revealing a sacred mantra. He merely had to look at someone and immediately palms were pressed together and heads bowed. They walked the trail under the glowering mid-morning sun and not a wisp of wind. The heat, even beneath the foliage, was oppressive.

Rama had enough of the excessive reverence when Ekavira, walking at the head of the group, started clearing pebbles away from the trail and calling out protrusions of roots and dangling branches for Rama to avoid.

'Stop for a moment,' said Rama.

Everyone stopped and turned in a blink, all their palms together like devotees before a murthi.

'This has to stop. I cannot suffer this anymore.'

'I was thinking the same, Swami.' said Anantha. 'It's

not right that you should go to the Malaya Kshatriyas. You should go back to the ashram. We'll bring them to you. That is appropriate.'

Rama was taken aback for a nimisha.

'Yes, Bhagawan. That is how it should be done,' said Chandragupta.

Rama stared at Chandragupta, his expression grim. Chandragupta quailed as Rama's raptor gaze stayed on him.

'Do not call me that,' Rama spoke slowly and clearly, staring at each of them. 'And that is not what I meant, Anantha. I want all of you to stop behaving like I'm a walking god.'

He could sense the reluctance. He lifted the Parashu and nicked his forearm with its edge. A little blood trickled through the break in the skin.

'I bleed. Like any mortal,' he said as he rested the Parashu against his thigh and drew Anantha's sword from its scabbard in the blink of an eye. The group gasped. Rama groaned inwardly. He should have moved slowly. He nicked himself again.

'Any weapon can make me bleed.' He made sure everyone saw his arm. 'I have many blessings by the grace of the gods. And many responsibilities. I remain mortal, I haven't become Bhagawan. Being a chiranjeevi doesn't mean I'm immortal. My lifespan has been extended far beyond normal. But it will end one day.' The group merely stared at him.

'There are many things I cannot do. I cannot fly, I can't shower gold from the skies, I don't know everything about everything, or grow a thousand arms.'

Really? the other voice inside him questioned. *You never know till you try*. Rama ignored it.

'There are some ordinary things I can't do. My brothers tell me my attempts at humour are really bad. My jokes are all lame.' No reaction from any of them. They stood stone still, not even glancing at each other. Rama sighed loudly.

'I'll try one now. What happens if an axe falls on your head?'

No one answered.

'You get a splitting headache.'

The group looked at each other, unsure of how to react. Nobody laughed.

'See? Bad joke.'

No one spoke. 'I don't understand. If the blade of the falling axe hit the head, one could've died,' said Ekavira.

'Very "cleaver" of you,' said Akrita in a jiffy.

Anantha snorted, a grin breaking out on his face.

'I got one,' Akrita continued. 'How does an axe chase away cows?'

'Para-shoo, para-shoo, para-shoo,' he said, waving his arms. Chandragupta laughed.

'It's worse than the first one,' Raikava chuckled. Only Bhamaha was disapproving.

'I understood that. Do you have another one?' Ekavira asked.

'I thought you'd never *axe*,' came Akrita's prompt retort.

Rama relaxed. Thank heavens for Akrita, the mood had changed. Akrita's easy banter would end the formality with which they behaved with him. They would fall back to their earlier camaraderie without even realising it. 'Walk on,' he said.

Ekavira and Akrita walked ahead, followed by Raikava, Bhamaha and Chandragupta. Rama held Anantha back.

'Do you get the sense someone's watching us?' he asked quietly.

'No, Swami.'

'Swami is good enough. Thank you for not calling me Bhagawan.' Anantha tried hard to hide his sheepishness but failed.

'Do you remember yesterday's incident around the campfire, Anantha? That boar Bhamaha couldn't sense.'

'What about it, Swami?'

'Odd that it fled like it did.'

'Maybe because you pointed at it.'

'It was close, Anantha. Too close to a group of humans, and too quiet. I didn't think about it then, but it struck me as improbable, and I remembered it in the morning. I can't shake the feeling we're being watched.'

Anantha moved to look around. Rama stopped him. 'Keep walking. I'll double back and check for tracks. I don't know if it is an animal or a human who's watching us. We've set a fair pace since morning. Anything or anyone following would've left traces. I'll catch up with you. Don't stop.' Rama stepped off the trail and disappeared into the forest.

He was back at the campsite in no time. He found the spot where the boar had been and trailed its mad rush back to its den. A solitary male, foraging for food. Rama could recognise its footprint now, and he tracked it further westwards in the direction they'd come from. He stopped at the muddy puddle the boar had soaked in, hunched down and examined it. The boar's tracks meandered to the river, new tracks made a few hours ago, but older ones led north, away from the puddle and towards where the trail should be. Rama estimated the distance. He was closer to the river than the trail, the river to his left and the trail to his right.

The trail was too far from the puddle for the boar to feel the need to investigate. It had a powerful sense of smell and could tell from here that the group was passing on and not staying in its territory. He tracked the boar from the puddle to the trail, and then he was sure. From there, its tracks ran eastwards, parallel to the path, in the underbrush and dense growth between the river and trail. It hadn't stopped, and it hadn't deviated to forage. Unnatural behaviour for a wild animal. It was being compelled perhaps? Someone was watching them, he was certain.

Rama stopped. The boar had followed for more than two yojanas. But why only from here? He moved further west, searching, identifying animals by their prints and watching where their tracks led.

He found the carcass of the civet. Killed and eaten by a leopard, and the scavengers had been at it too. He tracked the civet. No doubt, the civet was following them. So intent on tailing them, it hadn't been aware of the leopard lurking in the branches of the arjuna tree. The watcher had lost the civet, had somehow sensed the boar some distance ahead, and then used the boar.

Who could it be? The mantravadin who'd used Abhichara against him? There was powerful magic at play here. Rama couldn't think of anyone else. How was he watching me now? Rama slowly turned a full circle, senses alert, eyes darting. He checked the position of the sun to estimate the time and waited. A quarter of a muhurta later, he was convinced no animal was taking an undue interest in him. Yet, the sense of being watched was still strong.

He sped to the campsite, and from there, tracked the path they had set off on at dawn. He zigzagged, cutting across the trail and into the vegetation on both sides of it.

Dantakrura watched. He regretted the impulse that had made him vacate the boar's body the previous night. He had panicked when Parashurama had pointed straight at him in the dark and believed the man knew he was watching through the boar's eyes. The animal had fled the moment he'd let go of his hold on it, and his prey had grown suspicious. Parashurama now knew he was being followed. The avatara had sharp instincts. Dantakrura watched as Rama searched for tracks, moving eastward from the campsite, and grinned. He wasn't going to find any.

Sometime later, Rama stopped searching. There were no tracks following the group at all. He glanced at the sun, made his way back to the trail and sped towards the group. He caught up a few minutes later. His new-found speed never ceased to amaze him, and he wasn't even breathing hard despite the distance and the relentless heat. He told Anantha what he'd found.

'So, he isn't following now?' Anantha asked.

'What time is it, Anantha?'

Anantha glanced at the sun. 'A muhurta past noon, Swami.'

'Do you see it?'

'What?' Anantha looked all around.

'The hawk in the sky. That's how he's watching us. He uses that hawk and hides in the sun. He keeps between us and the sun so we can't see him in the brightness. Clever.'

Rama sniffed the air. 'Two muhurtas from now, we'll run

into rain. You can see him against the clouds then. Let's keep going.'

They walked quietly for a while.

'The child of the earth had anything to say while I was away?' Rama asked.

Anantha grinned, 'Oh yes. At the campsite, you were Bhagawan. After you told us not to call you that, the name became Uddhatr. He started talking after you left, though none of us were keen to hear. Soon, Uddhatr became Swami, and now it's just Parashurama. The experience of last night became a vision, then a dream, and now he questions what happened. He thinks some root or leaf we ate gave us all hallucinations. And then finally decided that it was a magic spell you used. Abhichara, to befuddle all our minds. Bhagawati knows what he'll say when we strike camp tonight.'

'All is maya,' said Rama. Anantha laughed.

'He won't stop about that Vishwaguru. He has an excuse for every failing we found in his guru. Bhamaha should've just elected himself Vishwaguru since the original disappeared.'

Rama chuckled, 'No, not disappeared.' Anantha waited, but Rama didn't continue.

'But how can he be so doubtful after last night, Swami?'

'A lifetime of believing the wrong teachings. The values and beliefs he's been taught have been internalised now. It is a matter of his ego. If the values fail or reveal their hollowness, he fails. And he won't allow that to happen. So, he will doubt his senses, and present it in the garb of healthy scepticism, as an enquiring mind or even as common sense. Anything that lets him assume some kind of moral or intellectual superiority. It is really his mind. It warps things to conform to his illusion of truth. That illusion is all he has to understand life, and he doesn't dare to break it. We always start by lying to ourselves before lying to others.'

Two muhurtas later, the rain hit them. It drizzled for a few nimishas, and then the rain walloped into the earth, drenching the forest and the group. The trail turned into a rivulet, and the bottom of it became a sludge that sucked at their feet as they scrambled for cover. They found shelter under the trees; the rain crashed through the foliage and branches in thick black sheets of water. Leaves, twigs and all sorts of creepy-crawlies fell on them. Insects climbed their legs. They brushed them off themselves and each other and waited, thankful for the respite from the heat.

As abruptly as it came, the rain disappeared. Rama motioned them to stay, watching the sky through the leaves. Clouds hid the sun still, and slowly the run of water on the trail abated. The forest burst alive with sound and scent as if the rain and relief from the heat had given it renewed zest. Water dripped from sparkling green leaves as Rama waited. The watcher would see an empty trail and would be searching now, waiting for them to emerge from the verdure.

Rama beckoned to Anantha, and they scrambled to the trail. The hawk was visible against the backdrop of the clouds.

'I see it now, Swami. Are you sure it is watching us?'

Rama nodded.

'It flies high. Could you have shot it if you had a bow?'

'We don't need one.' Rama replied. He pointed at the hawk, paused for a brief moment and raised his Parashu. The hawk veered north mid-flight, shrieking as it closed its wings to plummet down and away, to put the treeline between itself and Rama.

'Aren't you killing it?'

'Why kill the poor hawk, Anantha? The watcher knows we go east. If he scouts far enough ahead, he'll find your camp. It'll be too big to miss. He'd guess that's where we're going. Now, he knows I know, and I know that he knows. Let's see what happens. I'm sure the hawk will be back once the clouds disappear. Let's walk.'

They stopped for the night below the shade of a great ashwattha tree, the driest ground they could find, but still sodden. Even the firewood was damp, giving off more smoke than fire till, at last, the heat caught and the fire blazed. Anantha insisted on a watch; Akrita was given the first, and Rama was the last one before dawn. He accepted. Brahmamuhurta was ideal for dhyana. They ate and retired for the night in silence, Bhamaha having nothing to say.

Chandragupta woke Rama from a dreamless sleep. He fed the fire, went round the camp, watching, listening. Satisfied that no danger lurked, he went into dhyana. He scanned the group for any spells on them and didn't find any. When he eased out of dhyana, he found Akrita seated before him.

'I've been thinking of your question, Akrita. I still have no answer.'

Akrita frowned.

'What became of Arjuna? Did he just die, or did something else happen?' Rama reminded.

Akrita nodded. 'Don't you know any spells, Gurudeva?'

'I know the Atharvan spells, but I haven't used any of them. Why?'

'For protection against the mantravadin who used Abhichara against you. To fight him, to find out who he is.'

Rama smiled. 'He plays a game of cat and mouse and fancies himself the cat. He will show himself sooner than later.'

'What does he want? To kill you?'

'He used a fascination spell. It wasn't to kill; it was cast to control. To use me at his will or take away all my power. It's my power that he's after.'

'He can take away the power of avatara in you?'

'I really don't know if such a thing is possible, Akrita.'

'Are there any commonplace spells you can use? For these mosquitoes, and all these worms that know to crawl on us just as we fall asleep. To stop us from getting wet in the rain or to keep snakes away. I haven't seen so many snakes in one day. That king cobra we saw crossing the trail must've been thirty feet long. And the rain, it was black and left smears on everything.'

Rama wondered about the rain. The dried smears on their clothes and bodies were fine ash carried by the wind to the rain clouds. That much ash from the west could only mean Mahishmati's fires had died down, and the ash had dispersed. Maybe blown westwards by Vayavastras. Rama ignored Akrita's question and told him to wake the others.

Two days later, close to dusk, Rama sensed a subtle change in the forest. There was a strangeness to the rhythm and smells and a sense of wariness in the animals. He knew they were close and scanned the jungle as they walked the trail. Half a muhurta later, he saw the sentry, cleverly camouflaged atop his perch on the sal tree. He heard the piping whistle of a bulbul and saw Anantha and Ekavira suddenly look alert. It was a mellow bird call, and Rama guessed the sentry was signalling the sighting of familiar people and no imminent danger.

'Another muhurta before we reach?' he asked aloud.

Ekavira nodded and Anantha grinned sheepishly, knowing Rama had spotted the sentry he hadn't. Akrita rushed to him, whispering.

'You did cast spells, Gurudeva.'

'I don't know what you're talking about.'

Akrita was disbelieving. 'A lot of rain all around, but nowhere near us. No snakes, no mosquitoes.' Rama shrugged and offered no comment.

An ululation broke out as they turned the corner by the boulder. Bhargavi and dozens of women welcomed them with clay lamps in their hands. Cheers broke out from the men behind them. Women lined the path on either side, and the men showered flowers on them. Rama grinned at Bhargavi and then saw the two figures to her right. A man and woman, a rishi and patni.

A short, swarthy man with a formidable belly and a genial smile framed by thick black hair and beard. Rudrakshas adorned his neck, pooled on his wrists and around the topknot of his hair. Both he and his patni wore the white robes of ascetics, and the tripundra marked their foreheads. The lady was slim, a head taller than her husband and wore her magnetic beauty with ease and grace. Rama recognised them in an instant, though he'd never seen them before. They were unmistakable. A great rishi and an equally great rishika. Agastya and Lopamudra.

The women and men fell in behind the group as they climbed the gentle incline, the lights of the lamps like a serpentine sparkle of fireflies in the growing dark. Bhargavi completed the ritual welcome and applied the vermilion paste to Rama's forehead as the ululation reached a crescendo. And then there was a rush to touch him, to touch his feet, to greet him, to have him bless babies, to ply him with savouries and short-eats. Rama patiently stood for it all, not wanting to disappoint, not wishing to dampen their evident joy.

He saw Anantha and Ekavira hold court with a growing crowd hanging on to every word. Wide eyes and open mouths turned to him. Rama knew what that was all about. The talk spread from mouth to ear, gasps and exclamations spread like wildfire, and there was another rush to touch him and seek blessings. Rama sighed, hemmed in by eager hands and expectant faces and astonished eyes. He saw Agastya and Lopamudra watch from a distance, knowing smiles on their faces.

A long while later, there was no let-up in the throng pressing against him. Rama gently eased the people away from him and lifted the Parashu to his shoulder. The crowd *aah*-ed in awe and stopped cold. He raised the Parashu high. The crowd hushed and backed away, now eager to keep its distance.

'I'm here for some time. All of you will get to meet me,' he said loudly. He nodded to Bhargavi, Anantha and Ekavira, and they shepherded the crowd away. Rama made his way to the couple, prostrated before them, touching his hands to their feet.

'Parashakti bless you! Mahadeva protect you!' said Agastya. Lopamudra repeated the blessing. Rama rose with a smile. It was wonderful to hear 'Parashakti' from their lips.

'Let me look at you,' said Agastya as he held Rama by the shoulders at an arm's length. He peered at Rama's face and frowned. His pupils turned up and the whites of his eyes stared at Rama.

'Mahadeva!' Agastya exclaimed.

Rama heard a short, hard gasp from Lopamudra. She grabbed his right hand and examined his right thumb with the whites of her eyes. They stared at him for a long while, and Rama suddenly knew what it felt to have to look into pupil-less eyes that seemed to bore into one's soul.

'I see only two, seven are invisible. How is this possible?' said Agastya.

'See his thumbprint,' said Lopamudra. Agastya scrutinised it.

'Five symbols of Mahavishnu. The Parashu. Then the inverted triangle of Devi. The print keeps changing. Adbhuta!'

Rama didn't understand. He looked from one to another as they lowered their pupils.

'Come, come. Our tent is by the river. Bathe and finish your sandhyavandana. I'll get you a dhoti. We can talk after,' said Agastya.

Rama finished his sandhyavandana and walked into the tent. He found Anantha and Bhargavi inside. Lopamudra sat in padmasana with her eyes closed. Agastya gestured to the Parashu leaning beside the tent flap.

'You have mastered it and made it your own.'

Rama nodded.

'Mahadeva will be pleased. You must show me your moves.'

Rama bowed to show his willingness, and Agastya seemed to know about the Parashu.

'What were you talking about back then?' he asked.

'Do you have any knowledge of Jyotisha?'

'Not much. I only know the grahas and rashis,' Rama replied.

'I can read the grahas and rashis off anyone's face,' said Agastya. He pointed to Bhargavi, 'Makara rashi, Surya in Dhanus. Anantha is Karka rashi, Surya in Kumbha. I can list all the grahas and their positions. But I can't see the grahas on your face except two. Surya and Chandra are both exalted. Surya in Mesha, and Chandra in Vrishabha. You were born on Akshaya Tritiya. But I can't see the other seven grahas.'

Lopamudra spoke as if in a trance. 'Father sun, mother moon.'

'I really don't see value in these astrologers,' said Rama.

'Ah! Those charlatans and peddlers of remedies. One eye on the chart of grahas; one on your purse. Expensive remedies and expensive fees. They understand very little, and all they do is instil fear in people. They've brought infamy to sacred knowledge. A natal chart and the position of the grahas, when one is born, shows the prarabhda karma in this birth, what to do to burn it as much as possible before one dies and how not to add more bad karma to one's account. That's all. My karma tells me that I will find a shishya here. One of my best, and he will come south with me,' said Agastya. 'But I can't formulate your chart with just two grahas.'

'Does this have anything to do with being a chiranjeevi?' Rama asked.

Agastya ignored Bhargavi's gasp, but his eyes shone with excitement. 'A chiranjeevi before my eyes. Now what would the chart of one such be?' He put his hand to his chin, musing it over.

Rama waited a while and asked, 'What about my thumb?'

'Another conundrum. A thumbprint is another method of prediction. The Nadi jyotisha is unique to each person. I can tell everything about a man from his thumbprint. His name, his parents' names and even the name of the woman he'll marry. But again, I can't say a thing about you. The pattern of your thumbprint keeps changing between the seven symbols I mentioned earlier.'

'Seven invisible on the face. Another seven are visible on the thumb. Interesting!' Agastya lost himself in thought again.

Rama noticed the whorls and lines on the inside of his thumb. Nothing changed, everything was as ordinary as everyone else's. Just as he took his eyes away, he thought he saw a triangle. He peered again, and now it looked like an axe. He looked away and back, and the whorls on his thumb were shaped like a conch. Rama stared at Lopamudra in surprise. The rishika didn't say a word, her eyes still closed.

'Tell us your story, Rama. It would be a privilege to hear it,' said Agastya. Rama took a deep breath and began, telling them how it all started, providing every little detail Agastya requested.

When Rama narrated the incident of the beheading of Renuka, Lopamudra, eyes closed and palms pressed together, whispered, '*Bhavaranya kuttharika*.'

The axe that clears the jungle of samsara. Rama went quiet for a nimisha, thinking about the meaning of her words.

Rama repeated Jamadagni's and Renuka's words. *Tat Twam Asi*, and *sa ham*. Again, Lopamudra spoke.

'*Tat. Twam. Aayi.*' That. Thou. Mother. Three separate words.

Rama told them of the leper that Akrita was and the deluge of blood from Ma Chinnamasta's mouth. He waited for Lopamudra to speak.

'*Mrithyudaaru kuttharika.*' The axe that cuts the tree of death.

He spoke of the Panchagni and the amsha.

'*Haribrahmendra sevitha.*' She who is served by the Trimurtis.

A thrill ran through his body when he realised Lopamudra was describing Parashakti. These were the Supreme Goddess's names.

He spoke of the dream seeded by the Avadhuta. A dream that was more than a dream.

'*Jagrini. Svapanti. Suupta. Turiya.*' She who causes the four states: wakefulness, dreaming, deep sleep and transcendence.

Rama told his story, and Lopamudra whispered the names. The tent was quiet and solemn, like the sanctum of a temple, everyone listening to Rama with awe and Lopamudra with reverence.

He finished with his arrival.

'*Vindhyachala nivasini.*' She whose abode is in the Vindhyas.

Lopamudra opened her eyes. Dozens of names had been whispered, but Rama was sure there were more. A great longing to know those names rose in his heart, and he wondered if he could ask her. How many names? They couldn't be random ones; each was imbued with meaning. Meanings, he corrected himself. One that was apparent, and one or more that was hidden. One meaning for the mind, eyes, ears and lips. The others for the soul. Rishis and rishikas were maestros at hiding secrets in plain sight. Secrets revealed only to true seekers, to those who deserved to be told and whose karma allowed them to know.

Bhargavi cleared her throat, and Rama ceased his musing.

'What would the Uddhatr have us do?' she asked.

'I want to build an army. An army that wages a different war. I'll explain in a moment.' Rama asked Anantha to bring Akrita, Raikava and Chandragupta.

Once they'd arrived, introductions and salutations exchanged and all were seated, Rama continued, 'This is my plan. I want to train a small force of warriors that will spread out to the cities, ports and trade routes of Jayadhwaja's kingdom. A dozen warriors will go to each place. Chandragupta will help decide the places. The targets are the treasury, the enforcers and administrators of the unjust system, the guardians of the trade routes, the tax collectors, ministers, generals and spies. Slay them.'

'The upholders and enablers of the iron frame,' said Chandragupta.

'Yes,' Rama affirmed. 'Raikava and Chandragupta have the most travelling to do. In each city, they will identify Brahmins, traders, workers and even Kshatriyas who follow dharma. Who have defied or are willing to defy the system. They now have swords and fighters on their side. They will find courage in our strength. Use bards to spread the message of the revolt.

'Use guile and subterfuge. Once the attacks start, I want them to fear that they can be killed anywhere, anytime. Anyone can be the killer. The Malaya Kshatriyas have fought this kind of war before. Your army was trained to hit and retreat, and your squads to kill or die trying. This time you are up against larger forces and greater odds, and you will need both these elements.

'There is no cavalry, no rathas, no elephants in this army. Identify targets, kill and escape. Any fighting will be close combat. I will train you for that. I will give you a new weapon for melee fights where you are surrounded by a greater force of enemies. Mahadeva equipped me for my fight. It is my dharma to give you a weapon before I ask you to fight for me. Are your blacksmiths any good?' he asked Bhargavi.

'The best there are. Our swords are superior and highly prized. The process we use to make them is a closely guarded secret.'

'Rama, you can end this all yourself. Challenge Jayadhwaja. Slay him,' encouraged Agastya.

'Better the whole kingdom revolts than just one Parashurama,' said Rama. 'The people have endured tyranny for thousands of years. Every uprising has been brutally crushed. There will be anger in their hearts and revenge in their minds. The people need to be invested in their freedom. They need to feel that they too had a hand in winning it, and it wasn't just handed to them by me. Only what is hard-won is ever valued.

'A thousand stories need to sprout about their resistance and fight, to remind them to never let this happen again. And if it does, to give them hope that tyranny can be overthrown. This needs to be done to remind the Kshatriyas that they are guardians, not predators. That they owe to society as much as society owes them.

'Things will escalate once we start, and inevitably things will come to a head. There will be a battle of Akshauhinis and divyastras. I will be there to counter, to deliver the crushing blow.'

Rama sighed, 'Twenty-one Akshauhinis I put to the sword. So much killing has happened already. So many souls trapped in the Parashu. I must find liberation for them, so the cycle of rebirth and karma continues. I killed these men. I owe it to them to find a way out. It is my dharma. My atonement.'

Agastya nodded his agreement.

'Maybe the samrat will find good sense once he realises the situation is out of his control,' hoped Anantha.

'There will always be men and women in this world who want to see it burn. Pure evil. And then some want power and control and will go to any lengths for it. I doubt the samrat will see sense,' Agastya replied.

'Jayadhwaja is a cunning man. He believes it is his birthright to be the samrat, and he's not above using poison, assassins or any underhand way to get what he wants. He'd love being a tyrant, no chance of him changing for the good,' said Chandragupta.

'Does he have a mantravadin?' Akrita asked excitedly. 'Has he used Abhichara?'

Chandragupta and Raikava looked at each other. 'No,' both confirmed.

'But he did lead the campaign against the black magicians of Mayong many years back. He killed everyone he could find there, but if rumours were to be believed, he did spare the life of a prince, a child already adept in Abhichara,' Chandragupta added. 'There was some talk about the child's eyes.'

'Eyes?' Rama asked.

'Can't remember what. Something was odd about them, that much I remember.'

'There will be a lot more slaughter, Rama,' Agastya said quietly. 'This isn't a prediction but my thoughts. Everything about you is hidden from me, something I've never thought was possible. And there has been no prophecy after Apava's. Strange.'

It seemed like everyone in the tent had run out of words.

'Can you show me your moves now?' Agastya broke the silence.

Rama laughed.

They quickly exited the tent, Agastya leading the way to the practice grounds of the warriors. It was a rough circular clearing. Torches on high poles were lit around the perimeter as Rama walked to the middle. Word spread and the Malaya Kshatriyas gathered.

'Who will help show us the Uddhatr's powers?' Bhargavi called.

Three men stepped forward, not bothering to draw their swords. They surrounded Rama and lunged to tackle him to the ground. None touched him. In a blink, they were on the ground, reeling with strikes to the head, midriff and knee.

'Too easy. Three are not enough. This is not an ordinary man, he is the Uddhatr,' Bhargavi exhorted loudly.

Ten more stepped into the ring, three women among them.

'Draw your swords,' said Rama. They hesitated.

'There will be a reward for anyone who can touch me with their swords,' Rama challenged.

Eyes twinkling with excitement, they drew their swords and took their stances. The group surrounded him again, not rushing, waiting for him to show his hand. The attack came from Rama's right, four men moving in unison. He immediately realised it was a feint to turn him, so the real attack came from his left. He moved towards the feint as they expected. That's all they saw. He whirled and rushed the left flank faster than the blink of an eye. The six warriors didn't have the time to react. He kicked their feet out from below them, elbowed them just below the ribcages and twisted their wrists. Two nimishas later, the four on the right too had fallen, prone on the earth or on their knees, swords out of their grasp and utter disbelief on their faces.

'Is this the best the Malaya Kshatriyas can do? Are you so weak?' Rama said aloud.

'Call the squads. And call the bards,' Bhargavi ordered.

They gathered quickly, men and women, lithe of body, lean and sinewy, hard glint in their eyes. Twenty of them stepped forward.

'Not enough,' said Rama.

More came. Rama shook his head. A buzz rippled through the crowd as more and more warriors entered the ring. They stood ready, hands on the hilts of sheathed swords, watching Rama all the while.

'You will need the Parashu now,' Bhargavi taunted.

Rama held his arm out. The Parashu flew to him. He eased the one blade into the ground. The Parashu jutted out from the earth at an angle.

'If you can take it, it's yours,' said Rama.

'A hundred Malaya Kshatriyas in the ring. Make him regret his boast. Sing. Fight,' Bhargavi cried.

'Shame if you cannot draw a drop of blood,' said Rama. 'May you all die old, weak and toothless in your beds. May your enemies pity you.'

The hundred faces glowered. Outrage and resolve sparked in two hundred eyes. It wasn't a game anymore. It was a matter of honour.

The drums beat as one, and they drew their swords. They beat again and they touched their swords to their foreheads. And the bards sang.

Swing the swords, battle is life.
Swing the swords, battle is song.
Glory of the fight, shine of the sun,
Glory of the fight, magic of the moon.

The warriors twirled their swords to the beat.

Warriors' valour, mountains that pierce the sky,
Kill your foes, oceans their widows cry.
Sweat of our brow, the rivers of the earth,
Kill your foes, laugh at death and hope for rebirth.

Our battle roar, thunder in the sky,
Last breath of enemy, a lover's sigh.
Pyres of the enemy, the heat in our loin,
Gamble your life, what better coin?

Battle is life,
Battle is song,
Battle is love,
Make battle, make love, what more to life?
Glory to stand unbowed in crowd of foes,
Kill! On lover's bosom, forget your woes.

On sword edge, two lovers, death and life,
Guard and grip, husband and wife.
The blade is our goddess,
In battle, in life, she is solace.

Swing the swords, battle is life,
Swing the swords, battle is song.

Glory of the fight, shine of the sun,
Glory of the fight, magic of the moon.

At the last beat, the warriors only an arm's length away from Rama attacked, their swords swinging and thrusting. They found air. Rama was nowhere and everywhere. All they saw was a blur that whirled amongst them. When Rama stopped, more than twenty of them lay on the ground, clutching their sides, heads and wrists in pain. Their bodies surrounded him and the Parashu. The rest of them would have to pick their way through to reach him.

Rama didn't wait. He walked through the fallen bodies. Someone far to his left, a woman on the ground, clutching her midriff, drew a dagger from her waistband and threw it at him. He caught it in mid-air, twirled it around his fingers and threw it backwards without a glance. It hit the cheek of the blades of the Parashu exactly at the bindu. The dagger's blade crumpled inwards with a dull clink. He moved outside the ring of fallen bodies.

'The Parashu is there. I'm here. Grasp either the Parashu or me, and you win,' he said.

They threw themselves into the attack, some trying to maim Rama and others running for the Parashu. Groans and cries erupted. Swords dropped or were tossed harmlessly in the air. Bodies thudded onto the ground. Rama stopped beside the Parashu. Less than a dozen remained standing.

Those among the fallen who had recovered now scrambled for their weapons. Many rushed to the perimeter, arming themselves with spears, bows and arrows. They threw the spears and shot the arrows. Rama leapt, turning mid-leap to avoid the nearest missiles. He snatched a spear, and another one. The rest whizzed past or landed where he had been only a nimisha ago.

They threw more spears and shot more arrows. Rama whirled the spears. The Malaya Kshatriyas saw no spears in his hands, only two spinning chakras, the spearheads a blur of steel. The spears and arrows were slapped away. Rama charged, his spears spinning in a blur. One nimisha he was on the ground, the next along the perimeter and in another, he stood beside the Parashu. He stopped. Not one of the hundred remained standing.

The crowd stood in stunned silence.

'I hope you will take your training seriously,' said Rama as he moved to help the injured.

'Can I try?' said Agastya from behind him. 'I touch the Parashu, I win.'

Rama nodded, stepping further away. Agastya charged, his speed giving the lie to his girth and short strides. Rama blocked him, veering him off his course. The Malaya Kshatriyas rushed out of the way, dragging their fallen compatriots.

Rama's and Agastya's bodies melded into a blur as they attacked and counter-attacked. They moved around the Parashu at blinding speed, sometimes closer to it, sometimes further away. Kicks, punches and slaps were landed and countered. They leapt high and grappled low. The blows that landed rang loud. The crowd gasped, straining their eyes to match their incredible speed.

They were at it for a quarter of a muhurta when Agastya held up his hand, panting heavily. Sweat soaked into his dhoti and his torso glistened with it.

'I can't touch the Parashu,' he gasped.

Rama acknowledged with a nod, out of breath himself.

'But I did pin you down for a nimisha.'

'Yes, you did. Name your reward.'

Agastya shook his head. 'No. It is I who must reward you. For being able to stop me. None have before. Karthikeya himself taught me, but it seems his father taught you a little more. Mahadeva is mischievous sometimes.'

Rama laughed despite the panting. They grasped each other and walked to the perimeter as the onlookers cheered. Agastya collapsed on the grass outside the practice ground. Rama moved to do the same.

'So soon?' asked Lopamudra. 'My turn now.'

Rama pointed to the Parashu, still on the ground. 'There it is. Touch it and it's yours.'

'And what would I do with it? Chop wood? I have one for that.' She pointed to her husband. Agastya laughed. 'I want you to show me your moves. But slowly, so I can see everything clearly.'

Rama shrugged, wondering what this was about. He picked a spear from the ground and broke the stout staff in two. He dropped the half with the spearhead. Lopamudra stepped onto the ground and lowered herself, knees flaring out to the sides and up on her toes. She touched the ground with her hands, and brought them to her eyes. Rama performed his drills slowly. Lopamudra watched every move he made.

Stupid, this is, said the other voice. *So awkward and embarrassing*.

She rose slowly and moved forward, stepping softly, her body swaying as her arms moved in a sequence that was unlike his and yet the same. She finished and brought her feet together, standing straight with her left hand in a fist on her left hip and her right hand grasping the fist. Lopamudra waited for him to continue.

Rama stood awkwardly, unsure what to do, when the chime rang out. Agastya held a small pair of bronze cymbals, one in each hand. He struck them together, and Rama moved. A defensive drill—blocking strikes, turning the shoulder to avoid a thrust and swinging his arm overhead to strike with his mock sword. The chiming brought a beat to his movements and stopped when he did.

It rang again as Lopamudra moved, and this time it was slower. Lopamudra swayed like a paddy field in the breeze, like palm tops in the wind. She danced, and Rama stood transfixed at the sheer grace in her movements. The slowness that kept his eyes on Lopamudra's face and the mudras of her fingers. The expression on her face was that of a lover, teasing and seductive. The bhava—the feeling in her dance, in her eyes, in her face—was shringara, romance, and in her movements was lasya, grace. She had adapted his movements to dance to express love. And he hadn't ever seen anything so graceful.

Lopamudra's expression changed subtly, and so did the light in her eyes. The teasing lover of a nimisha ago was now a mother placating her child. The bhava had changed seamlessly. No bard sang, and except for the chimes of the cymbals, there were no other musical instruments. Yet she had conveyed her feelings through her exquisite dance. Rama looked to Agastya.

'The complement to the fury and pace of your battle dance, Rama. The opposite of it. Gentle and slow. The feminine to the masculine, acceptance to the defiance. The love to the anger. Lasya to your virya. The dance that enthrals. The dance of Mohini,'[5] said Agastya.

He struck the cymbals again, and Rama moved, the Parashu flying to his hand as he dropped the mock sword. He submitted himself to the flow of the movement, bringing forth the fury of the Parashu. He knew the beat now and controlled his pace to it. Rama kept close to the ground, moving, darting just inches from the earth. The beat changed, and he knew Lopamudra was dancing. The beat was in his head; he didn't stop. His movement was like a crocodile, he realised.

He changed his stance and movement, swaying now, thrusting and returning, turning on the spot. Like a snake with its hood open and moving from side to side. Joy erupted in him as he moved by instinct, remembering the moves he'd learnt through the Parashu and adding his own. The fury melted away. Ananda. Bliss blossomed. He danced his war dance around Lopamudra as she gracefully undulated and pirouetted. All inhibition was gone, all awkwardness forgotten and all was joy and grace. Virya and lasya wove beauty and abandon in the forest night, in a clearing on a mountain slope, before a thousand fascinated eyes and a million twinkling stars, as even the gentle chimes of the cymbals seemed to laugh in happiness.

He lost all sense of time. He lost all sense of self. And he found himself in dhyana. It wasn't the mirror before him; it was the banalinga. His banalinga, utter black with three white almond-shaped eyes. It seemed to smile back at him. Rama laughed, dancing in the nothingness, the beat still in his head. The banalinga turned transparent and became the mirror.

[5] Mohiniyattam

Rama danced before the mirror. He exulted at the thrill of it. He laughed, and the nothingness laughed with him. The beat vanished, and a sound replaced it.

Ram.

Rama danced to it. He glanced at the mirror and his reflection had sixteen hands, each with a Parashu. But each axe was single-bladed. Like his Parashu had split vertically in two. Rama stopped, and the golden energy body shone in the mirror. The three golden nadis moved upwards to the third chakra, just above the navel. The Manipura chakra. It lit and pulsed and settled into a steady glow. Rama danced again.

He didn't know when he stopped, but when he grew aware that he had, and where he was, he saw a great multitude of people surrounding the clearing, perched on branches and the slopes overlooking the ground. All their eyes were on him. Lopamudra stood beside Agastya. She had stopped long ago, and Rama had danced alone far into the night. He went to them.

Lopamudra assumed a stance as he came closer. Her right hand had the little and ring finger bent and held by the thumb. The index and middle fingers were straight and apart like scissors. The left hand was a fist.

'Do you know what these mudras together mean?' she asked. Rama shook his head.

'Not what. Who. This is the mudra for you. Parashurama.'

Rama prostrated himself at her feet. 'Maathey, teach me the names of Parashakti. Bless me with your vidya.'

'Rise, Rama,' said Lopamudra. A teasing smile played on her lips. 'I shall teach you the Lalitha Sahasranama. The thousand names of Parashakti. Only if you can guess one name from it. A name I haven't mentioned before.'

Rama smiled. 'I don't need to guess. I know one name.'

He pressed his palms together and said, 'Lasyapriya. She who loves grace.'

12

Serpent Sword

At the crack of dawn, Rama's selection of the warriors began. The message had gone out in the night, and it seemed almost everyone wanted to be part of it.

The warriors of the squads and battle-hardened veterans stood shoulder to shoulder with eager aspirants. Everyone would get to try. That was only fair. Rama had told Agastya, Lopamudra, Bhargavi, Anantha and Ekavira what to look for and how to test the candidates. They called the Malaya Kshatriyas forward a score at a time.

'Sit in sukhasana,' Rama told the volunteers before him. 'Now get up without using your hands.' He dismissed the ones who struggled or failed.

'Feet together. Take a big stride forward with the right leg. Bend the left leg till the knee touches the ground. Now stand up.' He dismissed all who had to lean forward to rise.

'Legs apart to the sides, feet twice the length of your shoulders. Squat till your thighs are parallel to the ground. Hold till I tell you to rise.' He dismissed the ones who gave up or whose legs trembled.

The tests grew harder. He wanted both the onlookers and

the ones he had dismissed to know they'd have a fair attempt and also have respect for the ones selected. And they did, cheering the aspirants on, urging them to give it all they had, commiserating when they failed. He judged their strength, endurance, agility and ability to swim and run long distances. It took a couple of days, but in the end, he had a thousand of the toughest Malaya Kshatriyas.

'Celebrate your selection and rest tonight,' said Rama. 'Meet me here tomorrow before Brahma-muhurta.'

Rama, Agastya and Lopamudra walked to the entrance of the training pit where Bhargavi waited with the workers.

'It's ready, Swami, just as you wanted it. But I don't understand it.'

The entrance faced east, with steps descending into a pit dug six feet deep into the ground. Rama climbed down, the rest following. Workers stood inside with torches, awaiting inspection.

The pit was rectangular, sixty-four feet long and thirty-two feet wide. The floor was evened with red mud mixed with powdered herbs to prevent insects, worms and infections. Roughly hewn wooden pillars extended from six feet below ground to fourteen feet above it. Long planks sloped from a central beam running the length of the pit to the pillars on the sides. The sections above the ground and the roof were thatched with palm leaves, leaving a little gap at the top of the walls to allow air to flow in. The southern wall had a raised platform cut into it for observers to sit.

'Good idea to escape the heat,' said Agastya.

'It is more, Maharishi. It is my homage to the spiritual path I tread. A path that began with my grounding in reality by the grace of Ganapathi. And I will not teach the art of violence without teaching dharma and my path too.'

'Is everything ready for the rituals?' he asked Bhargavi.

She guided them to the south-western recess, where seven semicircular, tapering steps were built into the corner, rising from the ground up to Rama's waist.

'The seven chakras, and atop it will be Devi's kalasha. I teach my students to fight, so the form of Devi to be worshipped is Bhadrakali. Fearsome and unstoppable.'

'Our Kuladevi,' Bhargavi crowed.

A brass lamp with five wicks stood before the seven steps. 'My homage to Mahadeva. The five wicks represent the Holy Panchakshari.'

Lopamudra stared at the seven tiers, lost in thought.

Rama pointed to two raised platforms on the western wall. 'The nearest is the altar of Ganapathi. A single elephant tusk will be placed there. My homage to the Deva. On the second platform will be the padukas of a revered ancestor, for the blessings of our pitrus.'

'Then the padukas of the mantravadin who foretold the Uddhatr. The padukas of Yogeeshwara,' said Bhargavi.

Beyond the second altar, mock swords, daggers, long and short staffs, and different weapons were arranged against the wall.

'We start tomorrow. May Parashakti bless us,' said Rama.

Jayadhwaja sat before the warlock, the fire pit burning low between them. The stench, the bodies, the pyres and the flies had all disappeared. Mahishmati was limping painfully back to life, but there was a long way to go yet.

'You've been busy, samrat,' said Dantakrura.

'Reinforcements have come. I, along with a handful of Maharathis, have used divyastras to incinerate the corpses to ash and blow them away. It's blessed to breathe clean air again and be rid of the damned flies.'

'There will be black rain across the land. The rain clouds will put the ash back on the earth.'

Jayadhwaja waved his hand dismissively. 'Better anywhere else than here. We've blown the ash eastwards.

'Your spell worked, Dantakrura. Good news pours in every day. One kingdom after another bows to me and hails me as samrat. What news do you have for me?'

'I watch him. He knows I watch and wants me to know that. He's no longer in the ashram.' Jayadhwaja stiffened.

'Where does he go?'

'East. But he remains south of the Vindhyas. I've found his army.' Anger bloomed in Jayadhwaja.

'So, he wants to rule. How strong is this army? You said every Kshatriya is bound by the spell. Who are these people?'

'They aren't Kshatriyas, but call themselves the Malaya Kshatriyas. They are a few thousand, and all of them are at the settlement Parashurama is residing in at the moment.'

'I've heard of them. A nomadic people searching for something. But just a few thousand? What can he do with these few?'

'Not something, samrat. Someone. The Uddhatr. That's their name for Parashurama. He trains a select few for some tasks. Along with Agastya and Lopamudra.'

'Another interfering rishi,' Jayadhwaja spat. 'Meddling in other's affairs when they should be sitting in tapasya somewhere. But how do you know all this? You said he knows you watch.'

Dantakrura tapped the pouch at his waist. 'I have a new pair of eyes, and I'm very careful. Parashurama scans the people around him often, checking for spells. So do Agastya and Lopamudra. The nimisha I see their pupils turn up, I exit my host's body, leaving no trace of my spell. But, another curiosity! Access to the Malaya Kshatriyas' eyes is hard to come by. I'm denied entry into so many minds because I cannot sense them. I've never seen something like this before. It isn't a spell, but there is a protection at play that I do not understand. I've had to spend days searching, but I think I've found a mind now.'

The warlock exhaled, 'It is tiring, nerve-racking work.'

'We'll rest when he's dead. What's more?'

'Parashu. Rama. Not one word, but two. We knew nothing of him before he got that name. We know the weapon is Mahadeva's blessing. What if I can take the Parashu away from Rama?'

'How will that ever be possible?'

'I don't know how, yet. Your father was invincible. Undying, un-slayable. Yet, Parashurama did both. He overcame your father's power. If he found a way, so can we. I have to think ...' Dantakrura's voice trailed off.

'My plan is simple, warlock. If my spies confirm Jamadagni is alive, I move east. Think hard. Let's exterminate this pest and be done with it.'

Jayadhwaja walked away. He would send a message to his spies to check Parashurama's whereabouts. Time was of the essence. To have his vengeance, to kill this upstart and then, the Ashvamedha, to prove to the world he was a worthy successor to Karthavirya Arjuna.

Dantakrura's thoughts raced, choosing and discarding spells and rituals. He fantasised about holding the Parashu. It sent a shiver of excitement down his spine. That would be glorious. The samrat could have the earth, but with the Parashu, he could take on Indra himself. He played with that thought. He would need his army. Dantakrura grinned. He knew exactly what kind of army he needed. And what of that self-righteous idiot, Bhamaha? He'd read his thoughts when he watched through his eyes, listened to him prattle about all kinds of visions. It was clear he disapproved of Parashurama and his ways. He had a weak mind, gullible and easy to dominate. Sometimes, it didn't need a maharathi to defeat an enemy. A mahamurkha would do nicely.

—

Rama lit the five wicks of the brass lamp.

'*Om Namah Shivaya*,' he intoned. Agastya, Lopamudra, Bhargavi, Anantha and Akrita repeated after him. He placed flowers and tulsi leaves on each of the seven tiers and the kalasha and bowed before it. He did the same at the altars of Ganapathi and the padukas. The others followed and then sat on the southern wall's raised ledge. The disciples walked in, stepping into the pit with their right foot first. They prayed at the three altars, touched Rama's feet and filed out. Except for thirty of them, the first to receive his instructions.

The men stripped to their loincloths; the women had an additional swathe of cloth wound tight around their bosom. They sat in padmasana or sukhasana as they shut their eyes and let Rama lead them through several breathing exercises. Sometime later, they watched as Rama stood before them and invoked agni into his right palm.

'Stare into the agni without blinking. Let agni be all you see. The agni is all there is.'

Rama waited for a few nimishas and continued, 'Close your eyes. As you inhale, imagine the agni coming from my hand to your navel and entering your body. As you exhale, imagine agni's energy spreading through your body.'

He let them breathe for some time, extinguished the agni and then said, 'Open your eyes. It would take several years to teach what I know and to lead you forward step by step. We don't have the time, so I will teach what is necessary for our intent.

'The navel is the centre of the body. It is the bindu of the body. The power in your blows and strikes is transferred from your legs and hips to your arms and shoulders through it. The first principle: be aware of it. It is the seat of balance and power, and what you call gut instinct. It is the seat of your will, confidence and discipline.' He led them through a series of asanas to energise the Manipura chakra and told them to practise them every day before the lessons.

'The second principle. The body becomes all eyes. In the heat of the fight, your perception of your opponent's next move, his weaknesses, where you need to move and what strike you need to employ all come to you in a fraction of a nimisha. It is the body that perceives all this through the learning of the exercise drills and the energy in your navel. For this purpose, it is a second brain.

'The training will put calluses on your hands. It's a sign of your discipline. Learn well, and you will have calluses in your brain. The sign of a true warrior. There are three requirements to be a warrior. Ekagra, ichchashakti and atmavishvasa. Focus, will and confidence. And three skills: simhasya garjanam, vyagrasya sheegram and marjara laghavam. The roar of a lion, the speed of a tiger and the light-footedness of a cat. We begin. All rise.'

Akrita called for the bards and scribes to come in. Rama demonstrated the movements and broke them down step by step. He called out the steps as the scribes wrote them on palm leaves and the bards repeated softly, committing them to memory.

Two muhurtas later, he dismissed the thirty students, urging them to rest in the afternoon and practise again in the evening.

'Lopamudra and I will teach the ones waiting outside, and we can dig two more pits. We can divide the work that way,' said Agastya. Rama accepted.

'This is good, Rama. I like this method of instruction.'

'Pashupati, in his wisdom, has adapted the movements of pashus to the human body. I will teach eight of these animal manoeuvres,' said Rama. He called for the next thirty students to come in.

'It is an art you are teaching. Warriors of the body, mind and soul. Name it.'

'That thought did cross my mind. What do you think of khalurika prayoga?[6]'

'Perfect!' Agastya exclaimed.

They called it a day when dusk fell. Rama made his way to the smithy. He described the weapon he wanted to be

---

[6] Kalaripayattu

made to the iron smiths, the length, width and thickness of it. He wanted four variations of it. Rama drew it out on a parchment and also the shield he envisaged for the weapon. The blacksmiths pored over his sketch, asking questions about the grip, the hilt and the weight. He answered their queries and told them to get started right away.

He was walking back to Agastya's tent when Bhamaha approached him. The man pressed his palms together in a silent namaste. Rama guessed he was having trouble deciding the right name to address him.

'You've come to meet the barbarian after so many days,' said Rama. Bhamaha grimaced and stayed quiet, unsure how to respond.

'You want something. Ask away.'

'When will all this training finish?' asked Bhamaha.

'Why?'

'So you can come to my homeland with your army. Like you said you would.'

Rama folded his hands across his chest and stared into Bhamaha's eyes. Bhamaha looked away from his powerful gaze.

'Ahimsa in thought, word and deed, you said. Is telling a lie not himsa, then?' Bhamaha wrung his hands, shamefaced.

'I never agreed to come. This training is to help people fight for themselves. To win their victories. To deserve their freedom. Why didn't you even try to qualify for the training?' Bhamaha stood mute. 'Those people who came with you, seeking the Uddhatr, do they all still think the same?'

'Oh! A few have lost their way. Two of them, a man and a woman, even got selected by you. Shame! Shame!'

'Then ask them to help you once their training is over.'

'I already asked. They refuse to come,' Bhamaha wailed.

'Their brains are finally working. Who'd want to risk their lives to fight for people who call them barbarians?'

'But ... but ... it's their duty.'

'What is your duty, then?'

'To uphold ahimsa.'

'Then go back and be slaves to Jayadhwaja's army. Maintain ahimsa that way. Stand by what you believe and die for it. There's some honour in that, though paltry. Your beliefs are not worth a handful of soil, but at least stay true to them.'

'But we will all die. The women will continue to be violated, the children whipped, put to the sword. Do you not care for children, Rama? Are you so hard-hearted?' Bhamaha was crying now.

'Show some courage, Bhamaha, and I will come. If you shirk from violence, show me some moral courage. Throw these foolish beliefs out of your head. Has nothing you've seen shown you how wrong you are? Have you understood nothing of what I've said?'

Bhamaha wiped away his tears and stood proud. 'The evolved will face many tests, many temptations to forsake their path. Only the truly enlightened will have the courage to walk the path, even if Mahavishnu says otherwise. There. I have shown moral courage. Don't break your word now.'

'That's not what I asked, Bhamaha.'

'An avatara refuses to help till I give up my beliefs. I do not. What greater moral courage is there? The deaths of all our children are on your head if you refuse.'

The utter, blind foolishness of the man irritated Rama. And he was back to being avatara now. He fought to remain calm.

'Did you ask Maharishi Agastya?'

Bhamaha went red in the face. Rama waited. Bhamaha gulped and stammered, 'He ... He ... told me my beliefs were wrong. He ... doesn't have the intellect to understand.'

He grew vehement. 'Both of you think dazzling people with your powers and illusions makes you special. The truly special are common, who have no talent, who are just ordinary. The ones who are like sheep. They are the ones closest and dearest to god.'

Rama sighed in resignation. There was no end to this.

'Did he call you a fool?' Bhamaha's face became purple in embarrassment. 'No need to answer,' said Rama as he walked away.

Rishi and patni were waiting for him in the tent. Rama gulped down water from an ewer and was about to discuss the training routines when Lopamudra spoke instead.

'Before you start, there's something I must ask. Do the seven semicircular tiers in the pit have no connection with the seven murthis in the temple you visit?'

'The tiers are the seven chakras. Nobody I've asked knows anything about the temple; even my father and Shukracharya didn't know. The old Mahadeva temple in Indrapuri is just a temple for them. Nothing changes for them the way it changes for me.'

'Then it is a revelation for you to understand. Many ways to the truth, and each way reveals a new facet of it. But the tiers got me thinking. There are so many associations with the number seven. The Saptarishis, for instance. You've met four of them now. Could the murthis be of them?'

Rama thought it over. 'If one of the murthis is of my father, I would have identified that clearly, don't you think?'

Lopamudra nodded. 'There are other significations. Seven horses of Surya, the seven worlds above us, the swaras of music and the dweepas, to name a few. But I don't know if there would be murthis of all these.'

Rama agreed.

'Then I thought of what you said, that it was all about the mothers. And the All-Mother. Could it be the murthis of Parvathi and the Kritthikas? The seven mothers of Karthikeya?'

'There is a murthi of Bhadrakali in the main sanctum, Maathey. Bhadrakali, Parvathi, Lakshmi and Saraswati are all feminine manifestations of Parashakti. Since a murthi is in the sanctum, would it appear in a row of seven again?'

Lopamudra shook her head. 'I'd say no. But, interestingly, you said "feminine manifestations". Do you know the story of Andhaka?'

'Ah!' said Agastya, nodding in agreement.

Rama looked from one to another. 'I know he's an asura Mahadeva had defeated.'

'Yes. But how?' asked Lopamudra.

'I don't know, but I'll be glad for a tale.'

'Once, Parvathi playfully closed Mahadeva's eyes with her hands. All the worlds and realms plunged into darkness. Mahadeva's third eye manifested itself on his forehead and shone like a million suns to restore light to all creation. Parvathi withdrew her hands in a nimisha, and the third eye closed. In the intense heat caused by the opening of the third eye for a single nimisha, a drop of sweat fell from Mahadeva's brow. From that sprang Andhaka, so named because he was born blind.

'Hiranyaksha, Hiranyakashipu's brother and Prahlada's uncle, adopted the boy. He became the asura's overlord after Prahlada. His intense tapasya gave him the power to conquer the three worlds.'

'How many times have we heard that, haven't we?' Agastya chuckled.

'But Andhaka coveted Parvathi and fought Mahadeva to kill him.'

'What?' Rama was dumbfounded.

'They fought a terrible war. Andhaka and the hordes of asuras besieged Mahadeva but couldn't defeat him. But, Andhaka had a clever trick, a devastating power that was wrought for him by ...' Lopamudra waited to see if Rama could guess right.

'Shukracharya.'

'Yes. The Daityaguru. Every drop of blood that spilled from Andhaka's body generated another Andhaka. Soon there were crores of Andhakas battling Mahadeva.'

'So Mahadeva incinerated them all?' asked Rama.

'Nothing worked, Rama. Until Parashakti invoked her magic. She sent seven warriors to aid Mahadeva, fight the countless Andhakas and prevent his blood from touching the ground. They killed them all and broke Shukracharya's magic, and Mahadeva impaled the original one with his trishula. But Andhaka didn't die. He survived a thousand years skewered by the trishula. He begged forgiveness, forsook his power and ego and prayed to serve Mahadeva. And Mahadeva forgave him. Andhaka serves as his attendant now.'

Rama listened, rapt in the story.

'The seven warriors were women. Together, they were called the Saptamatrikas. The mothers' seven. They were the shaktis of seven gods, named after them—or perhaps, it was these shaktis that inspired the gods' names in the first place. The Saptamatrikas are Brahmani, Vaishnavi, Maheshwari, Kaumari, Varahi, Indrani and Chamundi. The shaktis of Brahma, Vishnu, Shiva, Karthikeya, Varaha, Indra and Yama.'

'Mothers' seven,' Rama whispered, his eyes on the hemp carpet that covered the floor of the tent.

'I'm not sure, Rama. The murthis could be of some other deities, the Saptasindhu, the seven rivers, for instance.'

Rama nodded absently, lost in thought. After a while, he said, 'Let it stay with me a while. I won't think it over, just let it be. When I'm in the temple again, I may have some answers.'

Lopamudra smiled. The pupils of her eyes turned up. 'Are you ready, then?'

Rama nodded eagerly.

'I will not chant, Rama. And you will not hear. So how will you learn the Lalitha Sahasranama?'

Rama's pupils turned up. He went into dhyana and saw himself before the mirror. He imagined Lopamudra seated before him in the tent, and in a blink, she was in the mirror, the whites of her eyes staring at him. Rama looked into those eyes and waited. The sound of the nothingness filled his ears. He waited. Slowly, a murmuring came to him from all around. It grew louder like it was the nothingness itself. He heard Lopamudra's voice, and countless other voices in chorus. The moment she started her chant, the Parashu appeared before him. Not in the mirror, but beside him as if it too was in dhyana. The rune on it pulsed with the chant. Rama heard, repeated, learnt and sang. All the nothingness was devotion and bliss.

A long time later, the voices faded away. Rama stayed in

dhyana, the silence alive with contentment. Agastya appeared in the void, not as an image or reflection but as if he was physically present there. *Was Agastya in my dhyana or is it the other way round? Was this even possible?* Rama thought.

'Yes, possible,' Agastya's voice was soft. 'But I'm not here to teach you that. I came to reward you.' Agastya's lips didn't move. Rama was hearing his thoughts.

'The reward is a mantra,' Rama spoke in his mind.

Agastya's lips curled into a delighted smile, and his thoughts spoke in Rama's mind. 'A reward for a Brahmakshatriya. The Trailokya Vijaya kavacha. The armour for victory in the three realms which will complement your divine weapon.'

'Not rishi or avatara, but Brahmakshatriya, you say. You think the kavacha will manifest differently, Maharishi.'

'Yes!' There was laughter in Agastya's thought. 'I am curious about that. If learning the chakras has been such a vastly different experience for you, perhaps even this will be so.'

Rama pressed his palms together and bowed his assent. And they began, Agastya chanting and Rama repeating. Soon, it was just Rama chanting as Agastya watched. Rama sensed the heat grow in his body, gathering at his navel like a red-hot bindu. The heat spread out from his navel. Agastya gasped. Rama continued.

He stopped when he grew aware of a third presence behind him to his right, where Agastya had his eyes fixed. It was a figure of heat and light, seated exactly like him. A nimisha later, Rama understood it was his subtle body. And it wasn't in the mirror but right next to him. He could see the nadis and the chakras, and it was all sheathed in golden light.

'The armour has manifested as the golden light around your

sukshma sharira,' Agastya murmured in wonder. The subtle body flowed towards Rama, enveloping him, coalescing with his body. Its glow seeped into him from head to toe, settling just below the skin. Rama looked at Agastya in surprise.

'Always the unexpected with you, Rama,' Agastya spoke loud. 'Armour that lies within the skin! Do you feel different?'

Rama shook his head. He moved his arms and twisted this way and that. Nothing different. Agastya snapped his fingers, and they were both back in the tent and out of dhyana.

Rama pinched himself. 'Where is the armour, Maharishi?'

'Gone!' said Agastya. 'It manifested this time because I chanted with you. You need to get siddhi of it. You must chant the mantra many million times before you can summon it as you wish.'

Rama prostrated himself before Agastya, clasping the maharishi's feet.

'Win, Rama!' Agastya blessed. '*Vijayi Bhava*!'

Four days later, the swords were ready. The edges were unsharpened as Rama had instructed; he didn't want grievous injuries during the demonstration. The thousand disciples gathered around him in the practice ground, armed with swords, spears and shields. He held up the first sword. The thin, broad, flexible blade was coiled in a tight circle against the hilt and held together by his index finger. He released the coil, and the blade flopped down, hanging loose.

'This is the weapon I promised you. The Naga Khadga, the snake sword, is my homage to the spiritual path of the Ahi and the gods you worship. This blade is an arm's length. You begin the weapon's practice with this length.' He picked up a second whip sword with his left hand and held it at head height. The blade dropped to the ground, its length matching his height. He let both fall and reached for a third—this one was even longer.

'Attack!' Rama ordered.

The inner ring of warriors charged and the whip sword flashed, its blade whirling around Rama in a blur. The warriors jerked back. Some leapt; some tried to duck under its arc. Rama adjusted his swing to counter. The supple blade curled around the warriors' shields, slapping their heads, shoulders and upper arms. It knocked weapons out of their hands, hurting fingers and wrists. It wound around bodies, lashing them and bruising them as it withdrew. Rama bent a knee and lowered his arc. Cries of pain broke out as it lashed ankles, shins and knees, pulling some off their feet. The thrown spears were deflected or had their shafts shattered. The attack ground to a halt.

Rama spun faster and struck. The whip sword hissed and thrashed like a steel serpent, forcing them to break ranks. Moments later, he stopped still. Some clutched their limbs in agony, others backed away as far as they could. He dropped the sword and picked up the fourth—this one had two blades, each flashing in the sun and as ominous as a snake rearing to bite.

'The snake sword is a melee weapon, useful particularly when you are outnumbered and surrounded. When you fight at close quarters and in tight spaces, this can clear up space quickly. It gives the advantage of reach. Unlike a spear, it can kill at a distance and remain in your hand. The blades I used are blunt. I think you can assess the damage I'd have done if they were sharp.'

Rama picked up a shield. 'A buckler shield. Thicker, smaller and lighter. You have to be agile and fast-moving and cannot be burdened by big, heavy shields. You can strap this on your back easily, leaving your hands free. And it will protect against recoil and accidental curl backs when you use the snake sword. We start training with these as soon as you are proficient in other weapons.'

A month later, Rama watched with satisfaction as the disciples went through their paces. He'd trained them hard, demanded complete dedication and they'd risen to the task. They had some way to go yet, but he knew they would get there. The training had aroused great interest, and people thronged to watch in the evenings. Rama saw a few children armed with twigs and sticks, mimicking the drills. He ran to Agastya.

'The children, Maharishi. Let's train them.'

Agastya looked around, 'No lack of enthusiasm but, there are just three of us, and we don't have the time.'

Rama thought it over. 'I'll select a few. Give them more lessons and teach them advanced techniques. Train them to be acharyas, so they can teach others.'

'How will you select?'

'We'll have the thousand duel each other and pick the best.'

Agastya laughed. 'Let's do it.'

A couple of days later, the three of them had picked seven

each. Now, they had fourteen men and seven women, ready to undergo preparations to become acharyas.

Rama taught them unarmed combat—how to strike with the flat of the hand, elbows and knees, and where to apply pressure in the body to maximise pain, incapacitate or even kill enemies. Not having a weapon was no longer a disadvantage for them. All of them gathered in Agastya's tent. Bhargavi, Anantha, Ekavira, Akrita, Raikava and Chandragupta. Lists of spies, ministers and other important officers were drawn up and updated every day. Discussions on the cities, towns and other places to be targeted had everyone offering suggestions. Agastya held up his hand for quiet.

'You need an insignia, Rama. Something like a banner that people can recognise. It will rally the oppressed to your cause and give them hope. A symbol for the revolt and fight.'

Everyone agreed, and all wanted Rama to pick the symbol. He promised to think it over. A few days later, he showed them a symbol drawn on a piece of parchment. An umbrella made of palm leaves and a pair of padukas, and between them the Parashu.

'The umbrella signifies protection, the padukas our commitment to walk the path of dharma and the Parashu our fight for it.'

Deep into the night, Rama went into dhyana. He pictured the temple in his mind, and he was there, inside the outer wall. It was night there too, and no light broke the quiet darkness. He bowed to the murthis and walked to the panel. Agni flamed in his hand as he walked from Ganapathi at one end of the panel to Veerabhadra at the other, and back again. The seven murthis were hidden as before.

How could he reveal the shapes that were straining against the skin of stone? The Saptamatrikas. If only he knew more about them. He thought hard. There had to be something in common between the gods and their shaktis. And they were battle goddesses. They should be carrying weapons. No, Brahma carried no weapon.

He held the agni close to the first obscure murthi and thought of the vahana, the mascots or mounts of the gods. A hamsa, a white swan for Brahma. He looked at the murthi and focused his thoughts on that divine hamsa. The first murthi resolved from the stone before his eyes. He stepped back in excitement. These were indeed the murthis of the Saptamatrikas. Here was Brahmani carved in black stone. His eyes studied the murthi's posture, its arms and embellishments. He bowed and stepped to the next one.

Garuda, he thought, and Vaishnavi appeared. Nandin revealed Maheshwari and Paravani, the peacock, brought Kaumari out of the stone. He had no idea of Varahi's vahana, so he thought of the boar's face. To his delight, it worked. Next was Indrani. He thought of Uchchaisravas, and nothing happened. Puzzled, he imagined Airavata, the elephant. Indrani's murthi shone like a black pearl in the light of the agni.

The last one confused him to no end. He thought of the buffalo, the noose, the mace. Nothing worked. He mused over it and imagined a skull. Chamundi, the shakti of Yama, emerged from the stone. The panel was complete. Rama danced with the joy of seeing the seven shaktis for the first time. Hours later, he came out of dhyana and rushed to Agastya's tent to break the news to them.

Agastya was in dhyana himself, and there was palpable anticipation on Lopamudra's face as she motioned Rama to wait and remain silent. Agastya opened his eyes a few nimishas later. The whites of his eyes stared at Rama.

'Kael,' Agastya said. Rama didn't understand.

'Listen,' said Lopamudra.

Agastya continued,

'*Aaru tamarayil poothavan,*
Yaezhil nirkkum pon Velayudhan,
Yaezhu thaayarin varam pera,
Thandaiyin karuththu ninaitthu kolga,
Por theeyil nannaiya nee,
Arindukol pazham nee.'

Agastya stopped and blinked. His eyeballs dropped down, and he was beside himself with excitement. 'It's a prophecy, Rama. For you! The seven murthis are the Saptamatrikas, the seven mothers from Andhaka's story.'

'But I didn't understand a word. And Maharishi, I saw the murthis in the temple just now. They are the Saptamatrikas. How did you know too?' said Rama.

'Tamizh,' Agastya replied. 'A language taught to me by Mahadeva after I came south of the Vindhyas. I'll explain the meaning. I didn't see the temple or the murthis, Rama. Only the prophecy was shown to me.'

'*Aaru tamarayil poothavan*. He who blossomed on six lotuses. Karthikeya. Velayudhan means he who holds the divine spear, the golden Vel. *Yaezhil nirkkum pon Velayudhan* means Karthikeya stands at seven. Seven of what? That I do not know.

'*Yaezhu thaayarin varam pera, thandaiyin karuththu ninaikka*. To receive the boon from the seven mothers, remember the father's lesson.

'*Por theeyil nannaiya nee*. When you bathe in the fire of war. *Arindukol pazham nee*. Know that you are the fruit.'

Rama mused it over. Seven of what? Which lesson? I am the fruit? He shook his head, unable to understand.

'I can offer some insight on the fruit,' said Agastya. 'When Ganapathi and Karthikeya raced to circumambulate the three worlds, Karthikeya set off on his vahana, the peacock Paravani. Ganapathi merely circled his parents thrice and won the prize, a fruit. The fruit of knowledge.'

Rama's pupils turned up suddenly, and the visual flashed in his mind. Mahadeva with Parvati on his left, both seated on deerskin in Kailasa. To her left was Ganapathi, standing. He circled them thrice and then moved half a circle to Mahadeva's right to receive the fruit. *Three loops and a half!* Rama's eyes returned to normal, but he didn't utter a word.

'Karthikeya was miffed. He came south of the Vindhyas. Mahadeva met him on a mountaintop. The words he uttered to console Karthikeya were "pazham nee". You are the fruit of knowledge. It resides in you. That mountaintop is named Palani in honour of these words.'

Rama nodded his appreciation for the story, but he still didn't understand the prophecy. And he'd learnt not to take prophecies lightly. He would remember and think it over. He brought his hands together in pranaam, bowed his head and thanked Agastya for his insight.

They waited in the pre-dawn darkness. The ashram was eerily quiet, like the tomb of a stillborn child. They'd ridden their horses hard, the rage of the samrat the whip, and his thirst for vengeance the froth in the horses' mouths. They'd dismounted and walked half a yojana through the jungle like predators. Jayadhwaja gestured for his men to spread out, pointing at the silhouette of the hut that was his target. Light flickered in the hut's window, and the men froze. The light steadied and grew stronger, and the men slipped away into the night. The door of the hut cracked ajar. Yellow light poured out of it as Renuka stepped out and placed the clay lamp on the stoop. Jamadagni emerged behind her.

Jayadhwaja watched as they hugged. Jamadagni spoke to Renuka, but he was too far away to hear anything. An owl hooted. The signal. His men were in place, divyastras ready, drawn against the man who was a master of the Dhanurveda. Jamadagni turned at the sound. He looked straight at where Jayadhwaja lurked. The samrat froze. Did the Saptarishi know?

Jamadagni sat on the stoop, in padmasana, with his hands nestled in his lap. Renuka sat beside him, her eyes not leaving him for a nimisha. The warlock whispered in Jayadhwaja's ear. Jayadhwaja waited, and he waited some more. Both husband and wife seemed deep in dhyana. It suited his plans perfectly. A couple of nimishas more. Then he charged, drawing his sword. The signalman following hooted twice. The signal that the attack had begun.

The hut drew closer. The husband and wife sat immobile with their eyes closed. Jayadhwaja screamed his vengeance as he raised his sword overhead. Renuka startled. Her eyes flew open. The warlock's spells smashed into her, pushing her back against the wall of the hut. The magic wound tight around her, stupefying her into paralysis. It crawled into her mouth and stifled her tongue. Her eyes watched, helpless, frightened, frantic.

Jayadhwaja reached Jamadagni. The Saptarishi was still as a corpse. Jayadhwaja's sword sailed an arc that sliced through Jamadagni's neck. The cut was clean. The head toppled to the ground. The body stayed upright.

Jayadhwaja roared into the night, feral, triumphant. His men turned, shooting their astras at the other huts. Explosions and fires erupted. Angry vines of red, orange and yellow flames bloomed in the night. Jayadhwaja grabbed Jamadagni's head by the hair and spat at it. He held it high and roared again. He looked at Renuka and laughed, his voice high and maniacal. Jayadhwaja sat before her, sneering at her helplessness. He placed Jamadagni's head in her lap and pressed his palms together in mock salutation.

The earth trembled and ancient trees shook as the astras destroyed the ashram. Jayadhwaja walked away. The signalman blew hard on the trumpet. The attack stopped, and the men fell back. Dantakrura stared at Renuka and Jamadagni's headless body. There was no doubt about it. The Saptarishi was dead. He couldn't detect a hint of life in the body. There was no Atharvan magic at play here, no illusion to trick them.

A long nimisha later, the warlock angrily walked away with one question in his mind. Why was there no blood?

13

The Heart of Compassion

Rama ...

The agni disappeared from Rama's palm as he looked around in confusion. He listened hard. Only the usual sounds, the controlled breathing of his disciples, rapt in the fire meditation. He stood still, unsure if it was sound, memory or imagination that had caught him off guard. He waited a long nimisha. Nothing. He turned his attention back to his disciples.

Rama ...

Just the meekest hint of a whisper wafting past his ears, kissing the fine down on his earlobes and fading without entering them. His senses snapped alert. His pupils turned upwards, and he scanned each person in the pit with the whites of his eyes. He saw no spells.

He emerged from the pit. There was nothing unusual around him; he heard the gentle breathing of the disciples on the practice ground, the faint sounds of the settlement before dawn and the forest further away. He saw Agastya come out of his pit and look in the direction of the forest. Rama turned to the entrance of the third pit, and a puzzled Lopamudra was already there. He walked to Agastya.

Rama ...

He froze, two steps away from Agastya. The sound was still soft, but now it was a sound. He heard the sharp intake of breath a little behind him. Lopamudra had also come.

'Do you hear it?' he asked.

Agastya didn't turn, but he shook his head. 'I sense something ... I don't hear anything.'

'What do you hear, Rama?' Lopamudra asked, her voice low and a frown on her face.

'It sounded like my name.'

'I don't hear anything either. But there is some ... I don't know what ... A pulsing. A strange disturbance. Who's voice is it?'

Rama couldn't identify the voice. It was oddly neutral, without inflexion, without gender.

'I don't know,' he whispered, scanning the grounds and everyone in sight.

Rama ...

He heard it clearly. Now, a harsh, guttural voice. A sound from an unwilling mouth, or a mouth unused to forming words. Almost inarticulate, animal-like. Lopamudra rushed to Agastya's side.

'I felt it again,' she whispered. Agastya stood mute.

Rama ... Rama...

The sound was a whiplash. It pierced his ears and lodged in his brain like spiked arrowheads. White hot rage surged in the sound. The voice was inhuman, shrill, and it made his hair stand on end. He sensed rather than saw Agastya's hands clutch at Lopamudra's. In a nimisha of utter, terrifying clarity, he realised Agastya was looking away to the west. Towards ...

Rama ...

It was a wail of incalculable loss and grief. A desperate cry for help. It was his mother's voice.

'Go!' Agastya screamed, but Rama was already gone, running as fast as he could, the Parashu flying after him.

'I fear the worst,' said Agastya. '*Bhagawati rakshaam dehi.*'

Rama ...

He raced over sand, rock and water, hurling the Parashu at anything that stood in his way. He felt the mad thumping of his heart in his chest and didn't care; he pushed himself harder. His breathing grew shallow, but he didn't slow, desperately hoping for a second wind.

Rama ...

Sweat broke out on his body as the sun beat down, and it was whipped away by his speed in an instant. Rain lashed down, and he roared, drowning out the thunder.

Rama ...

He thought about the divine ratha for a fraction of a nimisha and dismissed the thought. He wouldn't pause to summon it, and it wouldn't be of much use through the thick woodland. A corner of his mind kept count of the number of times he'd heard his name. Ten times.

Two muhurtas before dusk, he flashed past the empty settlements. He could smell the smoke and see trails of it above the treeline. Rama careened into the ashram, slowing down to avoid crashing into the throng inside it. He pushed his way through the wailing and lamenting, his worst fears looping in his mind. He broke through the crowd and went numb.

Rama ...

Twenty times, a quiet corner of his mind whispered.

He stared at his father's corpse, his body in padmasana and the decapitated head in his mother's lap. Several bodies, lifeless and covered with sheets, lay within the circle formed by settlers, forest dwellers and injured inmates. The ruin of the ashram lay behind it all.

Jamadagni was gone. Rama knew it deep in his heart. He knew Ma Chinnamasta wouldn't work her miracle again. He didn't know how he knew, but the cold, cold certainty of it gripped his heart. The Parashu slipped from his hand, and he stood simply, losing all sense of time.

'*It is time*,' the three words emerged from his memory. This is what Jamadagni had meant. And Ma had known. That was why they had sent him away. The three words snaked in his mind, relentless in their poisonous cruelty. He felt something on his left shoulder as if Jamadagni's coarse beard was tickling his skin as he held Rama in one last embrace. Rama raised his hands to hug him back and caught empty air. He dropped his hands and stood. The son who'd gone with an embrace and returned to a corpse. Sweat flowed down his body and brow. He simply stood.

Vishwavasu slapped him.

'Rama, Rama!' he screamed as he shook him by the shoulders. Rama blinked and stared at his brothers standing around him.

'Look at Ma,' Vishwavasu screamed again.

Rama looked. She sat unmoving. He did nothing.

'I can't remove father's head from her lap. I can't move her,' he shouted.

Rama snapped alert, and his pupils turned up. He looked again. He saw the spells of paralysis of body and tongue. Rama burned it away. Jamadagni's body toppled.

Renuka wailed, long and desolate. His brothers rushed to her. Her cry didn't abate. She bent forward as her lament rose to the skies as if cradling Jamadagni's head in her womb. She snapped upright, raised her head to the heavens above and shrieked like Kali on the warpath and in the throes of bloodlust. The crowd shivered and hushed. After what seemed an eternity, Renuka went silent abruptly.

'Saptarishi Jamadagni is dead. Pay your final respects. Build his pyre,' Renuka said as she rose.

Her four sons and the inmates of the ashram rushed to do her bidding. Someone spread a mat on the stoop, and they moved Jamadagni's body onto it. Renuka clutched his head to her bosom and placed it on the mat at the neck. She gazed at her husband for a nimisha and walked away, going past Rama without a word. Rama stood and stared.

The pyres for Jamadagni and the dead inmates were built quickly, overflowing from the small space in front of the hut and spreading across the ashram. The surviving senior renunciates rushed to get things ready for the last rites. Someone thrust a pot of water into Rama's hands, to bathe and purify himself before the rituals. He emptied it over his head and stood.

His brothers moved Jamadagni's body to the pyre. The rituals started, the chants barely audible even in the stolid hush of the crowd. The crowd parted for Renuka. She had two pots of river sand in her hands and two lids for the pots. The man conducting the rituals called to Rama. He moved, leaving the Parashu where it lay, and did as he was told. The rituals, the chants, the circumambulation around the pyre—everything passed in a blur for him. Vishwavasu lit the pyre first, and the crowd rained flowers on it.

The fire caught and blazed as if Agni himself was paying homage to the Saptarishi. The fire rose higher than the trees, the flames dancing orange, blue, yellow, red and white. The heat pushed everyone back. Some fragrance filled the air, and the wood crackled to some ethereal music. The crowd watched, awe-stricken. Rama stood rooted at the foot of the pyre.

It burned deep into the night long, long after the other pyres had died out. The crowd didn't leave. They sat around, a vigil for the Saptarishi's last passage. Soft hands and low voices offered consolations and prayers. Rama didn't acknowledge them. He stared at the pyre and stood through the night.

Dawn broke quickly. All that remained was a cold heap of ash. Jamadagni's body had returned to the five elements. His soul had passed to another realm. He was now memory, sentiment and grey, powdery residue of wood, flesh, marrow, blood and bone. Renuka rose from the stoop where she'd sat the night through. She bent by the ashes with a pot in hand. She blew, and the ashes parted, drifting into the air. Renuka reached into the ash and picked up a single red-hot ember the size of a pebble. She placed it in the pot and shut the lid. The wind surged through the ashram, pushing people back. It swept the ashes away as it disappeared above the trees, leaving one small mound in its wake. Vishwavasu rushed to gather it in an urn.

Renuka rummaged through the ruins of her hut. She emerged with a cloth satchel slung across her body and the darbha in her hands. Something was in the satchel. She called her four eldest sons and spoke to them together and then one at a time. She handed Vishwa the darbha and whispered instructions. They protested, they cried and pleaded, but Renuka hushed them all. Rama didn't listen in. He stood impassive. She placed her empty pot and lid in her satchel, gathered the pot with the ember in both her hands and came to Rama.

She stood beside him, both staring at the elongated patch of black on the earth that was the pyre a few hours ago. They stayed silent for a long while. The four brothers stood at the stoop, tears in their eyes, bafflement writ large on their faces.

'Your brothers will perform the rest of the rituals,' said Renuka.

Rama understood the implication. He didn't react.

'Who?' he asked.

'Jayadhwaja and his Abhichara mantravadin,' Renuka replied.

'Don't look back,' said Renuka as she turned and walked away.

Rama went to the Parashu, picked it up and followed. He didn't look back.

She walked, and he followed a couple of paces behind. She didn't stop, and he didn't speak a word. Through day, dusk, night and dawn, Renuka walked. Through jungle, up mountains, upon grass and mud and on barely visible trails. She didn't rest or eat. He followed faithfully.

She baked in the heat of the day and shivered in the cold of the night, but she walked. North, always north. As if she were an arrow shot out of an incredible bow. He didn't ask where they were going.

On the afternoon of the third day since they'd begun, she collapsed with exhaustion at the foot of a tree. Her lips were dry and cracked, and she tried to swallow saliva. Rama looked around for a stream, a pond, at least a Haridrabha tree, and realised he didn't have to. He picked up the nearest rock and caressed it, whirling it between his hands. He let the water drip into her mouth, squeezing as much as he could, till the rock cracked and turned to dust. Renuka drank and slept. Rama didn't. He hadn't since he'd left Agastya's side.

She woke at dawn. She refused the berries Rama had collected, walking away without eating. He dropped the berries and followed. Her pace slowed, but she stopped only at dusk. Rama dripped water into her mouth again, and she slept hugging the clay pot with the ember. He could feel its heat inside the pot. He didn't wonder why.

They walked down the northern slope of the Vindhyas, and she walked faster as the ground evened out. The forest dwindled into scrubland, and then onto flat plains. They drank their fill at the rivers and streams they crossed but didn't carry any water from them. They walked past settlements and villages and took nothing from the kindly folk who offered their produce.

The plains were vast, with no shade or water for yojanas in any direction. She walked slowly, her feet hurting, nicked and bruised by gravel and sharp stones. She refused to let him carry her. The sun hammered down on them, and there had been no rain for days now. The cloudless sky embraced them with a stoic, heavy stillness. Rama lost all track of time. She leaned on him as she walked, always clutching the pot and refusing to part with it.

He cut her a staff from a lone, small tree, and she smiled. She hadn't spoken a word since the ashram. A muhurta later, she collapsed again from the heat. Rama raced to find a stand of trees. He found it yojanas away, cut branch and bough, and carried it back to build a small tent for her. He could've carried her, but she wouldn't have wanted him to.

Days passed; she could barely walk. She shuffled, dragging her feet painfully, her blood speckling the ground. Her clothes hung loose on her body, and her skin hung loose on her emaciated frame. The flesh had long withered away; her eyes were a shade of murky grey, sunken in their sockets. Her full cheeks now clung to the bone.

She had no strength to hold the staff, but she clutched the pot with brown, bony hands and claw-like fingers. Rama didn't understand, didn't protest or plead. His mother was a living corpse carrying an ember from her husband's pyre. He knew there was nothing he could do about it.

She fainted and slept three days in the bough tent Rama made for her. He checked her pulse. She was barely alive. Worry broke through the numbness in him. He'd long since given up trying to go into dhyana. His mind rebelled against it, and dhyana couldn't be forced. The pupils of his eyes no longer stayed up, and he couldn't form the agnikund in his mind. He did the only thing that came to mind. Rama prayed to Ma Chinnamasta. He struggled to hold that terrible image that had danced before his eyes as he prayed. He didn't give up, he couldn't lose his mother too. So, he prayed with all his heart. Deep into the night, he felt a thump around him. He opened his eyes as if in a trance. The bough tent glowed red from within. He scrambled to it on his hands and knees, desperate hope in his eyes. Renuka lay senseless, but her gaunt body was crimson. Her mouth was open, and her tongue lolled out. He searched for a rock but knew immediately that it wouldn't do. The Parashu came to his hand. He cut across his left palm. He let the blood drip into the mouth, forcing out as much as he could from the wound till the mouth closed. Rama collapsed and slept a dreamless sleep.

He woke before dawn broke, compelled by habit. Renuka was awake and waiting. She turned and walked. He rose, feeling immensely tired and weak. Yet, he followed.

They'd walked for weeks now, months even, and Rama still didn't know. He could see the snow-clad mountains grow closer by the day. They were far north of the ashram, at the foothills of the Himalayas. He lost count of the number of times he'd cut his palms. Both were an ugly mess of bruises and open cuts.

They climbed the foothills slowly, one lumbering step after another. The brown plains gave way to lush green, deep valleys and the burst of colour of the wildflowers. The cold nipped at them by day and chewed at their very souls by night. And Renuka still walked, all skin, bone and resolve. The Ma he had known was long gone. A haggard, dirty old woman who wouldn't speak was beside him now.

At last, she stopped before a lake, shimmering icy blue, cold and tranquil. She sat by it and gazed into the water, before turning her gaze south as if she could see all the way back to the ashram. The sun climbed down from its zenith, painting the snow saffron-gold and filling the valley with a soft glow.

She put the pot and satchel aside and sat with her legs stretched out. Her eyes shut and her hands nestled in her lap. She stayed that way for a long time.

She opened her eyes and sighed deeply. She reached into the satchel for the empty pot. Renuka walked with it to the water's edge, her back to Rama. He stood mute, watching, tired out of his mind like he'd lived a thousand lifetimes in the span of one.

'It is time,' said Renuka. She walked into the lake.

'Ma! No!' Rama cried in anguish. She stopped and turned.

'He was the love of my life, and now he's gone.' She licked her lips and let her mouth hang open, as if her jaws ached from the strangeness of talking after months of silence. She stayed quiet for a while before she spoke again.

'Jamadagni's gone, but the power of the Saptarishi stays in this world. You understand?'

Rama didn't. He just stared at her. 'Will you ever know love, my son? Jamadagni's soul departed before Jayadhwaja attacked. But what he did to my husband's body, the cravenness to spit on a Saptarishi and the glee he took in placing his head in my lap is beyond sacrilege. Beyond words I have. He must pay.

'You are a chiranjeevi. So many will live and die, and so will their descendants through the coming ages, but you will still live and breathe. For lakhs of years, Rama. We are only at the beginning of Treta. Don't invite loneliness into your life. Have iron in your heart, but don't let your heart turn to stone.'

Renuka went quiet for a long while.

'Today is Ekadashi. A good time to go. It is my time. Better I go how I want to go.' She looked at him as if awaiting permission. Rama knew it wasn't his to give. He wanted to carry her away, to plead, to look away, to follow her to wherever she went. He knew it would be of no use. He knew he couldn't stop her. He did none of it. He stood mute and stared at her. She waited. A long time later, he nodded.

Renuka walked into the water. Rama watched as the water reached her knees, her waist, her neck. And then there was nothing. Just the clear, still surface of the water.

He sat at the edge of the water. A gentle breeze wafted past.

Rama ...

He looked up. The wind grew stronger and colder, rippling the surface of the lake. He shivered. He saw the pot drifting in the lake towards him, propelled by the wind. It stopped at his feet, and the wind died away. He gathered the pot and slid the lid open. It was full of water. He closed it and opened the other pot. The ember glowed hot and red. He shut it and looked in the satchel.

A bunch of dry palm leaves strung together through a small hole at one end. It was the bundle that Jamadagni had in his hands when he'd returned with Shukracharya from the jungle. He read the first leaf. It had only two words. Karunya Hridayam. The heart of compassion.

Rama's heart broke. He curled up in the sand and wept in the fading light of the setting sun.

14

Tetractys

Ekavira brought him to Bhargavi as she sat on the makeshift ledge under the ashwattha tree, talking to Anantha. 'The sentries spotted him and alerted me. He's asking to meet the maharishi. I know this man, he's the Uddhatr's brother. Vishwa.'

'Inform the maharishi,' said Bhargavi as she went to the man and cupped his face in her hands. 'Agastya told us about the Saptarishi,' she whispered. Vishwa didn't react. His head stayed bowed. Agastya and Lopamudra came quickly with Ekavira at their heels. In a nimisha, Akrita hugged Vishwa close, crying his heart out. He had no words of consolation. Agastya sat on the ledge and waited.

'Ma and Rama have gone north,' Vishwa spoke softly. Nobody said a word. Vishwa stared at Agastya, willing him to respond, to say something.

'You will not see Renuka again,' Agastya said finally. Vishwa burst into tears and Akrita was stunned into silence.

'But the Uddhatr is gone too. What are we to do now?' said Bhargavi.

'You do what he tasked you with. He picked the best

fighters you have and trained them hard. It's been months since he left, and we have continued to train. I think it's time to begin the war. Send the warriors out to the places we'd decided. Remember, Rama touched the foreheads of the twenty-one leaders. He can speak to their minds if he wishes.'

'Will I see my brother again?' Vishwa asked.

'I do not know, Vishwa. I cannot see the path of his future,' Agastya replied. Silence smothered the group again.

'Ma asked me to come to you, told me it was time,' said Vishwa to Agastya.

'What did she say? What were her exact words?'

There was a sudden sharpness to Agastya's eyes and voice. 'That it was time for my unbecoming ...' Vishwa stopped as Akrita gasped suddenly. 'She said I've been chosen for something. She didn't say what. That I'd become Vishwa, I'd died and now ...' Vishwa stopped and started again, 'I don't know what her words mean.'

'You will once I narrate the saga of Parashurama. I don't think you know all of it,' said Agastya. Vishwa nodded without understanding and stood quietly again, working up his courage to say something important.

'I don't have much,' Vishwa's voice was leaden with grief, 'But Ma insisted I give you this as dakshina and ask if you will accept me as shishya.' He drew the darbha out of his cloth bag.

Agastya stared at the grass in surprise. His pupils rolled up, and he exclaimed, 'Darbha of the Vishwayonika! My child, I accept!'

Vishwa knelt before Agastya, dropped his bag and held out the darbha with both hands. Agastya accepted the offering, and it caught fire. The column of smoke rose thick and sparkling white. It reached the leafy canopy of the tree and descended on Vishwa's head, bathing him in water from head to toe. 'Fire father, water mother,' said Agastya. Vishwa pressed his palms together and bowed his head. Agastya placed his right hand on it, and Vishwa shook like a leaf in the wind. 'You unbecome Vishwa and begin anew now. I name you for the grass dakshina, the anointment of water and the burn of fire. You become Trinadhoomagni, and so shall you be called henceforth. Like the grass, you will burn, and new soil the ash will fertilise.'

Agastya gathered the ash of the burnt darbha into his left hand and smeared it across Vishwa's forehead with three fingers.

'*Om Namah Shivaya*! Welcome home, shishya.'

Time ... Relentless. Ticking away. Inconsequential to him. He'd lost track of it. He avoided being aware of its passage. There was a world out there, but he'd separated himself from it. He understood why but didn't know what to do about it.

Day and night ... They didn't matter. It was always dark in his cave except for the occasions he'd invoked Agni in his palm. The cave was halfway up a mountain and at the end of a tunnel he'd had to twist and turn and squeeze through to enter. The Parashu was there with him, and the satchel and some kindling he didn't remember gathering.

Food ... He hadn't eaten in a long time now, and there was no sense of hunger in him. The air he breathed and the water he'd melted off the icicles were enough. He knew how to keep the agni in his body burning so the cold didn't affect him.

This was all there was to him. Air, fire, water, earth. And his thoughts.

He glanced at the two pots. One with fire, the other with water. *Fire father, water mother*. He'd come round to understanding it, at least he thought so. He understood in his mind. But all his thoughts couldn't dispel the shard of icy numbness in his heart. No agni could melt it.

Jamadagni had been irascible once, and he'd changed. The master of Dhanurveda hadn't used a single weapon against Arjuna or Jayadhwaja. He'd said he was the balance to the Brahmakshatriya. Renuka's beheading had brought about a profound change in Jamadagni. That unspeakable violence against his wife and four sons had shaken him. It had to be done, no doubt, and Jamadagni hadn't shied away from the task. That eventful day flashed through Rama's mind. He knew the sheer desperation that would've coursed through his father, hoping that at least his youngest son would step up to the task. A task no son should be asked to perform. A task no son should agree to.

Jamadagni never forgave himself for slipping in the quest for the mantra, for what he'd done to Renuka and his sons and for what he'd asked Rama to do. Rama was utterly convinced that Jamadagni knew Jayadhwaja was there, lurking near the ashram on that fateful dawn of his death. How and when he'd known, Rama would never know. But Jamadagni knew he'd be beheaded and had accepted it. His ahimsa wasn't to run away and bemoan reality, but to face it with courage.

Both his parents knew when it was time to pass on. Rama would never know. Maybe it would happen in the next Manavantara, but even that was just a guess.

Renuka had made him walk away. To teach him this part

of his life was over, that being a chiranjeevi meant that death would never be a friend. He'd died once, and come back to never die again for yugas together.

Death wouldn't touch him. It could cavort and dance all around him. Entertain him, if he so wished. Or go about changing the garbs of the souls if he ignored it. For that is what death is. Death is a tailor. Yama was fearsome, but all he did was stitch your new garb with all your karmas, vasanas and desires, point out the wombs available for your rebirth and let you work things out yourself.

Renuka wanted him to know that a relationship that was a lifetime to others would be a few nimishas to him. Ephemeral, leaving wisps of memory and longing. She made him make a clean cut from the past. A harsh, hard way to do it, but she'd put herself through it too. And had finally gone her way, asking for permission she did not need. Enormous love was there in those few nimishas she'd waited ... All the love in the world. And all the hurt.

He looked at the palm leaves. A thousand times he'd picked it up to read, a thousand times he hadn't. He'd flipped to the last leaf and seen what was written there. *For Rama*, it said, and below were two syllables. *Pha* and *Da*. Jamadagni was still teaching. That too was all the love in the world. And all the grief.

Two pots. One with an ember that wouldn't die, the other with water that wouldn't spill. Two syllables. What was he to do with these?

He was the man in the mountain who wanted to go down to the people. To give them his treasure, his knowledge of the path, to deliver them from their misery. To show them the light, to speak to them the words their ears and souls needed. The souls that needed liberation weren't only in the Parashu, there were so many more in the world. The souls in the Parashu had shed the garb of their bodies, the ones outside in the world still had their garb on. They both awaited, but he didn't trust himself.

The fury at Jayadhwaja's insult to Jamadagni burned in him. And in that volcano of wrath was a shard of ice. The numbness. His mind could grasp it, but his heart didn't. And he didn't know how to reconcile the two. Have iron in your heart, but don't let it turn to stone, his mother had warned. The iron was there. So was that shard, slight but solid. As long as he had it, he was dangerous. To humanity, to life in this realm. For all he'd learnt of the path, he'd be the one to forsake it, to turn to adharma if he didn't melt that shard. And he didn't know how.

Maybe this is what the world called loneliness.

He lost count of the number of times he'd chanted the Lalita Sahasranama. That was joy and relief. It had blown away the blankness enveloping his mind. He'd chanted the mantra given to him by Agastya, and he had siddhi of the kavacha. He could go into dhyana now, he could see the mirror and the temple. The pupils of his eyes turned up, but the numbness in his heart stayed. The heart chakra in the mirror flickered dimly, barely there. He couldn't afford to have the light stay that way. He couldn't turn into the monster he'd killed. The world couldn't afford another Karthavirya Arjuna.

That is all there is to the world, hurt and grief. *Losers whine, and winners take what they want and care nothing for who objects*, said the other voice. Rama wondered what this was. This contrary voice, almost like a beast inside him. Perhaps it was always there, but had found voice only after he'd started this journey up the chakras. He dismissed it. He'd think about it later.

Time relentlessly ticking away. Suddenly of prime consequence. Days passed in furious thinking and desperate hope. If only he knew how to reach the guru. If only he knew the yantra for him. So far, the yantra hadn't come to him in dhyana, nor any mantra.

His own words flashed in his mind. Ekagra, ichchashakti, atmavishvasa. The intent was important, and he was clear. To reach Guru Dattatreya. A small idea sprouted in his mind. He didn't need the guru's yantra. He needed a yantra to reach out to him. Could he make one of his own?

Rama focused his mind, confidence coursing through him. He knew the basic forms, the bindu, the circle, the nested square and the lotus petals. The symbol for earth was the square, for water, the crescent and fire was a triangle.

Triangle! An upward-pointing triangle denoted male, and the downward, female.

Rama cleared the ground before him. He went into dhyana. His pupils turned up. He saw himself seated in the cave. He was in the mirror, in its nothingness. He drew the yantra.

Rama made three bindus of an upward triangle on the ground. They symbolised the Trimurtis, whose manifestation in this realm was Guru Dattatreya. He considered joining the three bindus to form a triangle but decided against it. The Avadhuta wasn't bound by society or the Shastras. He was free. There could be no lines for him, only bindus.

He stared at it, sensing an incompleteness. There should be more. He thought of his intent. To reach the guru. Who wanted to reach him? He, Parashurama. Who was he? A

Brahmakshatriya, an avatara, a future Saptarishi. Rama dismissed the options. It would mean little to the Guru. A shishya! A disciple was reaching out to the teacher. Rama smiled. He knew what to do.

In the mirror, his yantra appeared around him, like it had when Bhamaha had demanded proof. The beam of the amsha blazed from his forehead.

'Guru Dattatreya, your shishya calls out to you. For the blessing of your presence, for aid, for teaching,' Rama prayed in the cave and the nothingness.

The three bindus glowed red in the mirror. He drew two more, just below and to either side of the topmost bindu—they shone white. Between the red and white bindus, he added three more. Then, in the last row between the red ones, he placed two additional bindus. As soon as he made them, all turned white. It was a triangle of bindus. No lines at all. A dasabindutrikona.

He needed a hymn, a mantra to go with this sacred geometry. He didn't know any hymns of the guru, but if he was reaching out, it had to be something special. Something of significance. And then the answer came to him. Syllables! His journey was the path of beeja-mantras, and though he didn't know the beeja-mantra of the guru, he could still use syllables. A syllable for each bindu!

Rama stared at the triangle, his mind racing. Four lines of bindus. Ten bindus in total. If this yantra, instrument, was to work, he had to compose a tetractys verse. The first line of one syllable, the second of two and so on. And a fifth line of ten syllables, the total number of bindus. He composed carefully, taking his time till he had his verse ready. He pressed his palms together in prayer and chanted.

Te
Shishyah
Upaiti
Tvaam sankatena
Shrunu praarthanaam aagaccha guro!

Your
Shishya
Approaches
You in dire need,
Hear my prayer and come, O great guru!

To the guru, he surrendered his five senses. Five of the seven white bindus turned red. He surrendered his mind and his sense of self. The last two bindus in the lowermost row turned red. Rama pressed his palms together and whispered, '*Om Gurave Namaha!*'

In the mirror, he surrendered his yantra into the ten bindus.

The tetractys came to life. The bindus rearranged into one single point, then into a circle, then into a bindu within a circle. White lines flashed through them, forming triangles and polygons. The shapes changed. The mirror disappeared. A triangle of light formed, a circle also of light touching the apexes. Circles upon circles of lotus petals bloomed, radiating from the triangle, and all within a nested square. Rama saw the yantra for a fraction of a nimisha before the nothingness itself filled with light. He floated in the soft brilliance and serenity.

In the cave, the Avadhuta sat before him.

He was a being of light, his mortal frame suffused with an extraordinary radiance. Only the faint contours of his body could be glimpsed in it. His face was benign and smiling. Softly arcing, long eyebrows were the only evidence of hair on his body. No beard or topknot. No rudrakshas or japamalas. Long arms with slender fingers. A feeling of grace and auspiciousness filled the cave. The guru chuckled, and Rama's heart leapt with joy.

'You have reached me, Rama.' His lips didn't move, but that ever-so-gentle voice was in Rama's head. The guru looked at the yantra and smiled. 'The Saptarishis have taken measure well. You come up with a way when none seems to exist. Ingenious to use syllables as sulba, the thread to create a sutra. A formula of simple progression for your hymn.'

Rama didn't know what to say. He suddenly didn't want to say anything at all, only bask in that divine aura.

'The man in the mountain wishes to go down into the world but distrusts his heart. He fears it may turn to stone. What do we do about it?'

Rama sat silent, his mind blank, his soul filled with the sight of the Avadhuta.

'We are in the mountains. The air is pure and the flowers bloom.'

And in a blink, they were in a meadow below an audumbar tree. The air had a snap and fragrance to it, of flower and hope, possibility and joy, beauty and grace. It filled Rama's lungs with prana, his heart with the warmth of home and his mind with sacred chant. The mountains around them embraced the skies, kissing clouds into existence and pouring their love into clear, tumbling streams. The blades of grass were their stories of love infinite, the snow their imperious nobility. Thousands of blooms of every colour possible danced the glory of that vast love, and the wind carried the music from their hearts.

'When in the mountains, sing! Sing of life, of love, of how to live and how to die. Sing the lessons you learnt and wish to teach. Sing of dharma and valour. Sing the song in your heart.'

'Rama, sing and heal. I wish to hear Parashurama's geeta.'

Rama made to speak, but his tongue didn't utter a word. He'd chanted the hymns of the Vedas before but had never sung like this. He didn't know the words of his song. He didn't know the tune of his heart. Rama didn't know if he had a song.

He thought of Renuka and Jamadagni. The two pots and the palm leaves appeared before him. All the love in the world.

He thought of all that he'd been through. The Parashu appeared before him. All he'd learnt of life and truth.

He looked into the gentle eyes of the Avadhuta. And Rama sang ...

Namah, to pitrus old, whose whispers thread the breeze,
To my guru, the sage of boundless sight,
To Mahadeva, lord of bhasma and peace,
I bow where silence carves the atma's delight.
To Devi's lotus feet, my mortal heart's release,
This lyric I offer to Thy crimson effulgent light.

O Mother! Womb of stars and timeless sea,
Thy grace awakens hymns of eternity.

Storm of my grief dims not devotion's fire,
To Lalitha, my song soars in mystic flight.
Her glance ignites the embers of sorrow's pyre,
A warrior's love that pierces mortal night.
No blade can rend what bhakti does inspire,
Her name banishes all plight.
O Tripurasundari! My atma's fervent desire,
In Thee, my spirit takes wing higher.

She is the dawn, the dusk, the breath between,
The pulse of the earth, the void where universes play,
In Her dissolve all forms, seen and unseen,
She is the chit that holds both silence and the fray.
No shore confines Her tide, Her entirety no eye can glean,
She weaves the worlds, yet stands beyond their sway.
O Sarveshvari! In Thee alone I find,
All gods and the brahmanda enshrined.

In Her, the dark and light embrace as kin,
Parashu and kamala bloom from single root,
She dances joy where sorrow's reign begins,
Her maya cloaks the truth in veils astute.
Beyond the states—waking, dream, sleep's thin grin—
Her stillness mocks the mind's unyielding suit.
O Mahamaya! Your lila, both fierce and tender spun,
The Many and the One in You are one.

To know Her is life's unyielding quest,
To chant Her name through toil and fleeting breath,
In worship's flame, the soul finds truest rest,
To merge in Her transcends the sting of death.
No creed, no clan can bind what She has blessed,
Her love annuls the chains of rebirth and death.
O Mahakali! Goal of all my earthly strife,
To merge in Thee is the purpose of my life.

In Shiva's tandava, worlds take flight,
Shakti's pulse bids all to breathe and grow,
Their union spins the braid of day and night,
A dance where stillness meets the river's flow.
She is life's unyielding might,
He holds the void below.
O Maheshvari! Thou are both, the One Supreme!
Life's water and death's ember within Thy boundless dream.

With sight, I see Her hues in sky and flame,
With sound, I hymn Her nada pure and deep,
Touch offers strength to bear Her sacred name,
Taste savours grace, scent wafts where roses weep.
Through chakras seven, kundalini's claim,
Ascend to Her in rapture's sweep.
O Parashakti! The five senses bow, the serpent wakes to sing,
Her throne is within, where mortal souls take wing.

She loves the clash of shastra in Her name,
The axe that carves through pride's brittle crust.
She craves the sage who masters shaastra's flame,

Whose wisdom turns ego's boast to dust.
In battle roar, Her laughter stakes its claim,
In dhyana, Her compassion we must trust.
O Sarvamangala! May Thy devotees arise
With might and truth to storm adharma's lies.

To thy feet, O Mother, this I lay,
A warrior's boldness, a poet's fragile plea,
Take Thou this song, my very being, I pray
And bind me ever in bhakti to Thee.
No boon I seek but to never stray,
Thy glance alone is my soul's eternity.
Shree Matrey Namaha! My heart's last call,
Thou are the One, the Only, the All in all.

Rama closed his eyes and nestled his palms together in his lap. A deep silence settled over him. A languid warmth spread across his chest, and he was enveloped in an embrace, gossamer soft and divine. He slipped into dhyana, and he found nothing there. No mirror, no temple, no nothingness. He sat on a mellow golden light that rose and drifted around him like drifting snow. All around him was a wall of white that tapered like a dome to a pinnacle above him.

No, it wasn't a wall. He could discern faint lines in the white, broad at the level he sat, and gracefully arcing upwards to the point of the pinnacle. Like ... like closed petals. Twelve petals. And he knew where he was. He was in the lotus of his heart chakra, the Anahata. His heart filled with gratitude to Guru Dattatreya, and in the white silence came a thrum that he could *see*. The thrum of the beeja akshara of the Anahata.

'Yam,' Rama intoned, letting the vibration of the syllable

play over him. With a burst of extraordinary bliss, the twelve petals of the lotus opened out and away from him. His heart leapt with joy. There was nothing around him. All was dark. It was just him seated on the lotus, floating on nothing.

Then there was light, and it came from below the lotus, spreading golden rays as the dark slowly receded. Rama felt an indescribable urge to look down at the source of the light. The lotus tilted, the light in it somehow holding him steady. The green stalk of the lotus twisted away from him like an iridescent serpent. At an incredible distance, the stalk disappeared into the navel of a gigantic sleeping being. His body was blue, of a radiance that boggled the mind, but Rama's heart sang a rhapsody of bliss. He had four arms that held a lotus, a mace, a conch and a discus. He seemed afar and all-encompassing, an arm's length away and somehow within him ... within everything. Rama brought his hands together at his chest and chanted, '*Om Namo Narayanaya*!'

Narayana transformed ...

A being with the five symbols of Mahavishnu emblazoned on his arms, shoulders and chest. The being was him. Rama, the avatara. The eyes opened, golden light emanated from its body and the dark disappeared. It looked at him, the Rama in the lotus, the mortal Rama. The implacable gaze of dharma in the eyes of the being bored through him. In response, the amsha's light emanated from his forehead in response.

Narayana smiled, and Rama's entire being vibrated with joy beyond compare.

'My avatara ...' said Narayana.

Narayana's gaze turned compassionate, full of love for him, the human who had undertaken the arduous journey to spark the Amsha and fulfil its potency. Compassion for the heartbreak, the grief, the fury and the superhuman effort. Narayana reached with his index finger. Rama extended his own, and the incredible distance was bridged. In the infinitesimal gap between their fingers, the shard of his heart shattered into dust. The fingers touched, and an incredible warmth spread through Rama's body.

'You have my aid,' said that divine dhwani, that celestial sound. Rama blinked, and he was back in the cave.

The guru sat before him, smiling. His index finger was on Rama's chest, exactly above his heart.

Guru Dattatreya withdrew his finger. 'You have been wedded to your purpose, Rama. Driven to seek answers, and relentless in your pursuit. You forgot to be kind to yourself. You became all avatara and forgot you are mortal. Rama, you are both. You told everyone to treat you as a human being but forgot to remind yourself. Now, you are in balance.

'Sometimes, a pause will take you further on your path than ceaseless striving. The shard is gone, and you know to never allow it to form again. But it leaves a scar. A reminder that there has been a wounding and a healing. The scar is the fort, the circle that will keep shards from forming again.'

Rama bowed to the guru.

'Do you realise it was inevitable that I would come to you? Even if you didn't find a way to reach me?'

'How so?' asked Rama.

'The concern you have for your shishya. Your urge to help him along his path. His devotion to you. All this would have compelled me. How can I treat my shishya any different?'

Rama bowed again. The guru placed his right hand on Rama's head. Rama's pupils turned up on their own accord.

'*Athatho Deeksham Vyakhyasyamah*,' he said. 'I will explain what Saptarishi Jamadagni saw but didn't understand. Only I can do that because it concerns the other disciple of mine. The one that strayed from dharma, the one you slew. Arjuna.'

'Two syllables your father left for you. One I will explain, the other you need to realise. Pha is the Beeja-akshara to invoke Arjuna. You are the avatara that killed him, and his soul lies trapped in your Parashu. He awaits judgement. I grant you the power to deliver judgement. Arjuna has unbecome, has died, and you will decide what becomes of him now.'

Rama thought awhile. 'You have set me a test, Gurudeva. How can I use the syllable?'

The guru smiled and stayed silent. Rama wondered why. Then it struck him.

'I don't know how to reach the souls trapped in the Parashu. I must discover that first.'

Still, the Guru waited, and it finally dawned on Rama.

'*Devastam sarvarupah pasavo vadanti, vyakta vak-ascha avyakta vak-acha*. All forms of life, and even objects, speak a language of their own, whether articulate or inarticulate. The Parashu too has a language. So, I must find its beeja-akshara. You want me to *see* it.'

'Well deduced,' said the guru. 'You've already seen the beeja-aksharas of four chakras. You are the master of the Parashu. Only you can do this. Enough, for now, Rama. The world awaits. There will come a time when you will join me as shishya. Until then ...'

'Wait!' Rama exclaimed.

'Did you know I will die and become a chiranjeevi? Did you already know what would happen? And what will happen in the future?'

'I knew you would both die. What would happen after

your death depended on the choice you made. "The fork in the path of dharma", remember? You chose right. You turned possibility into reality. So, we are here now.

'As for the future, Maharishi Agastya told you he doesn't see all the grahas. Even nadi jyotisha fails. The prophecy, too, is for you to understand. It means you decide, Rama. Break the world or build it, your actions will decide it. Not doing anything is an option you have forsaken.

'In times like this, it is always better to follow one's counsel. Your instincts have led you true thus far.'

Rama nodded.

'Do you know why you are a chiranjeevi and a future Saptarishi?'

Rama smiled. 'You sent me a shishya right at the beginning. Akrita is a blessing to me. He taught me to be a guru. I think you intended that. After the Saptarishis took measure, it struck me that you desired to teach this path to many and also to someone in particular. Someone who needs a guru who knows the Vedas and the path of the Ahi. That's why I was chosen.'

'True,' said the guru. 'And why chiranjeevi? And what does it mean to be one?'

Rama shook his head. He didn't know.

'Because the particular person is an avatara. He will be born in Kali Yuga, and he will seek you as a guru. A guru of shaastra and shastra. And who better for this than a Brahmakshatriya? His name will be Kalki.'

'Kalki,' Rama mused, 'the destroyer of foulness.'

'A chiranjeevi is one whose body heals faster than it decays. This extends the lifespan enormously and slows ageing. There will be other avataras to meet. What you must do when you meet them is for you to realise. So much for you to learn. So much more than you think. Await my call, Rama. Three and a half times, I've come to you already.'

Rama prostrated himself before the guru. A nimisha later, the light disappeared, and the cave was as before. Three and a half times? Rama mused. First at the Naga grove as an Ahi and now. Why did the guru say three and a half then?

15

Pha

Rama squeezed out of the tunnel that led to the cave. He wondered why he hadn't cut his way through with the Parashu. The cave had been a womb in the mountain, a place to heal his heart and emerge restored. Restored and dirty, Rama mused as he looked down at himself. He was plastered with grime and dust, his dhoti sickly brown and his hair and beard had grown long and was caked with dirt. He whirled the Parashu, and it wasn't any heavier. He hadn't lost his strength, and he still didn't feel hungry. Remarkable.

It was a little past dawn, but he didn't know which day it was. He wondered about Akrita, Agastya, Lopamudra and the Malaya Kshatriyas. From this high on the mountain, he could see much of the heavily wooded valley. Winding through the deodars and pines was a stream. Rama descended to make his way down to it.

He washed his dhoti and loincloth, spread them out to dry and swam naked in the stream, enjoying the cold, white purity of it, glad for the use of his muscles and the fresh air. He clambered out after a long, lazy swim and perched on a rock, letting the sun dry him out as he mulled things over. A couple of muhurtas later, he dressed and checked the satchel. The pots and the palm leaves were intact. Again, his mind baulked at reading Jamadagni's words, and he didn't understand why. *For Rama*, the last leaf said, and the two syllables were below. Did that mean the rest of the leaves were not to be read by him? So many answers were still left to be found.

Rama searched around for some shade and settled down in padmasana. He went into dhyana and looked at himself in the mirror. The Anahata chakra glowed in the shape of a six-pointed star within a circle of twelve lotus petals. Two triangles, one pointing upwards and the other downwards, formed the star. He'd seen the four beeja-aksharas for the four chakras, and the beeja-akshara for Ganapathi when the god had appeared before him. How was he to find the beeja-akshara of the Parashu? It had been with him for long. He'd mastered it, but he'd never seen its seed syllable.

He imagined the Parashu and meditated upon it. No sound came to him in the nothingness. He focused on the rune. It glowed in his dhyana, yet no sound. A long while later, he eased out of dhyana. It was well into the night. Time had slipped by fast.

Rama stretched his legs. Not tired, not sleepy, not hungry. He paced about, not thinking, not worrying. He went down to the river, washed his face drank some water and went into dhyana again at midnight.

As he gazed at the chakras in the mirror, a realisation dawned. He had to focus on the next chakra, the the Vishuddhi chakra in the throat area. To *see* the beeja-akshara and bring it from Para to Vaikhari, from *seen* to *spoken*. All the previous syllables had come to him during action or because of it. This time, he was seeking the syllable in dhyana, and he didn't know what to do or expect. He gazed at the faint pulsing light of the fifth chakra and emptied his mind. Nothing happened, but he waited. Ever so slowly, he grew aware of a vibration, inarticulate and distant. He didn't grasp it or pursue it. He simply waited. And the vibration, the spandana grew louder. It was there, around him, waiting for him to *see*.

Rama's mind raced as he thought of what to do next. How does one hear with the eyes? *See* the sound? People who'd grown hard of hearing guessed words they couldn't hear by the movement of the lips of the speaker. One could see a bee at a distance and imagine the buzz of its wings. But these were sounds the hearer already knew, sounds they'd heard before. It was one sense using memory to compensate for the lack of input from another.

Rama paused his train of thought. Compensating. The five senses worked in tandem but separately to provide inputs the mind then made sense of. He had to get them to cooperate, not compete or compensate. And he knew what to do.

Rama imagined a bindu in his mind and surrendered his five sense organs to it. The syllable burst into his mind. He *saw* it in his mind, the sound of it, the intonation of it. And his mind chanted along. *Ham*. The mantra of the Vishuddhi chakra. The chakra glowed in the mirror. It was a circle ensconced in a downward-facing triangle, which was itself inside a circle of sixteen lotus petals. He continued to chant, happy he'd succeeded. He lost himself in the chant, oblivious to the mirror and the nothingness. Only the bindu existed for him.

His chant stopped on its own accord, and utter silence enveloped him. The bindu disappeared, and all his surrendered senses went blank. Intense white light blazed.

Rama was somehow sure that it was not in his mind, it was in his consciousness, in his soul. Notes of some divine music wafted towards him. Strings pulled and plucked with grace, giving off a joyous melody. A veena played all around him. He didn't know if he heard saw or breathed or felt or tasted the notes. It was all at once, and he could not differentiate. All he knew was that it was absolute bliss. He lost the feeling of having a body; he was all soul, all joy. As if his atma had touched something that was the same as it, but was indescribably immense. An immensity of ecstasy.

In that bliss, the hymn came to him, to his soul, whole and unmistakable. The white faded, and the nothingness and mirror formed before him. His senses functioned as normal. He chanted the beeja-aksharas of the five chakras in turn, starting from the Muladhara at the base of his spine and moving up. He brought forth the light in his forehead and invoked agni into a yagnakund before him in the mirror. The rishis described sound at four levels. Vaikhari of the mouth, Madhyama of the breath, Pashyanti of the eyes and Para was telepathic. Rama recited the hymn he'd *seen*, the truth he'd realised, at all four levels. With proper pronunciation as Vaikhari, with all the pranashakti he had as Madhyama, learning and devotion in his heart as Pashyanti, he surrendered his mind to the truth, the satya of the hymn as Para.

> '*An no yagnam Bharati tuyam etu, Ila manusvad iha cetayanti,*
> *Tisro devir barhir edam syonam, Saraswati svapasah sudantu.*'[7]

---

[7] *Rig Veda*, 10.110.08

May Bharati attend this yagna. May Ila awaken our consciousness. May blissful Saraswati come. The three who hurt not, but sit in truth.

Again, all was white, only the agni burned yellow-orange. Rama invoked the Parashu and held it afloat in the flames. He pressed his palms together and prayed.

'Three goddesses of truth, I bow to you. I've been given the power to judge a soul in the Parashu. By invoking the three of you, I've promised not to hurt. I submit to your judgement. Judge me, my intention and my truth.'

Three white hands emerged and wrapped themselves around the Parashu's shaft.

'Be warned! Hurt, and you will be damned. Speak asatya, and you will be damned. Dishonour the hymn, and you will be damned.'

One feminine voice, soft and tremendously powerful, but shared and spoken by three goddesses. His hymn had invoked extraordinary power, and he had to abide by their rules. He bowed his acceptance. He focused on the Parashu's rune. It glowed white.

'Speak to me,' he told the Parashu. 'Reveal your essence.'

And it spoke in his mind. It revealed its beeja-akshara, its primordial spandana that birthed it. A sacred secret known to Mahadeva and none else. Rama bowed to the Parashu. He wouldn't bring the syllable to his lips; he wouldn't reveal this to anyone. It was the truth of the Parashu meant for him alone. He chanted it in his mind.

The Parashu blazed brilliant white. The three hands let go, and it sped vertically towards him, the rune level with the light on his forehead. It disappeared as it touched Rama's forehead, and he was pulled into a world nestled deep within the Parashu.

Millions of thumb-sized sparks of light floated in the dark, dead silence. Rama turned a circle. They were all around, stretching away without end. The area they encompassed was flat, without feature, without light. This realm of the Parashu was a world of its own. Rama looked down. There was no terrain underfoot; he was standing on nothing. Nothing in this world except perpetual darkness filled with all these tiny sparks.

He wondered what the first soul would have experienced here. Perhaps utter terror. The first life taken by the Parashu. By some being wielding the Parashu before him. He thought of the first life taken by him. The asura in the battle between the deva and the asuras from so long ago. His heart went out to the sparks, the atmas trapped here by him. Could they not speak? Could they not see him? He had to find a way to free them. It was his duty, his dharma. He stood still awhile, a silent body in an ocean of silent souls. The light on his forehead had gone out. He brought it forth again.

A ripple swept through the souls as if they were suddenly aware of him. They came closer, unsure, nervous and disbelieving. Rama stood quiet, wary of making any sudden movements.

'Save us.' The voice was like a whisper. Rama startled.

'*Rakshaam dehi.*' Another voice, distinct from the first. And they all spoke, surrounding him in a sphere of light, their voices neutral but pleading.

'Give us our chance at rebirth and redemption.'

'We pray. Do the gods hear us?'

'Maybe they've heard now. Else he wouldn't be here.'

They knew him. They knew he was the one that had killed them all. Yet, hope and expectation filled the voices. There was no trace of enmity or hurt or vengeance.

Rama pressed his palms together in pranaam. 'I will liberate you. I promise.'

The voices were quiet for a nimisha.

'So, not now. But when?' Rama couldn't identify which atma spoke.

'Soon. I give you my word. Soon.'

The souls went mute. A few moments later, Rama spoke. 'I come here under an oath of truth. I cannot speak asatya. Soon, I promise.'

'Why do you come now, avatara?'

Rama wondered how they knew. 'I come to find Arjuna.'

'Why?'

'To judge him.'

A scintilla of surprise seemed to run through the souls.

'Again? You passed judgement when you slew him.' Rama didn't reply. 'Will you judge us?'

'I cannot,' Rama replied.

'There is no Arjuna here, only souls. No man, no woman. No mortal, no deva, no asura. And no names. Names are for things, not souls.'

'I can find his atma.'

The souls went quiet again. They moved, and the sphere around him disappeared. The souls gathered around his knee, surrounding him closely and stretching away beyond the scope of Rama's vision. They were silent, waiting.

Rama focused his intention and called with his mind. '*Pha.*'

One spark of light moved. It drew closer and stopped at

an arm's length, at level with Rama's eyes. Rama gazed at it. It was no different from the others, a soul that had cast off the garb of the body. Was this Arjuna, or was it a trick? No, a soul couldn't lie. And it had to respond to the beeja-akshara that was the essence of its birth.

The guru had bid him judge Arjuna. How was he to do that? The soul before him didn't speak. Rama stood uncertainly before them all.

'The guru sent you,' said the soul at last, and Rama nodded. 'He gave you the authority to judge. But what is the secret to identifying me? How did you call me forward? What explains this inescapable urge to come before you?'

Rama didn't speak.

'I accept your authority,' said the soul. Rama bowed to it.

'I don't know what to do,' Rama confessed.

'Restore my body,' said the soul.

Rama was amazed. Was that possible?

'It's possible for you,' the soul said as if it was reading Rama's mind.

Rama focused his mind, imagining Arjuna's body as he'd seen him in the temple in Mahishmati.

'Pha,' he said in his mind.

Karthavirya Arjuna stood before him. All majesty and might and sardonic smile. The smile changed to one of welcome. He inclined his head slightly.

'I bow to the avatara,' Arjuna whispered.

The other souls gasped and inched closer. Nervous anticipation ran through them. Arjuna looked around.

'I faced my killer on prithvi. I face my judge and liberator here. What world is this?'

'All of you are trapped inside the Parashu,' said Rama.

Exclamations of shock rang in Rama's ears. Arjuna stared, slack-jawed.

'How long have we been here?' he asked at last.

'More than a year.'

'Feels like aeons. So many lives were taken by you. A hundred-fold more than I have slain through my life. And all in three days.' There was no anger in Arjuna's voice, only wonder.

'What happened on the battlefield? How did you come back to life?'

'With the blessings of Parashakti,' Rama answered. Arjuna didn't understand. He waited for Rama to continue. 'Perhaps you will understand someday. But now I've come to judge you.'

Arjuna nodded. 'I have so many questions, but none of it matters. I accept your judgement, whatever it may be. Pronounce it. Do I get a glimpse of swarga before I'm sent to naraka?'

That was the root of the quandary Rama was in. He'd thought about myriad punishments, but the hymn had changed all that. The Parashu had revealed its beeja-akshara in the hands of three goddesses who had come 'to hurt not'. The dread weapon of himsa people flinched away from had revealed its essence through ahimsa. That hymn had come to him from the Supreme Consciousness, from Parashakti. He hadn't composed it. And it was the first hymn he'd *seen*. The three goddesses were *Satya Vak* manifest, the truth in thought, word and deed. He was bound by oath not to hurt. Would punishing Arjuna break that promise? But he did not doubt that the man who'd plunged the world into misery deserved just that.

Rama's mind raced. Arjuna waited patiently. It was a long wait.

'You and I are tied at the hip. Before me is the man I should've been, and before you, the man you never will be. The man you would never want to be.' Arjuna broke the silence. 'Are you samrat now?' Rama shook his head. 'You should be. You would make a good one, I think.' Rama didn't react. 'Power should be wielded and seen to be wielded. And you have enormous power. What will you do with it?'

'Destroy what you have created. Too big a man sat on the throne. Now, he stands before me. Too many small men will covet the throne. A big man's ego thought the throne too small. A small man will disguise his inadequacy with his lust for power. Both kinds make for petty tyrants. The world has suffered enough. I will shatter your empire.'

Arjuna stared into Rama's eyes, his face bereft of emotion, and replied quietly, 'Ego and the lust for power. So akin to dhatura. Easy to find, fatal to use.' Arjuna turned away and looked into the distance. 'I remember the beginning of our story.' Rama stiffened ever so slightly; Arjuna didn't notice. 'The dream. Me in the desert, you in the grove. I knew it bodes ill for me, but the desert has its own addictive power, its own treacherous beauty. And I didn't want to give it up. Too painful to acknowledge the truth, even to myself.' Arjuna sighed and looked again at Rama. 'But without water, the desert can kill you. There was too little water in me. My ego, the heat of the desert, the power lust, the sands. And I didn't look for water either. The desert was my heart. Maybe it all started with a small grain of sand. I don't remember. I lived too long.'

Rama looked away. This wasn't the Arjuna he expected,

shorn of vanity and ego. 'It always starts with a grain ... Or a shard,' Rama murmured.

'Not the Arjuna you expected?' Arjuna smiled as he spoke. Rama was surprised at the innocence of the smile. 'Death can do that. That's perhaps why mortality is a blessing. I've had a long, long time to amass enough grains of sand to make a desert ... In my heart and the lives of others. Pride is a woeful thing.'

'Pride is much maligned, Arjuna. Too many things disguise themselves as pride: ego, self-importance, vanity ... It is hubris that is true sin and folly. I fell prey to it once, forgot my pitrus and called it pride. Hubris is the need for self-aggrandisement. Genuine pride is to seek what is great and *be worthy* of it. Pride's twin is humility. He shows you what is attainable by you. Where the brothers work together, there comes achievement. But hubris can disguise himself as either of the brothers. Hubris masquerading as humility is humble brag, and as pride is boastful self-depreciation.'

'Does the world and its trappings and its luxuries hold no fancy for you?'

'The trappings are to give you joy, aren't they? The woodlands are home to me. I find joy there. And there's enough water. A Bhargava always has agni with him. The grove of the heart must never wither ... That's all it takes.'

'You hate this world? Yet love it enough to change it?'

'I don't hate it. I'm from it, and it gives me an arena to tend to my dharma. I must leave it better than I found it. That is my love for it.'

'Do me a kindness, Rama. Answer two more questions for me?'

Rama nodded.

'What happened to my queen?'

'She died before you in the temple. Devi herself showed her the true visage of her karma and burned her life away.'

'She was a bad one. As ego-driven and power-hungry as me. And she was a good one. Loyal to the end. I was the love of her life ... Good and bad ... So entangled, so hard to untwine. So hard to understand dharma. My second question. How did you become a Brahmakshatriya?'

'By true repentance, by burning false emotion through the Panchagni tapasya.'

'I didn't know it could be done this way. Thank you for your answers. I accept your judgement, whatever it may be. That is my repentance. And there will be no false begging or excuses. I did what I did. Now I'll have to pay for it. My deeds of adharma are indeed long. It shouldn't be hard to decide.'

Rama stayed quiet, still thinking it over. Did the guru know the hymn would reveal itself to him? Did he know he'd face a moral dilemma here? Rama mused. *To unbecome, to die, to become.* The words flashed in Rama's mind. Akrita had asked him what Arjuna had become.

Rama made his decision. Arjuna had to become something. He focused his intention and mentally intoned the beeja-akshara again. Sahasrabahu stood before him. Arjuna looked down at himself in surprise. The souls retreated in shock.

'I proclaim judgement, Arjuna. You will keep the form of Sahasrabahu, the source of your hubris and power. And your punishment is this. I proclaim you the Finder of Lost, Stolen and Misplaced Things. You will be at the service of mortals, devas and asuras.'

Arjuna gaped.

Rama invoked agni in his open palm. 'Every time anyone

calls out to you for aid in remembering misplaced things or finding lost ones, you, Sahasrabahu, will respond. If you help find the lost or misplaced article, two of your thousand arms will drop off. However, if you are unable to help, you will grow two more. When all your hands have disappeared, you will change from Sahasrabahu to Arjuna again, be reborn and have your chance at redemption. You will not be of prithvi, nor have a physical, mortal form. You will have a subtle energy form and exist in the ether until all your arms have vanished. Do you accept?'

Arjuna stared awhile and then spoke. 'Gracious of you to ask acceptance when you've been given the power to judge, and I've already submitted. I accept.'

Rama thought hard for a few nimishas before he continued, 'Hold your right palm over the agni.

'May this mantra invoke Sahasrabahu to the task. May it be chanted a thousand times to honour his form and ability.

'*Om Kartaveeryo Namah,*
Raja bahu sahasravaan,
Thasya smarana mathrena,
Gatham nashtam cha labhyate.[8]

'O Agni! Your devotee beseeches you. Be a witness and bind Sahasrabahu to this judgement. Carry my decision to the guru, the rishis, the devas and the asuras. May they spread the news in the three realms. May the guru, the gods and the rishis find my judgement fair and just.'

The flames leapt from Rama's hand, whirled around the

---

[8] Kartaviryaarjuna Stotra

two of them and shot straight up, far into the darkness. Then, it disappeared. Sahasrabahu closed his eyes. A few nimishas later, he laughed loud.

'Clever Parashurama! To use my thousand arms and my ability to read minds to punish me without punishing me. I could be finding things for all eternity.'

'I've the read thoughts of people before me. Thoughts that were present in their minds. I don't know how well I can read the memories of people to remind them of things. It never struck me to read memories. I presume I have to learn to do it.'

It wasn't a question. Rama stayed mute.

'And I don't know how many minds I'd need to read to find stolen articles. I'm about to find out, aren't I?'

Rama nodded.

'I will heed your judgement, O avatara. Let this be my penitence.'

He bowed to Rama. A nimisha later he disappeared. The souls rushed to Rama, whispering a thousand questions.

'Where did he go?' Rama had no inkling. He didn't answer.

'What about us?'

'Is this what will happen to us, too?'

Rama held up his hand for quiet.

'I will release you all,' he said.

'Do you know how, avatara?'

'No. But I will find out.'

Rama chanted the secret beeja-akshara of the Parashu and focused on returning to the yagna. The world of trapped souls disappeared. The Parashu was again in the agni of the yagnakund, held by three white hands.

'You have not hurt.'

'You spoke the truth.'

'You honoured the sacred hymn revealed to you.'

Rama bowed to them. The white blinked out, and so did the Parashu and yagnakund. Rama eased out of dhyana.

Jayadhwaja sprawled before the throne and stared at the crown placed on it. A lone lamp cast its weak light on one side. The sheer white of the court fought with shadow and the dark, and lost. The disc with a thousand spikes fared no better. His brothers walked to him and called out. Jayadhwaja didn't respond. Shura lit more lamps as Vrishasya knelt before Jayadhwaja. He gestured for a lamp and Shurasoma rushed one to him.

'Jyeshta,' Vrishasya whispered as he gently shook Jayadhwaja's shoulder. Jayadhwaja stared ahead, the whites of his eyes showing above the pitch-dark pupils. A beady, reptilian gaze on an expressionless face. Vrisha gathered close with another lamp and looked him over. Dirty clothes, scant stubble on the face, grimy fingernails and the smell of sweat.

'How long since you bathed, jyeshta?' he asked. Jayadhwaja's tongue flicked out of his lips before he spoke.

'He wanders ... lost and forlorn.' The brothers glanced at each other, ignoring the smell of Jayadhwaja's unclean mouth. 'He's here now, standing by his throne.'

'There's nobody here but us,' said Shura.

'Father is here. He searches for redemption. For restoration of glory. I am here, Sahasrabahu. I will redeem your glory. I am enough.'

'Jyeshta, wake up,' Vrishasya shouted as he shook Jayadhwaja as hard as he could. Jayadhwaja blinked and looked at his brothers in surprise.

'When did all of you come?' he said as he sat up.

'We've been here a while. Who are you talking to and why haven't you bathed?' said Shurasoma.

'Just thinking aloud,' said Jayadhwaja. He looked down at himself and grimaced. 'Guess I forgot, been busy. Anything important?'

'No. It's just that we haven't seen you too often nowadays,' said Vrisha.

'Fine then. I'll clean myself and then we can talk,' said Jayadhwaja.

'A small matter, jyeshta. A few women have been killed,' said Shurasoma carefully.

Jayadhwaja shrugged.

'All ... er... women of the streets,' Shurasoma continued. 'Thirteen of them. All were killed brutally. Cut to shreds.'

'Increase the sentries then. Why bring this to me?'

Shurasoma held out a small purse. 'Only royals use this. It was found at the site of a murder.'

Jayadhwaja froze momentarily, but Shurasoma noticed.

'Someone's being naughty and trying to have some fun on the side. Why connect it to the killings?'

Jayadhwaja waved his dismissal. 'Just increase the patrolling. I'll see you tomorrow. I need my rest.' He walked away, and the brothers dispersed. Only Shurasoma stood staring at Jayadhwaja's retreating back.

Jayadhwaja returned a couple of muhurtas later, still unwashed. He checked to see if his brothers were still waiting. The court was empty. His brothers had left, but they had lit every lamp and torch in it, even the ones on the balconies. The white of the walls and the gold of the throne and crown glared boldly and majestically, and Jayadhwaja felt himself shrink before it. Annoyance twisted his lips. 'Stupid brothers I have. Just cannot leave me alone.' He squatted before the throne and stared at the crown again.

A long shadow etched itself across the throne and the golden disc behind it. The crown almost disappeared in the shadow's embrace. A fragrance rushed past, filling Jayadhwaja's lungs but itching at the insides of his nostrils. It could mean only one thing. Dantakrura had come.

Jayadhwaja watched as grotesque shadows swarmed across the floor, some snaking around and up the pillars, hanging from the curtains, lounging on the seats. Blotches of black and grey erupted across the expanse of white marble as if the shining stone had caught the pox. Something reptilian with six forked tongues and scales that slithered across its body suddenly stood upright on three legs. It was an oily black silhouette that moved slowly, but it cast a shadow of its own. The creature paused and darted forward. The shadow stayed. A new shadow formed as the creature moved, and then the shadow multiplied sixfold. It snorted and slobbered and the six shadows mewled with fright and ran from it. A whip-thin tongue flashed out of its mouth, caught the first shadow and stuffed it down its gullet. Lamps died out around Jayadhwaja, but no smoke rose from the wicks and torches. He looked up at the far ceiling. He couldn't see it. Bulbous smoke massed like boulders above the court.

'You've finally come out of the cremation grounds,' said Jayadhwaja.

'This can do as well. So this is the famed court of Arjuna,' Dantakrura laughed contemptuously.

'You laugh at it? You see no power in the throne and crown?'

'Oh, there is power! So much of it. But ...'

'You don't want a samrajya, no riches either. What do you really want, warlock?'

'I haven't lied to you. I'm oath-bound to you, samrat.'

'You haven't spoken the entire truth. Tell me now.'

Dantakrura paused a nimisha and replied, 'Surely you have deduced by now. Think!'

Jayadhwaja shrugged.

'The first gift I gave you. Oil spelled with Kshatriya blood. It gave you unquestioning loyalty.' Jayadhwaja remained mute. 'Bhargava blood, samrat! That's what I want. There is much magic in blood, and I want the blood of a Bhargava male.'

'The Saptarishi had none. You should've found and killed his sons. You missed your chance.'

Dantakrura stared at Jayadhwaja. The man did not even wonder why there wasn't any blood in Jamadagni's body. So consumed by his vengeance and lust for power. But it had frustrated him like nothing before. Why wasn't there blood? Did Jamadagni know this was what he so desperately wanted? Maybe the Abhichara he'd used to trap Parashurama had alerted Jamadagni. He'd have recognised the spell immediately. If only we'd known Jamadagni was alive before that spell was used. It took extraordinary power to make blood vanish ... Almost as if Jamadagni had pre-empted their attack. The warlock was certain. Jamadagni had surrendered his prana before Jayadhwaja had severed his neck, and the samrat was oblivious to this. They wouldn't have found a drop of blood even if they'd cut his body to pieces.

So near, yet so far. He'd rushed from Mayong to Mahishmati as soon as he knew of the battle. He'd been watching Jayadhwaja for a long time now. But alas! Arjuna had been cremated before he could arrive. There had been no time for a ritual to stop it, and he'd lost Arjuna's blood, too. What a treasure that would have been! He'd lost the blood of a Saptarishi and of Sahasrabahu, the most feared, powerful man in the three lokas. He wouldn't miss the third time around. The blood of an avatara! The Aghoris can treasure their skulls. Skulls had their uses, but blood was worth a thousand skulls if one knew what to do with it.

'Their blood wouldn't do, samrat. Bhargava blood, yes. But not special. Not good enough for me.'

'That wretched avatara's blood then. What will you do with it?' Jayadhwaja turned to face Dantakrura.

'Ascend! To heights no mortal ever has. I don't want that pretty little bauble these rishis dangle in front of everyone. Moksha. That is for fools. I will sit with the gods. As their equal, not as a quivering devotee. Mortals will fear and worship me.'

'That's not possible!'

'There are ways! Abhichara doesn't concern itself with good and bad. That's for foolish philosophers. Abhichara sees what's possible and simply does it. And there is no one better at Abhichara than me. If ... NO! When I succeed, I will be a deity. I will make Shukracharya reveal the Mrita-Sanjeevani to me.'

Jayadhwaja gaped.

'One's ambition must be tall and proud, samrat! And mine is taller than Kailasa!'

'So that's why you haven't killed that wretch!'

'He will kneel, samrat! At your feet, while you sit on that throne and wear that crown. He will hold up wine and food for your pleasure. Or perhaps clean your sandals. He will be your loyal, obedient devotee!'

Jayadhwaja crowed with delight. The shadows sniggered along with him. Jayadhwaja looked all around him, searching for something. He turned to the warlock finally, looking into those pinpoint pupils. 'Where is my shadow, warlock?'

'Oh! Right here!' Dantakrura laughed as he pointed straight back at Jayadhwaja. Jayadhwaja looked down at himself, utterly confused. The warlock and the shadows roared with laughter.

16

The Battle of the Parashu

Dawn broke as Rama finished his sandhyavandana and emerged from the river. He wondered if he should find himself food, maybe some fruit or stem from the trees and shrubs around. He wouldn't mind a bite or two, but he wasn't really hungry. He dropped the idea. He felt really light, of body and mind. And light of heart too. The bleak despair was gone, he had been healed of it by Guru Dattatreya. He glanced up the mountain to the dim outline of the cave. The man in the mountain had emerged from his cave and was now ready to go to his people.

The satchel with the clay pots was on the ground before him. Fire father, water mother. He had an inkling of what he should do with the ember and the water. The enormity of what his parents had done filled him with wonder. And love. Their sacrifice and teaching wasn't just all the love in the world. It was also all the love *for* the world. They had thought beyond the destruction of the iron frame, and left him their power to build what came after. The two pots contained their legacy endowed to this world, for the salvation of the millions that had died, and the purification of the ones that had strayed.

Would the world have the wisdom to see and understand the greatness of Renuka and Jamadagni? There would be devotees of Guru Dattatreya, and the bards may sing of the epic saga of Parashurama, but how many would know that there would be no Parashurama without the Saptarishi and the Mahavidya. *Who cares?* said the other voice in his mind. *It wouldn't matter to my parents.* Rama paid attention, this contrarian voice was important. It had urged him to be samrat, give in to Shukracharya and lie with Bhumi. It was part of him and he needed to do something about it. Rama mulled it over for a while, before dismissing all thought. It was time to be on his way back to his friends and shishyas.

He scooped up the satchel and froze. His senses warned of danger, and his eyes scanned this way and that. A sudden stillness was in the air. A quiet that screamed immense power and numbing terror, as if the world were holding its breath. Rama's hair stood on end. He saw no one, heard nothing. Even the Parashu had gone disturbingly quiet. It hadn't responded to his alertness and readiness to face whatever it was that was out there. It lay on the ground a couple of paces away from him. Rama stepped forward and reached for it. It rose and sped away from him.

Utterly surprised, Rama reacted instantaneously, extending his hand and willing the Parashu back. The Parashu shuddered to a stop in mid-air. It buckled and shook in a frenzy as if trapped and buffeted by opposing forces. Rama looked past it and saw the being who had stepped into the clearing.

A man whose hair was made of flames. Orange-yellow and an angry red, bursting from his head with a ferocity that caused Rama's eyes to water. He was taller than Rama, and his skin was as black as night. As black as ... Rama's mind paused. As black as the banalinga. There was no tiger skin wrapped around his waist. He was clad in snakes, as dark and silent as him. Big and small, thick and thin, they swarmed across his waist and thighs. They twisted to form his janeu and circled his neck, unbothered by the flames. No beard on the face, but a grimly set jaw. Three eyes studded the face exactly like the eyes on the banalinga. The eye on the forehead was closed, but the two below were open and stared unblinkingly at Rama. They were incandescent white, and they had no pupils at all. His hand was extended for the Parashu, and an ominous smile played on his thin black lips.

There was no doubt in Rama's mind who this man, this being, was. It wasn't an Aghori this time, but the same divinity in another form. Rama wasn't about to make the same mistake again. He stopped willing the Parashu to return. He prostrated on the ground.

'*Om Namah Shivaya*! Blessed am I for your darshan. I beseech refuge at your feet, Mahadeva!'

The Parashu lingered in mid-air, absolutely still. Mahadeva stood silent. Rama raised his head, alarmed by the silence and the immobility of the Parashu. A nimisha later, he willed the Parashu towards Mahadeva. It sped forward and settled gently at Mahadeva's feet. He sent the Parashu back towards Rama. It hung above Rama now, waiting for him to rise and grasp it.

'You are a dangerous man,' Mahadeva's voice boomed everywhere, inside and outside him. 'I would have taken the weapon from you. But you did the one thing that would have prevented that.' Mahadeva paused a nimisha and repeated, 'A dangerous man.'

Rama rose, his palms pressed together in prayer, unwilling to grasp the Parashu. He had no idea what Mahadeva was talking about.

'You know the beeja-akshara of the Parashu. None of those who have used it before have ever known it. Nobody besides me has known it. You've learnt too much. You know so many divyastras. There's too much power in your hands. And you are a chiranjeevi. Dangerous!'

Rama stood mute.

'I don't need your Parashu. I have my own.'

A Parashu appeared in Mahadeva's extended right hand, a replica of Rama's weapon. Rama stared in amazement.

'So, you have mastered the Parashu? Prove it. I've come to take your head! Fight!'

Rama's jaw dropped in shock. Mahadeva didn't wait. He flung his Parashu at Rama. Rama acted on reflex. He grasped his weapon and swung. Blade hit blade with a sickening, bone-jarring, teeth-rattling chime. Part moan and part scream. Something tiny dropped from a tree beside Rama, hit the ground and lay still. The flung Parashu hurtled back to Mahadeva. He charged. An infinitesimal snatch of a nimisha later, Rama sprang to meet it. The blades struck each other with a roar that echoed off the mountains. Rama's pupils turned up. He called forth the fury of the Parashu, and it came flooding to him. He wouldn't back down. Rama would prove himself a worthy disciple and honour Mahadeva with a fight like none other. He counter-attacked.

He thrust the Parashu at Mahadeva's chest and met air. Rama saw Mahadeva not in three but sixteen places at once.

Ready to strike in sixteen different ways. It didn't bother Rama, nor did it surprise him. He had learnt a great deal, and his prowess was much more than when he had last fought Mahadeva. He spun and leapt faster than thought, lighter than a feather, avoiding the strikes. Rama turned mid-leap to smite down on the head of the flame, and the blades crashed into each other again.

'*Namah Shivaya*,' Rama intoned mentally as he defended slashes and cuts from all around him. Mahadeva didn't slow or pause like before. He moved faster. Rama willed himself to match the speed. Everything was a blur, and the Parashus whistled a relentless scream as they flashed past. Rama focused on the rune, and it glowed. He imagined it spinning inexorably. The chakra of time. Try as he will, it didn't slow. None of what he'd done before worked now. It befuddled Rama for a split second, and that was enough time for a kick of enormous power to land on his chest. Rama flew yards across the clearing and smashed into a tree trunk, splintering it and causing the shards to explode outwards. The sap showered out, dropping on and around him.

Rama's vision spun, his breath rushed out of his lungs and his chest seemed to be of water. He was surprised he'd survived. He'd been kicked with the strength of ten Sahasrabahus. Rama scrambled and leapt sideways just before Mahadeva's Parashu crashed through the tree trunk, running clean through it. The tree crashed down, and Rama leapt again to avoid the branches.

Fight, said the other voice suddenly. *Surrender*, it said a nimisha later.

Alarms went off in Rama's mind. That strike would have killed him if he hadn't scrambled away. This wasn't a test.

Mahadeva had come to deliver death. Fury erupted in Rama. He considered hurling his Parashu but thought better of it. Perhaps he wouldn't get it back. It felt safer in his hands. He gripped it harder and launched himself at Mahadeva.

As he fought, Rama cleaved his mind and looked in the mirror in his dhyana. There, he saw ... nothing. It was only him in the mirror, whirling, lunging, twisting. He couldn't see his opponent. The blades crashed into each other again. In the mirror, Rama's Parashu stopped abruptly, crashing into nothing at all. Rama brought forth the light in his forehead. He still couldn't see a thing in the mirror.

He thought of Sahasrabahu's power, of Agastya's reward and the divyastras. He baulked at all the options. It didn't feel right to him. And it didn't seem that any of that would matter at all. He would fight with what he had. He thought of the beeja-akshara of the Parashu. If the Parashus were the same, he could call the other one to him and disarm Mahadeva. Somehow, he was sure even this wouldn't work. He tried anyway, and nothing happened.

They fought at blinding speed, each intent on dominating the other. Rama lost sense of time. Out of the corners of his eyes, he saw fallen trees and smashed rocks and wondered when that had happened. He was oblivious to all but Mahadeva and his Parashu. And he was tiring. He was fighting as hard as he could, bringing all his learning and power into the duel, and he hadn't landed a blow or a strike yet. *Think!* he urged himself.

But think of what? Rama's mind jostled for answers, for anything at all that could aid him, but he found nothing. He wondered if he would lose, if he would die. Something sparked in his mind. He was a chiranjeevi. He couldn't die. But

Mahadeva could still hurt him; he could lop Rama's limbs off. A grotesque image formed in Rama's mind. Of Mahadeva's Parashu slashing through his head, splitting it into two vertical halves. The thought lowered his concentration. He took a false step and had to twist awkwardly to avoid the blades as they flashed past a hair's breadth from his throat.

'Shive!' Rama prayed. 'Show me a way to honour my guru.'

Mahadeva attacked with vehemence. Death. Chiranjeevi. Rama couldn't wrap his mind around the dichotomy of it. Another thought arose. The form Mahadeva had chosen. He hadn't come as an Aghori this time. He had come as ... Veerabhadra! Something clicked right in Rama's mind at last. Veerabhadra. Born out of Mahadeva's dreadlocks that were ripped in fury and pain from his scalp. Born to desecrate Daksha Prajapati's ill-fated yagna and behead him. To avenge the self-immolation of Ma Sati. And the temple! How had he forgotten? The panel of the Mothers' Seven, with Ganapathi on the left and Veerabhadra on the right.

He brought forth the temple in the mirror. He bowed to the murthis of Bhadrakali and Shiva and approached the panel. Veerabhadra's idol danced. The furious, lightning-fast dance of battle. Rama recognised the movements as the murthi danced, sensing they were being mirrored in the clearing. He cried out in exultation. Rama unleashed the joy he found in battle, the delight in his power and prowess, the calm confidence in himself and the call of his blood to dominate. He forgot his tiredness and flung himself at Mahadeva. He would fight his god, his guru ... and win!

For the first time, Mahadeva had to step back from the barrage of strikes Rama let loose. But Rama couldn't find an opening, a slip or a misstep to press home his advantage.

Mahadeva read his moves as clearly as he read Mahadeva's. They fought on.

Rama stood in the temple watching the murthi dance. It struck him that he had always been inside the temple. He had never seen it from the outside. He willed himself to do so. The new vista took his breath away. The temple was now high above him, with a triangular gopura and atop a mountain. The mountain in Indrapuri he had circumambulated. Triangle! An idea sparked in his mind.

In the clearing, Rama roared. Raw, animalistic, feral. He roared from the very depths of his being. Mahadeva paused. Watching, waiting. Rama danced like a madman, like an Aghori prancing with abandon among burning pyres, like a man possessed by a drunken spirit, like a leaf twirling in the eddies of the wind.

In his dhyana, he imagined a vertical triangle on the upper half of his face. Its lower corners rested at the centres of his pupil-less white eyes, and the apex rose just above his forehead, at the start of his hairline. At the centre of the triangle, he formed a bindu—precisely where the sixth chakra resides. The Agya chakra. A second mirror formed in his dhyana, showing him his subtle, sukshma energy body. The sixth chakra on his forehead, between the eyebrows and below the light of his amsha, pulsated dimly. He didn't wait for the beeja-akshara; he knew it from the very depths of his soul.

'Om,' he chanted, focusing on the throbbing chakra. It burned white, and Rama saw the form of the chakra. An inverted triangle enclosed in a circle with two lotus petals on either side. Shiva and Shakti. The archetype masculine and feminine. Consciousness and energy. The duality that rose from the unity that was Parashakti, the mother of all there was, is and ever will be.

The mountain disappeared in the first mirror and a magnificent yantra replaced it. A thrill of utter, inexplicable joy coursed through Rama. Nine interlocking triangles formed, four pointing upwards and five downwards, all around a bindu. Two concentric circles formed around the triangles, one of eight lotus petals and another of sixteen lotus petals. A nested square around the circles completed the yantra. *Navayoni chakra*, said Rama's mind. *The chakra of Sri Vidya, of Parashakti herself*, said Rama's soul.

'Sri Chakra!' Rama cried out in bliss.

The bindu rose upwards, and the yantra took on a three-dimensional form. Entire universes, and all things animate and inanimate, seemed to revolve around it as the point rose. Rama tried to see it all and failed. His mind reeled at the immensity of the sight. For a fraction of a nimisha, he saw fully-formed the three-dimensional yantra. Atop it, right where the bindu was, a linga appeared. A linga made of darbha grass. The yantra disappeared in a flash, and the mountain was back in the mirror.

'Vishwayonika!' Rama whispered in awe.

This was the secret of the Saptarishis that had to be self-realised. The Vishwayonika and the banalinga were the same. The Saptarishis, Guru Dattatreya, the devas and asuras, the Aghoris and mortals, all prayed and worshipped the same divinity. Their forms and names, rupa and nama, were different, but ultimately, they were all the same. Each chose the name and form that appealed to him or her the most. He knew this, but he had *seen* it now! Rama marvelled at this lila. The darbha grass was to honour Ganapathi, and the start of the journey, the Muladhara chakra. The mountain was a physical manifestation of the Sri Chakra. This was the true Meru! It existed in every plane of existence, and he had been blessed with a glimpse. Rama's heart sang with joy and gratitude. The mirror with the mountain blinked out. Mahadeva waited.

Rama stopped his frenzied dance and faced him. The sukshma sharira vanished from the second mirror. Rama saw himself in it. He still couldn't see Mahadeva. But he knew what he had to do. He had surrendered the Parashu. Now he would give Mahadeva what he said he would take.

In the mirror, he raised his Parashu. He would make a bali, a sacrifice. A bali of his mind and submit to pure consciousness, to Shiva. He lopped off his head in the mirror. Astonishingly, he disappeared in the mirror and Mahadeva appeared. In the same form and place as in the clearing, as Veerabhadra.

In the clearing, Rama whispered, 'I am Shiva.'

Two Veerabhadras faced each other. Rama hurled his Parashu at Mahadeva. Mahadeva smiled. The Parashu crashed into his forehead and shattered into a million shards. One shard remained embedded in his forehead. Mahadeva pulled it out. A scar remained. Rama froze, aghast and terrified at what he'd done. He had acted on instinct and now he berated himself for it. He was yanked out of dhyana. His forehead exploded in pain like his head had been severed in two.

'Your instincts are right, and so am I,' said Mahadeva. 'Dangerous man, you are. I wondered how you would face this challenge and extricate yourself from this predicament. And you've found an unusual way out. And you have unknowingly and temporarily manifested a state of being. A state of being Shiva. I shall cherish this scar.'

Mahadeva laughed, and the throbbing pain in Rama's

forehead vanished. Rama fell at Mahadeva's feet, begging for forgiveness.

'Well-fought and well-thought, Rama. Rise.' Rama stood, mute and meek as a lamb.

'Look at the scar, Rama.'

Rama looked at it. It opened. He looked into the utter blackness of it. He was inside it.

Rama saw distant fires in the throbbing darkness. Some powerful resonance pulsated all around him. He could feel his entire body quiver like the sound was the heartbeat of something gargantuan, something you never wanted to irk or displease. His fingers tightened on the Parashu's staff, surprise blooming in his eyes at the oddness of it. He looked at his right hand. The staff stretched away behind him, yards into the gloom lit by a half-moon. The blades were enormous—one buried in the earth, and the other looming in the sky, gleaming dully. Rama glanced at the moon. Half dark, half lit. Ashtami, he deduced, the eighth day of the lunar cycle. A waning moon, lit on its left. Krishna paksha, the dark lunar fortnight.He tugged at the Parashu; it barely moved forward and then stopped. Rama looked around. No vegetation, no undulation of the earth, no trail and nothing visible except for the fires and the moon. Starless sky, coarse black earth and an angry darkness. He looked again at the moon, and verses from the Lalitha Sahasranama flashed in his mind. His lips moved unbidden.

Ashtami chandra vibhraja. She who has a beautiful forehead like the half-moon.

Mukhachandra kalankabha. She who has a thilaka of musk on her forehead like the black shadow of the moon.

Charu chandra kaladhara. She who holds the sixteenth phase of the moon on her forehead.

He grasped the Parashu with both arms and tried to lift it out of the earth, bending his back and bracing his legs. He failed. Mystified, he decided to leave the Parashu and make for the fires. The fingers of his right hand stayed curled around the staff. He couldn't let go. Something howled in the dark.

Rama snapped alert, the hair on his arms standing on end. He waited for something to emerge from the gloom. Nothing. He dragged the Parashu with all the strength he had and moved towards the fires. A faint gurgle started, and soon, there was a dull rattle behind him. He walked on. The two sounds grew louder and more painful, making him look back as he walked.

The Parashu tore a great rent in the earth as it raked through it. Out of the rent poured blood, thick and red-black. Out of the blood, thousands upon thousands of skulls tumbled up and out, liked uprooted weeds. Rama stared at the horror. Finally, he turned and walked on. The sounds became agonising again. A savage howl lanced through the sounds. It sounded closer.

He heard the dull thuds of sprinting paws, the crack of skulls breaking under them and the sick squelch as the paws lifted out of the blood. Rama stopped and turned. He saw the great black hound bounding towards him, looming in the sky, a hundred times bigger than any shvana he'd ever seen. It raced past him, towards the fires, dwarfing Rama as it passed overhead. Rama braced as the wind growled in the hound's wake, threatening to topple him.

The wind died down, and Rama walked on. The fires grew closer and with a gasp, Rama saw that they were cremation pyres. Thousands of them. Beyond them was a river, silent and swift. Something, some being of terrible, terrible power, was in those pyres. He could feel it in his bones. Every instinct told him so. The reek of flesh, burning and rotting, hit him like a fist, pummelling into his lungs. The stench of coarse madira overwhelmed him. He stopped and stared at the sky-high flames. The hound emerged and bared his fangs at him. The gurgle and rattle died all at once, and a deathly silence enveloped everything, even the crackle and pop of the flames.

'You come to Kashiiii ...' came a voice made of a thousand whispers.

Rama froze. He knew who this was. He was in the presence of unimaginable power, of the divinity that had severed Brahma's fifth head with a mere fingernail! Bhairava!

'What do you bring?'

Rama looked at his right hand. The staff was no longer there. He was holding a skull, his fingers stretched across the top of its head. He shook his hand furiously. The skull stayed stuck. It cackled eerily. Rama saw a chain of skulls attached to this one and glanced back. There was a sea of blood and innumerable skulls cackling in it. They all went quiet all of a sudden.

He brought his palms together; the skull caught between them, and whispered.

'Lord of the storm,
Eater of sin,
Master of Time,
Cleaver of Brahma's head.
I bow to you, Bhairava!'

Absolute silence met his words, though the flames still danced and the river, the holy Ganga, flowed.

Rama was at a loss. Had he made a mistake? Why had the Parashu disappeared? His mind fumbled for an answer before it clicked into place.

When comes the dreaded weapon from Mahakaal's forge! He had been blessed with the potential in the Parashu. He had understood it, mastered it, and used it to defeat ego and ignorance. He'd realised the Parashu embodied both Shiva and Shakti.

The rhyme of the Parashu! It wasn't merely to teach him to master the Parashu. It was homage to the guardian of Shiva and Shakti's path, Bhairava! He chanted it.

'Cleaver of Minds,
Flame of Fury,
Binder of Spirits,
Striker of Fear,
Bringer of Mrithyu,
Devourer of Souls,
Drinker of Blood,
Beware the One,
Who holds golden and true,
Mahakaal's Parashu.'

Insane laughter broke out as soon as Rama finished. It washed over Rama and rolled into the distance. The skull in his hand disappeared, so did the sea of blood and the skulls in them. From the flames stepped ... a boy. Maybe eight years old and clad in a loincloth. He twirled the golden Parashu in his left hand like it was a toy.

The boy stopped before Rama. Rama knelt, clasped the boy's feet and touched his head to them. 'Bhairava! Accept my worship and grant me your blessing.'

Rama raised his head. Bhairava placed his right hand upon it, and Rama felt a bolt of lightning run through him. His pupils turned up, and he was in dhyana. There was no temple, no mirror, just him and the nothingness, and five gargantuan faces floating before him. Four faces in the four cardinal directions and the fifth face atop the other four and facing upwards. Rama revolved around the faces like the earth around the sun. The nothingness filled with a sound sacred, deep and sublime. Like his soul, nay, all souls in existence were singing some divine melody. He *saw* crores of mantras emanate from the lips of the five faces. Rama was thrilled to the bone.

The five faces of Shiva! He recalled their names as he paid homage: Sadyojata, Tatpurusha, Vamadeva, Aghora and atop them, Eshana. This was the source of the mantras the rishis *saw* in their meditation. The fount of Shruti, the sacred hymns. From here he received the hymn that manifested the three goddesses. So many mantras still unheard, unseen, unrealised. So much more to learn. For a fleeting nimisha, he thought he saw a sixth head beneath the other five, but the vision disappeared, and he was before Bhairava again.

Bhairava exhaled forcefully and Rama fell back, crashing into something that wasn't there a nimisha ago. He looked down and around and found himself on a throne. His throne. The one he had made from the burnt Sal tree. He looked up and right before him was a dark image. A twin image of himself on the throne, bathed in shadow. Rama stared. His hand moved involuntarily. So did the hand of the image. Rama froze.

'What does this mean?' he pondered.

'I am samrat. I rule,' said the shadow Rama.

'Half littt ... Half darkkk. Dualityy ... Only one should sittt ...'

Bhairava inhaled, and Rama was back on his knees. The throne and image disappeared. Bhairava clasped the Parashu with both his hands, just beneath the curve of its twin blades. He pressed both his forefingers on the runes on either side of the cheek. The Parashu split vertically. Bhairava held the two single-bladed Parashus in each hand and twirled them. He brought them together and whispered the beeja-mantra on the Parashu. The Parashu was whole again. He threw the Parashu to Rama. As Rama caught it, he raised his left leg and kicked Rama in the chest. Rama careened backwards at an incredible pace. The fires and Ganga disappeared in a blink. He landed on his back with a thump and stared up at Mahadeva.

'Ask a boon, Rama,' he said, smiling down at him.

'Teach me, Mahadeva. About the mountain, the temple and the wondrous sight I glimpsed.'

'You need to learn more, child. Learn the secrets of the sukshma sharira. Go into dhyana now. Form the mirror and see your chakras in it.'

Rama did as he was told. He saw his energy body in the mirror. Suddenly, he sensed Mahadeva's presence in the mirror, although he could see nothing but himself. He felt a finger touch the Agya chakra on his forehead. The image in the mirror changed. Rama saw only the Muladhara chakra—its vibrant colours, the beeja-akshara, its layered meanings and significance and the sacred aksharas inscribed on each of its petals. The yogasana and pranayama for it. He saw the three main channels, the Ida, Pingala and Sushumna nadis. He witnessed the processes of cleaning the channels and felt the rise of the kundalini and the Ahi lying coiled in the Muladhara. It progressed upwards through each chakra, and Rama's mind was boggled at the enormity of the learnings he needed to fully understand. What he had realised during that battle with Arjuna was so tiny in comparison. And there were so many chakras! He could see at least two more on his face. And above the Sahasrara! Chakras that pulsed beyond the physical body. So many more! The kundalini shakti reached the Agya chakra, and the finger lifted. Rama startled and broke out of dhyana.

'So much to learn. It will need many lifetimes to know it all,' said Rama.

'That is why you are a chiranjeevi.'

Rama paused a nimisha and blurted, 'Mahadeva! I don't remember a thing now. I've lost that knowledge.'

'No, Rama. It's not lost; it is just waiting to be learnt. You need to learn yourself. Guru Dattatreya will call you to him and teach you more. I will reveal more to many others, and you must learn that too. To unbecome, die and become. The wheel of time, Rama. Things become, grow, decay, unbecome, die and become again. The wheel turns on. Kali Yuga will come. Knowledge will be lost or corrupted. When the next Sat Yuga starts, you will teach what you've learnt. So, learn. Muladhara is Prayag and Agya is Kashi. This is your pilgrimage. The one Jamadagni spoke about. A pilgrimage of learning.'

Rama smiled. The Saptarishi was teaching from beyond. He glanced at the satchel lying unscathed in the destruction of the surrounding forest. Mahadeva spoke before Rama could ask. 'Those are for you to figure out.'

'You reached the Sahasrara chakra once and you may again. But to reach and go beyond? That will happen only once your learning is complete. This path needs learning and enormous courage and determination. The path itself is Brahmakshatriya.'

'What lies beyond?' asked Rama.

'There are many beyonds, Rama. More than even the enlightened comprehend. But, I promised you a boon. I bless that you can manifest the physical mountain when you wish. But it will not be visible to ordinary mortals.' Mahadeva touched his thumb to Rama's Agya chakra again. 'Call, and it will appear.

'I also grant you a divyastra. Since you do things your way, I will let you decide the potency, the invocation and the counter to it. I will let you name it. Decide, Rama.'

Rama thought long and hard, but he couldn't make up his mind. He eased into dhyana, focused his sankalpa on wanting a divyastra and waited for the answer to come. He held his mind blank and didn't form the yagnakund or the mirror. Utter exhaustion, both physical and mental, crashed over him. He accepted it and breathed slowly. He waited, unaware of how long he stayed in dhyana, but all he could see were the two clay pots in his hands, one with water and the other with the burning ember. His pitrus gathered around him as he sat, watching as if to see what he would decide. Rama gently came out of his meditation.

'I have decided, Mahadeva. I invoke not the power of a devata. I invoke the power of a lineage. Of the Brighus themselves. I invoke it with water and fire.'

Mahadeva smiled. 'The counter?'

'Time itself. It works for a certain time only. The duration will depend on the spiritual power of the invoker.'

'You bring the enormous power of the lineage of Brighus into a weapon,' Mahadeva said. 'This much power isn't to be trifled with. I must place a limit on it. As a Brighu, only you can invoke its full potency. If you were to teach this to another, it will simply multiply an arrow a million-fold.'

Rama bowed his acceptance.

'The mantra will come to you in dhyana,' said Mahadeva. 'Name the astra.'

'Bhargavastra.' said Rama, and Mahadeva laughed.

'Here, Bhargava Rama, the Parashu stays with you. I had come to take it away. Instead, you win a divyastra from me.'

The Parashu flew into Rama's hand. 'Those souls in the Parashu. How long have they been there?'

'Ever since you slew them. I have liberated all the ones slain by others who used the Parashu before. None knew the beeja-akshara or how to free them. You have entered the Parashu. Find how to get them out. Let that be your atonement. You have all that you need. You have mastered so much of it. Not all but close. Yet you've missed the simplest thing.'

Rama stared in confusion.

'Parashu!' Mahadeva laughed. He snapped his fingers, and it restored the forest.

'Blessings upon you, Rama,' he said as he walked away. He went to the thing that had fallen from the tree. It was a small sparrow. He picked it up, caressed it softly and smiled. The bird came to life and flew to the nearest branch.

'Da!' said Mahadeva. He vanished.

The world seemed to spin around Rama. He fought for balance but collapsed to the ground. He hadn't a mite of energy left in his body. Hunger and thirst assailed him. He heard distant cries and fast-approaching footsteps. His eyes closed.

'Gurudeva!' he heard Akrita's worried call.

'Water! Bring water!' Anantha screamed.

'I've got it,' said Bhamaha.

Rama felt water trickle down his throat. He drank greedily and swooned away.

17

The Navel of the Earth

Jayadhwaja sat chanting with Dantakrura amid the elaborate mandala. The fire pit blazed furiously and the copious fumes rose to the high canopy under which they were seated. The thick ropes of smoke glided across its length to the open sides and then rose to the sky, suspended in the air like a greasy, malignant cloud, swelling, bubbling and frothing. The cloud held steady, impervious to the gusts of wind that shook even the tents that were a good distance from the canopy.

The number of tents and pavilions grew by the hour, encircling the spot where the samrat and the warlock sat chanting on three sides. Vassal kings, maharathis and soldiers had gathered here at the samrat's orders but they were wary, nay terrified, of pitching their camps any closer. Unseen things lurked around the enclosure, things that snickered and snarled and made one's heart go cold as ice in utter terror. No one even looked that way at night.

The tents stretched away for hundreds of yojanas to the west, south and east. Jayadhwaja faced north as he sat, and no one wanted to be in his line of sight. Men, animals and activity teemed in the three directions—workers laying camps in each army's preferred grid, clearing shrubs and trees, building stables and smithies, kitchens and vaidyalayas, and digging latrines. Convoys of food, meat, water and animal feed swarmed into the camps, and fleets of carts transported waste out of them. The great armies of Bharatvarsha were gathering here, along with the foreign legions summoned by Jayadhwaja.

A ceaseless movement driven by the extraordinary needs of a humongous gathering of a hundred Akshauhinis—a moment never before witnessed in itihasa. It was less a gathering and more a country by itself, and it had only one aim, one anthem—to kill that man who was called an avatara and end the mayhem his followers had unleashed across their kingdoms. Stories about Parashurama were legion, often contradictory; he was a saviour for some, an enemy to a few, demon for others, but everyone gathered here knew that they were at the crossroads of history. There would be a breaking of the world or a smoothening of it from here on, there would be a pralaya of blood or unchallenged dominance, continuity of their lineage or obliteration of legacy. They were astounded by the annihilation of twenty-one Akshauhinis in Mahishmati, and by the power that was being harnessed under the canopy.

The soldiers, handymen and generals whispered prayers at night and stayed put in their tents, only rushing out warily to calm frightened horses and elephants, war dogs and beasts of burden. They kept their torches and lamps burning through the night, to banish shadows that had fang and claw, venom and fume. Unseen horrors lurked at corners and prowled the passages between camps. Many slept in the shrine-tents of their ishta devatas. Incessant prayers sprung from mind and lip and heart.

Dusk crept upon the camps and canopy, and Jayadhwaja continued to chant the mantra Dantakrura had given him. Both had chanted together at this very spot for months now. Those unseen watchers had chanted along with them, guttural and ferocious. Their numbers had grown again, Jayadhwaja was sure of it. No longer just hundreds of them. Now there were Akshauhinis, and Jayadhwaja relished it. The gnashing and snarling had taken hold of him, he was one of them now, and he trembled with joy. He had found welcome and belonging, and this was his clan and tribe.

His brothers approached fresh from their ritual baths, wet dhotis clinging to their legs and fright on their faces. They sat behind Jayadhwaja and stared into the fire, ignoring the chill that ran down their spines, and the crawling and itching on their skins.

The sun dipped below the horizon. Dantakrura held up his right hand. The chanting came to an abrupt halt. A deathly stillness rushed into the quiet, the fire froze and the world seemed to pause. The fire exploded into black, slithery fumes and was extinguished. Smoke stung their eyes, wormed into their nostrils and leached into their skin. It stained their clothes before slowly clearing away. The heat was incredible, burning their lungs as they breathed. The mandala had disappeared, and the warlock held a black astra in his hands. His pinprick pupils danced feverishly as he placed the astra in Jayadhwaja's open palms.

'Ranasthambini! You have attained the siddhi of it. The power is yours, samrat. Use it well. Bring that avatara to heel!' Dantakrura crowed.

'It doesn't kill, warlock. It makes the target immobile. That's all,' Vrishasya found his voice.

'That's all?' Dantakrura exclaimed. 'The astra has the power of a Mahavidya. Devi Bagalamukhi. There is no counter. This ritual we just finished had to be done with utmost precision and focus. Otherwise, the power would have turned on us. But we succeeded! Renuka is dead, and we have the power of a Mahavidya now. Physically manifest as an astra, no less! Does the import of this escape your puny minds?'

'There are other astras to kill. Even an ordinary arrow would do. But we must capture him alive.'

'Why?' Shura asked.

'The power of the avatara and the Parashu. We need him alive to extract that power. After that, he's as good as dead.'

'The plan is stupid, jyeshta,' Vrisha told Jayadhwaja. 'That man has that divine bow and knows many divyastras. Kill him and be done with it.'

'It takes enormous power to be the samrat of the world. Don't you want to get it all back? Should your jyeshta be lesser than his father? Arjuna had the power, and the lifespan, to do it. Do any of you? And Arjuna had Brighu by his side when he started. Your jyeshta has me.'

'The Parashu is a divine weapon. It will need tremendous spiritual power to wield it. None of us have it,' said Shurasoma.

The warlock smiled.

'You mean to harness it for yourself!' Shurasoma turned to his eldest brother. Jayadhwaja stayed silent. 'What if he turns against you, jyeshta?'

'I've sworn a blood oath!' Dantakrura screamed. 'On my heart's blood! I cannot break it.' He paused a nimisha. 'And I've sworn it only to him.'

Shurasoma glared at the warlock. 'How can you harness his power?'

'His blood! Blood is liquid life. It is the seed of power. Spill enough, and you are a great conqueror. Staunch its flow, and you are a saviour. It can spring rivers of tears and quench revenge of the heart. Draw it out, infuse it with Abhichara and you have power!

'You have the blood of kings. Bah! Cheap ... but the blood of an avatara! It is a thing marvellous.'

The brothers stayed silent, doubt dancing in their eyes. Dantakrura watched them, and muttered, 'No other way. Unless one of you is prepared to undertake decades of tapasya to earn the power. Revenge can wait, I guess.'

'No!' Jayadhwaja spoke at last. 'My armies from the other dweepas are back. I have a hundred Akshauhinis. No more delay.'

'I have an army too, samrat. An army like none other, an *un-mortal* army. It is at your service,' said Dantakrura.

Something about the way Dantakrura said it put a sudden chill into the air.

'You do not have the spiritual power either,' said Vrishasya.

'There are ways.' Dantakrura laughed. His pupils danced in a frenzy. Vrishasya blanched and looked away.

'The killings haven't stopped. Our men have been targeted and slain across the land, in cities and on trade routes. It becomes increasingly difficult to collect taxes and police the subjects. These assassins seem to know whom to kill and when. No official moves without an armed escort, yet they die ... in the streets, in their homes. Traders throw up their hands and say they've been warned against paying taxes. Priests have disappeared by the score. Farmers refuse to part with produce. Treasuries are looted, and tax collectors are killed. We continue to lose money ... and honour,' said Shurasoma.

'Word of the avatara has spread like wildfire. It is all that people talk about. The avatara to end the tyranny of kings. Parashurama is breaking our world,' said Shura.

'He is shattering it,' said Vrishasya.

'I cannot do everything for you. If you don't know how to run a samrajya, why strive for one?' said Dantakrura.

Vrishasya had no answer.

'It must be the people he was training. Where are they now?' asked Jayadhwaja.

Dantakrura shrugged. 'I watched Parashurama, not them.'

But he had watched, and there were thousands of minds to possess and eyes to access through them. At least when Parashurama had reached the camp. But then, a curiosity! No spell of his could pry into the minds. They were protected. And the wonder! He couldn't detect any traces of a protection spell. He had found one mind at last and was making do with it.

'Jyeshta, Parashurama's emblem is everywhere now. Our officers dread it, but the common folk celebrate it. They openly demand taxes be reduced, and only a sixteenth portion of the farm produce be taken. Songs of praise for these killers and of contempt for us are popular now.'

'A king's chhatri, his weapon and padukas. Remember that vision of him? The rishi wants to be samrat!' Dantakrura spat.

'Maybe we can reduce taxes?' Shura suggested in a small voice.

Jayadhwaja turned in anger and disbelief.

'We can't,' said Vrishasya quickly. 'Hundred Akshauhinis camp here. We have to pay them. And feed them.'

'What songs?' Jayadhwaja asked.

Vrisha pulled a damp, folded piece of cloth from his

waistband and handed it to Jayadhwaja. It was a square of dirty, damp white cotton with the emblem on top and six scribbled lines below ...

Fool Jayadhwaja, not so brave,
Not a king, just a knave,
He searches his stools in the morning,
Even there, he hopes to find a coin,
Won't pay his barber for a shave,
May he soon rot in a grave.

Jayadhwaja threw it to the ground and stamped on it in anger. Shura handed him another. Jayadhwaja glowered. He opened the cloth and read.

Samrat has a mouth and stomach, but no heart,
Eats all our food, loud his fart,
Takes all our coin, greedy mutt,
He puts it, you know, up his enormous ...

Jayadhwaja didn't finish. He screamed in rage and tore the cloth. No one spoke for a long while.

'The balance of power tilts your way, samrat. Jamadagni and Renuka are dead. Parashurama hides in a cave,' said Dantakrura. Jayadhwaja didn't respond.

'There's more. He emerged from the cave a while back.'

Dantakrura paused. How to explain what he didn't understand? He'd watched from the eyes of the sparrow ... That axe had sped from Parashurama's hands and hung in mid-air. The man talked to nobody at all. The Parashu dropped to the earth, and suddenly he was swinging it. And then everything went blank. He couldn't remember a thing. The next thing he saw was Parashurama falling in exhaustion and his compatriots running towards him. Something *had* happened, but what? He decided not to mention it and gazed away into the distance.

Shurasoma pointed to the small figurine made of black wax. It had four arms and stood upright. Around it were five black stones. 'Is that ...?'

'Yes! Surprised?' Dantakrura laughed. 'It is Mahavishnu. There are ways!'

'Parashurama is an avatara of Mahavishnu. I have taken the measure of him. Now I must counter his extraordinary power. And for that, you all have roles to play.'

The warlock reached into the hot ash of the fire pit, scooped a handful of the ash and smeared it across Jayadhwaja's forehead, lips, chest, navel and armpits. He repeated the same with each brother. Dantakrura picked one stone from the five around the figurine, examined it and handed it to Jayadhwaja. The stone had a rune on it. A square nested on all four sides.

'Earth,' said the warlock. He pointed to a spot a few paces away. 'Bury it there at dawn.'

'This isn't just any stone. This is a shaligram!' Jayadhwaja whispered. Dantakrura smiled knowingly as he picked another that had a crescent rune and handed it to Shurasoma. 'Water.' He handed Shura the shaligram with an upward triangle. 'Fire.' The one with diagonal lines went to Vrisha, 'Air.' He placed the last one with horizontal lines in Vrishasya's hands. 'Ether.'

'Ride now,' Dantakrura ordered. 'Ride along the four cardinal directions. Stop not for food, water or rest. Ride through the night until dawn breaks. As the first glimmer of the sun appears on the horizon, bury the shaligram and return.'

'Why are we doing this?' Shura asked.

'For a man of incredible power, I need an extraordinary trap. These stones are the answer. They are infused with the power of the five elements, the panchamahabhoota, and are meant only for the avatara of Mahavishnu. After you bury the shaligrams at dawn, the magic will come alive. The magic of each element will come together and form a grid. A mandala of power. Then, we wait. Wait for Parashurama to step into the field of magic ... then you will see. He's north of us now. That's probably where the magic will take hold of him. But I take no chances. Let him come from any direction,' Dantakrura explained to the brothers.

He raised his face and hands to the sky and screamed, 'Let him come! I will have him and it will be glorious!'

'Why should he come here?' asked Shura.

Vrisha answered before the warlock could reply, 'This army. A hundred Akshauhinis. It is just bait!'

'Yes! BAIT!' Dantakrura roared. He laughed and around them rose an obscene snickering and slobbering. 'And this is the perfect place for it. That's why I insisted this yagna be held here.'

'I don't understand,' said Jayadhwaja.

'An ancient name, samrat. There is enormous power in the earth here. This place is Nabhi Prithviya. The navel of the earth. Here we will cut the umbilical cord that connects that wretch and his power. His blood will spill, and he will wail like a baby.'

Dantakrura walked away into the deepening dark.

'I don't trust the warlock,' said Vrisha.

'Abhichara! This is wrong, jyeshta,' said Shurasoma.

'You have a better idea, then?' asked Jayadhwaja. No one replied.

'You don't want to do this?' Jayadhwaja asked Shurasoma. Shurasoma shook his head. Jayadhwaja's eyes bored into him. He whispered, the menace unmistakable. 'But you will do it anyway, won't you?' Shurasoma gulped and nodded. He glanced around nervously, as if he sensed something waiting to pounce on him.

Suddenly, there was a change in the surroundings. It thrummed with excitement as if those profane maws were salivating at the stench of rotten flesh. The warlock was running back to them, his amulets flying about him, his pupils dancing furiously.

'I have it!' Dantakrura screamed. 'I have the Parashu! I have taken it away from that wretch!' He reached the brothers and stood panting, drinking in the astounded expressions on their faces with glee, his wild eyes looking all around the six of them.

'Samrat! My man has the Parashu! He carries it to me as we speak. Parashurama will not have it back!'

Jayadhwaja rushed to embrace Dantakrura. 'Once we are done with him, I will pound these assassins into dust.'

'Destiny calls, samrat. Be prepared,' said Dantakrura. 'He's lost the Parashu, and he'll come for it. Get our troops ready to battle. We are too many this time. Even an avatara cannot match one hundred Akshauhinis. We will win!'

'We win!' Jayadhwaja screamed. The brothers shivered as they stood rooted to the spot, frightened to within a heartbeat of their deaths at the foetid breaths that hit them from all around, the unclean touch that made their skin crawl, the power in the insane sounds that erupted in the millions and threatened to turn their brains to mush.

Bhamaha rode as hard as he could, scared of the beast he was astride, afraid thieves would waylay him, terrified he'd come across Malaya Kshatriyas. The voice in his head wouldn't let him rest. The axe was strapped across his back, and the blades were wrapped in an old cloak. And he was terrified of it, too. Terrified that those keen, menacing edges would nick him somehow, cut off an ear perhaps or come to life suddenly and plunge into his head. At least he didn't have to look at it. He was hungry and regretted leaving the bags with the supplies behind. But he had been so excited, so nervous. He'd picked up the axe, scrambled to the nearest horse and ridden away as soon as that false avatara, Akrita and Anantha had swooned from the spelled water.

He had to find food for himself now and feed for the horse. But he had coins hidden in his waistband, in his boots and in his loincloth. The warlock had warned him the axe would be heavy, and he'd shown Bhamaha how to prepare the special paste and the spell for it. Bhamaha almost threw up when he thought of the ingredients he had to find for it ... newt blood, bat droppings and so many more unclean things. But it was worth it. The warlock had promised a spell to turn the violent men in his homeland as docile as lambs. But he had been clever. He'd bargained for more. He wanted the men to repent, to make amends to the children of the earth through lifelong servitude. The warlock had agreed and revealed the secret spell. Bhamaha chanted it under his breath. The warlock would deal with this false avatara, and Bhamaha would bring peace to his land. He would return and be called by the name his people knew him by. The name he had assumed so long ago. Vishwaguru!

Bhamaha rode on, trying to forget the two eyes with pinprick pupils that seemed to control every thought in his head. He stopped his chant and whispered to himself, 'Hero! That's what I am. A hero!'

End of Part 2

Author's Note

After the release of *Rama of the Axe*, two most common questions I've been asked in interviews and podcasts are: Is this how the story actually happened? And, is this what is in the Puranas? I've penned this note to throw some light on these and other connected questions, and how I approached the story itself. I do not intend to bore you with a list of creative liberties taken or deviations from the story in the Brahmanda Purana, but I will give you a few examples.

The tone of both the books is one of deep devotion. At the very start, I was clear that I do not intend to write Parashurama as a mere mortal who later came to be considered an avatara. A naturalistic retelling of Parashurama's story can be interesting, and many readers seem to like the ancient stories framed this way. But I think it robs the story of the one thing that is imbued in the Puranic corpus–divinity. Consequently, Parashurama's journey loses its divine purpose and becomes a tale of just revenge, duty or obedience. Still enthralling, no doubt, but lacking in fullness.

Some incidents aren't in the Brahmanda Purana—Renuka manifesting the Mahavidya Chinnamasta, for example. That comes from folklore and legends connected to the Yellama Temple in Saundatti, Karnataka. The character of Veera/ Nandin, the verse about the Parashu, are my additions to the story, as also, redefining the meaning of Brahmakshatriya, or attributing sentience to the Parashu. Inner motivations, dialogues and spiritual encounters are my imagining, inspired by meditation on Parashurama's divine essence, and his role as an instrument of dharma. The spiritual or mystical moments reflect my vision of divinity's presence, crafted to honour the spirit of the Puranas, and to illuminate Parashurama's sacred path. Perhaps the best example of creative liberty I can give you is not including the culling of twenty-one generations of Kshatriyas in the book, but using the number twenty-one in various parts of the story. I'll leave you to find out the instances.

Such liberties have been taken to highlight Parashurama's character arc, and to lend fullness to the storytelling—a blending of scripture with my heart's interpretation.

This book is a map of unchartered territory, limited only by my imagination and available information. The most consistent reaction I've got during the writing of Part 1, and after its publication, is—I thought Parashurama is an arrogant and violent man. It struck me that we are looking at, or all we see in popular media, is just the shadow of the avatara, a misperception or unawareness of him, not the avatara himself. This book is a dramatisation of the philosophy, life lessons and spiritual path of Parashurama. An attempt to integrate the shadow we've all been looking at with the actual self of the avatara through the path of the chakras. Ambitious or foolhardy, you, dear reader, get to decide. It is not to bring Parashurama to life (he is more *alive* than all of us), but to help us see him clearly, and to perhaps understand.

It has been an extremely tough but rewarding journey. To connect temple architecture (Rurujit Vidhana, the layout of the temple Parashurama accesses in his dhyana is the real-world layout of various Devi temples established by him; for instance, the Sri Kurumba Bhagavathi Temple, Kodungallur, Kerala) to Kalarippayattu and the Urumi. Since I couldn't find Sanskrit words for them, I had to coin *Khalurika Prayoga* and *Naga Khadga*, respectively. To pen a tale that traverses from a Rig Vedic hymn to a tantric text (see footnotes), from a question—how was Parashurama made a Saptarishi?—to the surprising connection to Tamil, it has been hard to find answers and facts. I hope the Trikona Prashna chapter convinced you that Parashurama deserves to be a Saptarishi. It is a fictionalised portrayal of Parashurama's wisdom and what I understand of dharma.

A good story is like the five koshas of Hindu yogic philosophy. The plot is the Annamaya kosha, and the emotional energy of the story is the Pranamaya kosha. The character arc and character motivations are the Manomaya kosha, the theme and insights, form the Vijnanamaya kosha. Finally, the joy of connection with the divine, the transcendence a story evokes, is the Anandamaya kosha. I hope this story satisfies all five, was interesting, and brought you closer to the glory of Parashurama, as it did me.

Faith plants the seeds of truth, fiction waters it with wonder. Where one ends and the other begins, I cannot say. To those who are quick to dismiss such stories as myth, and to those who love such stories but are irritated or embarrassed by the word 'mythology', I leave you with this quote:

History recounts the bones of what was, mythology weaves the soul of what endures. Myth unveils truths too vast for mere facts to hold. Where facts falter, stories soar to reveal the eternal.

Acknowledgements

My heartfelt thank you to the readers for making *Rama of the Axe* such a big success. I'm enormously grateful for the privilege of writing for you.

As always, my wife Radhika, my sister Priya and my mother remain first readers, severest critics and strongest supporters. Friends who've been kind enough to read and give feedback and information—Bharathi V., Monisha, Shalini Puthiyedam V. and Rekha Achyutuni of Hindu Parenting Podcast, and Vijaykrishnan Iyer of Bharat Narratives—thank you for the kindness and indulgence.

The team at Westland—Karthika V.K., Sonia Madan, Vidisha Ghosh, Abhirami Lal, Amrita Talwar, Saurabh Garge, Satish Sundaram and others who have worked behind the scenes—thank you for your keen eyes, sharp minds and endless patience. Thank you to Nithin Rao Kumblekar again for the wonderful cover.

Big thanks to the team at Scratches to Curves—B. Vivek Anand, Aditya Kumar, Karan Parekh, Ishan Verma, Sandeep Ananda Das, Akanksha Bankar, Kiran Shanth and Milan Patel. The trailer is simply magical. Thank you, Rohit Umashankar, for bringing it all together.

Onward then, new enemies and old friends, new questions and ageless answers await Parashurama.

Part 1 was the story you only thought you knew.

This book, Part 2, is the story you don't know.